Praise for Archer Mayor's Joe Gunther Series!

"I have a soft spot for quiet writers like Archer Mayor, whose unassuming voice and down to earth style stamp his regional crime novels with a sense of integrity. The strength of these narratives has always come from the author's profound understanding of his region and from his hero's intuitive ability to relate to the people who live there."

> — Marilyn Stasio,
> *The New York Times*

"Superb  —*Publisher's Weekly*
> *(starred review)*

"It is our good fortune that Mr. Mayor's skills are equal to the vigor of his imagination."

> —*The New Yorker*

"Mayor's elegiac tone and his insights into the human condition make [each book] a fine addition to one of the most consistently satisfying mystery series going."

> —Thomas Gaughan,
> *Booklist*

"Archer Mayor is producing what is consistently the best police-procedural series being written in America."

> —*The Chicago Tribune*

"As a stylist, Mayor is one of those meticulous construction workers who are fascinated by the way things function. He's the boss man on procedures."

> —*The New York Times*

The
Disposable Man

The
Disposable Man

Archer Mayor

AM press

PO Box 8648, Essex, VT 05451

www.archermayor.com

Library of Congress Cataloging-in-Publication Data
    Mayor, Archer.
    The disposable man / Archer Mayor.
        p.   cm.
    I. Title
    PS3563.A965D57   1998   98-19551 CIP
    813´.54—DC21
    ISBN 978-0-9798122-8-6

Designed by Dede Cummings Designs / Brattleboro, Vermont

Printed in Canada
1   2   3   4   5   6   7   8   9   10

This book is printed on FSC-certified, 100%
post-consumer recycled acid-free paper.

To Leete Ekstrom and Bob Backus,
good storytellers both,
with great affection and many thanks.

Acknowledgments

As always, I am indebted to a great number of people for the nuts and bolts of the tale that follows. I write these stories in part so that I can meet people who know about things that stir my curiosity, and I appreciate their time and patience in sharing that knowledge.

In addition to these people, I would like to especially thank the proprietors of the Windham Hill Inn, in West Townshend, Vermont. They allowed me to use their very real and pleasant establishment as the backdrop for part of this story, despite my assuring them that I planned to link its name to all sorts of skullduggery.

For their forbearance and good humor, I owe many thanks. To the reader, I should point out that while the inn does exist, the people inhabiting it in *The Disposable Man* do not. Nor does it have a terribly smelly tree planted in its front yard.

In addition, I mention near the end of the book a business called Cartographic Technologies. Again, while this organization does exist, and its proprietors were of enormous help to me, I have taken great liberties both with their personalities and in how they conduct their business. My deepest thanks for their enthusiastic help.

To them, therefore, to those working in the following organizations, and to many, many others, my gratitude.

The Newfane Greenhouse
The Brattleboro Police Department
The Vermont State Police

The Middlebury Police Department
The NewBrook Fire Department
The Windham County State's Attorney's Office
The Windham County Sheriff's Office
The Vermont State Medical Examiner's Office
Mr. & Mrs. Ed Sawyer

The
Disposable Man

1

R ON KLESCZEWSKI DROVE WITH BOTH HANDS ON THE WHEEL, HIS eyes intent on the twisting dirt road ahead.

"Do we know for sure this isn't a dog or a dead deer or something?" Tyler asked from the backseat.

I twisted around to face him. "Not according to Sheila. She checked it out. It's definitely a man."

J. P. Tyler scowled silently into his lap. "A suicide, I bet," he said glumly. The forensics expert of my four-member squad, he was along for good reason, but he'd been having a bad day and was obviously convincing himself the rest of it had just vanished down the tubes. I was counting on his natural curiosity to resurface once we reached our destination.

A sudden lurch made me turn back toward the road.

Ron smiled apologetically. "Sorry. Don't guess this sees much traffic."

He nervously drove us through a huge muddy hole, accelerating to make sure we didn't get stranded in the middle. Trees to both sides of us canopied overhead, allowing only an ineffectual dappling of late summer sun. I checked their crowns in vain for the first faint blushings of the coming fall foliage, always first to appear in the high, colder hills surrounding downtown. We were off of Ames Hill Road, west of Brattleboro, an area as seemingly remote as Vermont's deepest backwoods, and yet only fifteen minutes from the office. Half our department's beat looked like this, yet we were perhaps the fifth largest community in the state.

"There it is, up ahead," Ron commented, easing us around a copse of trees and up a final, narrow driveway to an opening haphazardly cluttered with beaten trucks, rusting cars, one police cruiser, and half a dozen barking dogs. Directly before us was a small, open-sided barn, filled with a battered assortment of woodworking equipment and an ancient generator. To our left, connected to the generator by a heavy electrical cable, an outhouse-sized cabin, with one closed door and no windows, sat perched on the edge of a large concrete slab covered with a plywood deck.

"What the hell is this?" Tyler muttered, fingering the door handle and suspiciously eyeing the circling dogs.

"Doesn't look like anybody's here," Ron echoed, craning his neck.

I watched the dogs for a moment, reading their body language. I'd spent enough time in Vermont's most isolated region—the Northeast Kingdom—to know the careful protocol of a newcomer. Despite our now being some two hundred miles south of there, almost touching the Massachusetts and New Hampshire borders, I recognized the need to follow the old rules.

I opened the door slightly, sticking a foot out first for the dogs to sniff, before slowly emerging from the car, my empty hands visibly open and slack by my sides. Cool, wet noses filled my palms in flurried, competitive greeting.

"Hey there," I murmured, slowly crouching, running my fingers lightly through shifting tufts of hair. "How's it going?"

The dogs were light, dark, tall, short, rangy, and compact. All were scruffy, their hair thick and matted. Their eyes stayed watchful throughout this ceremony, their haunches muscled up in preparation for instant fight or flight.

They skittered away as the door to the distant shed opened, revealing a tall, slim woman in a police uniform. She paused at the top of a stepladder connecting the ground to the concrete slab and waved at us.

"They're okay," she called out. "The owner wants to meet you before I show you what we got."

"All of us?" I asked.

"Just you, Lieutenant." She laughed suddenly. "Maybe you guys can play catch with your new friends."

"Not goddamn likely," Tyler said under his breath, having tentatively joined me by the side of the car.

I crossed the rutted parking area, circling a pickup truck perched on cinder blocks, and approached what now looked more like a tool shed balanced on the edge of a missile silo hatch. It was all situated slightly higher than where we'd parked, so that as I drew abreast, I discovered a row of three narrow basement-style windows lining the edge of where the slab emerged from the earth.

Sheila Kelly tilted her head toward the broad, flat expanse as I climbed the four-step ladder to join her. "It's a work in progress," she explained. "They put in the cellar a few years back and capped it. Someday they're going to tear this thing off," she patted the shed wall, "and replace it with a log cabin. Least that's what the owner says. His name's Billy Whitehurst—he found the body. He's a little twitchy about letting too many people on his property, though. That's why the introduction."

I nodded. "That's fine. Is it far from here?"

"Not too. Maybe half a mile up the road you came in on, and then into the woods a bit."

I now saw the shed's sole purpose was to protect a set of stairs leading into the basement. Below us dim lighting revealed the bottom few steps and the poured cement floor beyond. I gestured to Sheila to lead the way.

The atmosphere that rose to meet us was clammy, cool, and aromatic—enriched by decaying food, unwashed bodies, and stale, unmoving air—both curiously sweet and rancid. Daylight barely seeped through the three cloudy windows I'd noticed earlier and was anemically assisted only by a single bulb hanging over a distant kitchen sink. A man stood there, with the water rushing, laboring over something I couldn't make out. His back was turned toward us.

Lining the damp walls were counters, stacks of boxes, two bunk beds—one cradling a small, wide-eyed child—and a clothes dryer being emptied by a silent, furtive woman in a tie-dyed skirt. In one corner was an ominous-looking bank of interlinked car batteries connected to a fuse box, which, I assumed, ran to the generator in the barn outside. The other three corners were demurely walled off with bedsheets nailed to the ceiling joists.

I imagined a family living here for several years and tried not to think of the psychological toll.

"Mr. Whitehurst?" Sheila said as we crossed the cool, sweating floor. "This is Lieutenant Joe Gunther, our chief of detectives—the police officer I told you about."

The man at the sink turned away from what I now recognized as the heart of a carburetor and looked at me from under a shaggy pair of gray eyebrows. I didn't offer to shake hands, nor did he, both of us following the same code of conduct I'd recognized was in play from the start.

"You want some coffee?" he asked.

"I'm okay, thanks." I leaned my hip against the counter, waiting him out.

He wiped his hands ineffectually on a red rag he extracted from his back pocket and poured himself a cup from a nearby coffee machine. His fingers left dark smudges on the dingy white plastic.

"Hell of a thing, something like that."

"How did you find it?"

"Checking the woodlot with one of my boys. There's a soapstone deposit a little ways from here, with a small quarry. Every time we're near it, the kids fool around with it—chip some off, or mark it up. It's soft and easy to work. Supposedly, they make talcum out of it. Years back, somebody had plans—that's how the quarry got started—but they crapped out. One of these days, maybe I'll do something with it. They use slabs of it for woodstoves and heating stones. You can cut it with a chain saw it's so soft."

I nodded, my silence as eloquent as any verbal prompting.

He took a deep swallow of coffee. "Anyhow, the boy found it first. Called me over. I saw right off what it was. Sent another of my kids to call it in on a neighbor's phone."

I glanced at Sheila.

"I took a look, just to confirm it, but that's all," she said. "There's another unit there now, sealing it off."

"You recognize the body?" I asked Billy Whitehurst.

He shook his head. "Guy's facedown in the water, but he's wearing city clothes. Nobody I know."

"And you didn't touch anything."

"Nope."

"How 'bout any traffic around here recently? Or something that might've set off the dogs?"

"Been pretty quiet."

"When was the last time you visited the quarry?"

"A few weeks ago."

"Is there another way to get there, other than right by your driveway?"

"The road goes on through. It's rough—nobody else lives on it—but you can do it if you're in the right kind of rig."

I scratched my cheek, glanced out the dim window, and pushed away from the counter. "Okay, Mr. Whitehurst. If you don't mind, we'll go take a look."

He nodded silently and watched me until we'd both almost reached the foot of the stairs, before addressing what was really on his mind. "This going to be a big deal? Lots of people and what-all?"

I shrugged. "Not if you don't want it to be. It's your property. We have to have access, especially if it turns out to be something bad, but you can stop anyone else from coming on your land, same as always. Promise me you won't use the dogs, though, okay?"

He pushed his lips out slightly but said nothing.

"For our part," I added, "we'll keep the location out of the papers. That work for you?"

"All right."

I emerged as from a dank grotto and tilted my head back to face the sunlight, the warm smell of the nearby woods clearing the dampness from my nostrils.

"Think he might be involved?" Sheila asked after shutting the door.

"I doubt it. Just happened to be in the wrong place. You ought to check him out when we get back to the office, just to be sure. Could be Mr. Whitehurst is a retired ax-murderer."

We waded through the dogs toward the others and eventually backed both cars down the driveway to the road. Ron gingerly followed Sheila for ten minutes more, until we found another patrol car parked to one side. We both pulled over behind it, tilting precariously on the edge of a ditch. Tyler—short, thin, and still pissed off—struggled to lug his equipment cases out of the uphill door onto the road. "Jesus, Ron. It's not like we'll be holding up traffic."

Ron smiled and lent him a hand, recognizing as I had that the bite was out of his bitching, and that it wouldn't be long before the J.P. we were used to had returned. Whatever it was that had gotten us all out here, any field work was better than the office drudgery we'd saved him from.

In fact, Tyler's road to recovery barely took him five paces.

He set down his cases like a weary airport traveler and stood a moment in the middle of the road, getting his bearings. Suddenly he crouched and touched the dirt at his feet. "This is the quickest way to the site?" he asked Sheila.

She nodded.

"So it's the logical place to park if you're going to dump a body," he said, almost too softly to hear.

It was more than a simple statement of fact; there was also a hint of reproach in his voice. Three cars were now parked where a previous one might have paused in the commission of a crime, obliterating all hopes of identifying either tire tracks or trace evidence.

Tyler straightened, apparently unconcerned. "Doesn't matter. That, though," he added, pointing at the woods, "is something else. Did anyone think to restrict people to a single corridor in and out?"

Sheila smiled and pointed to a rock by the side of the road. "I put that there when I first got here. The rest of the way's marked with surveyor tape."

We lined up at the rock and gazed into the trees. Bright pink scraps of plastic ribbon, tied to branches twenty feet apart, stretched uphill into obscurity.

"I chose this spot because I saw fresh tracks over there," Sheila added, pointing just beyond the parked cars. "Well," she then corrected, "maybe not tracks exactly, but some crushed plants and scratch marks in the dirt."

Tyler's eyes gleamed. "Nice work." He wandered over to appraise her discovery.

Ron Klesczewski turned toward our car. "I'll call for one of the Fish Cops to see what they can pick up."

The Fish Cops was the nickname for the wardens at Fish and Wildlife. The term was one of affection, since we all knew the best of them could track a squirrel over bedrock. At least that's what they had us believing.

"Sheila," J.P. called out. "Where did you say the body was?"

She pointed into the woods. " 'Bout a quarter mile that way."

He returned to us, his brow furrowed. "Whoever it was wasn't taking any chances. Looks like he took a route where he could leave as few tracks as possible."

Each of us hauling one of Tyler's cases, we set out on Sheila's blazed trail, leaving Ron behind to radio in. Five feet into the woods, it became obvious that protecting the integrity of a potential crime scene wasn't the only reason to have marked a pathway. The surrounding trees became almost instantly indistinguishable from one another, looking as dense and untouched as remote Canadian hinterland. Without those plastic pink flashes of color, we would have been hard-pressed to know what direction to take, or how to find our way back to the road.

One hundred and fifty years earlier, Vermont had consisted almost entirely of farmland and pasture, wrested from a prehistoric virgin forest that had given the lumber industry a lucrative start. Now, some eighty percent of the state looked like our present dense surroundings and gave visiting tourists the erroneous impression that they were traveling the same paths used by the Abnaki Indians. Only the odd stone foundation or field wall gave a clue to the truth.

Several hundred yards up our gentle ascent, the trees thinned out, the earth beneath us yielding to moss- and lichen-covered rock, and we found ourselves following the spine of a long, rocky crest, like ants traveling the length of a sleeping dinosaur. Here the surveyor's tape was pinned in place by small stones.

"Clever," Tyler said. "A spur of this same surface is what I noticed near the road, where those scratchings were. Guy obviously knew the terrain."

"Unless," Sheila cautioned, almost hopefully, "we're talking about a hiker who just tripped and broke his neck."

J.P. didn't bother looking back. "Wearing a business suit?"

No one answered him.

There was no view from the ridge. The forest surrounding the outcropping we were traveling was too tall to allow for one. But it was brighter, and a small breeze brushed our faces, easing the claustrophobia of moments earlier.

The figure of a man suddenly rose as from the earth itself, standing up near the edge of the clearing. He waved at us. "Hey, Lieutenant. Over here."

Patrolman Ward Washburn came our way, speaking as he approached. "The quarry's right there. It was kind of hard to rope off."

He led us to the edge of a sudden drop-off—a small quarry cut into the stone like a bite into a wheel of cheese. A yellow streamer of tape marked "Police—Do Not Cross" lay awkwardly on the stone, until it reached the woods at the foot of the quarry and began looping more authoritatively from tree to tree. Between the base of the small cliff we were standing on and those woods, nestled in the palm of the crescent-shaped quarry, was a pool of dark, shallow, stagnant water. Facedown in its middle floated a small, thin man, spread-eagled, his arms extended as though desperately signaling a bus to stop.

The odd thing about him, though, wasn't his attire, which looked like a throwback to the fifties. It was more the lack of it. His feet were bare.

J. P. Tyler smiled slightly, at last wholly in his element. "Well, it ain't no deer."

2

ALFRED GOULD, THE ASSISTANT MEDICAL EXAMINER FOR Brattleboro, sat back on his heels by the water's edge. The corpse, stiff with rigor mortis, lay faceup in the embrace of a wide open body bag, like a wet, unpliable parody of a Christ figure. His face was a blotchy purple, his hands and feet puckered and made slightly translucent by prolonged immersion. And yet his distinctly Slavic features—those of a man at least in his sixties—were recognizable, if no longer terribly appealing. He hadn't been in the water long enough to suffer real damage, nor had any aquatic animals chosen to make a meal of his face.

I asked the obvious first question: "Any idea what killed him?"

Gould glanced up at me. "The ME'll have to confirm it, but I think this had something to do with it."

He reached under the body's chin and spread the flesh at the throat with his latex-gloved fingertips. A deep but grotesquely bloodless wound yawned open like a slice into a large piece of fish, extending across the neck to below each ear.

"I'd say he was garroted, probably with a thin wire. Not what I'd call a weapon of opportunity."

"And he's not the typical age for a crime of violence, either," I muttered, as Gould grabbed each of the body's arms and folded them in with a loud cracking sound so he could close the bag.

Ron Klesczewski, by far the most sensitive of my crew, let out a small groan. "So he was dumped. Why the bare feet?"

Tyler, his preliminary photographs, site maps, and measurements completed, was wasting no time getting back to work after waiting for Gould to finish. Straddling the body bag like a strawberry picker astride a row of plants, he rummaged through the soggy clothing, looking for anything interesting.

"That's easy," he said without looking up. "We might've been able to trace his shoes, at least to country of origin—same reason all the labels have been cut out of his clothes."

Gould looked back at the body, his brow furrowed. "You think he's a foreigner?"

Tyler straightened. "It's just a guess. Why else would you remove those kinds of identifiers but leave the fingertips and face intact? We could run print checks till next Tuesday and get nowhere if we don't even know what country he's from."

"There's Interpol," Ron suggested.

"They need a country reference, too. There's no such thing as a central international print file. Anyhow," he added, stooping over again, "there're a ton of places that don't share with Interpol or anyone else—either that or they're so disorganized it amounts to the same thing."

We silently watched him as he continued his search. The sticky mud and strands of vegetation clinging to the corpse sent up a cloying odor of rot.

"Maybe the Fish Cops'll come up with something," Ron persisted, the perpetual optimist.

Tyler, his voice showing frustration, spoke directly to the body again. "They better, 'cause I'm getting squat here—not a fiber, not a ticket stub, not a candy wrapper. Nothing. But I won't be surprised if they don't." He swung his head around and glanced at me suddenly, repeating a theme he'd introduced earlier. "Whoever did this knew what he was doing."

His hands at the victim's belt buckle, he abruptly froze. "Uh, oh."

There was a small clicking sound as he manipulated the buckle and smoothly extracted a nasty-looking knife blade. He held it up in his gloved hand so the sun reflected off its short, lethal double edges. "Cute," he said.

I leaned forward and looked at it carefully. "I guess we can rule him out as a lost tourist."

The facilities of the state's medical examiner were brand new. After years of borrowing clinical space in Burlington's Fletcher Allen Health Center, and doing her paperwork in a rented office above a dentist on Colchester Avenue, the ME had finally come into her own.

She greeted me at the door of the waiting room with an unusually gregarious smile, simultaneously shaking my hand and lightly patting me on the back. A tall, blonde, formal woman of indeterminate age and occasionally formidable frostiness, Beverly Hillstrom was also a doggedly curious perfectionist, traits I'd never shied from aiding and abetting. Frequently in the past, she had waived fees, brought in outside consultants, and spent extra time on cases when she'd thought I might benefit. I had no idea if she did this for other departments or investigators. I'd heard some cops refer to her as a coldhearted, bureaucratic bitch. I expected, however, that she repaid in the currency she was dealt—coin for coin. Over the years, we'd become close and trusted colleagues, despite the fact that we still only referred to one another by our official titles.

"This is an unexpected pleasure, Lieutenant," she said, guiding me through a general office area to a coffee machine, where she offered me a cup. "Were you just in town, or did word of our Taj Mahal finally prove irresistible?"

I smiled and shook my head to the coffee. "I was curious, I will admit."

"We are the unlikely beneficiaries of a market-driven, politically sensitive war between the Dartmouth–Hitchcock Medical Center in New Hampshire and this place." She waved her hand overhead. "The entire hospital has been overhauled to compete. We just caught hold of the coattails. Actually, half our facility is shared with either the hospital or the university, but considering what we got, I'm not begrudging them a single square foot."

She suddenly looked at me over her reading glasses, belatedly struck by the unlikeliness of my merely dropping by. "We haven't completed your John Doe, by the way."

I smiled at the veiled warning. "I'm not here to speed things up."

The warmth returned to her eyes. "Interesting answer— meaning it warranted a three-hour drive over a five-minute phone call. Must be big."

This time, I laughed outright. "Don't I wish. I'm afraid 'weird' is a better word. We found this guy over eight hours ago, and we still have no idea who he is, where he's from, how he ended up where we found him, or even how he came into our jurisdiction. It's almost like he fell from a balloon."

Hillstrom opened a rear door onto a broad, brightly lit hallway and turned left, leading us past an enormous scale, mounted flush with the floor. She didn't comment on it, but I recognized the significance of that item alone. In the past, cadaver weights had been estimated—everyone in the autopsy room had been allowed a guess, and the median had appeared in the formal report. That scale was a sign that Vermont's medical examiner had finally been paid some respect.

"Well," she said, rounding a corner and heading for a broad door at the end of the hall, "if it's any help, the balloon couldn't've been too far off the ground, because there's no evidence of any fall beyond the height of the quarry wall. And that was postmortem, by the way. He was killed earlier, and probably elsewhere."

She fitted a key to the door and swung it back, ushering me across the threshold. We entered a large, high-ceilinged, well-lit room equipped with a skylight and two complete workstations—twin autopsy tables attached to a long, single counter like boats nosed up to a dock. There were four people in the room: Harry, the pathology assistant; Dr. Bernard Short, Hillstrom's young and brand-new second in command, whom I'd met only once before; Ed Turner, the ME's investigator on loan from the Vermont State Police; and my blotchy-faced acquaintance from the quarry, who was lying naked on the far table with his torso split open. Dr. Short was holding his small intestine in both hands.

"Gentlemen," Hillstrom announced as the door swung shut behind us. "You all know Lieutenant Gunther, I believe?"

A chorus of mumbled greetings rose from the group, accompanied by Turner's "Long trip, Joe. This guy special?"

The question was as much from simple curiosity as from the ME's official law enforcement liaison, onto whose turf I'd just stepped. In times past, homicide victims especially were routinely accompanied by a department baby-sitter, equipped with pictures of the murder site for reference. As a goodwill gesture to everyone, however, the VSP had eventually assigned one of their own to gather whatever evidence the ME found, forward it to the crime lab in Waterbury, take photographs, lift prints, keep up the paperwork, and generally stand in for the often uneducated neophytes we'd all depended upon before. It had been such a success that the appearance of a cop like me, instead of a FedEx package bearing photos, was now as unusual as it had once been commonplace. And it obviously made Ed Turner wonder why.

"I don't know," I answered him. "I was just telling Dr. Hillstrom that we can't find anything on him. We're thinking he may be a foreigner, but that's all we've got so far. My inner bloodhound got the better of me, I'm afraid. Hope you don't mind."

Turner's face broke into a smile. "Hell, no. Good to see you again."

Dr. Short was looking at me quizzically, entrails still cupped in his hands. "Why a foreigner?"

"The missing shoes and the clothing labels. If they'd been American, they wouldn't have been removed."

Short nodded thoughtfully. "Could be. The dental work reminds me of some of the horrors I saw in South America, out in the boonies— very crude."

I approached the table and gazed down at the familiar face, cleaner now, slightly cut and blanched where the purplish lividity had been prevented by stones pressing against the flesh from the bottom of the shallow pool. Contrary to popular belief, floating bodies do so head-down, that part of their anatomy having the most mass. Hillstrom joined me.

"Right now, it appears cause of death was a ligature around the neck, as Dr. Gould surmised in his report," she said. "Something as thin as piano wire—it's almost an incision wound."

"Never seen one of these before," Ed Turner added, "'cept in that *Godfather* movie. Think it was a hit?"

I merely shrugged.

He pointed at a damp pile on a distant counter. "We ran an ultraviolet lamp over him before and after we undressed him, to check for trace evidence. We didn't find anything, so I removed all the pockets for the lab. Thought there might be drug residue or something." He paused and then added, "You been having any action like that back home?"

I shook my head. "Not really. Were you pointing a finger specifically at South America, Bernie? Or just saying the guy's dental work was from out of the country?"

Bernie Short was now weighing his burden in a large, shiny bowl attached to a scale. "No, no. I'm not *that* much of a world traveler. You'd have to have a forensic dentist or someone analyze the alloys in the fillings—different countries have different amalgam mixes." He paused and then hedged his bet. "For all I know, he might've grown up in West Virginia and had some horse doctor work on his teeth."

"I don't think so," Beverly Hillstrom said softly. She was standing at the body's feet, examining his toes. "Did anyone take note of this?"

We all gathered around her. Harry spoke first, "They look like tattoos—one on each toe. Pretty faded, though. I can't make it out."

"I shouldn't think you would," Hillstrom said. "Unless I'm mistaken, these are Cyrillic letters."

A long silence greeted her remark. She left us and crossed over to a phone mounted on the wall. She quickly punched in a few numbers and waited a moment. "Betty? Find Timothy Cox in my Rolodex, and if you can reach him, tell him I've got a tattoo I need interpreted—soon as he can. Thanks."

She hung up and faced us. "A neurologist friend. Works upstairs. Spent five years in Moscow teaching. It's worth a try. If he doesn't know, we can go through more formal channels."

"Absolutely," I agreed. "Can you tell me any more about the garroting?"

"Not much," Bernie Short said. "It was done from behind. Death was almost instantaneous, although not quite. We found scratches around the neck wound and some tissue under the nails, indicating the victim tried to claw the garrote away. It's probably his own skin, although we'll test its DNA to make sure it doesn't belong to someone else. But that's basically it, excepting a small laceration to the top of the head. He was definitely dead by the time he went underwater. Judging from my findings and the documentation Al sent with the body, I'd say someone pitched him into the quarry from the top of the small cliff. As you know, time of death is always tricky. Al's notes say the body temperature was the same as the environment, so cooling was complete. Yet rigor was still in full force."

He'd removed the bowel from the scale and was opening it lengthwise on the counter with a scalpel, checking its contents. "Notice the slight discoloration around the abdomen—a shade of light green in the right lower quadrant?" he asked.

I did see something that looked like bruising.

"First signs of putrefaction. On the other hand, while the corneas are cloudy, they haven't begun to bulge, which they would've later on. Also, there's no insect infestation. 'Course, the only skin exposed to the air were the heels—the rest being either clothed or underwater—and blowflies don't like that part of the body much."

"So maybe more than a day, probably less than two or three?" I interpreted.

Hillstrom patted my arm. "Very good, Lieutenant. We'll have you in a lab coat yet. Unfortunately," she added, glancing at Bernie Short and obviously using me to caution him, "he may also have been placed in a freezer for three years and then thawed. For all the tricks of our trade, I can still only guarantee that someone's time of death occurred sometime between when he was last seen alive and when his body was discovered."

Visibly abashed, Short resumed in a slightly quieter voice, "Two other details you might like: it looks like he had a moderate meal just a few hours before he died, although what it was I don't know; and according to the lividity pattern, he was dumped not long after death, so he didn't spend the night in a car trunk or something, although lividity overall was lessened by some pretty serious blood loss—the garrote cut into the carotid."

I tried to ease him out of his embarrassment. "Tell me more about the scalp laceration."

Short made a discouraging face. "Can't say if it happened before or after death. There was some vegetable matter caught in his hair near the site, but I don't know if it was related to the wound. He was pretty grubbed up."

Ed Turner cleared his throat and motioned to an evidence envelope nearby. "What we collected's in there, if you want to take a look. It's mostly tiny bits and pieces, though—probably crap already in the water."

"Incidentally," Hillstrom said, "don't take the suggestion that this man ate shortly before death as gospel. They've done endless studies, trying to pin a predictable rate to the digestive process and have gotten nowhere. Depending on a person's metabolism and state of mind shortly before death, food's been found in the stomach, far downstream, and everywhere in between, even hours following ingestion."

She smiled and let her protégé off the hook with one additional comment: "Which doesn't mean he didn't eat shortly before he died."

"There's nothing else?" I asked in the brief silence following.

Short readied himself to cut through the scalp from ear to ear, just above the occipital portion of the dead man's head, in order to expose the cranium and subsequently the brain.

"There might be," Hillstrom admitted, nodding in his direction. "We're not quite finished, and there are some tests to be done. We've taken blood, bile, vitreous humor, and urine samples for tox scans, along with a blood standard for DNA typing. It's possible we'll pick up something later as a result, but I wouldn't hold my breath."

Short, having finished his incision, peeled the face down under the victim's chin like a rubber mask. He pointed to a small bloody stain on the glistening skull while Harry took a picture. "Definitely looks like that head laceration was perimortem." He hesitated slightly under Hillstrom's gaze and added, "I would guess it happened as he fell, since it's not compatible with an attack wound—too minor. 'Course, that's just a guess. He could've bumped his head before he even set eyes on the person who killed him."

Hillstrom smiled. "No, I would agree with the first suggestion. It's reasonable and logical."

Short let out a small sigh and reached for the bone saw. As its high-pitched whine filled the room, Hillstrom resumed her conversation with me. "We took a complete set of X-rays and made a listing of all moles, scars, and signs of prior surgery for future reference, but I imagine his teeth and fingerprints alone will suffice if you ever come up with a possible identification."

"Are you going to include a hair sample with the tox scans?" I asked.

She gave me a surprised look. Her answer, I guessed, was as much an olive branch to Short as a response to me. "That's a good idea. I wouldn't have thought of it, since drugs weren't a known factor. But where identification is the goal, everything should be considered."

I noticed Short smiling as he put aside the saw and began working the top of the cranium loose, and I realized that despite their curious way of communicating, they probably made a good team.

Bernie freed the skullcap and held its bowl-like interior up to the light. "Yeah—there're no signs that blow to the head caused any cerebral damage."

Hillstrom moved to look more closely, suddenly interested. "Yes, but see that yellow-green color on the inner table of the calvaria?"

"Tetracycline?" Short asked.

"Right," she agreed, and explained to me, "tetracycline leaves a permanent stain here on everyone who's ever used it. It's a common enough finding in the U.S., where it's routinely prescribed for infections, but it's rarer in less developed countries. If the assumption is correct that this man is a foreigner, and of Slavic origins as his features suggest, this could be an interesting finding."

"Can you determine what caused the infection?" I asked.

Short began to shake his head, but Hillstrom, for once not watching him, merely shrugged her shoulders, making him instantly freeze.

She was smiling as if to herself and said, "Well, there is one small test we could try—more for fun, really."

She picked up a long, thin probe from the counter by her side, and stepped up to the corpse's midriff. She took his uncircumcised penis in one hand and gently inserted the probe up his urethra. After a minute, she withdrew the probe and laid it back on the counter.

"Strictures?" Short asked.

She looked pleased. "Yes." She turned to me: "I found an obstruction—probably scarring caused by a bout of gonorrhea, which could have been treated with tetracycline. It's entirely conjectural, of course, so don't take it too seriously. We have no way to really prove it. I just thought of it because of the tattoos and the man's age. In a rough-and-tumble life, a man is likely to contract an STD at least once before he goes."

The wall phone buzzed, and she crossed over to pick it up. "Hillstrom."

She listened for several seconds, said, "Thank you, Betty," and hung up, explaining, "I thought the wording might catch his attention. Tim's on his way."

I hadn't bothered forming a mental image of Hillstrom's Russian-speaking friend, but when he was shown through the door by one of her staff, I was somewhat taken aback. Instead of a skinny, stooped academic, with maybe a goatee and thick glasses, a man in the casual dress of a businessman—sport jacket and slacks—balding, sharp-eyed, broad-chested, and thin-lipped, entered the room as if he were about to address a board meeting.

"Beverly, what are you up to?" he demanded, taking the rest of us in with a glance and a curt nod.

Hillstrom knew better than to bother with introductions. She took Cox's arm and led him to the autopsy table. "We have a John Doe with a curious set of toes. What do you make of them?"

Perching a pair of half-glasses on his nose, Timothy Cox bent at the waist and peered at the row of letters, keeping his hands by his sides. After no more than half a minute, he straightened back up, removed the glasses, jammed them into his breast pocket, and announced, "We're tired."

"That's what they say?" I asked, after a moment's stunned silence.

Cox allowed a small, pleased smile. "Right. In the old Soviet

Army days, you'd mix an excess of vodka with boredom and a barracks artist, and this," he pointed at the toes, "was often the result. It was considered a classic infantry badge, way back when." He glanced up the table at the discolored face. "And judging from his looks, this guy'd be about the right age. My bet is you've got yourself an old-time Russkie here."

3

I REACHED BRATTLEBORO LATE THAT NIGHT. THE TRIP HOME HAD been by the sepulchral gleam of a full moon, washing the tree-covered mountains and the undulating road with the colorless light of a hundred-year-old photograph. Vermont at night has always made me think of the eighteenth century, when its few inhabitants surrendered the darkened fields and forests to the mysterious elements that helped fuel Indian folklore on one side and settlers' fears on the other. To this day, even in a car flying down the interstate, I see the vast spaces between the occasional lights as teeming with nocturnal life, most of which is watching me as I pass, a meaningless blur, no more than a shiver of wind.

I took Exit Two, considered checking in at the office, but turned right instead, toward West Brattleboro, making another right up Orchard Street, where I shared a house with Gail Zigman. It was time to be home—to be one of those glimmering lights.

Still, I paused on the street opposite our address, killing the engine to better savor the moment. The house was large—even enormous—with a garage, an attached barn, a back deck so big a huge maple looked comfortable sticking up through its middle. It was two and a half stories tall, Greek Revival in style, with white-painted wooden clapboards and a slate roof. It was surrounded by a lush, sloping lawn and sat in the moonlight like a display in some celestial shop window. Not long ago, it would have been as foreign to me as a mansion in Rhode Island. And now it was home.

It was Gail's doing, of course. An erstwhile hippie of the sixties, come to Vermont to exchange a wealthy urban lifestyle for a nearby commune, she'd eventually migrated to town, become a successful Realtor, earned a place on half the boards available, been elected a selectman, and fallen in love with me. Now she had a dependable bank account, worked endless hours as a brand-new assistant state's attorney, and was as happy as I'd ever seen her. It had been a long road, almost destroyed by a violent rape a few short years ago, and this house was the visible reward.

Which sometimes left me feeling a little odd. Briefly married, a widower for decades thereafter, I'd been a cop my whole adult life. I'd lived in this town since my mid-twenties, most of that time on the third floor of an ancient Victorian pile, in a cheap apartment remarkable only for the shabbiness of its furniture and its excessive assortment of books—my only recreation. The son of a farmer who'd fathered me late in life, I knew nothing of the financial achievements that had marked Gail's past. The house opposite me was ours in name, and represented a move I'd made without regret, but I had yet to form an attachment to it. It remained the home a rich person would own, and within its embrace I always felt slightly like an intruder.

I restarted the engine and pulled into the driveway, the night abruptly torn away by the blinding glare of two motion-detector spotlights. Walking from the car to the kitchen door, fumbling with the several keys I needed to gain entry, I squinted up in vain at the stars for a final farewell, defeated by the artificial brightness. Perhaps that was another cause for my uneasiness with this house: it had been purchased after the rape, which had occurred in Gail's own home, where she'd been happily living alone. This substitute, while fancier by far, was like the memorial of an event that would never fade from memory.

I found Gail in bed upstairs, surrounded by folders, legal briefs, and sheets of yellow notepaper. She didn't usually work in bed, having an office down the hall, which prompted me to ask, "You okay?"

She caught my meaning immediately, holding out her arms for an embrace. "Yeah. Just feeling lonely."

I kissed her and sat on the edge of the mattress. "Tough day? I noticed no one from your office showed up at the scene this morning."

She lay back against the pillows. "It was a zoo. Court appearances all day, one secretary out sick, Carol still on vacation. Once Jack heard it was probably a dumping, he didn't see much value in sending anyone out for a drive in the countryside. What was it like?"

I smiled appreciatively. Jack Derby was her boss, the Windham County State's Attorney. A relative newcomer on our political landscape, he was a natural pragmatist. "He had it right—pretty day for it, though."

She began collecting her homework, dropping it on the floor. "Who was it?"

I rose and removed my jacket and shoes. "Don't know. That's why I went up to Burlington. We don't often come across bodies so totally stripped of identifiers—it was like he'd been dry-cleaned. Even his clothing labels were missing."

"Was Hillstrom any help?" Gale asked, settling back on a now-clean bed, killing the reading light beside her. She was wearing pajamas, and her hair was spread out on the pillows behind her. The only remaining light came from a small lamp on the dresser, which threw soft shadows on her face.

"A friend of hers was. Pegged some tattoos the guy had on his toes as Russian."

"That's pretty exotic."

I returned to her side, sat back down, and took her hand in mine. "That may be all it is. So far, none of it amounts to a nibble, and it might stay that way. Still, I asked them to keep the tattoos to themselves, just in case we need them later."

She closed her eyes and sighed. "Well, it's good to have you back. I missed you all day for some reason. More than usual."

I let go of her hand, reached up and unbuttoned the top of her pajamas. A smile slowly spread across her face. Her leg pressed against mine and her hand slid onto my thigh. I went down to the next button, and the one below that, until I could peel back one-half of the top.

"Welcome home," she murmured.

The shouted warning appeared from nowhere as soon as I touched the doorknob. "Don't open that."

I froze in the police department's short hall-like entranceway, and stared at the seated man signaling me from behind the bulletproof glass lining one wall. I leaned toward the speaking hole cut into its middle. "What's going on?"

Barry Givens, the graveyard-shift dispatcher, explained, "They put down a new floor last night. It's still drying. You have to go around."

I waved and retreated to the public corridor splitting the Municipal Building in two—along with the police department's offices—and walked farther up to an unmarked door generally used by the patrol division. We were undergoing yet another renovation, this one to accommodate an updated dispatch center to handle the town's police, fire, and EMS simultaneously. A good idea in itself, it also conformed with the state's ongoing effort to join the 911 emergency response system, something Vermont had avoided until it had become virtually the sole holdout in the entire country. One of the nation's least populated states, Vermont was also chronically broke, two factors that had put 911 on the back burner for too long.

I let myself in using a key, walked through the quiet Patrol Room, and crossed over to the chief's corner office next door. It was before seven in the morning, my people were just beginning to show up, Patrol was closing out the shift, hunched over their keyboards, and Chief Tony Brandt was already at work, sitting at an enormous, rough-hewn, cubbyhole-equipped pine desk he'd built himself.

All was as usual.

Brandt was an unorthodox mixture of the old and the new. A lifelong cop, a New Englander born to small-town habits, he had nevertheless evolved into a modern administrator/politician. He ran the department from his oversized desk, from lunches with Brattleboro's movers and shakers, from meetings in offices of people who saw government as children see playgrounds. He cajoled and threw hardballs when necessary and draped a protective mantle over the department and all its employees. The rank and file sold him short for this sometimes, saying he'd lost his touch for the street, but he got them new equipment when other town departments were left wanting, and he was receptive to suggestions when he thought they had merit. No longer a good ol' boy, perhaps, he'd become a damn good boss instead.

He had also once been an inveterate pipe smoker, something both his doctor and new town regs had finally curtailed. Still, I'd gotten used to forever seeing him through an aromatic haze, and—his health not-withstanding—I begrudged the new appearance of his office nowa-days, with its crystal-clear atmosphere.

He peered up at me as I entered, the early morning sun glinting off his gold-rimmed glasses. "How was Burlington?"

I waggled my hand back and forth equivocally. "So-so. The guy might be a Russian, he might have been killed one to three days ago—or three years ago and then put in a deep freeze— and he probably had a meal the same day he died."

Tony stared at me for a moment. "That's it?"

"Basically. He might've had the clap once, too. The Russian part comes from some Cyrillic letters he's got tattooed on his toes. That and he had bad dental work."

Tony stared thoughtfully at his desktop. I remained silent. "You having a briefing about this soon?" he finally asked.

I checked my watch. "Fifteen minutes."

"If it's all right, I'd like to sit in."

There were six of us around the table: Tony, Ron, J. P., myself, and the two remaining members of my crew—Sammie Martens, my second-in-command, and Willy Kunkle.

I began by passing out a sheaf of papers. "These are copies of the ME's preliminary report, which basically says what we saw yesterday is what we got. The addendum about the tattooed toes is mine. I asked Hillstrom to keep that part of the autopsy under wraps, just in case. One additional tidbit: the dead man was apparently once treated with tetracycline. Hillstrom's Russian expert said that access to that stuff over there is pretty much a black-market deal, which implies this guy had those kinds of connections. Ron, you handled the inquiries from here. What's the status so far?"

Ron Klesczewski paused, fingering his notepad. Despite his years on the squad—even being my second for a couple of them—he remained a curiously tentative soul, much given to self-doubt. His strength, just as J.P.'s was forensics, had always been document searches and paper flow. And although I'd seen him stand unflinching in a firefight, he'd always struck me as being too nice a guy to be a cop.

"It's a little early yet," he now answered. "But as soon as you called me with the Russian angle from the ME's office, I faxed the FBI, INS, DEA, Border Patrol, ATF, all the area drug task forces, the state police of New Hampshire, Vermont, Massachusetts, and New York, as well as all in-state law enforcement agencies. When the crime lab produces his fingerprints and a decent photograph, I was thinking we could enhance and expand the bulletin nationwide and forward the prints to the FBI."

"Good," I agreed. "But no feedback so far, right?"

He shook his head.

"Sammie," I asked next, "what about the neighborhood canvass?"

Sammie Martens—small, wiry, high-strung, and aggressive— had come to us from the Army. Still in her twenties, she'd replaced Ron as my number two through sheer willpower, working harder, smarter, and for longer hours than anyone else in the entire department. The cost had been the total sacrifice of a private life, something I'd vainly encouraged her to cultivate for sheer sanity's sake. Had she not proven her intense loyalty to me time and again—and had I really cared about such things—I would've felt the hot breath of her ambition on my neck. As it was, I was happy to know that whatever happened to me, the squad would be in good hands.

"Zilch," she answered shortly. "There aren't many people living up there to start with, and none of them admits to hearing or seeing a thing."

"You check with anyone regularly traveling those roads?" I asked. "Maybe a delivery truck driver saw something."

"Right," Willy Kunkle said with a laugh. "UPS is up there all the time, delivering Brookstone nail clippers to their upper-class customers."

Ron took note of my suggestion in his pad. Sammie just gave Willy a withering look which he ignored. Kunkle was the office renegade—surly, impatient, opinionated, but with a talent for police work bordering on pure instinct. His left arm totally crippled by a bullet years earlier, Kunkle had a quality I alone seemed to value. As impossible to categorize as he was to control, he was my best weapon against those regular customers who treated us with arrogant dismissiveness. When the crunch was on, and I truly needed answers, Willy was the one I sent out, although I often worried that his tactics—whatever they were—would eventually land us in court. Unfortunately, such redeeming opportunities were all too rare. The rest of the time, he seemed content to simply be a pain in the ass.

J.P. looked up from reading my addendum. "Are we assuming this John Doe was a Russian?"

"Not necessarily," I answered. "It's a strong possibility only. I'd love to have Interpol fly it by the Russian police, but until we get more on him, it would probably be a waste of time."

Willy crumpled his Styrofoam coffee cup and tossed it into a nearby trash basket. "Waste of time anyhow. Those guys are too busy robbing banks."

"I think," I continued, ignoring him, "we ought to release a cleaned-up photo of him to the local papers, play the 'have-you-seen-this-man' angle, and hope we get lucky. In the meantime, maybe we can brainstorm a few other ideas. Any suggestions?"

"The killer lives in the area—we know that much," Willy said.

J.P. nodded in agreement. "At least the person who dumped him does. He knew the terrain and he knew how and when to approach it so no one would notice him. Fish and Wildlife is still working the site this morning, but as of last night their tracker was pretty impressed."

"So maybe an outdoorsman to boot," I suggested.

"That local knowledge combined with the body's lividity pattern suggests he was killed in the area," Sammie said. "Is there any way to identify the gastric contents? Maybe we can tie it to a nearby restaurant."

I shook my head. "I was told that's a dead end."

"He was probably driven to near where we found him," J.P. said. "And given what the garrote did to his neck and the lack of any blood at the scene, we're talking about a car or some absorbent material that's pretty bloody."

It was a statement of fact—something merely to remember, but it stimulated Willy to ask, "How did he get here in the first place?"

"Good point," I said. "Ron, put out inquiries to train, bus, taxi, and rental car companies as soon as we get his photos." I looked around the table. "What else? How 'bout motive?"

"Mob," Sammie said immediately. "It looks like a hit—a strike from behind with no sign of a struggle—and we've all been reading bulletins about how the Russian Mafia's on the move. Plus there's that tetracycline/black market angle."

"Implying a drug war, maybe?" I asked.

"*I* haven't heard anything," Willy stated flatly, which, given the circles he traveled in, meant something.

Tony Brandt spoke quietly for the first time. "The Canadians have." He looked at Ron Kleszczewski. "You better add RCMP, Quebec Provincial Police, and the larger urban agencies up there to your list. It wouldn't be the first time their troubles began leaking south."

There was a hesitation in the room as everyone groped for something to add. Getting to my feet, I finally let them off the hook. "All right. That's probably enough for now. A couple of things, though: it's early yet, so don't let this take over your lives. Wait for our inquiries to generate something solid, and try to clear your desks of ongoing cases in preparation. Also, don't let this Russian mob angle give you tunnel vision. For all we know, some benign foreign uncle was knocked off by his woodchuck nephew for the inheritance."

Typically, Willy had the last word. "Sure," he said, "an uncle equipped with a buckle knife."

Two days later, we were stuck where we'd started. The papers had published the picture we'd supplied, which the state crime lab had made acceptably presentable, all our teletyped inquiries had been sitting on other people's desks for well over twenty-four hours, and every officer in the department had talked to his or her snitches. Nothing had popped to the surface, including from the FBI, which had reported a "no match found" in record time.

Homicide cases have a limited shelf life, and I was beginning to fear our mysterious John Doe might melt away with as many questions as he'd stimulated.

Until I received a phone call from Beverly Hillstrom.

"Lieutenant, I hope you don't mind my calling—I'm not even sure I'm not breaking a confidentiality of some sort—but I've had a couple of visitors I thought you should know about, unless, of course, you sent them yourself."

I hesitated a moment, completely at a loss. "No," I answered slowly, hoping that wouldn't prompt her to retreat.

I needn't have worried. She'd clearly made up her mind before dialing the phone. "Two rather frosty gentlemen in suits came by to look at your John Doe."

I sat up straighter in my chair. "Who?"

"One was from the FBI—named Frazier. The other was introduced as 'Philpot.' The implication was that they were a team, but Philpot never showed any identification."

"What did they want?"

"That's why I called. They didn't really want anything. Frazier presented the proper paperwork and asked to see the body, but when I did the honors myself, out of pure curiosity, all they did was glance at the man's face, thank me, and take their leave. I wasn't sure what to make of it."

"I don't either," I admitted, "but I'll try to find out."

She sounded surprised. "You know Frazier? I'd never met him. He seemed pleasant enough—a bit formal."

"Yeah. He heads the Burlington office. 'Formal' isn't a description I would've used, to be honest. He never struck me that way."

"I think it was Philpot. I got the impression Frazier was there purely as decoration—to get my door officially open. Maybe he was just feeling uncomfortable."

I mulled that over for a moment. "Did you tell them we thought the body was Russian?"

"I wasn't overly friendly."

That was answer enough. I'd seen her in that mode. "Let me dig around a little. You want to hear the results?"

I could almost hear her smile over the phone. "Well . . ."

"You got it," I interpreted, laughing, and hung up.

My hand still on the receiver, I pondered what Hillstrom had told me, resisting the impulse to call Walter Frazier directly and ask him what the hell was going on. The unannounced presence of the FBI was curious enough, but nobody I knew named Philpot was assigned to either their Burlington or Rutland offices, and he, combined with the already mysterious John Doe, made me want to do some homework before confronting Frazier.

I picked up the phone and dialed an internal number. "What's the latest news?" I asked Sammie once she'd answered.

"Nothing yet."

"How 'bout the dailies. Anything there?"

The dailies were our own internal log—the official diary of everything the department did around the clock, whether it resulted in further action or not.

There was a pause as Sammie checked my request. "Nothing stands out," she reported a moment later. "There was an inquiry from the sheriff's office—it doesn't say what they were after. Want me to chase it down?"

"Yeah. I'd like everything checked for the next few days. The FBI's been sniffing around our pal with the Russian toes. I'd love to find out why."

Sammie knew better than to suggest simply calling them up. Despite serious advances in interagency cooperation, skulduggery and exclusion remained time-honored practices. It often paid well to do a little spadework before holding that first conversation.

"I'll call you back," she said instead.

It took her under ten minutes, and she delivered the news in person, appearing at my door with a satisfied expression. "I guess I know why you're still the boss."

"Oh?"

"That inquiry from the sheriff was about an abandoned rental car near Stratton Mountain, left parked at the filling station just north of the access road. They're asking if anyone's reported it missing. So far, no one has."

She let the significance of her last sentence sink in before raising her eyebrows. "Wanna go for a ride?"

4

I WAITED UNTIL J.P. TYLER PULLED HIS HEAD OUT OF THE RENTAL CAR'S trunk before breaking what I thought had been an extraordinarily gracious silence. Locked into a stuffy, windowless garage to ensure the integrity of a potential crime scene, Sammie and I had watched him powder, scratch, vacuum, and snip at almost every surface the car had to offer, receiving very little information for our patience.

As Sammie took another surreptitious glance at her oversized watch, however, I thought a break in the pattern was due.

"So, J. P., what're we looking at? Good news?"

He was holding a plastic spray bottle in one hand, and a flashlight rigged with a dark red filter in the other. His expression read of slightly veiled irritation. He was not a man who enjoyed an audience.

"It's got promise."

He crossed over to a long workbench against the wall and exchanged what he was carrying for some nail scissors and a small evidence envelope. Sammie sighed but kept her peace.

I did not. J.P. had milked this as much as I was going to let him. Besides, I could tell from his barely perceptible smile that he felt he'd already won the game. He could afford to be magnanimous.

"So spit it out."

He placed the scissors on the car's bumper. "It's no home run, but it's better than what we had. I lifted several fingerprints from the interior, most of which look like they match our John Doe. That would make him the probable renter of the car, in my book. There are others, here and there—kind of in odd places, actually, which make me think they came from someone on the rental company's cleaning crew. But that's about it. The rest are smudges, which might've come from any-one. The nice thing is that what I got is very clear. Rentals are much better than regular cars that way—almost like clean blackboards, as far as fingerprints are concerned. Once we locate the franchise he got this from, we'll check their time and personnel files, find out who cleaned it, and see if we can rule out the other prints."

He then shrugged. "Unfortunately, that's about it for the interior. I'll run the dirt I found on the gas pedal by the crime lab, along with what I vacuumed from the seats, but I don't expect much. And there was basically nothing else—no candy wrappers, no personal items, not even a road map. And," he held up a finger, "no luggage. It's almost like he drove the car a hundred feet and then abandoned it."

"Or someone made it look that way," Sammie added.

"Or he did himself," I said, the visitors from the FBI still fresh in my mind.

They both looked at me.

I explained. "Nothing else about him seems normal. The suit, the belt knife, the tattoos, even the way he was killed. They're all pretty weird. Why not the possibility that he cleaned out his own rental car before dumping it? The one thing we haven't even bothered with so far is figuring out what someone like this was even doing here."

Sammie chewed on that for a moment, and then asked J.P., "Was the steering wheel wiped clean?"

He shook his head dismissively. "No, but it didn't need to be. Steer-ing wheels are lousy for prints. Everything ends up smudged."

He turned toward the trunk again. "Anyhow, none of that's the really interesting part. I found bloodstains on the carpeting back here."

I stood next to him and stared into the dark recesses of the immac-ulately empty trunk. "A lot?"

"Enough for analysis. I'll send some clippings to the lab and have them cross-check the DNA with John Doe's."

I shook my head. "No. What I meant was the ME said his carotid had been cut, that he'd lost enough blood to affect lividity. If all that blood's not here, it's got to be somewhere else."

J.P. nodded. "So we either have a seriously stained site somewhere, or a blanket or tarp that's soaked in the stuff."

We all stared at the car in silence. Finally—hopefully—I muttered, "Well, that's something," although none of us were entirely sure what that was.

That night, the bedroom was dark and empty. Gail was in her office at the end of the hall, nestled in an oversized armchair and surrounded by the stacks of paperwork that seemed to follow her like doting pets. Not that I was any better. I'd been doing some late-night homework myself.

I leaned over and kissed her forehead, jostling her reading glasses with my chin.

"Hey, kiddo," she said. "Did you get hold of Walter?"

I'd told her of Walter Frazier's visit to Hillstrom's lab. I found a narrow clearing in the middle of a small couch opposite her and settled down. "Yeah. I thought I'd wait till after hours. I figured if the FBI was being coy, maybe he'd share a few secrets off the record. We've worked pretty well together before—he doesn't play the Bureau's usual game of excluding local law enforcement."

She removed her glasses and polished them against her shirtfront. "And did he share?"

"Oh, yeah—no problem. I could've spared myself the cloak-and-dagger. He said it was standard practice for the Bureau to ride shotgun when another federal agency needs to fish in home waters without a license."

She stopped polishing and looked at me closely, suddenly caught by the excitement I'd been stifling. "What's that supposed to mean?"

I laughed, still incredulous about my discovery. "Remember Philpot? The guy I told you about? Turns out he's CIA, dispatched from Boston on orders from Langley."

* * *

Early the following morning, Ron Klesczewski stepped into my office with a single sheet of paper, which he laid on my desk.

"Just came in—the Logan Airport branch of that rental car company. We faxed 'em the John Doe photo, which they definitely matched, and they kicked this back. Interesting reading— mostly for what it doesn't say."

I sat forward and peered at the document under the light from my desk lamp. It was a rental application filled out in the name of Boris Malik. "Address: Paris; driver's license: international, original issue Lebanon; company address: Moscow."

I stopped reading and sat back. "Let's follow this up—push whatever buttons you need to gain access to all passenger lists on international flights arriving at Logan in the three hours before he rented that car."

The intercom buzzed and the dispatcher's voice floated into the room. "Joe, you have a call on three—the caller wouldn't leave his name."

I punched the speakerphone on. "Hello?"

"Lieutenant Gunther?" The man's tone was soft, almost sleepy.

"Yes."

"Would you mind taking this call off the loudspeaker?"

I looked at Ron and motioned to him to pick up the phone on the desk just outside my office. I already had a sneaking suspicion who this might be—or at least where he was calling from.

At a nod from me, Ron and I lifted our receivers simultaneously. "This better?" I asked.

"Much—thank you. I assume you either have someone listening in or a tape recorder running. That's not a problem. I just thought it might be more discreet not to have this conversation broadcast all over the station."

I put my feet up on the desk. "What's on your mind?"

"My name is Gil Snowden. I'm calling from Virginia about a John Doe you recently discovered."

"That reminds me of a guy I met once," I said. "Years ago— very clean-cut, well spoken, an obvious Ivy Leaguer—who told me he'd gone to college in New Haven. Are you being coy that way, too?"

He allowed a theatrically embarrassed chuckle, and said, "Okay, I work for the CIA. I was wondering if you'd be interested in having a conversation. It might help you put this case to bed."

He left it hanging there. Ron raised his eyebrows at me questioningly.

"You mean down there?" I asked.

"It would be friendlier face to face."

I tried looking at the possible angles, but had no idea where to start. "I'll have to get back to you," I hedged. "I'm not my own boss here."

"Not a problem," Snowden answered smoothly and gave me a phone number. "Call me anytime."

Tony Brandt swiveled his chair around so he could stare out the window, two fingertips of his right hand just grazing his lower lip. It was at moments like this that I knew he missed his pipe the most.

"Frazier didn't tell you anything?"

"Supposedly, Philpot—if that is his name—didn't tell *him* anything. Frazier asked who the guy was, hoping for a little buddy-buddy breach of confidentiality. All he got was a one-liner about how the Agency had been looking for someone, but that our John Doe wasn't him—that they had no idea who he was."

Brandt's eyes stayed fixed outside. "And you're not swallowing that."

"Not when Snowden tells me he can put the case to bed. They're obviously reading from two different playbooks—one says to stiff us, and the other to scratch our ears till we roll over and go to sleep."

"Then why go to Langley? Won't they just shovel you more bullshit?"

I turned both my palms heavenward. "What else have we got? A virtually dry-cleaned body, a near-sterilized car, and not a single murmur from all the inquiries we sent out. Ron told me this morning we're not even getting crank calls for the picture we put in the papers. That's a first. I'm not saying Snowden's going to spell everything out like he's implying. But I am hoping he'll let *some*thing slip."

Brandt finally turned back to face me. "We can't afford to *fly* you down."

* * *

I don't often travel beyond the three states surrounding Vermont, but when I do, I'm amazed at my small world's insularity. There are just over half a million Vermonters—not quite as many, it seemed, as were crowding the Boston–New York–DC corridor the day I drove south. Like the sole contemplative member of some gigantic herd, I began to wonder if I was even remotely in control of my choice of destinations, or merely being influenced by some massive migratory urge. Trucks, cars, pickups, and upscale four-by-fours by the thousands, along with their apparently transfixed drivers, seemed as drawn by the same irresistible magnetism that was pulling me along.

And that was just the most immediate contrast. Beyond the traffic was the scenery, slowly changing from farmland to mall to suburb to something that eventually looked like a city without end, punctuated now and then by a sudden upthrust of taller buildings, appearing like some cataclysmic collision between tectonic plates.

Which may be, in fact, what makes the approach to downtown Washington as unique as it is, at least from the north. Where Hartford, Springfield, New York, Baltimore, and all the rest have recognizable city centers projecting a sense of purpose, DC is essentially flat, lacking the glass-and-steel towers most other urban clusters erect to justify their existence.

From the outskirts, there is only a gradual sense that the gritty, commercialized, outlying carpet has yielded to something more focused. Trees appear alongside avenues, traffic becomes leavened with buses, taxis, and the occasional limo, and the buildings—increasingly pompous by the mile, if no taller—cease being either residence or business, and become that third, more mysterious creature: the government office, where things indefinable, arcane, and even faintly menacing are allowed full leash.

I headed west of the city, to a cheap but survivable motel in suburban Arlington that Tony Brandt had recommended. It was within walking distance of a Metro station, and thus all of DC, allowing me to move without the hassle of looking for a parking place.

This convenience had nothing to do with my trip's stated goal, of course. CIA headquarters are in Langley, Virginia, northwest of

Washington, and far from any subway system. My desire to reach downtown was purely sentimental, for the city, whatèver its faults, does one thing remarkably well: it honors the dead, sometimes with admirable emotional flair. From soldiers to politicians to leaders of various causes, all seem to be remembered on a sliding scale of tastefulness. My appointment with Snowden wasn't until the next morning, and by leaving home well before sunrise, I'd purposely given myself enough time to visit two of Washington's less-touted memorials.

The air was hot and muggy, even late in the afternoon, so it was with some relief that I dropped off my bag at the motel and immediately sought refuge in the Metro's air-conditioned depths, bound for Judiciary Square station.

On my way to pay homage to a few specific dead, I pondered once more the man whose death had stimulated this trip.

The mystery surrounding most killings, of course, is not in discovering who did it. By and large, that's as challenging as following a trail of blood from one room to the next, where some distraught friend or family member is found holding the weapon. The mystery is in the why—why this person? Why now? Why this sudden rage?

If we actually do have a situation where the culprit is not in the immediate vicinity, then we're usually faced with two alternatives: a series of leads that takes us to someone we can then present to the State's Attorney, or—on very rare occasions—a dead end that grows more hopeless by the day.

The investigation I was facing, however, followed neither of those norms. While apparently a dead end, it also seemed to be growing in scope. Invited to a city renowned for its lack of clarity, I had no illusions that the CIA would lift the veil from my eyes. Which left me wondering what I was being drawn into— and why.

Although quiet, smooth, and remarkably clean—attributes for which the Washington Metro was justifiably famous—the subway ride to Judiciary Square was long and predictable, and by the time I arrived, my mind had been dulled by the blurred succession of trains, stations, and thousands of blank faces sealed behind glass. The familiar discomfort of being in close quarters with so many withdrawn people had begun to envelop me.

I half fled for the exit, toward fresh air and open space, climbing flight after flight of stairs, dogged by the memory that Washington's subway system had supposedly been designed to double as a bomb shelter. When I finally reached the foot of the last steep escalator and looked up the sun-bleached exit shaft, I saw the sweltering swatch of flame-blue sky with the same relief I'd felt upon entering the Metro's air-conditioning earlier.

The illusion of returning to the land of the living was just that, however, since the escalator delivered me to the heart of my destination—the broiling hot, dazzlingly bright National Law Enforcement Officers Memorial. From a cool, muted subterranean world of stone-faced commuters, I'd ascended into a three-acre, oval frying pan made of white-hot marble, in which, at the moment, I was the only human being.

The memorial, with an imposing bronze plaque at its center depicting an officer's shield superimposed by a single rose, extends out in a series of widening topographical parentheses, made variably of colonnades, trees, and shaded walkways, and finally, at its outermost edges, of two pathways banked by a continuous, curved, knee-high marble wall, inscribed with the names of over fourteen thousand law enforcement officers killed in the line of duty.

Only a few years old, the memorial reflects several standard monument styles—from archways to statuary to a shallow pool of running water. But the most effective is the homage to the Vietnam Memorial, wherein a seemingly endless list of names is arranged as randomly as the ways in which those officers were slain.

Sweat already trickling down my sides, I crossed to a softbound directory housed in a weatherproof case and squinted against the sun to look up three names: Frank Murphy, John Woll, and Dennis DeFlorio.

All had been members of my department—Murphy, the man I'd replaced as chief of detectives; Woll, a young patrolman; and DeFlorio, one of my own squad. But contrary to the implied heroism of this formal, austere setting, none of these friends had died catching bullets intended for the civilians they'd served. Murphy had been killed in a mundane car crash, Woll's murder had been staged to resemble a suicide, which by that time his own miseries had made all too believable, and DeFlorio had been blown apart by a car bomb.

I collected the reference numbers for each of them and entered the tree-canopied pathway to find their names, grateful for the shade, reminded of the dense, multihued woods of Vermont. As I sat on the rounded stone bench facing the inscribed wall, exchanging silent greetings with my three friends, my chagrin became less for their loss and—typical of most mourners, I think—turned back onto myself. I began recalling all that had brought me up to this point—the daily exposure to despair, deception, and misconduct—and wondered why I'd made some of the choices I had.

Law enforcement had never entered my mind as a youth on the farm, any more, I guessed, than it had those of most of the people now etched on this wall. But somehow that's where we'd all ended up, perhaps wanting to be of use to others, or seeking shelter against the vagaries of a capricious upbringing, maybe hoping to find some measure of elusive self-confidence. There are those who believe police officers become so merely to compensate for personal inadequacies. But by and large, I'd found that most cops just sort of end up in the job, after which the good ones do their best to make it count, despite the airless niche in which society has placed them.

In the final analysis, it was the pure normalcy of the people on this wall, and that they'd died doing something few people understood, that saddened me most.

I stayed there until the sun had dipped low enough on the horizon that I no longer needed the trees for protection, and then I headed off on foot to complete the second half of my pilgrimage.

The Korean War Memorial, located near the base of the Lincoln Memorial, was so new it didn't appear on most tourist maps. Almost a half century old, with casualties rivaling Vietnam—although lasting a mere fraction of that struggle's length—Korea's conflict remained a footnote war, treated almost as a post-World War Two afterthought—a fact the memorial's too recent appearance served more to highlight than to dispel.

Returning to the United States after my stint in it, I'd been struck by the lack of fanfare greeting us, especially given what vets had encountered a mere seven years earlier. At the time, I'd been deeply offended, feeling my teenage sacrifices had been cavalierly dismissed. Now, I knew such reserve probably had more to do with the nation's emotional numbness. The Nazi/Japanese Axis had bathed the globe in blood, and the Soviets were threatening to do the same using nuclear weapons. What chance was there for a local boundary squabble, so equivocally viewed by our own leaders that they avoided calling it a war? It would be fifteen more years before the country took a deep breath and voiced its outrage over Vietnam. And by then Korea, never resolved in any case, had been all but forgotten.

Brought low by the long drive, the listless subway ride, the blistering barrenness of the law officers memorial, and my own ruminations about a case without issue, I worked to clear my head by walking all the way, even though it was almost a mile and a half distant. I stopped to eat a sandwich at a neighborhood deli and saw my first sustained human interaction since leaving home. The counterpeople were loud and gregarious and treated their customers with the casual irreverence of long-standing friends. It was an easy, open exchange, as restorative as the food I ate, and sent me on my way in a much better mood, as I rationalized that much of what had been plaguing me was no more than a provincial prejudice against a huge urban environment.

It was dark by the time I reached the reflecting pool but not much cooler. The tradeoff for walking had been a reminder of just how tenacious southern heat can be. It radiated off the sidewalk, as from a wood stove in the middle of winter, and filled the air—in a startling paradox—with the familiar parched odor of warm silage, the acres of cropped grass around me substituting for the farm fields of memory. The jacket I'd been wearing had gone from being slung over my shoulder to being held uncomfortably in one sweaty hand.

But I had no complaints. This part of Washington, especially at night, subdued most petty complaints with its sheer wide-open majesty. The pale-lit Washington Monument, a red beacon at its apex, looked otherworldly in the surrounding darkness, its daytime absurdity replaced by the mysterious murmurings of its Egyptian forebears. And its aura spread outward like a thin mist, snagging on the spotlit architectural oddities that belted the Mall like an ancient ring of mountains. I took it all in, from the Capitol to the museums to the gargantuan, recumbent federal buildings, with the happy acceptance of a willing tourist. I walked the length of the quarter-mile pool—Lincoln's tomb-like tribute reflecting in the water like a ghost—and yielded utterly to the theater of it all, using the countless historical cues to carry me back to my past.

Finally, thus summoned, a pale scattering of distant shadows caught my eye through the trees to the left and brought my journey to an end. I stood stock still in the darkness, in the here and now, and saw the defining image of myself as a nervous, isolated teenager on the threshold of self-discovery.

Scattered across a gently stepped slope, only barely illuminated by concealed, muted spotlights, a company of soldiers silently hovered in the gloom, as if frozen in mid-step by the distant, dying flash of a random artillery flare.

I abandoned the sidewalk and cut across the warm grass, all discomfort forgotten, transfixed by the nineteen nebulous bronze statues that formed the centerpiece of the Korean War Memorial. As I approached, their details emerged, commingling with memory. Clad in windswept ponchos, their weapons held with the ready casualness of umbrellas or shovels, they were lean with hunger, fatigue, and worry, and their faces, barely caressed by the thoughtfully directed light, were by degrees exhausted, pensive, frightened, and resigned. The closer I got, the more clearly I could see the slightly blurry photographs I'd sent my mother from beyond the ocean, and that reside still in the albums by her side.

It is a beautiful monument, low-key and reflective. A mixed service company of slightly larger-than-life soldiers—sculpted by a fellow Vermonter—ascends a series of shallow, planted terraces reminiscent of rice paddies. Ahead of them is a pool and a flagpole, to their right a low, black polished granite wall, sandblasted with the smoky images of over a thousand people looking out, like half-seen specters, representing the millions who served with the likes of me. The countries that contributed to this ephemeral, poorly remembered effort are etched in stone, along with the numbers of people sacrificed—over fifty-four thousand of them. It is a quiet place, designed for pensiveness and reminiscence, and alone in the night I gave in to just that, slowly pacing the walkway that encircled the site.

That quiet, however, was offset by occasional urban interruptions, the most jarring of which were periodic low-flying jets heading for the nearby airport. I was strolling in an easterly direction when a particularly noisy example made me stop in my tracks and turn around to watch. Instead of focusing on a startlingly close airplane, however, I came face-to-face with a rough-looking, bearded man standing a mere ten feet behind me. He and I, witnessed by nineteen well-armed silent soldiers, were the only ones within sight.

At first, he seemed as surprised as I was, his eyes widening and his body stiffening, and then he whirled around as I had and stared down the empty walkway. He looked back at me, his eyes suspicious. "Whaddya lookin' at?"

His voice was slurred and thick. "You," I admitted.

"What's wrong with me?"

"I don't know. What're you doing here?"

His mouth set in an angry line. "You sayin' I can't be here?"

"Not necessarily."

He considered that, found it acceptable, and loosened his stance, looking almost athletic in the process. He wasn't old— at most in his mid-thirties—and his clothes, while far from city wear, were more rough than ragged.

He gave me a conspiratorial smile. "You do me a favor?"

He took a couple of paces toward me, which I didn't like. Only half consciously, I moved my jacket before me, holding it loosely in both hands.

"I need some money," he continued. "I gotta get enough for bus fare. You give me something?"

I stepped back as he drew nearer, the hairs on my neck tingling. "Isn't this a pretty strange place to be looking for bus fare?"

His eyes narrowed, and his right hand dipped to his side. There was a metallic click and a flash of reflected light. I surprised him by leaping forward, the jacket held taut between my fists. He came up with the knife, startled by my sudden proximity, and I caught the blade in the folds of the coat, twisting it away and to one side. Inches from his face now, enveloped in his breath, I saw his mouth open in pain as he let out a shout. I then brought my knee up between his legs with all my strength.

The results were mixed. On TV that would've been the end of it. In fact, as he crumpled, he grabbed me around the neck with his free arm, rolled with his hips, and sent me staggering toward the nearest soldier. I tripped over the low curb separating the walkway from the terracing and stumbled with a dull clang into the statue, twisting around to keep my eyes on my assailant.

I'd dropped my coat in the process, the knife still within it, and it now lay between us on the ground. Doubled over, one hand clutching his groin, he dove for it the same time I did, just as a clear shout rang out in the night.

"*Police*. Stop where you are."

I got to the jacket first, but only because my opponent pulled up at the last second, rabbit-punching me in the neck instead of fighting for the knife. As I collapsed onto the cement, the flat switchblade hard against my chest, I saw him run off into the darkness toward Independence Avenue.

Heavy footsteps ran up behind me. "*Don't move*."

I twisted around to look up at a young patrolman, standing over me with a gun in his hand. "I'm the *victim*."

He looked at me nervously and then glanced up to where the other man had vanished.

"I'm also a cop," I continued, very slowly reaching for my back pocket. "I'm going for my badge."

I extracted the worn leather folder and flipped it open.

The patrolman slowly lowered his gun, his disappointment complete. "Shit."

* * *

The DC police were sympathetic and helpful, giving me aspirin and an ice pack for my neck. They listened patiently to my account, took a few notes, and when they were done, they even drove me to my Arlington motel. But I wasn't asked to look through any mug books, or to give a detailed description to an artist, and when the switchblade was recovered, I noticed no effort being made to preserve any fingerprints. What I'd suffered, I was told, was a typical attempted mugging—one of the mandatory accessories of any large city. I was wished a pleasant visit, given a generalized apology for having witnessed the back end of the welcome wagon, and left to my own devices.

That night, however, as I lay watching the passing car lights play across my ceiling, I found myself unable to be as casually dismissive. While not a city dweller, I still knew the makeup of the average mugger. The man I'd wrestled with had not been such a creature. I'd sensed duplicity and purpose in his eyes, beyond the presence of any cash in my wallet.

As the hours slipped by, the more I replayed what had happened, the more I believed our meeting to have been no simple random act.

5

THE ENTRANCE TO THE CIA IS DISARMINGLY PLACID. A LARGE sign off of Virginia Route 123 announces its presence, the initial access road is empty, treelined and free of any obvious security, and when the first man-made obstacle is encountered, it consists solely of a kiosk equipped with a camera and a loudspeaker. I announced myself there, showed my badge to the camera as requested, and proceeded to a visitors' center farther down the road. Only then, leaving my car to enter the small building, did I glimpse my final destination at the end of a woodsy corridor—gray, massive, and studded with antennae.

The security people behind the counter were polite and efficient, dressed in cheap uniform jackets decorated with identification tags listing numbers and letters only—no names. I was asked to fill out forms, to explain once more my purpose for being there, and was issued a parking pass and a visitor's badge. A phone call was made to the main building, and I was given directions to the parking lot opposite "the old main entrance."

The sun and the heat were back, making the surrounding forest shimmer in the haze of hot air bouncing off the parked cars and sticky asphalt. As I slammed my door in the VIP lot and squinted up at the monolith across from me, I was struck by its IBM-gothic harshness—all brutal, straight cement lines and jutting angles, punctuated by row upon row of blank, characterless windows.

To one side, in startling contrast, was a statue of Nathan Hale—the twenty-one-year-old Revolutionary spy caught on his first time out—standing with a rope around his neck under some shade trees. Either the guys behind that choice had seen patriotism and nobility where I also saw amateurism and failure, or someone with a wicked sense of humor had been given too much leash.

Through the wide bank of glass doors, I entered an enormous marble lobby, freezing cold and soaring high, buttoned in place by the CIA's oversized seal, mounted like a religious icon into the floor before me. The reverent tone was picked up by a lone statue of founder William "Wild Bill" Donovan, a glassed-in honor book of CIA dead, and a wall-mounted excerpt from St. John's famous gospel, "The truth shall make you free." There was a certain majesty to all this self-esteem, along with a sense that perhaps too much was being made of it.

A small woman, her graying hair in a tight bun, stepped forward from a distant row of elaborate turnstiles to greet me. "Lieutenant Gunther?" she asked pleasantly, extending a hand. She didn't introduce herself.

"You step in past the first barrier," she explained, escorting me up to one of the turnstiles and entering what looked like a cow pen for humans, "and place your badge into the slot," whereupon the bar behind her rose to lock her in. "After the computer has processed the badge's information," she continued as the bar before her ducked out of the way, "you can proceed. But," she smiled broadly, turning on her heel and holding up her identification, "don't forget your badge."

I followed suit indulgently, half wondering how much coded information I was sharing, and joined her on the other side.

She tapped my breast pocket. "Great. Just clip it there for the rest of your stay, and follow me."

We climbed a flight of four steps, and turned left into a broad hallway.

"Impressive lobby," I commented.

She laughed. "A little like a mausoleum, if you ask me. There's a newer entrance that's much friendlier. I can show it to you later, if you like."

"Far from Nathan Hale?"

"Right—the bearer of mixed messages. Still, I suppose there's a lot of truth to that, if you think about it."

She was right, of course, which made me feel a little guilty about my instinctive first reaction.

"You work with Mr. Snowden?" I asked as we turned right into a second hallway.

"Off and on. I'm sort of a gofer—more fun than being a secretary."

"And what does he do, exactly?"

She gave me a bright, disarming smile. "We don't often get people this far into the building who don't know why they're here."

Touché, I thought, and dropped it.

We were now walking alongside a long row of large oil portraits.

She noticed my interest. "All the past directors." She pointed to Richard Helms. "That's where I came in, under the last of the patricians—or the last of them that acted the part."

"Is that good news or bad?" I asked.

She shrugged and answered freely, showing none of the coyness she'd just displayed. "Neither, I suppose. Like all bosses, they've varied in quality. Casey loved the job too well; Turner hated it. Bush was my favorite. He was the nicest."

We entered an elevator at the end of the corridor and rode to the seventh floor. When the doors slid open, I was surprised at the cheerfulness of the decor—pleasant lighting, soothing carpeting and walls. And every door we passed was painted a different color.

Again, my guide anticipated my question before I asked it. "It all used to be battleship gray, as you'd expect. This happened almost overnight. Scuttlebutt has it someone was paid a fortune to suggest that brighter colors make for a happier workplace. I'm not complaining about the results, though. Here we are."

She gestured to a door labeled "7-25J"—none of the doors had names on them—and entered without knocking, ushering me into a windowless room that to the very last detail looked stolen from an upscale hotel, with a blank computer filling in for the TV set.

"Mr. Snowden will be with you shortly," she said and left me alone.

In fact, it wasn't all that shortly. I got to familiarize myself with my fashionably bland surroundings for fifteen minutes before a side door opened and a slender man with thinning hair and dark-rimmed glasses entered, a single folder clutched to his chest like a shield. I guessed Gil Snowden to be in his mid-fifties, and my instincts told me he'd been waiting me out on the other side of the door, a notion suggested by the sole mirror in the room looking suspiciously like the one-way observation window we had back at the PD.

The possibility didn't predispose me to like him.

He gave me a limp, moist handshake before officiously barricading himself behind the dark wooden desk. "Lieutenant Gunther," he spoke in the same sleepy voice he'd used on the phone, "it was very nice of you to come down on such short notice. I hope you had a pleasant flight?"

"I drove."

Snowden had been pretending to study the contents of the folder. My terse reply made him look up. "Everything go all right?"

I tried jarring him a little. "Till I got mugged last night."

He smiled sympathetically. "Yes. So I heard. I am sorry. Not the best introduction to the city. I'm glad you got off lightly."

I was seized by the same chill I'd felt before being ambushed the night before. "How did you hear about it?" I asked. "The local cops made it sound like it was right up there with a parking ticket."

His smile didn't change, but he sat back in his chair, exuding a smugness I'd missed earlier. "We have different interests from them."

"In me or the man who tried to knife me?"

"Both, actually. But you're sitting here now. I don't know where he is."

"Implying you know who *he* is."

He waved a hand carelessly. "It doesn't matter. What counts is that he missed."

I shifted my gaze to the wall behind him for a moment, rethinking my position. It was in Snowden's interest to play up the Big Brother image, regardless of what he knew, but he obviously did know something, and that alone gave weight to some of the paranoid fantasies that had kept me awake last night.

"Is the man we found in Vermont connected to the mugger?"

"Possibly. Part of that depends on what you can tell me."

I looked at him incredulously. "What I can tell *you*? We've got nothing on that case. I came down here so you could tell me something."

Snowden shook his head and laughed softly. "Lieutenant, forgive me, but I bothered to find out a little about you. Very tenacious man— 'Like a dog with a bone,' from what I heard. Don't you think 'nothing' is understating things slightly?"

I took my time answering, suddenly suspicious. He'd dug into my background, he knew about the incident last night, and his own people had visited Hillstrom's lab to check out the corpse. Yet now he was pleading ignorance. It was possible he didn't know how little we'd discovered, or that he was concerned we might know more than we did. More likely, we'd stumbled over something we hadn't yet recognized. If so, nothing he'd said so far had made me want to use him as a confidant.

I spoke slowly, hoping my genuine befuddlement would help hide the little I planned to hold back. "As far as I know, we have a dead floater with no identifiers. We don't have a single lead—nothing. We put feelers out everywhere—you know that—but we've gotten nothing back. That's why your phone call was so interesting. You did say you'd help me put this case to bed."

I left it short and simple, giving him a choice to either share his knowledge or nail me with the omission of the tattooed toes, the buckle knife, or the fact that we'd traced the rental car to Logan Airport.

Not surprisingly, I suppose, he ducked the choice entirely, leaving me as up in the air as before. "Lieutenant," he said, leaning forward and resting his forearms on the desk. "Around here, we are so instinctively suspicious of everyone and everything, we often end up confusing the very people we're supposed to be working with. What I should've said on the phone was that *we* would put this thing to bed—take it off your hands, so to speak."

This time, I didn't need to fake any confusion. "You're allowed to do that? Operate within the country?"

Snowden was already straightening in his chair, smiling and waving his hand to interrupt. "No, no. Of course not. I didn't mean it that way. Let me explain. You have a dead body and no leads to follow. I happen to know that's with good reason. The man you found was simply deposited in your area—pure happenstance. He doesn't have the remotest connection to Brattleboro or Vermont or even the U.S., for that matter. He was a foreign national, a man we've been watching for years, and he was taken out by other non–U.S. citizens. His ending up in Vermont was a fluke. I'm not asking you to drop the case or even to tiptoe around anything. You can beat the bushes all you want. I'm just saying you won't find anything. My comment about putting the case to bed was a clumsy way of recommending you don't waste too much overtime on this one. But it's up to you. I am sorry about the poor phrasing—too many years working in Washington."

I just stared at him, a response he obviously hadn't anticipated. After an awkward silence, he added, "After all, what's to be gained? Your job, like mine, is to protect and to serve. The people who killed this man are long gone, so no one needs protection from them, and running around for weeks discovering that fact won't serve anyone, least of all your taxpayers. Letting this one slip to the back pages will save you a lot of aggravation, and if things work out the way I think they will, it won't be too long anyway before I'll be calling you with some news that'll satisfy everyone."

"Meaning the CIA will locate his killer or killers abroad and hold them accountable?"

"Something like that. I'll give you enough that it'll look like a real-life spy thriller. 'Course, it'll be a bit on the vague side. But the locals should get a kick out of playing a minor role in some international intrigue."

I gave him an acquiescing smile, now absolutely positive I wasn't going to play ball with him. "Sort of amazing, isn't it, you getting me all the way down here just to tell me not to waste taxpayer money? This kind of thing happen often?"

Snowden became very still. "I'm not sure what you mean."

"That you make such an effort to tell a local cop to lay off. I mean, let's face it, you people aren't the only ones who're overly suspicious by nature. I'm a little that way myself. Why didn't you just let us charge around till we ran out of gas?"

He let out a small sigh. "I can see my homework about you was pretty accurate. Look, I won't go into details—there are some national security angles I can't divulge—but I'd be lying if I didn't say that your fading away quietly would be a big help to us. I meant what I said about doing what you want, though. Despite what the media says, we don't mess with the Constitution. But what you found is a tiny fragment of something we've been working on for years. Kicking up a lot of dust won't do you any good, and it could make things harder for us, so I guess I'm asking you to look at the big picture, and ask yourself if searching for something that isn't there is in anyone's best interest."

"And I'm to do this totally on faith, even though you won't tell me anything because of national security?"

He laid his hands flat on the table, his smile erased by the tone of my voice. "Well, apparently not." He rose to his feet. "Lieutenant, I guess you'll just have to do what you have to do, for whatever reasons. I was hoping for a little interagency cooperation, but maybe those days are gone. It's becoming that kind of world—everybody covering his ass, and to hell with what's good for the nation. Too bad."

He crossed the small room and pulled open the door. The same woman who'd escorted me here was standing in the hallway, apparently summoned by mysterious means.

Snowden nodded to me as I passed him, but didn't offer his hand, which was just as well. I might've been tempted to tear it off. "Sorry to have wasted your time, Lieutenant. Have a safe trip back."

It was dark. The rain outside hammered on the skylight over our bed with a comforting futility. I was lying facedown on the bed, a large towel beneath me, and Gail was straddling my hips, alternately oiling and massaging my back, which was sore from hours of driving in lousy weather, not to mention the odd knife fight.

"So what do you think you've stepped into?" she asked, bearing down.

"No ghost of a notion. I ran it by Tony, but he's as confused as I am. We can't tell if they know everything and are being cute, or know almost nothing and want to know more. Snowden basically told me to lay off the investigation, but there again, that could've been just to fire me up. One thing is for sure—he lied about Boris Malik, or whatever his name is. Told me he'd been dumped here out of convenience—a foreigner killed by other foreigners now out of the country—and that finding any evidence, or linking the case to anyone or any place local would be impossible. We know that's bullshit, since whoever did the dumping knew about the quarry and how to approach it."

Gail paused to apply more oil. "Which leaves you back where you started?"

"Not quite," I admitted reluctantly.

She resumed her handiwork along the tender back of my neck, forcing me to reach back and stop her.

"Ease up a bit. Something else happened down there," I continued. "You probably would've heard about it soon anyhow, the way news travels. I was mugged by a guy with a knife. Nothing much happened," I added quickly to her quiet intake of breath. "He came at me, I threw him off, and then he disappeared, right after he chopped me in the neck. But I'm having trouble believing it was as random as the cops're claiming."

She stretched out next to me to look into my face. "You sure that was all of it? Just a near thing?"

I kissed her forehead. "Promise. I kicked him in the balls, and he took off. The neck's a little sore is all."

She laid her head on the towel and closed her eyes briefly, one hand still stroking my back. I understood her concern. I'd almost been killed by a knife a few years back, and when she'd been raped, her attacker had used a knife to torment her. Such symbols had become evil icons to her, as had sharp noises in the night, the need for locked doors, and a wariness of things implied but perhaps not meant. They represented a skittish undercurrent beneath an otherwise hard-driving, intelligent, utterly self-possessed exterior.

I kissed her again. "Thanks for the back rub."

Her eyes reopened. "Want more?"

"No. That did the trick."

There was a long pause before she asked, "So what made this not a random mugging?"

"I don't know. For one thing, it happened at the Korean War Memorial. If I were a mugger, I wouldn't've been skulking around a totally empty area, probably famous for its police coverage. For another, I never heard him coming. I just happened to turn around to look at an airplane flying over. And finally, Snowden knew all about it early the next morning—at least he seemed to."

Gail raised up to prop her head in her hand. "He *knew* about it? How?"

"That's what I asked him. He pulled the all-seeing-eye routine, implying he even knew who the mugger was."

"Why would he tell you that?"

"To impress me, to hoodwink me, to scare me. You name it. Whatever it is, it worked. I left his office so full of theories I had no idea which one might be right. We've practiced disinformation at the department now and then, either to flush someone out or to get the press to cut us some slack, but this took the cake."

"But why go to all the trouble?" Gail asked.

"Specifically? I have no idea," I answered. "But it keeps boiling down to a single common denominator. Regardless of whether the CIA is hoping we'll drop it or pursue it, we've obviously stepped into something pretty interesting, and I would love to find out what the hell it is—and why the FBI is apparently also being kept in the dark."

I waited for Ron and J.P. to squeeze themselves into my two office chairs, one wedged between a couple of filing cabinets, the other shoved under a tiny side table loaded down with files. Each man knew to move slowly and cautiously, having suffered paper landslides in the past.

"You both get the memo on my trip to DC?" I asked.

J.P. nodded. Ron asked, "How real is the CIA connection?"

"Real enough, not that we can do anything about it right now. For the moment, I'm pretending they don't even exist. What did you two dig up while I was gone?"

Ron started off, cradling a thick folder in his lap, which he patted apologetically. "Not much on the paper trail. All the inquiries we sent out are still dangling, including the ones to Canada. INS and DEA have nothing on their books. I drove to Boston to look over the airline passenger lists personally, but Boris Malik doesn't show up anywhere, meaning he either used another name, or he picked up the car at the airport as a decoy. In the three hours before he rented the car, planes came in from all over the place, including Moscow, but without a name, I don't guess it matters. I kept the lists just in case another alias crops up, but otherwise, it's a dead end."

"You talk to the rental people?" I asked.

"Yeah, but there again . . . The girl who did the paperwork recognized him, but she couldn't remember if he had luggage or not, or if he said where he was headed. She wasn't even sure if he was alone. She did say he had an accent. It was the only reason she remembered him at all—'cause they had such a hard time communicating."

"What about the credit card?"

"Counterfeit. The charge went through to some poor bastard in Illinois. The name on the card was Malik's."

"He didn't ask for any maps or directions?"

Ron shook his head.

I looked at J.P. "You fare any better?"

He smiled, despite the absence of a file folder of any size. "I think so. I got two items linking the car trunk to the dead man. The first is a definite blood match, and the second might give us the leg up we've been looking for, although to give credit where it's due, one of the crime lab guys discovered it. Remember the debris collected from Boris's hair and clothes? Most of it was pond scum, but there was a single leaf fragment that caught this guy's eye. He's an amateur botanist—studied it in college—and this thing looked like nothing he'd ever seen. So instead of just sending it down the pipeline for someone else to figure out weeks from now, he took it to a consultant after work. Turns out it came from a ginkgo tree—a *Ginkgo biloba*, to be exact—native to China, so it's pretty rare."

He was about to continue, which I knew he could do for a quarter hour if properly stimulated, but I was too curious to wait. "How rare?" I asked.

J.P. blinked at me a couple of times, caught off guard. "I don't know—maybe a couple of hundred in the state. But that's not really the point. See, these trees aren't like most. They're distinctively sexed. Male trees are separate from female trees."

I began to smile, despite my impatience, and decided to leave him alone.

"When I was going through the trunk of the rental car," he continued, "I collected what turned out to be a tiny sample of flesh from a ginkgo seed, which is unique to the female. It was gooey and didn't smell too good. I didn't know what it was then, of course, except that it was some sort of plant, but after the leaf was identified, I drove it up to the lab yesterday afternoon, just before quitting time, and they confirmed it."

"Which leads us where?" I asked belatedly, realizing he'd come to an end.

"I don't know yet, but if we could locate all the female ginkgo trees in the immediate area, it might give us a location." He hesitated a moment. "Of course, that could be easier said than done. I was going to start calling a few local naturalists, botanists, and the like. See what I could find."

I raised a finger. "I have a better idea. Come with me."

Newfane, Vermont, is about twelve miles northwest of Brattleboro on Route 30, a broad, beautiful, winding road that follows the meandering West River up the valley toward the ski slopes of the southern Green Mountains. During foliage season, every October, the road fills with out-of-state cars and buses "from away," crowded with tourists soaking in the idyllic mixture of hills, trees, and sun-dappled water. Most of these people make a stop at Newfane village—to shop, take pictures, gather leaves, and walk around a quaint clutter of ancient white clapboard buildings bordering a huge green commons complete with church, courthouse, and meeting hall.

This, over time, has helped transform Route 30 into one of the major noninterstate arteries into the state's center, and make Newfane a stepping-off point to many inland destinations. Which is why I immediately drove J.P. up there.

Just south of the village proper, across from Rick's Tavern, was the Newfane Greenhouse, one of the best nurseries in the area and—what interested me most at the moment—a favorite destination for the upwardly mobile. I was counting on the ginkgo's rarity to translate into an appropriately high price tag—and on the greenhouse's staff to know who could afford one. J.P.'s notion of chasing down naturalists hadn't been bad, but no one I'd ever met in that line had ever had two dimes to rub together. I was hoping the ginkgo was less a natural phenomenon and more an upper-class commodity.

It wasn't too busy when we arrived. The summer was winding down, and while I was still impressed by the activity in the parking lot, it was still less than half-full.

J.P. and I got out of the car, looking out of place in our coats and ties, and walked into the only building that wasn't a plastic-sheeted greenhouse. A young man greeted us from behind the service counter. "You need any help?"

"Yeah," I said. "We're looking for some information about a really rare tree—a ginkgo. You know anything about them?"

He pulled a face and shook his head, smiling. "I can handle the run-of-the-mill stuff, but that sounds more like Jay's department. Hang on a sec."

He reached under the counter and retrieved a portable radio. "Jay?" he said after keying the mike.

"Yeah," came the answer after a pause.

"I got two gentlemen here asking about ginkgo trees."

"Be right there."

The young man replaced the radio with a laugh. "You must've pushed a button with that one. He's knee-deep in mud, working out back."

A woman approached with a tray full of small plants, and we faded back so the clerk could work the cash register. A few minutes later, an impressively tall, skinny man wearing a baseball cap and an open face ambled into the building, rubbing his hands on a mud-encrusted pair of khakis.

He smiled broadly as he drew near. "Hi. I'm Jay Wilson. You the ones interested in the ginkgos?"

I walked with him to an unpopulated corner of the room, speaking quietly. "Probably not in the sense you'd like, I'm afraid. We're from the Brattleboro police—sort of on a research trip."

Wilson's bright disposition remained undaunted. "Neat. What do you want to know?"

"I guess for starters, do you sell them?"

"I do when I can find 'em. They're pretty hard to get. Even as high-priced as they are, they move like crazy."

"So there're a lot of them around?" J.P. asked, disappointed.

"Oh, no. Offhand, I'd say fifteen to twenty tops in the whole county. Their rarity's part of the appeal. Not that they're fragile or anything," he added quickly, as if we were customers. "They're quite hardy—grow almost anywhere. Interesting tree, actually, and a real beauty. One of the oldest on the face of the earth. I read they were, around two hundred and thirty million years ago, native to North America, which is ironic, since their only native habitat these days is eastern China. That's what makes 'em so pricey."

"I gather they come in male and female varieties," I commented.

He seemed to dismiss the idea. "Well, they do, but that doesn't really matter. People only buy the males. It's all *I* ever sell."

We both stared at him. "Why?" J.P. finally asked.

"The females have seeds—orange grapey things about an inch long, coated with a messy pulp. They not only litter the ground, but they stink to high heaven—the pulp does. They're famous for it."

"How many females do you think are in Windham County?" I asked.

He considered that for a moment. "Probably no more than three or four, but that's just a guess. They're a little sneaky. For the first twenty to even fifty years, the males and females look pretty much the same. It's only after they fruit that the females come out of the closet. So there're probably several supposed males out there that're getting ready to surprise their owners. I got called about one just recently. Guy wanted to know how to deal with the seeds. I told him he was screwed. Even picking them up won't work, since they're designed to break open when they land. The season only lasts six weeks, though, starting in late summer. I said he should try to work it to his advantage, make it a selling point somehow. Asians actually eat the seeds—consider 'em a delicacy, after the pulp's been removed—and they're hot right now in the herbal medicine market. Supposed to treat everything from Alzheimer's to hearing problems."

He gave a sly smile. "They're also sold as a sexual enhancer—that's why I thought he could turn it into an advantage. He didn't sound too convinced, though. Maybe he couldn't figure out how to phrase it in the brochure."

"Brochure for what?"

"He runs the Windham Hill Inn, just outside West Townshend."

6

THE DRIVEWAY TO THE WINDHAM HILL INN IS MODEST ENOUGH—
a dirt lane branching off from the road between Route 30 and
the tiny village of Windham some seven miles farther north. There is
an official state sign advertising the place—small, sedate white letters
on a dark green background. Vermont does not permit billboards, a
decision with which the inn had obviously tastefully concurred, since
not even the mailbox continued the message.

The darkened lane meanders a short distance past a house or two,
closely shaded by a crowd of trees before cresting a small hill and issuing into the light of a vast opening.

It's a theatrical setting. From right to left, on a gentle downhill
slope, are a pool, a tennis court, a huge converted barn, a discreetly
landscaped parking area, and the main house of the inn itself—old,
brick-clad topped by white clapboard—all looking like a watercolor
of the English countryside. Beyond it hovers a view of thousands of
acres—fields, forests, and haze-blurred mountains—and standing
front and center, visually connecting the barn and the main building,
towering in sharp contrast to the breathtaking but hazy horizon, was a
tremendous, fan-shaped tree, unlike any I'd ever seen.

I had stopped the car on the crest, and now cast a glance at J.P.,
whose eyes were glued to the tree. "The ginkgo, I presume?" I asked.

"It's huge," he murmured.

I rolled down into the parking area near the tree and killed the
engine.

"Okay," I said, turning toward him. "Soft-shoe time. We're here unofficially, no bones to pick. We're working on something vague, checking a variety of neighborhoods. If we can avoid mentioning any interest in the tree, so much the better."

"Do we even admit we're cops?" he asked.

We opened our doors simultaneously. "Let's play it by ear."

We were met by a cloying, nauseating odor—a stunning counterpoint to the beauty surrounding us.

"Jesus," J. P. gasped. "It smells like shit."

"Or vomit," I agreed, "Wilson didn't even come close."

J.P. was looking around him in shock. "I guess. The little bit I found in the car trunk smelled bad, but I thought it was something else—a dead piece of skin or something." He glanced over at the main house of the inn, artistically swathed in flowers, bushes, and a couple of carefully pruned fruit trees. "I don't think keeping the tree out of the brochure is such a good idea. This guy could have a lawsuit on his hands."

As if in response, the front door swung back, and a tall, white-haired man with a tanned face, slight belly, and broad shoulders appeared on the threshold. He waved and called out, "Hi, there. Welcome."

I waved back. J.P. was still glancing about, suddenly aware that I'd parked right in the middle of a blanket of the pulpy seeds. He lifted his foot and checked the sole of his shoe with disgust.

The man approached, shaking his head, but only speaking once he'd come within earshot. "I am sorry. You've just been introduced to our ginkgo tree, I'm afraid. It doesn't last long, but it's a mess while it does."

He shook our hands. "I'm John Rarig, the owner. You'll be glad to know this is the worst of it. We've put shoe scrubbers at all the entrances, the only rooms we're using right now face away from the tree, and the dining room's on the other side."

Neither J.P. nor I said anything immediately, forcing Rarig to shuffle his feet a bit, put his hands in his pockets, and lean back to stare up to the top of the towering offender. I guessed him to be in his mid-seventies but in terrifically good shape. He sighed resignedly. "I know, it still stinks. There's no way around it. It's probably been there thirty years or more, as beautiful as any tree I've ever seen. In the fall, it turns an electric yellow, like it's been plugged in—amazing. It only started doing this this year."

"I know," I admitted, mostly to spare myself another botanical lecture. "We heard all about it from Jay Wilson at the greenhouse."

Rarig looked at us in surprise. "How did you know about my tree?"

"We didn't. It came up in conversation. It sounded interesting, so we came by to check it out."

J.P., yielding to curiosity, had stopped worrying about the slimy pulp and was instead taking a tour of the tree in its midst, circling the thick trunk and looking up into its branches. The tactic of avoiding all mention of the ginkgo had obviously been amended.

"Are you naturalists or something?" Rarig asked, showing his confusion.

I gave him what I hoped was a disarming smile. "Cops, actually—out of Brattleboro. I'm Joe Gunther. That's J.P. Tyler. Wilson made this tree sound so weird, we came up on impulse. I hope that's all right."

Rarig was still smiling, but I felt the intensity of his eyes. "Sure—I wish I could turn it into a tourist attraction. Charge admission and make up some of what it's costing me."

"Cut into the clientele, has it?" I asked.

He gazed unhappily at the converted barn we'd passed driving in, his voice flattening now that he knew we weren't customers. "Even after closing every room facing this damn thing. I've got twenty-one of them, grand total, so that's only five or six I can't use. But it still doesn't matter. Guests are pretty understanding about most things, like when we were fixing up that barn—all the construction noise and trucks and workmen—but this really gets to them. Gets to me, too."

Having finished his survey, J.P. circled back toward us. "Why don't you cut it down?" he asked.

Rarig looked at the sloppy, stained driveway. "I probably should. It's just that for the rest of the year, it's like the focal point of the whole place—ties it all together visually." He turned toward the main building and gestured with his hand. "Why don't you come in for a cup of coffee or something? Get out of this stench."

We fell into line behind him as he led the way, still talking. "It's also worth an incredible amount of money—thousands and thousands of dollars. Plus, I'm the new kid on the block—only owned the place for four years—and it's been here forever. I'd hate to come across as the turkey who destroyed the prize ginkgo 'cause he wanted to make a buck."

"Where did you live before?" I asked.

"DC. I worked for the State Department. Gray life in a gray office inside a gray building. I couldn't wait till the pension reached its max. I was out of there so fast I don't even remember packing. I didn't come straight here, of course. Took me ten years of roaming around the country before I found the best it had to offer." He laughed and showed us how to dampen the soles of our shoes in a soapy pan and then scrub them against some stiff brushes bolted to the door stoop.

The interior of the main building was a blend of English pub, old family home, and New England antiquities. It was dark, comforting, heavy in wood and wool accents, and decorated with somber oil paintings and weathered brass knickknacks. Rarig led us down the short central hallway, around a cherry wood bar area, and back to a grouping of overstuffed armchairs overlooking the back lawn, a small pond, and the woods beyond. The chairs reminded me of ones my mother still had at home—a little old, a little faded, and utterly relaxing.

As soon as we'd sat down, he pulled open a drawer from under the coffee table at our knees and handed me a magazine. "This'll give you an idea of why I'm so ambivalent about that tree."

It was a two-month-old copy of the *New York Times* Sunday magazine, dedicated to "Great Escapes in New England." It was doubled-back to an article featuring the inn, in which the ginkgo was resplendent in an opening, edge-to-edge color photograph.

"I see what you mean," I murmured, leafing through the article.

The following shots were standard fare—the view, the inn, the barn, down the long, narrow dining room at night, complete with candles and contented guests. One picture, of the entrance hall, caught Rarig himself reflected in a wall mirror, looking distracted and morose. It had obviously been his intention to be out of the photographer's way at the time.

I returned the magazine. "Very impressive. That must've helped business."

"It didn't hurt. Of course they were here before it started stinking like a sewer." Rarig passed it over to Tyler and then went about pouring us cups of coffee from a fancy thermos parked on the table. As he did, I watched his profile, still digesting the improbable coincidence of his having come from the very city where I'd almost been stuck with a knife.

"You ever been back to Washington?"

He gave me my cup. "Not even maybe. I missed my own retirement party. They called me and said I had a certificate or something coming. I told 'em to mail it. It never arrived."

He handed a second cup to J.P. and sat back, cradling his own before him. "No. If I never see another city again, that'll suit me just fine. This life is no feather bed. You get cranky guests, leaky roofs, and bursting pipes in the winter—the place was built in 1823—but they're the kinds of problems you can actually fix. Not some vague matters of policy set in place by a bunch of on-the-job-retirement bureaucrats."

I took advantage of the reference to ask, "You have many cranky guests?"

He took a sip before answering. "Not really. There's a New Yorker right now who's a little thin-skinned, but I get the feeling he's got problems back at the office—it's nothing personal."

"I suppose a lot of people come up here to get away from it all, kind of like you did."

"Oh, sure," he said. "They can never resist bringing their cell phones, of course, but they tell themselves they're relaxing, and I suppose that's half the battle. We try to make them feel like it's real."

He sighed deeply. "This isn't the way I'd really like it, though. Twenty-five years ago, this place was almost a commune. The guests had to pay, of course. But they all ate family style, at one huge table, from a fixed menu. And everybody mixed in—the employees and the guests, everyone's kids. Must've been like the Waltons. It caught a little flak for that, of course, especially from the local cops. The owners were pretty left-wing. Unmarried mothers-to-be, Vietnam War protesters, illegal immigrants—people like that hung out here a lot, mostly as temp help. But I really like the idea of one big family, all sharing the same experience, getting rid of the elitist image most inns try to pump up."

Rarig paused, staring at the ceiling, and then blinked a couple of times, clearing his throat and looking straight at us. "Can't do it, of course—economics. Nowadays, people expect the French cuisine, the four-star treatment. I'd be cutting my throat, turning it back into a hippie hangout."

He shook his head mournfully. "That's the only reason I really am considering cutting the tree down. On the other hand, late summer isn't the best time for us anyhow. People have to get back home. Maybe I could just shut down for a month and a half . . . It's a tough decision."

"How long do your guests stay, on average?" J.P. asked, speaking for the first time since we'd sat down.

"Two days—a standard weekend—but we encourage them to stretch things out a little. The third day is half price, and the fifth is on us. Right now we have twelve guests, and for about half of them this is their fourth day, which is pretty unusual."

"Any that've been here longer?" I asked. According to our calculations, the man with the tattooed toes had been killed eight or nine days ago. I knew such an obvious question might tip our hand, but I also couldn't see what we'd gain by letting more time slip by.

Rarig slowly leaned forward and gently placed his half-empty coffee cup on the table, as if it were full to the brim. He stayed slightly hunched up and looked at me closely, his head tilted. "No. What is this all about?"

J.P. and I exchanged glances. He raised his eyebrows and shrugged almost imperceptibly. "We're investigating a murder, Mr. Rarig," I said, "and we suspect the inn is somehow connected."

He didn't move. "How?"

I didn't have much to lose. If he was tied into all this, my being coy would be purposeless, and if he was as innocent as he seemed, he could do us some good.

J. P. answered for me. "We have compelling evidence the killing took place here."

Rarig sat back again, smiling slightly. "The tree, right?"

"Why do you say that?" J.P. asked.

It was a silly question, occasionally workable with one of our run-of-the-mill clients, whose gullibility often seemed without bottom, but not with John Rarig, who was patently nobody's fool. J. P. Tyler was a scientist by instinct, a little slow to discern such human subtleties.

Rarig laughed softly at his awkwardness. "Two cops drop by, a long way from their home turf, having discussed ginkgo trees in New-fane. Sure sounds like a research trip to me. Did your dead body have a branch clutched in one hand?"

But while no wizard at interviewing, Tyler had a fetish for discretion. He merely stared back.

"Have you been around here all week, Mr. Rarig?" I asked.

He crossed his arms, the informality of our get-together now utterly gone. "Yes."

"Do you recall anything unusual happening eight or nine days ago, day or night?"

"No, but then I don't live at the inn. I have a house just over the hill—well out of earshot. No one reported anything, though."

"Did any guests leave ahead of schedule around then, or show any signs that something was wrong?" Tyler asked.

Rarig hesitated. "I'd have to check the register, but nothing comes to mind."

I took the bait. "Could we look at that?"

Rarig avoided a direct answer. "What makes you think it was one of my guests? What *is* your evidence?"

"It's the tree," I told him. "Specifically, one of the seeds."

"And one of the small lower branches has been freshly broken," J.P. added, touching his hair. "About head high."

To give Tyler his due, it was a nice bit of timing. Rarig pushed out his lips and expelled a small sigh, staring straight ahead. "I see," he finally said.

"So?" I prompted.

He looked uncomfortable. "We've got a very good reputation here. You saw the article. Word gets out I handed you my guest list, I could lose my shirt—maybe even end up in court. I don't suppose you have a warrant?"

I in turn ducked that. "We're not exactly Keystone Kops, Mr. Rarig. We could check them out without their even knowing it, at least initially. If we found something suspicious, the person involved would probably have more to worry about than smearing your reputation."

Rarig shook his head. "I better call my lawyer and get some advice. I don't want to be unfriendly, but I'm way out of my depths here, and I don't want to lose everything I've put into this place."

I was impressed by the sincerity in his voice, which I also knew meant nothing whatsoever.

"What about your employees?" Tyler asked. "How many are there?"

His answer surprised me. "Twenty-five, not counting me, although only five of them are full-time salaried."

"Could we have *their* names, at least?" I asked.

Again, he didn't answer immediately.

"There are Labor and Industry files we could consult," I prompted, being somewhat less than truthful. "Tax records, Department of Health, disability insurance. It would take time, but—"

He waved his hand and stood up. "All right. I don't see the harm there. I will warn them about what I've done, though."

J.P. and I joined him. "Fair enough," I said. "When can we expect them?"

"Would tomorrow be too late? That'll give me time to call my lawyer, too."

I shook his hand. "That'll be fine."

He led us back to the front door, where I removed the retouched photo of the man in Hillstrom's cooler from my pocket. "You ever see him?"

He looked at it carefully. "He's the one in the paper, who was found in the quarry."

"That's right."

He returned the picture. "No. I'm afraid not."

He looked me hard in the eye as I put the photo away. "Look, I do want to cooperate. You understand that, don't you?"

"Yes, I do," I told him. But I hadn't the slightest idea.

We'd been driving for five minutes in silence before I asked Tyler, "Tell me more about the broken branch."

"It was around the back of the tree, near the trunk, out of sight of where we parked."

"You think it could have caused Malik's head injury?"

"It was the right height. And the stump had been trimmed with a knife—clumsily—and the broken piece removed. I checked the whole area. That could be innocent enough—we can ask whoever it is who takes care of the grounds if he found it and threw it away after trimming the stump. But it might mean the killer did it to hide any trace evidence on the wood. A tidy guest might've done it, too, I suppose," he added after a pause. "So much time's gone by."

"What could you see from there?"

"A pretty good view of the inn. At night with the interior lights on, I'd guess you'd have a clear shot of the whole first floor, at least toward the front. And that's where most of the activity takes place, what with the dining room taking up ninety percent of the back side. I checked how the night lighting's rigged. From what I could see, a floodlight mounted across the walkway on the wall is aimed directly at the other side of the trunk, throwing a shadow where I was standing."

"So—a nice, discreet observation spot."

"I'd say so. I'd have to go back at night to make sure. There is something else," he added after a pause. "If Malik was standing there, it would give us another explanation why his shoes were missing."

"Maybe. What about Rarig?" I asked.

J. P. frowned thoughtfully. "He plays straight enough. I hope we don't get any shit about the guest list."

"We will. We also might be able to find out who some of them were through the employees. *That* list I think he'll give us, to buy us off."

"Meaning he does have something to hide?"

"Not necessarily. His concern's legitimate—reputation's a word-of-mouth thing. What sticks in my craw is that magazine article. Not only did Rarig appear in it just once, by accident, but he keeps the article tucked away."

Tyler gave me a skeptical look. "It's in a room where all the guests get together before dinner every night."

I shook my head. "No, no. That's not what I mean. A few million people've already read the thing, after all. It's the body language. If *you* ran that place and got that kind of attention, wouldn't you frame the article and put it where people could see it?"

"Maybe. I suppose so."

"It's the fact that he didn't, and that he stayed out of the photos in the first place, that bugs me."

Tyler slowly began to smile. "And that he originally came from DC."

7

JOHN RARIG LOOKED AROUND MY OFFICE EARLY THE NEXT MORNING, no doubt struck by its small size and state of disarray. Brattleboro was once described as a champagne town with a beer income—a reference to its population's affinity for catering to all causes while being hard-pressed to pay for them. The police department, along with all the other municipal services, was allowed no fat in its budget, as my office decor amply testified.

I gestured to a plastic guest chair. "Please, have a seat."

He stayed standing in the doorway. "No, thanks." He reached into his back pocket and extracted a folded sheet of paper, which he handed to me. "That's a list of my employees. My lawyer wanted me to tell you to pound sand, but I disagreed. If someone who works for me has broken the law, I want to find out about it. The guests are another matter, at least until you can get a warrant, but this one's on me. I did put out a memo, though, that I was cooperating with the police, so they know you'll be coming. I thought that was only fair."

I glanced over the sheet. "That's fine, and I appreciate the cooperation. It's not like we're loaded for bear, anyhow. We're just hoping to solve a puzzle. It could be your place had nothing to do with any of this." I smiled and added, "That we're barking up the wrong ginkgo tree."

He smiled weakly. Turning to go, he paused. "Try to respect their privacy, okay? These are good people—at least I think they are. They've

70

helped me enormously—kept a dream alive. I don't want anyone to think I've abused their trust."

I rose from my desk and escorted him down our small hallway to the building's central corridor. "Mr. Rarig, we do this a lot. For every thirty or forty people we interview, only one ends up holding the bag. We're not out to abuse people."

He nodded and shook my hand. "Will you let me know how things are going?"

"I'll keep you informed," I said, solely to pacify him.

I stood in the doorway, watching him walk toward the exit where the parking lot's located. His shoulders were slumped and his gait hesitant. For the first time since I'd met him, he looked his seventy-odd years.

Despite the circumstances that had led me to him, and the deep suspicions I had concerning him, I'd also been touched by his asking me to watch out for his employees. The reference to their helping him achieve his goal had struck a chord—at once poignant and lonely—the comment of a single man who'd made the best he could of the end of his life, to the point of calling it a dream come true.

We were in the conference room, just the three of us, making the table look larger than it was. My office would've worked also, but I'd wanted space enough for all of us to take notes comfortably.

I passed out copies of Rarig's employee list, noting with amused satisfaction how it was received. Sammie picked it up in both hands and stared at it, as if willing it to confess. Ron aligned it squarely before him on the tabletop with his fingertips—a document worthy of preservation and respect.

"Twenty-six names," I said, "including John Rarig's, to be split between the three of us. The chief won't give us any more manpower, since it doesn't look like we've got a tiger by the tail. But chances are we can whittle the numbers down pretty fast. Start with the usual criminal record checks—NCIC, Vermont CIC, and the in-house criminal files of VSP and all bordering state police agencies. Check our own archives, and as soon as you peg a home address for each name, call any contacts you might have in other municipal departments to see what they have— you never know who might be on a snitch or suspect list. And don't forget the sheriff's office."

Both of them were writing this down, so I paused briefly to let them catch up. "If we don't get lucky with any of that," I continued, "we can check out public records. Start with Motor Vehicles. They'll give you a lot to go on—description, address, date of birth, what's been registered, and so on. From there, you can go to the appropriate town clerks for more. Push comes to shove, and they don't own a car, use the phone book to at least get an address. All we're after at this point are the basics—name, rank, and serial number. As individuals begin standing out, we can dig a little deeper, just so we know more than they think we do when we talk to them. Right now, though, nobody gets the third degree," I added, remembering Rarig's plea. "If there's a bad guy in the bunch, chances are he'll pop up before the others even know we've been snooping around."

"What're we going to do about the guest list?" Ron asked.

I sat back in my chair. "Not much. When we get to talking with the employees, we should ask for any names, hometowns, and anything else they might remember. Maybe they'll be a little less discreet than Rarig."

"They're going to know that's against the rules," Sammie cautioned.

"True," I said, standing up. "But there're all kinds of ways to extract information. They don't have to see you coming."

Around one that afternoon, by now immersed in the details of chasing down my nine allotted names—to little effect—I got a telephone call from Stan Katz, the editor of the *Brattleboro Reformer*. Katz and I went back many years, from when I was just a detective, and he was the paper's distrustful cops-'n'-courts reporter. It had never been a friendship—far from it, on occasion—but we'd grown toward a mutual respect. When the paper had almost hit bottom a few years back, briefly becoming a sensationalist tabloid under the misguided management of an out-of-state owner, Katz had led the charge in an employee buyout. Now laden with a financial burden as well as his editorial responsibilities, he was a far more thoughtful and forgiving human being, which, given his start, made him just bearable—some of the time.

"Joe," he said, "long time, no harassment."

"Which makes me very happy. How's life?"

"Lousy. Don't let anyone tell you that when the nuts take over the nuthouse, things run any smoother. No wonder the Communists went belly-up. I was calling about the dead guy in the quarry. Anything new?"

"What happened to Alice?" I asked. Alice Sims was the current police beat reporter.

"I gotta take a break from this management crap once in a while. Alice'll write it. I'm just helping her out."

"I don't know what she'll write," I said. "We still don't have a name, a motive, a weapon, or anything else. The last press release still says it all, including the Boris Malik pseudonym."

"Does that mean the guy was Russian?"

Through the sheriff's initial inquiry, the rental car's existence had finally leaked, along with its connection to Logan Airport, but we'd still managed to keep the tattooed toes and the buckle knife under wraps. "Could be. But we got nowhere checking flight manifests into Boston, and the car rental people were a dead end."

I paused a moment, reflecting on my present efforts, and considered how this conversation might be turned to my advantage. "To be honest," I added, "there's a growing feeling the body was just dumped here. We haven't found any neighborhood ties—no reports of strange sightings or sounds or missing persons that might fit. And the fact that the car was abandoned on one of the busiest roads in southern Vermont supports the theory. We've shared everything we got with the appropriate agencies, including the Canadians, and nothing's come back."

I was hoping he wouldn't conjure up Kunkle's logical question about the knowledgeable choice of the quarry as a dumping spot. He didn't, opting instead to pounce on my purposefully bored tone of voice. "Meaning you're doing nothing?" he asked incredulously. "It's a murder, for Christ's sake."

"Of course we are, Stan," I said wearily. "We're conducting interviews and digging up what we can, but let's face it, we don't have a hell of a lot to go on, and off the record, the troops aren't all that enthusiastic. There's nothing to charge them up."

"I can sympathize," he conceded after a moment, sounding disappointed. "I thought when you found him we had something hot."

"Not so far, and I don't see anything on the horizon."

We hung up after a few closing comments, and I leaned back in my chair, thoughtfully staring at the phone. With any luck, tomorrow's article would reflect my lack of enthusiasm. It wouldn't make us look like the FBI, but it would take the edge off the interviews we'd be conducting over the next few days. If the people we were talking to thought we were just going through the motions, the chances of one of them letting something slip increased.

It was a long, tedious two days before Sammie, Ron, and I reconvened at the same conference table. Instead of three copies of a single sheet of paper, we each now had folders bulging with information about John Rarig and his employees, most of which, I knew, would eventually prove useless. But our business was like the orchid breeder's in one sense—founded on the knowledge that success only comes after endless disappointment.

Which certainly described my results. I'd uncovered no "hits" whatsoever, a fact I thought it politic to keep private until later. "Okay," I said, "what've you got?"

They'd apparently exchanged notes earlier. Ron spoke up first, "One for me, two for Sam. I've got a woman with a small string of offenses—shoplifting, check bouncing, operating an illegal day care. Name's Marianne Baker. She's been clean for five years, employed by the inn for three of them as a housekeeper. Lives in Jamaica." He placed the piece of paper he'd been reading from flat on the table. "Hardly on the Most Wanted list. Worst thing about her is the company she keeps. She's living with a guy with a history of violence, including some he did down here. Ever hear of Marty Sopper?"

I had. "Petty theft, assault, disorderly conduct, disturbing the peace?"

"Yeah," he answered, "among others. He did a couple of years for a drug deal—beat up the kid he was selling to. Like Marianne, not a headliner, but he likes to use force."

I cocked an eyebrow at Sammie.

"Bob Manship and Doug DeFalque," she said. "Bob was nailed for assault four years ago and given probation. Apparently nobody liked the guy he totaled, so the SA just went by the numbers, but the cop I talked to said Bob could've earned himself a murder rap if someone hadn't stopped him. It was over a woman—the victim's wife. He used a hammer."

"Jesus," I murmured.

"Been clean since," Sammie resumed, "and was a good boy up till then. Might've been just a flash in the pan, but the weapon impressed me, too. He works as the inn's dishwasher. The same cop admitted he was a nice guy—normally very quiet. I talked to his probation officer, too. Same basic report—steady, quiet, dependable, and remorseful about what he did. The woman in the case moved away, by the way. Manship lives alone."

She picked up another document. "Douglas DeFalque. No crimes of violence and no criminal record, but multiple mentions as a fellow traveler. Born in Quebec, he's lived on one side of the border or the other all his life, and from what I could find out, makes a tidy sum on the side as a smuggler. Both the Quebec Provincial Police and the U.S. Border Patrol have him on their hot sheets, but nobody's ever caught him red-handed."

"What does he smuggle?" I asked.

"Cigarettes and booze going north, aliens, drugs, and bear gallbladders going south—gallbladders are a hot item in Taiwan and China. They use the bile for medicine. It's pricey and it's regulated, so the black market demand is pretty high. I asked the Mounties to check him out, see who his associates are. They're still looking into it, comparing notes with other agencies, but it looks like he's a free agent, probably working with the biker gangs, and increasingly with the Russian mob."

There was a brief silence in the room as Ron and I digested that. Sammie smiled. "I thought you might find the last bit interesting."

"What does he do at the inn?" I asked.

"A waiter. The people I talked to say he's very smooth—good-look-ing, nice French accent, well liked by the ladies. He's seasonal, though. Only works during the crunches. That's what gives him time with his other pursuits."

"Is he working there now?"

"No, but he was two weeks ago. He left four days after we think Boris got whacked. He's around, though. Lives in Jamaica. I got the address."

I propped my chin in my hand, looking at them both. "Top of our list?"

Ron shrugged. "Looks that way. He's got everything except a known propensity for violence."

"Unless he contracts it out," Sammie suggested. "Didn't J.P. say Boris was probably spying on the inn from under that tree, hiding in the shadows? If DeFalque knew about that, he might've set him up."

I shook my head. "Whoa. That's a long way from finding a seed in Boris's hair. You may be right, Sam, but we need to sniff around more first. Do we have anything at all on the other names?"

They both shook their heads, Ron adding, "A few vehicular cita-tions—DWI, speeding, a minor accident or two. Two of the women I checked live together and got cited for disturbing the peace after an all-girl party a few months back. Nothing stands out, though. What did you find?"

I didn't even bother opening my file folder. "Nothing, really. Same as you—parking tickets, whatnot. John Rarig seems to be legit. Career Washington bureaucrat. Like he said: gray office in a gray building."

I asked Sammie, "How long before the Mounties report back on Doug DeFalque?"

"Should be today—noon at the latest."

"Okay. Let's get more background on him in the meantime. Locate any co-workers or neighbors who might be willing to talk. If he's as smooth as you say, he's either rubbed a few people the wrong way or titillated the gossipers. Ron, I don't want us to forget that a guest might've been involved in this thing. See if you can find out who was staying there at the time. And don't just interview the employees. If we can find a chatty guest who'll rat on the others, that would help, too."

Ron Klesczewski appeared at my door several hours later, a smile on his face. "I may have discovered the snitch from Heaven."

I peeled off my reading glasses and tossed them with relief on a pile of paperwork. "Do tell."

"Dottie Delman, eighty-three years old—rules the counter at the general store just outside West Townshend. Her brother owned the inn before it was an inn, her family tree rivals Moses', and from what I heard, she's both wailing wall and oracle for half the people in a ten-mile radius, meaning she probably knows more about what's happening at the inn than the owner."

"You haven't talked to her yet?"

"No, but I will unless you want first dibs. I got a lead on somebody else, too." He checked a note he was carrying. "Marcia Luechauer—however you pronounce it. She's a teacher at Deerfield Academy, in Mass. She was a guest during our time slot. Rumor has it she was very outgoing, made a lot of friends, and might be willing to talk."

"You take one, I take the other?" I suggested.

"That'd be great, if you have the time."

It was a typical equivocation, and a glimpse of the self-effacement that was also his best asset. It disarmed the very people who clammed up before the likes of Willy Kunkle, or even Sam, and gave Ron the upper hand in any interview demanding a delicate touch.

"I'll go down to Deerfield," I said.

Deerfield Academy epitomizes the blue-blooded image of the Yankee aristocracy. Like Eton in Great Britain, or a dozen other WASP-sounding schools around New England, it has stood for generations as the springboard to the Ivy League and the world of high finance beyond. I'd heard from a southern friend of mine that boarding schools in his neck of the woods were places to lock up rich juvenile delinquents, which had made him wonder why New England had so many of them. I'd set him straight on the difference, but the dichotomy had stuck with me. My interest in traveling the half hour to Deerfield was partly to discover whether my friend hadn't been closer to the mark than I'd been led to believe.

Initial impressions were mixed. The academy is located in the heart of a near-perfectly preserved historic village of the same name, both of which straddle a broad, straight, tree-shaded avenue. Taken together, they look like a cross between a movie lot and a museum exhibition—not bad for a reform school. But driving past one classic, cedar-roofed icon after another, I began wondering if so rarefied an atmosphere might not in fact be a little confining.

The school itself, at two hundred years old, is more monumentally imposing than the village, with brick buildings, ancient beech trees, and acres of manicured lawns, so that as I parked in front of an Independence Hall look-alike, I was beginning to feel thoroughly intimidated.

Getting out of the car, I caught sight of a skinny, mop-topped young man walking away from me, wearing gray trousers, a wrinkled blue blazer, and flaming red canvas high-top sneakers.

"Excuse me," I called out.

He swung around and approached smiling, revealing himself to be a she—a perfect tomboy. So much for being confined.

"Hi. Can I help you?" she asked, her lively, gleaming eyes making me smile in turn.

"Yeah. I'm looking for someone named Marcia Luechauer. A teacher? She told me to ask for Mather dorm."

"Oh, sure—Ms. L.—that's what we call her. She's cool. Mather's where I live. I can take you there, if you'd like."

I bowed slightly to this touch of courtesy. "I'd be delighted."

We fell in side by side as my guide headed for a crosswalk.

"What grade are you in?" I asked.

"I'm a sophomore."

"And you like it here?"

"It's neat. I wasn't sure at first. I thought it might be too stuck-up—two hundred years of grand tradition. But the teachers are cool, the kids come from all over, and I'm having a great time. They work your—" she abruptly paused and glanced up at me. "They work you hard, though."

We crossed the street to a pathway between two old wooden dorms.

"I thought this was a boy's school," I commented.

She let loose that infectious smile again. "Used to be. Girl-power won out." She pointed to the building on the left. "That's Mather."

We entered, and I followed her up one flight of stairs to a closed door with a hand-lettered wooden sign reading "Ms. L.—Knock if You Dare." Behind us I could hear girls' voices echoing down the hall, interlaced with snatches of music and the occasional slamming of doors.

My companion knocked, saying as she did, "She must be expecting you. This is usually open." She peered at me for a moment and then added, as if to set me at ease, "You'll like her. She's really nice."

The door swung back to reveal a small, round-faced woman in her fifties. "Scout," she exclaimed to my friend, "who've you rounded up here?"

Scout looked nonplussed for the first time. "I don't know. I forgot to ask."

I stuck out my hand. "Joe Gunther. We spoke on the phone."

She smiled and ushered me in. "I thought so." And she winked at Scout. "Just pulling your leg. Thanks for playing tour guide."

Marcia Luechauer escorted me through a colorful, sun-filled apartment to a living room facing the street where I'd parked, and pointed to a sofa under the window. "Tea or coffee?" she asked.

"Tea would be nice," I said. "I need a break from coffee. Cream and sugar, too, if you've got it."

She laughed. "They're the only reason I drink anything hot." She crossed through to a door leading into a small kitchen, still speaking as she set to work. "On the phone you said you wanted to ask me some questions about my trip to Vermont. That certainly was a mysterious invitation, especially from a policeman. I'm not in trouble, am I?"

I spoke to her as she passed back and forth across my line of sight. "No, no. I'm actually hoping you can give me some help. It concerns your stay at the Windham Hill Inn."

She appeared at the door, looking startled. "The inn? What happened there?"

"That's what I'd like to ask you. I just found out by accident that you'd been there. Mr. Rarig would want me to make it clear he didn't divulge your name, by the way."

"Oh, good Lord. I don't care. I had a wonderful time." There was a loud *ding* from behind her, and she vanished again.

"I don't know how I can help you, though," her voice said from the kitchen. "I don't remember anything happening that might be of interest to the police."

She reappeared carrying a tray, which she placed on a low table between us, perching herself on an armchair opposite me. "I'll let you do the honors. There's sugar, but I prefer maple syrup—one of my many Vermont afflictions. I love your state, incidentally. It's one of the reasons I work here."

I poured both syrup and cream into my tea, having, like Ms. L., an unapologetic sweet tooth. "What dates were you at the inn, exactly?"

"The fifteenth through the eighteenth. I left at noon."

For simplicity's sake, we'd settled on the sixteenth for Boris Malik's death. "And which room did you have?"

"It was a little thing on the top floor, facing the front."

"And the ginkgo tree?" I asked, startled.

She paused, her cup halfway to her lips. "Yes. Why?"

"John Rarig said he'd closed off all those rooms because of the smell."

She laughed, something I now realized she did all the time, obviously to the delight of her young charges. "I have almost no sense of smell left. That's about the only time it's worked to my advantage. I told him I really wanted the sun through my window, so he made an exception. It had the fringe benefit of making my room very quiet as well." She cocked her head toward the dorm. "Not that noise is a big problem with me."

"On the night of the sixteenth, then," I asked, "do you remember hearing anything unusual—voices maybe, a shout, the sound of a car very late?"

She paused to reflect. "There was a car. I don't know what time it was when I heard it, but it was the middle of the night. I'm afraid I didn't look out the window, though. I just rolled over and went back to sleep."

"Was the sound familiar? Had you heard that particular car before?"

She shook her head. "No. It was just a car. I am sorry."

"No. That's all right," I assured her. "We ask a lot of questions, but they're not all important." I handed her a picture of the rental car. "Was this car ever parked in the lot, or anywhere else that you noticed?"

She made a face, considering the photo. "I'm not doing very well here. It might have been, but I'm not big on cars. They all look like this to me."

I passed her the retouched mug shot of Boris Malik. "How 'bout him?"

She wrinkled her nose. "Ooh. He doesn't look very good. Is he dead?"

"Yeah. Sorry about that. The photographer tried to fix him up a little, but it's hard to do well."

She returned the pictures to me. "No, he doesn't look familiar. I don't suppose you could tell me what this is all about, could you?"

I sighed involuntarily. "Don't I wish. It's a bit of a mystery, and to be honest, the Windham Hill Inn may not play into it at all. We're doing a lot of fishing right now, hoping to get lucky. Rumor has it you got friendly with several of the other guests."

"Oh, yes," she smiled, more comfortable now. "That's partly why I take these trips. Every short vacation, I choose a different inn, usually in Vermont. Maybe it's being surrounded by kids all the time, but to me a vacation means meeting other people, preferably from far-off places. And inns are good for that, especially if you can't afford to travel far. The kinds of guests they get are often world travelers. They're fun to trade stories with."

I thought of our hoped-for Russian connection. "Did you meet any globe-trotters at the Windham Hill Inn?"

"Several. There were the Widmers, an elderly couple from New

Jersey. They'd spent an enormous amount of time in Saudi Arabia. He used to be in the oil business—"

"How elderly?" I interrupted as gently as possible.

But she cocked an eye at me nevertheless. "Ah. I see what you mean. No geriatrics need apply. How strong a person are we talking about?"

It was my turn to smile. "Pretty strong. On the other hand, we're not sure we're just talking about one person, either."

She nodded. "Okay. Well, in any case, better scratch the Widmers. They were both pretty feeble. Let's see . . . There was Roger and Sheila Brockman. They were middle-aged, and in good shape, too. Played tennis all the time. Sheila had the eyes of a tiger, I thought. One of those professionally skinny women, complete with tummy tucks, face-lifts, and all the rest. Roger was the traveler there. Sheila mostly stayed home and shopped, from what I could tell. But he'd been to the Far East quite a bit—Hong Kong, Singapore, Beijing. An investment banker. Not what I'd call a nice man, but an observant one. He noticed things, and he had a wonderful way of describing them."

"He mention Russia at all?"

She frowned. "No, not that I recall."

"Anyone else?" I asked.

She thought a moment. "There was another couple. I don't think they were married, but they didn't seem like sweethearts, either. I didn't see much of her. She was either feeling poorly, or just not very social, but she kept to their room for the most part. Her name was Ann, I think. I never did catch a last name. His was Howard Richter, and he'd definitely been to Europe. We got into a long conversation about traveling the canals over there, and he was quite knowledgeable. Otherwise, he struck me as a little aloof. In fact, I kind of wondered why they were even there. They didn't seem like the type."

"Does the inn serve breakfast?" I asked suddenly.

"Yes."

"The morning of the seventeenth, did you notice any of these people—or anyone else, for that matter—acting differently, or missing altogether?"

Marcia Luechauer had placed her cup on the table earlier and now steepled her fingers before her chin, her eyes fixed on some distant object out the window. "Let's see, that would've been my last full day there. Ann didn't show—no surprise there. The Brockmans were there, in tennis whites. Howard ... Let's see ... He did come down—late—and I waved to him from across the room. He acted as though he hadn't seen me. I remember thinking he and Ann must've had a fight, because he looked pretty ugly. But like I said, he was naturally a little moody." Her eyes suddenly widened. "Actually, the one who struck me oddest of all that morning was Douglas, my waiter. He was French-Canadian, and normally as smooth-talking as a bad commercial—one of those God's-gift-to-women types. He was downright cranky that morning and didn't look as if he'd slept at all."

I couldn't suppress a small laugh. "You have a phenomenal memory. You should be a cop."

Her eyes gleamed. "I think that would be fascinating. Has any of this helped?"

"Absolutely. We may have gotten a little sidetracked, though, when we focused on the world travelers. Was there anyone else who stood out, for any reason at all?"

"The Meades," she said instantly. "They were from New York City. She was a lawyer, he was a doctor—Ed and Linda. They both had cell phones, briefcases, perpetual creases between their eyes. I've run into people like them, using the inn circuit to try to get back together—try a second honeymoon, I guess. I don't think it works. It certainly didn't in this case. They barely spoke to one another. He'd go hiking, she'd borrow a bike. Their dinners were almost totally silent. But there was an odd quality to them that really struck me. It wasn't hostility. It was coldness. They treated everyone the way they did each other—no favorites. They gave me the creeps. They might have been robots."

A brief silence settled between us as I continued scribbling notes in my pad. "Other than that," she resumed, "it was a pretty typical group—couples making the fine foods tour, people just getting away for a few days, some old folks enjoying their retirement ... and me," she added brightly, "the spinsterish busybody."

"Bless you for that," I told her. "I wish everyone I interviewed was as observant."

I rose to my feet and headed toward the hallway. "Are there any last thoughts before I go? Anything more about Douglas, for instance?"

She joined me, shaking her head. "No, I'm afraid not. Other than that one morning, he was his oily self from start to finish."

"And no one else with overseas baggage?"

She laughed. "Not that I could tell, aside from John Rarig, of course. But him you know about."

I tried to pause as nonchalantly as possible in the doorway. "How do you mean?"

She looked up at me, surprised. "That he's been to Europe—speaks fluent German."

"He told you that?" I asked.

"He didn't have to. We were talking about wine one evening, and he pulled out a bottle of Gumpoldskirchen Veltliner. It's Austrian, from the Wachau district, and he pronounced it like a native."

"Sounds like you just did, too," I commented.

She burst out laughing, "With a name like Luechauer? I should hope so. I was born over there, and I'm the German teacher here. Anyhow, there's all sorts of German, I suppose, like anywhere else. His wasn't the school-taught kind. It was regional. He could only have picked it up by living there."

I reached for the door and pulled it open, letting in a flood of youthful noises from down the hall. "How did Rarig look the morning of the seventeenth?"

She paused reflectively and then answered, "Tired. He had bags under his eyes."

8

"How deep did you go into his past?" Sammie asked me.

"Usual paper trail, a couple of phone calls. Obviously, he could've gone to Europe on vacations, but nothing indicated John Rarig ever lived in Austria, or anywhere else outside the U.S. Marcia Luechauer said he spoke the language like a native. That takes time."

"Or intensive, intelligence-grade teaching," Ron said softly.

"If all this is CIA," Sammie said, "then we're up a creek. We're not going to be able to touch them. They'll just pull the shades like Gil Snowden did in DC and turn into the Cheshire cat."

I held up my hand. "Hold it. We're getting ahead of ourselves." We were back in my office, with the door closed—cramped but private—the only ones left after an already long day. "There's obviously some CIA involvement here, but let's not turn it into a full-blown conspiracy. If all this was really national security and cloak-and-dagger stuff, the FBI would be sitting here, not us. They sniffed around Hillstrom's office and apparently didn't take the bait. We are reasonably assuming a man was killed on our turf—a straightforward homicide. It would be nice to know who he was and what he was up to, but when you get down to it, our real job is to nail his killer. There's no reason to think we can't do that."

"Yeah," Sammie retorted, "except that if it really was no big deal, the CIA wouldn't've asked to talk to you, and they wouldn't've lied about knowing Boris in the first place. *That* was obviously bullshit."

I closed my eyes briefly, fighting the urge to tell her to back down for once in her life. Although, plagued as I was about that supposed mugging, part of my irritation stemmed from the chance she was right. "Luechauer fingered Doug DeFalque, too, Sam. What more have you dug up on him?"

She was obviously unhappy about being cut off, but her expression also told of something surprisingly like embarrassment. "RCMP reported back," she said quietly. "They have nothing connecting him with the Russian mob."

Ron stared at her. "This morning, you said he was a free agent working with biker gangs and the mob."

Sammie turned sullen. "I was right about the bikers. The mob angle was unofficial. My contact's pretty good up there, and it sounded solid when I heard it. Guess I was wrong."

"That's okay," I said quickly. "It was a theory. They're part of this process, too. What else did you find out about him?"

"I poked around his neighborhood in Jamaica. I have a friend who lives up there, and another one at the sheriff's department who actually knows him. They both confirmed he was a bit of a dirtbag—Mr. Smooth around teenage girls, not too swift with anyone else. He's been seen in town pretty consistently for the last few months. I asked a contact at Customs if they'd run his plate this summer, since they're keeping tabs on him. Last legal crossing he made was in early June, just before the tourist season, when the inn started using him on a regular basis. If Boris was whacked for some sort of international activity, it doesn't look as if DeFalque was part of it. Also, despite having a loud mouth and a swagger, he's never taken a swing at anyone I could find, so using a garrote seems pretty out of character."

"That confirms what I learned from Dottie Delman," Ron said. "She called him a slimy little worm. He's impregnated a couple of girls and left them high and dry, he shirks his debts and talks big, especially when he's been drinking, but he's also very good at ingratiating himself when he needs a job, a favor, or a loan, which probably explains his job at the inn."

I rubbed my eyes with the heels of both hands. "All right. Doug

DeFalque may be slipping from our number-one spot. Putting John Rarig to one side, what did either one of you learn about anyone else?"

"I think we can scratch Bob Manship, too," Ron said. "Dottie confirmed what everyone else was saying—he got into a jam, but he's a good boy. Always has been, always will be. Dottie thought he's been taking the whole thing way too hard—that the woman he creamed the other guy for didn't deserve either one of them. But Dottie's an old-fashioned sort. In any case, Bob lives like a monk now.

"Marty Sopper—" he went on, consulting his ever-present notes, "Marianne Baker's boyfriend—might be another matter. Dottie called him mean straight through, and thought he'd slice his mother's throat for the price of a Coke. She made Marianne sound like the typical abused spouse—a totally dependent target. Marty doesn't have a steady job. He works wherever he can, or just rips off Marianne, so he fits someone who could be hired to use a piano wire, but we hit a dead end when we come to the international angle. Dottie doubts he's been beyond Brattleboro, much less into Canada. He tends to work his own patch."

"How long was he living down here?" I asked. "We sure got to know him well enough."

Ron checked his cheat sheet. "Only two years. He was born in Wardsboro, so I guess he thought this was the big city. Too big for him, apparently—he still bitches about it, and about us especially. Says we were a bunch of Nazis. This is not a sophisticated man."

"And presumably not clever enough to sneak up on someone, strangle him, ditch him without leaving a trace, and then keep quiet about it," I said.

Ron chewed on his upper lip for a moment's silence. "I guess not."

"Scratch Marty Sopper," Sammie muttered darkly.

"Not yet," I cautioned. "But let's leave him alone for the moment. Luechauer gave me some new names. Ron, did Dottie mention any guests named Meade, Richter, or Brockman? Ed Meade was a New York physician—a real ice cube. Luechauer said he gave her the creeps."

Ron shook his head. "Dottie wasn't much good on the guests.

Her bread and butter's the neighborhood. I tried to see if she'd picked up any names from her inn contacts, but it was pretty useless. By the time she hears about them, they've been reduced to 'the white-haired couple from Florida,' or 'Mr. Attitude with the big ears.' There's a lot of typical flatlander resentment. Actually," he added, "as ironies would have it, Luechauer was the only one I did hear about—she passed with flying colors."

There was a knock at the door. Harriet Fritter, our administrative assistant, stepped in and handed me a fax. "Just came in—RCMP."

I read it over carefully and handed it to Sam. "The Canadians say Boris Malik is actually Sergei Antonov, one of several point men for the Russian mob, reportedly over here to set up operations. They pegged him through fingerprints, dental records, and the face shot we sent them. They don't seem to have any doubts about it."

Sammie passed the report to Ron. "That doesn't do us much good."

I placed my feet on my desk and crossed my arms, staring sightlessly out the darkened window that separated my office from the empty squad room. "No. It doesn't. If anything, it lets more air out of our tires—heightening the suggestion we were just a dumping ground for an out-of-town argument. I wonder where the Canadians are getting their information?"

Ron stared at me in confusion, struck by the implication. "What do you mean?"

"RCMP is a gigantic organization—about six of our major federal alphabet soups rolled into one. It's interesting to me that we've gotten three pieces of information from them recently, two of them contradictory. First we're encouraged to think Doug DeFalque might be dirty, then that's canceled. Next, we hear absolutely nothing about Boris for days on end, and now he's suddenly a major player for the mob. It's almost as if someone's either doing a lousy job of feeding us information, or just trying to tie us up in knots. I'm hearing echoes of how Snowden dealt with me."

Sammie looked disgusted. "Great. We're getting nowhere here."

"Oh, I don't know," I reassured her. "Taken separately, nobody looks particularly outstanding, but if you combine, say, Marty Sopper with John Rarig, things begin to pick up."

They both stared at me. Sammie spoke first, "Rarig with a sudden European past, and Sopper with the morals of a mongrel and a temper to match."

"I'd love to look at Sopper's closet for ginkgo seeds, and under his mattress for a new sack of gold," I murmured.

"Maybe we can," Ron said, his eyes bright.

"Right," Sammie added, "through Marianne Baker."

I smiled at their quickly recovered enthusiasm. "Like you said— 'maybe.' Remember what Dottie said about her, though. If she's willing to be the man's punching bag, she's not going to be inclined to squeal on him."

"She won't have to," Sammie continued. "As far as the ginkgo seeds are concerned, all we have to do is either get invited into their apartment, or get Marianne to admit that on the night of the sixteenth, Sopper's shoes smelled to high heaven. If we don't tip our hand that we're targeting her boyfriend, she might even admit he had blood on his clothes, or was out all that night, or said something that might place him at the quarry. We just have to get her conversational. It might take time, but she could be the key to establishing probable cause, after which we really could start cooking."

Despite the sudden energy in the air, I yawned and checked my watch. It was closing in on nine o'clock. "Okay. Let's do it. See if we get lucky. Ron, you keep after Marty Sopper. Find out everything you can about him. Does he have a bank account? Has he been throwing money around lately? Any recent change in habits—gambling, drinking more, whatever. Has he suddenly settled any long-standing debts? Paid off back taxes? See if you can establish a daily pattern, and whether he broke it the night of the sixteenth. Did any neighbors hear anything unusual then?

"Sam," I continued. "Go after Marianne. Take your time, use whatever approach you want. Meanwhile, I'll see what I can find out about our German linguist, Mr. Rarig. If he is or was CIA, and the paper trail I followed is bogus, there have got to be holes in it somewhere. I'll try to find people who knew him back when—boyhood friends from his supposed hometown. Things like that. If he's hiding something, maybe that'll be big enough for probable cause, too."

I got to my feet. "Right now, though, we better hit the sack. Tomorrow'll be a long day. But let's keep each other updated as we go, okay? No dropped balls, and no idle chitchat. If anyone gets wind of what we're up to, we'll probably be left with nothing."

Sam looked at me closely as we gathered by the door. "You really think the CIA is looking over our shoulder?"

I shook my head. "That's overstating it. I actually meant don't tip off Sopper or Rarig. The CIA's obviously interested, but I don't buy into the Hollywood hype about their being everywhere and knowing everything. I think Snowden's curious about Boris, but he's also probably as ignorant as we are."

I ushered them out ahead of me, worried my own doubts could be read on my face.

West Brattleboro is tenuously attached to downtown by Route 9, otherwise called Western Avenue. It is the only road crossing over the interstate that bisects our jurisdiction like a knife through a cake, and is predictably busy at most hours of the day, especially, like now, when the neighborhood ballpark empties out. It is also posted at a snail's speed limit, which about one in every ten cars observes. However, on a road this narrow and congested, that one is usually enough to reduce traffic to a crawl.

I was therefore absentmindedly watching the taillights ahead, and my rearview mirror, when I was struck by the silhouette of the driver behind me.

It was no more than a flicker at first—a memory twinge similar to what I felt a dozen times every day. In a town this size, where I'd worked for well over thirty years, I knew hundreds of people. And given the rural Vermont habit of waving to every driver one knew, I'd trained myself to associate faces with names pretty quickly.

Of course, here I didn't have a face to go on—merely a backlit outline seen in reverse through two layers of glass. It was exactly this odd lighting, however, that stimulated the notion I should know this person and put an ominous edge on my curiosity.

With time, it was all I could do to keep even one eye to the front. Finally, just shy of where I was planning to turn right onto Orchard Street, the car before me stopped completely, allowing somebody into line. At that point, the headlights of the mysterious vehicle came close enough to be blocked by my car trunk, just as some oncoming lights lit up the driver's face, fully revealing his features. In that fraction of a moment, I recognized the man who'd tried to knife me in DC.

Without thought or hesitation, I threw my car into park, stepped into the street, and pulled out my gun. Aiming with both hands, I pointed it at the now darkened figure behind the wheel and shouted, *"Don't move. Police."*

A squeal of locked tires and a crash right behind me drowned me out, making me jump to one side to avoid being hit. Simultaneously, the man I'd been aiming at threw his car into reverse and slammed on the gas, sending up two putrid plumes of burning rubber between us.

I began running after him, saw his car collide with the one behind him and slither out into the opposite, now wide-open, lane. *"Stop,"* I yelled, still waving the gun. But he fishtailed into a noisy one-eighty and disappeared down the road, both taillights broken. I ran back to my car to give chase and radio in, realizing that by yielding to impulse, I'd forgotten to note either the vehicle make or its license number.

Angry now as well as alarmed, I reported in, asked all units for assistance, and hit the switch to my blue lights, all before noticing I had nowhere to go. The two cars I'd caused to collide were now blocking me in entirely. Defeated, I got back out to help direct traffic, hoping to hell the man they'd catch would be the same I'd met that night in DC.

I hung up the phone and sat forward, my elbows on my knees, my chin in my hands. Gail stretched across the bed and rubbed my back. "Was that Tony?"

"Yeah—still no hide nor hair of the guy. By now everyone's thinking I've lost my mind."

"What were your options, Joe? You reacted on instinct."

"Instinct should have told me to radio it in and play bait until other units could corner the son of a bitch."

"You might've done that if you hadn't almost died of a knife wound a couple of years ago and relived that experience just last week. You made light of what happened in Washington, but it must've been like a nightmare come back to life. Seeing what you saw tonight—nobody should be surprised you did what you did."

I laughed shortly and turned toward her. "I had my gun out in the middle of traffic, like in some stupid cop show. It's lucky I didn't shoot someone."

She hesitated a second. "You were aiming at the man who attacked you, right?"

I went back to looking at the rug. "The man I *think* attacked me. I can't swear it was him. Sammie, Ron, and I had been working late, talking over the case, and at the end, Sam said something about the CIA looking over our shoulder. I played it down, but driving home I kept thinking about it, and about the guy who mugged me—how unlikely that all was, and how Snowden seemed to know all the details right after. I might have projected my paranoia onto some innocent slob who just happened to be behind me. He's probably on his fifth scotch at home right now."

"Except that from what I just heard, he's totally vanished, and nobody's reported being attacked by a gunman in traffic."

I got up and began removing my clothes, by habit dropping them into a laundry basket, and draping the next day's selection over a chair by the door, something I did in case I was called out in the middle of the night.

"There could be a ton of reasons for that," I explained. "Calling the cops is the last thing a lot of people do in a crisis, including the law-abiding ones."

"That doesn't explain why a dragnet couldn't find the car. You called it in immediately."

Naked, I pulled back the sheet and dropped back onto the bed, leaning against the headboard. "No . . . I just lost my cool—totally."

Gail extinguished the light. Moonlight through the skylight bathed us both in a colorless wash. "Which only makes you human," she said, sliding over next to me and interlacing my fingers with her own. "How is the case going? Have you found anything yet?"

"Nothing solid. We think we have a lead, but it's pure conjecture right now. We're basically flipping over every rock we can find, hoping there'll be enough for a warrant under one of them."

She slid her arm up and tugged at my shoulder. "Come on. Lie flat. Try to get some rest. You keep chewing on this all night, you really will go bonkers."

I did as she asked, and eventually her deep, even breathing told me she'd followed her own advice. I had doubts I could do the same. The shock of what I'd done, the blindness with which I'd simply reacted without thought, would not be neatly tucked away for the sake of a good night's sleep.

Exhaustion will have its way, however, no matter the impediments, and soon I found myself in a deep, dark, and threatening dream state, fighting ghosts from within and without, none of which made sense or gave solace.

As it turned out, it didn't matter anyway. When the phone dragged me back awake, the room was still dark, the moonlight still obliquely on the wall, and I was just as tired.

"Yeah," I muttered into the receiver.

"Joe." It was Willy's voice. "There's been a smash-and-grab at Lord's Jewelers. They're talkin' a bundle. I figured you'd want in on it."

I blinked a couple of times, trying to clear my head. "Okay. You at home?"

"Headin' out now."

"That'll give me time to dress. Pick me up on the way."

9

LORD'S IS LOCATED DOWNTOWN, NOT FAR FROM THE DUNKIN'
Donuts, where Western Avenue, here called High Street, T-bones
into Main. It is in the heart of the nineteenth-century, red-brick canyon that gives Brattleboro its identity and, for all that, is the fanciest
jewelry store in town.

It wasn't looking too purebred when Kunkle and I pulled up to
the curb across the street, however. Cut off by yellow police-line tape,
decorated by two squad cars parked out front, and sporting a huge
hole in its plate-glass window, the store resembled a riot scene.

The impression was enhanced by the crowd of people gathered
around the outside of the yellow tape—a precaution usually reserved
for homicide scenes.

We elbowed our way through the onlookers, ducking under the
tape. An officer, standing on the edge of an apron of shattered glass,
nodded to us as we passed by, heading for the front door.

"What's with all the people?" I asked him.

He gestured to an alarm mounted to the wall above the door. "That
thing went off. Woke the whole neighborhood up—it's why we had to
string the tape. People must be pretty bored."

"Not too subtle," Willy commented, surveying the mess. "Somebody had to've seen something."

I cast a glance over my shoulder. The wall of old buildings opposite loomed up like a dam, studded with lit windows framing people
lounging comfortably, taking in the action. Although it was the town's

commercial center, Main Street was also home to a largely financially challenged population. It added irony to the polish of all the ground-level stores that some of their closest neighbors couldn't afford the clothes they'd need to come in to get interviewed. These people might've been bored. They also—many of them—didn't have jobs to go to in the morning.

J.P. was already working the interior, instructing various Patrol personnel on how to set up the video camera and lights. Kunkle had been the detective on call, but J.P. hadn't wasted time getting everything into motion.

"Whatcha got?" I asked him.

He looked up from his assortment of equipment, a man in the midst of doing what he loved best. "Seems like a smash-and-grab so far." He waved his arm toward the broken window. "Whoever it was used a brick, both on the plate glass and the counter just inside, picked up what he could reach, and disappeared. I've already got canvass teams out looking for witnesses. The back door's secure, and none of the rest of the store was disturbed. So far, it's looking pretty straightforward."

"We know what's missing yet?"

"No. I couldn't find the manager, but the alarm's also hooked up to the owner's house in Springfield, Vermont, and he's already called us from the road on a cell phone. He should be here pretty soon. Maybe he knows the inventory. I think it was quite a haul, though. The store's been running ads—had its best stuff out."

I nodded to Willy. "See what you can find in the office."

Willy disappeared toward the back as I wandered up to the front window, being careful where I stepped and keeping my hands by my sides. A display case with a tented glass top had been placed parallel to the window, so that it was both visible from the sidewalk and accessible from inside. The breakage hadn't been quite as random as Tyler had implied. The thief had actually punched three connected holes in a row in order to get at the entire case and had left his weapon of entry—an old red brick—almost as a calling card. It lay where jewelry and watches had once delicately gleamed, resting on a velour pad, surrounded by shards of sparkling glass like some negative-chic statement.

He hadn't made a clean sweep—various items remained scattered in odd corners. One necklace was even draped over a jagged tooth along the bottom of the window, just shy of the outdoors.

"Pierre," I called out to the officer guarding the front.

He turned toward me, staying outside the debris on the sidewalk. "Yeah, Joe."

I pointed at the necklace. "If this almost made it out, other pieces might have. They could be mixed in with the glass out there. Don't disturb anything yet, but just keep it in mind."

He looked at his feet as if expecting something to move. "Will do."

A tense, disheveled man suddenly appeared out of the darkness, waving at me from the other side of the police tape. "I'm Henri Alonzo. I'm the owner."

I knew that. I also knew him to be an officious snob. I nodded to Pierre to let him through and met him at the front door, offering my hand. "Joe Gunther, Mr. Alonzo. Good to see you again. I am sorry about this, though."

He made to brush by me to approach the smashed case. I grabbed his arm to stop him. "Hang on. We haven't dusted all that yet. Keep your hands in your pockets and watch where you step. And move slowly."

I released him and accompanied him to the window, where J.P. was already taking pictures from the far end.

"Do you know what was on display?" I asked Alonzo.

He was shaking his head. "Where's Richard? He would know better than I."

"He the manager?"

"Yes. Richard Manners."

"We haven't been able to locate him yet," J.P. answered.

Alonzo straightened and stared at me, ignoring Tyler entirely—superior to superior. "God damn the man," he snarled. "He's worse than a bitch in heat. Call his girlfriend's home—Lisa somebody . . . What the hell is it? Goodfriend—that's it. Christ, how do you forget a name like that?"

Willy Kunkle had reappeared from the back and was standing behind us. He nodded as I turned toward him. "I'll call."

"Was it a valuable display?" I asked Alonzo.

"Hell, yes, it was valuable. Over a hundred thousand all told—oh, my God." He suddenly reached for the necklace hanging from the shard.

I caught his wrist in midair. "Remember."

His face flushed. "Jesus Christ. You think that'll have fingerprints on it? It's just waiting for someone to walk off with it."

I pointed to Pierre, standing six feet away, all by himself. "I don't think so, Mr. Alonzo. If you don't know what was in here specifically, maybe you can help us out in the office—find an inventory sheet or something. None of this will be going anywhere for a while. Have you called your insurance company? They'll want to send somebody down here, too."

Alonzo looked at me in disgust. "Of course I have . . . Jesus." And he stormed off toward the back of the store.

Two hours later, we were still hard at it, all of J.P.'s efforts completed, trying to determine the extent of Alonzo's loss. Richard Manners, it seemed, was as disorganized a manager as he was attentive to Miss Goodfriend, and helping him sort through his paperwork was proving quite a job.

In the midst of it all, Willy appeared at the cramped office's door and tapped me on the shoulder. "Chief wants to see us."

I raised my eyebrows. "He outside? At this time of night?"

"At the office. He sounded pissed off."

It was an unusual request, and a poorly timed one. Nevertheless, I rose from my chair and pointed to Willy. "All right. You take over here, and I'll see what's up."

Kunkle shook his head. "He said I had to come, too—to stick with you."

I scowled at that, making no sense of any of it. Unless one of our selectmen had called Tony in a fit, demanding immediate satisfaction, I couldn't imagine why I was being called on the carpet. I left the office and waved to J.P., who was packing up the last of his toys. "Take my place in there."

Willy and I left the store and crossed the road to his car. The predawn air was refreshing after the stuffy back office, and I breathed deeply to cleanse my lungs. "Why'd he want you along?" I asked Willy. "You gotten your ass in a crack again?"

"Not that any of you would know," he said tersely. "He made it sound like you were the one on the shit list."

Located at the far end of Main Street, the Municipal Building was all of two minutes away. Like most of its neighbors, it dated back over a hundred years, but it was placed on a hill and equipped with a Transylvania-style spiky roofline that, in the faint blush of dawn, made it look like a medieval prison.

Tony Brandt, looking grim, met us just inside the locked door leading into the Officers' Room. "Come with me, Joe," he said as soon as we'd entered.

Shrugging to Willy, who for once made no sarcastic comment, I followed Brandt back to the adjacent room and into his office in the far corner. There, also standing and looking unhappy, was Gail's boss— Jack Derby—Windham County's State's Attorney.

"What's going on?" I asked them, by now fully aware this was no minor political flare-up.

"Someone called Jack at home with an anonymous tip, Joe—"

"Not that I believed him," Derby interrupted nervously. "I just thought we should cover our butts."

Annoyed, Tony resumed, "A bystander at that jewelry store scene said he saw you put something in the outer breast pocket of your jacket."

My face flushed. "Bullshit."

"That's what I said," Tony agreed.

I reached into my pocket, felt something hard, and pulled out a shiny, diamond-studded brooch, obviously worth a small fortune.

The only thing I was aware of for a moment was the rapid beating of my heart. "What the hell is this?" I asked softly. I could feel the sweat prickling my forehead.

Tony looked as stunned as I was and cast a glance at the State's Attorney, no doubt wishing that Derby hadn't fielded the call. In his absence, we might have had more room to sort this out. Now, all decisions were already out of our hands.

I placed the jewel on his desk and heard it click against the wood surface. I felt as though my skull had picked up a low internal hum, as from a motor that's been dropped into low gear. "I don't know how it got there."

"And yet, there it is," Derby said gently, sounding extremely uncomfortable. The newest arrival on our small but intense political scene, it was obvious he felt he'd had a smoking bomb dropped in his lap.

I raised my hand to my temple. "Look, I surveyed the contents of the display case as soon as I got to the store. I was careful. I watched where I stepped. I didn't touch a goddamn thing."

"Were your hands in your pockets?" Tony asked.

"No," I answered angrily, "but they weren't rummaging through the merchandise, either. I kept them by my sides . . . At least, I think I did. I may have moved them around—who the hell knows? But I didn't tamper with the evidence."

I picked up the brooch again and studied it. "It wasn't there," I finally said. "I would've remembered it. And it doesn't belong to Gail. I sure as hell would've remembered that."

They both looked at me wordlessly, and I realized the trouble I was in. Without cause or reflection, I knew in my heart why the SA had been called by that snitch, instead of Tony or the department switchboard, and I knew that the brooch would figure in the inventory being compiled back at the store—that Richard Manners would swear on a stack of Bibles it had been shimmering front and center when he'd locked his doors at closing time.

A flurry of possibilities suddenly filled my brain, all demanding priority. "Must be Manners," I whispered.

Tony stared at me. "What?"

"Richard Manners, the store manager. He's a real goof-off. His boss thinks so, anyhow. And his records are in chaos." Another thought crowded that one out. "Or one of his clerks could've done a number on him. He never would've known." Another pause. "Unless he's cleverer than we think, and he's leading us by the nose."

I lapsed into silence.

The quiet in the room was eloquent. Still, Jack commented, not without kindness, "We're still stuck with how it got into your pocket."

I dropped my chin and looked at the floor for a moment, a confused torrent filling me from the feet up, threatening my breathing. I felt I could see into everyone's head, as if I were reading lines from a play. I knew they were waiting for me to say something incriminating, that all I'd said so far had already been tucked away for future misinterpretation. Somebody outside this room had started a process in motion, involving just the right cast of characters, in order to build a case against me—and it was based on the assumption that all cops in a bind are deemed guilty until proved otherwise.

That's how the system maintained its integrity.

"I'm leaving," I said suddenly. "Any problem with that?"

"Where're you going?" Tony asked, his face showing genuine concern. I moved to the door. "Home."

He reached out and touched my shoulder. "This'll go away, Joe. We just need to figure it out."

"We could try to do that here and now," Derby added, almost plaintively.

I pulled the door open and saw a small, silent cluster of people in the far room, looking at us. Anger half closed my throat, images of Snowden, Rarig, the mugger, and of Henri Alonzo's peeved expression crowded my mind. "You know goddamn well it's already beyond that. I'm gone."

I walked home, alone in the dawn's tepid light, my heart and mind in a turmoil, hoping the fresh air might help me to think, and yet paying it no attention. That I'd been carefully positioned into this corner went without saying, but the why and by whom of the equation had too many options, and therefore none at all. And the how had me baffled, too. The more I stalked into the coming day, hearing only the awakening birds over the sounds of my own footsteps, the more confused and enraged I became. Reaching the spot in the road of my other recent claim to fame—now marked by a few shards of plastic and two ugly strips of burned rubber—didn't help any.

Gail met me in the driveway, wrapped in a thick robe, obviously forewarned by Tony Brandt. "You okay?" she asked as I drew near.

"Not hardly," I said bitterly. "I feel like a cat that's been staked out on the highway."

"What happened exactly? Tony didn't go into details."

"That smash-and-grab I went to. They say I stole one of the jewels when I was at the scene. They found it in my pocket. Christ, I reached in and *handed* it to them."

She'd left the kitchen door open, and we entered together. "How did it get there?" she asked.

I looked at her peevishly. "How the hell do I know?"

I saw the hurt in her eyes and reached out for her shoulder. "I'm sorry. It's crazy. There're just too many possibilities."

She steered me over to the island in the middle of the kitchen. "Sit. You missed dinner last night. I'm going to make us waffles." She held up her hand as I opened my mouth. "Don't argue. We need to think this one out, and do something while we're at it. In fact, don't sit. Make us something hot to drink—tea, coffee, whatever floats your boat. And slice up that cantaloupe."

It was, of course, sound advice. I put myself to work.

"Okay," she resumed, reaching into cupboards and pulling out what she needed. "Let's go back to *when* somebody could have planted that jewel. Maybe that'll open up some doors."

I was by now mimicking her actions on the other side of the kitchen. "I tried that. It could've been anytime, and if they were good, or somebody I knew well, they could've even done it when I was wearing the damn coat. It was my breast pocket. Ever since handkerchiefs went out, it's almost never used. Somebody could've slipped it in there a week ago, and I wouldn't've known."

She paused to look over her shoulder. "A week ago? I thought you said it came from the jewelry store."

"It did . . . No, let me back up. We think it did. The inventory's still being done, but the store manager's so disorganized I doubt he'll be able to swear when he last saw it. It could've been missing for days."

She pointed at the pocket. "It doesn't have a flap. If you took the coat off and threw it over the back of a chair, the brooch might've fallen out. Whoever went to all this trouble would've thought of that."

The obvious truth of that startled me, and made me doubt my own ability to think this out. "You're right."

"So it was probably done this morning. Who were you standing close enough to that he might have had a chance?"

I shook my head. "That doesn't work. Willy picked me up—" I suddenly froze. "Shit."

"What?"

"We parked across the street. We had to push through a crowd to get in the door, and I ducked under the tape. Someone could've . . . No."

"Why not?" she asked. "That sounded plausible."

"How would they've known where I was going to cut through the crowd?"

"Where did you? Directly opposite the door?"

"Yeah."

She smiled hopefully. "That's logical—exactly what the guy would've expected."

I thought about that for a moment. "Maybe. It seems a little wobbly. If we'd parked on the same side of the street, we would've entered the scene from a different angle."

"How big was the crowd?"

I made a vague gesture. "Bigger than I would've expected. The alarm drew them out. A dozen maybe."

"That's not many, Joe. He sees you coming, he moves to intercept."

I paused in the middle of putting the filter into the coffee machine. "I don't remember anyone in motion. I don't think anyone even saw us coming." Again, I was struck by the idea's fancifulness. "It's such a long shot—putting so much faith on my having the right kind of jacket, presenting it at just the right angle at just the right time—not to mention the skill involved in pulling off something like that."

"Be worth checking out," she said simply, pouring milk into a bowl. "A good pickpocket could've done it, working in reverse. Maybe you should look at people with that kind of background."

More to mollify her than from any conviction, I said, "Pierre was positioned outside, facing them all. Maybe he saw something, or could remember who was there."

"All right," Gail said, with assumed authority. "That's a possible how. I'm guessing Kunkle could have done it, too, along with whoever else was there, but that's pretty unlikely. Agreed?"

"Yeah. Plus, neither the manager nor the owner ever got close enough to me."

"Okay. Let's go to the why."

I measured out enough coffee for one cup. Gail never touched the stuff. I was going to boil water for tea for her. "That's the one I was thrashing out all the way here. It could be anything, from this CIA thing I'm working on to some bastard I put away twenty years ago."

"If the latter's true, maybe the timing's important. You could match pickpockets with past cases and recent prison release dates and maybe come up lucky."

I turned away so she couldn't see my obvious skepticism. "I suppose." In fact, I couldn't remember ever dealing with a pickpocket. It seemed like a profession straight out of Dickens.

"Or," she went on, vigorously beating the contents of the bowl, "it might be connected to a current case—someone hired by somebody you're squeezing."

I opened my mouth to put the brakes on all this when I was struck by the reasonableness of what she'd just said. Once again I flashed back to the Korean War Memorial. "Like my mugger, you mean."

She poured a ladle of waffle mix onto the electric griddle and closed it, checking her watch. "Could be."

I walked over next to her and placed the kettle on one of the gas burners. "It still doesn't tell us a goddamn thing." I grabbed a cantaloupe and a knife but did nothing with either. "I mean, say the CIA tried to have me killed and now is trying to land me in jail, the question still remains, why? I haven't done anything unique. Some kid found the body, the ME's office sliced it up, the crime lab came up with that stupid ginkgo seed. I've just been a cog in this whole thing. Why do I deserve all the attention?"

I'd been using the knife as a baton throughout this speech. Gail pointed to it and said gently, "Cut the cantaloupe, Joe."

I did as she asked, my confusion unabated. "This might make some sense if I thought it was leading anywhere. But even sniffing around the inn, we still don't have enough for a warrant."

"You might with time."

I scooped the contents of the cantaloupe out into the compost bucket. "Maybe, but that misses the point. I was mugged in DC before I knew much of anything, and whoever ordered that couldn't have known a ginkgo seed was going to suddenly appear to lead us to the inn. That's too crazy."

Partly to my regret, that quieted her down. I sliced and prepared the rest of the melon in total silence.

Finally, Gail checked her watch again, opened the griddle, and extracted four waffles, which she placed on two plates. Her voice missing its earlier strength, she asked, "So what's the department do now?"

I set out the mugs, syrup, and utensils and sat opposite her. "They have to find out if the brooch came from the store. Maybe, if the manager's as much of a jerk as his boss thinks he is, that'll be the end of it. But I doubt it. After that, it'll be by the numbers, and you know what they are—paid suspension, while everyone sets out to prove at least possession of stolen property, and maybe grand theft. They have to come up with intent, knowledge that I knew it was hot, but the way things're going, I'm sure they'll be able to do that. Christ knows how.

"If whoever called this in had phoned the PD instead of Derby, I might've had some slack to play with. But he obviously knows how things work. Derby's hands are tied, and the whole department's been cut out of the loop. This'll have to go to external investigators."

Neither one of us had made a move to eat the breakfast we'd prepared. It sat there between us, looking increasingly unappetizing. Gail finally let out a deep sigh. "You want to blow this off?"

I merely tilted my plate over the compost bucket and set it in the sink. I turned on the water to wash things up, but Gail placed her hand over mine to stop me. "Leave it. Let's go to bed."

Two hours later, Gail had left for work, and I was sitting on the back deck, under the large, ancient maple tree that thrust up through its middle, my feet propped on the railing, a cup of cold coffee forgotten in my lap. I heard a car park in the driveway around the corner, but I didn't move or call out. My mood was such that I didn't much care who it was, or if they discovered my whereabouts. So much else was being done without my involvement, I figured this could take care of itself, too.

It did. Within a minute of the engine's dying, Sammie Martens appeared on the lawn below me. "I figured you'd be out here," she said, climbing the wooden steps.

I didn't bother answering.

She dragged another Adirondack chair next to mine and settled into it with a sigh. "How're you holding up?"

"Great," I answered. "Want some coffee?"

She shook her head, keeping silent.

"Am I officially dead in the water yet?" I finally asked.

"They established the brooch was theirs," she admitted. "But I wouldn't worry about it. It's not like you haven't been walking the straight and narrow for longer'n I've been alive." She paused and added, "You have any ideas?"

I thought of the gist of my long conversation with Gail, wondering how many times I'd have to repeat it with others. "Nope."

Blessedly, Sammie took me on faith. "We gotta dig deeper" was all she said.

"How're things at the office?" I asked after a moment.

"Confused. It's too early yet. The younger crowd's looking for the bogeyman. When they find him, they'll settle down, either believing you're dirty or you were set up. That'll make 'em all feel better. The rest of us—the chief included—see this as a no-brainer. Some klutzy kind of frame."

I glanced at her profile, impressed at the total confidence in her voice. "How are *you* doing?"

She gave me a tired smile. "Pissed off says it best right now."

I laughed and squeezed her forearm. "Thanks, Sam."

Later that morning, close to noon, it was Tony Brandt's turn. I was on the couch, unsuccessfully trying to nap. This time the sound of a car engine sent me to the kitchen door in my stockinged feet, more eager now for company, even if—as I sensed was likely—he was the bearer of poor tidings.

"Hey, Joe," he said, passing by me into the house. "How're you holding up?"

I followed him in, pointing to the coffeemaker, to which he nodded. "That's kind of up to you, right?"

He accepted the cup I handed him, and sat heavily on one of the stools parked around the island. "I hope you weren't thinking this would just fade into nothing. Derby's involvement pretty much guaranteed that."

I heard the words with sadness. We were old friends, and had shared many a trench against politicians, bureaucrats, and adverse popular opinion. That was not the case now. Tony was here as my boss, to lower the boom—however gently and reluctantly.

"So what's the verdict?" I asked him.

"Paid suspension for the moment. Derby says he'll pass because of Gail—kick it over to the attorney general's office. I haven't heard who's going to handle it there, yet. It's up to them whether they use the state police, or have their investigators run the case." He sighed heavily. "I can't believe it..." He turned and looked me straight in the eyes. "I know you left the office this morning 'cause you could see the writing on the wall, but do you have any idea what happened? *Why* it happened?"

I hesitated before answering, hoping to suppress all the emotions that rose inside me like a flock of startled birds. I went to pour yet another cup of coffee for myself but didn't. I crossed instead to the kitchen window and looked out onto the maple tree. "Don't take this the wrong way, Tony, but given how things're looking, would you answer that question if you were me?"

He didn't comment, but I'd made his job a little easier—officially at least. He quietly slid off his seat, placed the half-full mug on the counter, and walked toward the back door. "Better get a lawyer, Joe, and watch your back."

He paused on the threshold. "If you need any department resources—under the table..."

"I know," I answered quickly, before he said any more that he shouldn't. "Thanks."

Gail called that afternoon. "You heard about it going to the AG?"

"Yeah. Tony dropped by."

She was suddenly concerned. "You tell him anything?"

Gail hadn't been a deputy state's attorney for very long, but I was by now very much on her turf. She more than anyone knew the rules of engagement.

"No, counselor," I said with a short laugh. "I told him to go away— nicely."

"I'm sorry, Joe." Her voice was soft, supportive. The irony was, she was in much the same position as Tony. She was just taking her time coming to grips with it.

"Well," she resumed, "they've made up their minds. It's going to Fred Coffin. You know him?"

"Not personally, but what little I've heard isn't good."

"He was a guest lecturer when I was in law school. He's not a nice man. Very arrogant, very ambitious."

I felt my stomach turning sour, only partly because of a wholly caffeine diet. "I take it he's not going to let VSP do the investigation."

"No. He wants total control. His people should be down here pretty soon."

The AG's office was a busy place, having the entire state as its juris-diction. Cases submitted to it sometimes took weeks to reach the top of the pile. The fact that two investigators were possibly already on their way was not a good sign.

Gail took advantage of my silence to ask, "Have you eaten yet?"

"Yeah," I lied. "I had a little snack. I'm doing okay. You?"

Her voice dropped a notch, implying an open office door. "It's a little weird. I can't figure out if it's like I just lost a family member, or came down with a communicable disease. It's about as cheerful as a funeral parlor. I can't wait to come home."

"I can't promise you much of an improvement."

"I love you, kiddo," she said. "That's always been a godsend to me."

I looked at the floor for a moment, at a loss for words. "I love you, too," I finally answered, knowing the words were a pale reflection of what lay behind them.

Kathleen Bartlett, a no-nonsense pragmatist and a friend from years back, was head of the Attorney General's Criminal Division. She was also Fred Coffin's boss. I called her immediately after my conversation with Gail.

"This is Joe Gunther."

She didn't answer at first, obviously choosing her words. "Not a good idea, Joe."

"Pretend I'm a law student, just after the basics."

"What kind of basics?"

"Tell me about Fred Coffin."

"He's good. He's a climber."

"Where's he aiming?"

"Probably a judgeship. Probably more after that. He's got to move fast, though. The governor likes tough prosecutors, but he's ambitious, too. If he leaves office and some wimp takes over, Fred's out of luck."

"Why was I given to Coffin?"

For the first time, I sensed the concern Bartlett had been masking. "It wasn't my call, Joe. The AG knew you and I were friends, and Fred lost no time making a play for it."

"You make it sound like I'm in trouble."

"You are, regardless of the facts. You trust the system here, and Fred'll tear you apart, 'cause guilty or not, by the end, he'll try to make sure you're out of a job and that he's smelling like a rose. I recommend you hire a barracuda of a lawyer, play dirty if you have to, and don't call me till you've been certified one of the good guys again. Okay?"

"Thanks, Kathy."

"Don't thank me. Just cover your ass."

10

RICHARD LEVAY HAD BEEN A CRIMINAL LAWYER FOR THE BETTER part of two decades. In the compact, often interchangeable legal world of Vermont, he'd also done stints as a prosecutor, a judge, and a law professor, but criminal law remained his first love—and the profession to which he paid the most fealty. He came to my house within thirty minutes of my calling him.

There is a perception about cops and lawyers that makes them as compatible as oil and water. It is often accurate, certainly for some. Willy Kunkle, for example, was not a man I sought out to hear nice things about lawyers. I, on the other hand, had become—very slowly—a little less quick to condemn. A necessary evil, like anything from prisons to warning labels, lawyers still represented a service that almost all of us, sooner or later, would end up using—some of us more reluctantly than others.

Physically, Richard Levay was an unimpressive man. Small, slight, balding, and perpetually looking either startled or confused, he compensated for his appearance with an infectious enthusiasm and a focus bordering on magnetism. He made no excuses for defending the amoral, the degenerate, and the criminally aimless. In fact, he cheerfully admitted that most of his clients were crooks. But they had as much a right to a defense as the rest of us, he claimed, and while his goal had never been to set the guilty free, he felt honor-bound to make sure the prosecution stayed on its toes. In the past, that had often pissed me off. Right now, it was just what I was after.

I invited him into the living room as the phone began ringing. I pointed to the couch and picked up the receiver.

"Joe? It's Katz."

"I'm not talking to you, Stanley."

"You shitting me? You're in so deep, what harm could I do?"

"Thanks for the vote."

"I'm the only hope you got. Think about it. Cop gets caught, people assume he's dirty—no ifs, ands, or buts. The prosecution's not going to listen to you, your lawyer's going to tell you to shut up, and everyone else is buying tickets to ringside. You talk to me, you talk to the world, Joe. I'm the only way you get the truth out—"

Richard had gently removed the phone from my hand. "Stanley?" he said politely. "This is Richard Levay. My client doesn't want to speak with you."

I saw Richard nod his head several times and then add, "Anytime. You know how I like a good debate."

He hung up the phone, although I could still hear Katz's voice.

Richard resumed his seat. "Lesson number one: don't talk to anyone."

I sat opposite him. "Thanks for coming so fast."

He waved that away. "Happy to help, and just so you know up front, I'm waiving my fee."

I opened my mouth to protest, but he interrupted. "If I start losing my shirt, I'll let you know. Till then, those are my terms."

"Thank you."

"Okay, in a nutshell, what happened?"

I told him, virtually minute by minute, everything I did the night before. Occasionally he took notes; rarely he asked a question; but mostly he simply listened. At the end, he took a deep breath, let it out slowly, and said, "Not good. You have any idea how the brooch got in your pocket?"

"A few theories I kicked around with Gail, the best one being that somebody slipped it to me when Willy and I pushed through the crowd to get into the store. But that doesn't hold much water, and I can't prove it anyhow. A better bet is probably the CIA, and I doubt they'll be too forthcoming."

Levay looked at me as if I'd just admitted to seeing pink elephants. "The CIA?"

I told him about Boris, my visit to DC, the mugging, the near-shooting on Western Avenue, and the off-chance that John Rarig was somehow connected to it all.

Richard rose and walked over to the double glass doors, his hands behind his back. He rocked on his feet a few times and then faced me. "You think you could maybe not mention that little story again?"

"Too wacko?"

He tilted his head in acknowledgement.

"May be a bit late for that," I conceded. "Both the chief and my squad know about it. It's an ongoing case, after all."

"But there's no connection between it and last night's smash-and-grab."

"Not yet."

"Let's keep it that way," he said decisively and returned to his chair. "The fewer complications, the better. Who have you spoken with since you left the PD this morning?"

I thought a moment and suppressed an urge to lie. Kathy Bartlett had told me right off she didn't want to be pulled into this and had spoken to me purely out of friendship. But my loyalty to her was matched by my trust in Richard. What we said here was privileged, and he would have no reason to mention Kathy later. On the other hand, he might need to know about that conversation in case someone else tried to blindside him with it.

"I talked to Sammie Martens about what was going on with the squad, to Tony, who just dropped by to give me an update, and confidentially to Kathleen Bartlett to get some feedback on Fred Coffin."

He raised an eyebrow. "How confidentially?"

"Very. Just the two of us, briefly, and we didn't discuss the case. She said I was in up to my neck, but that was about it. She told me to hire a barracuda, and to break the rules if I had to."

"Ouch," Richard said softly. "All that on an open line."

I was suddenly hit with a chilling notion. "You think my phone's tapped?"

His eyes narrowed slightly, and he hesitated before answering. "No. Actually, I was wondering about a big office like the AG's, with all those lines, all those extensions. Wouldn't be the first time someone picked up a phone and accidentally eavesdropped." He leaned forward in his chair, his elbows on his knees, looking more like a shrink than a lawyer. "You were thinking the CIA again?"

I caught the tone of concern in his voice. "Not necessarily."

"Joe," he said slowly, "I've got only one thing to worry about here, which is that trinket in your pocket. I think we might be able to deal with that—maybe even duck it. A jury, for example, might be made to love that theory about someone in the crowd planting the thing on you, regardless of what you think of it. But if the CIA and mugger-hit-men come into it, that's going to introduce a whole other dimension, and I'll be honest with you, I'd prefer that didn't happen."

He began wandering around the room again, idly touching lamp-shades and photographs and the leaves of various plants with his fingertips. "And there's something else. You mentioned Gail. Have you and she discussed all the permutations of this together?"

I stared at him, feeling a sense of dread wash through me.

"She's a deputy state's attorney, Joe," Levay continued. "And you and she are not married. None of what you two talked about is pro-tected, and I seriously doubt Fred Coffin will overlook that. She will be deposed."

I rubbed my forehead, that odd humming back in my brain. "I think we even touched on that—watching what we said. Maybe I'm making that up. But we went ahead anyhow."

"Through that deposition, the CIA angle will probably come out, along with your somewhat unfortunate overreaction on Western Ave. Witnesses to that should have some pretty colorful descriptions."

I didn't say a word.

"Did you tell Gail you were going to call Bartlett?" he asked.

"No," I answered with relief. "That was spontaneous. I only thought of it after Gail and I talked on the phone this afternoon."

"Good. At least he can't reach Kathy that way." He smiled. "Well, don't worry about it. I can probably stop the CIA from being mentioned in court. And, if not—given the right jury— we'll just make the CIA look like the KGB. Who knows? This is a business for the nimble-footed. We'll have to be better at it than he is."

He crossed the room and opened his briefcase, replacing his pad and pen. "I wouldn't worry right now in any case. They haven't even begun the investigation, which could take them a while. I'll call Fred and let him know I've been retained, and then we'll just wait for the other shoe to drop. Best case scenario: they actually find the anonymous caller, who turns out to be a retired pickpocket."

He snapped the case shut and headed for the door. "Don't get too glum early on, keep your mouth shut, and only talk to Gail about the weather and what's for dinner. Give her my best, by the way, and tell her not to worry."

He paused before leaving. "About what Bartlett said—playing dirty? You'll leave that to me, right?"

"You got it, Richard."

Gail came home late that night, her shoulders slumped and her eyes vacant. She entered the kitchen, where I was sitting in front of a stack of six cookies, and barely cast them a glance, much less gave me a lecture.

"You look bushed," I said, taking her portable computer and brief-case and laying them on the breakfast table. "You had anything to eat? I could pull out a can of soup."

Without saying a word, she draped her arms around my neck and gave me a long, quiet hug. We stood there, I rubbing her back, for several minutes before she finally broke away, sat in one of the Wind-sor chairs by the bay window facing the driveway, and kicked off her shoes. "I'm not hungry."

I settled on a stool nearby and extended a cookie to her, which she took automatically. "I take it this was not a good day."

She chewed thoughtfully for a few seconds before admitting, "I kept trying to figure out what it felt like. I just spent the day doing what I do, nothing more. Everyone was polite, nobody avoided me— although your name never came up—but I was feeling victimized. I finally figured out it was like standing on a scaffold with a blindfold, with a bunch of people working under the trapdoor, trying to figure out why it wasn't opening. 'Let's make a little small talk while we sort this damn thing out . . .' I felt like I was betraying you by not grabbing them by the collars and telling them this was all such shit."

I handed her a second cookie. "You can't do that, Gail. You've got to just lock it in a corner of your mind. It'll drive you nuts otherwise. Sammie thinks it'll all blow over soon anyway."

She glanced at the cookie in her hand as if it had appeared from out of the blue and stuffed it into her mouth, ignoring my lame attempt to cheer her up. "I don't know if I can pull that off," she said in a muffled voice. "If Fred Coffin's people put together a case, I'll be up the creek in two ways. Not only will Derby have to park me where I can only work cases you've never come close to, but I'll be dragged into this anyhow once Coffin asks me if you and I have discussed what happened to you."

I pursed my lips and nodded. "Yeah. Richard Levay was here this afternoon. Told me the same thing. I am sorry. I should've kept my mouth shut."

This time, she half rose out of her chair and stole three cookies off my stack. "I'm the goddamn lawyer, for Christ's sake." She took a bite. "Sure wasn't thinking like one then. What did he say?"

I hesitated. She glanced at me, winced, and very gently thumped her forehead with the heel of her free hand. "Okay, okay. Never mind. Christ—what a day. I should've stuck to selling houses."

I leaned over and kissed her cheek. "Bullshit."

By late morning the following day, I'd gone to pacing through the house like a frustrated ghost, searching for something to do, too restless to finish it once I'd begun. Books were left open next to three different chairs, two TVs were muttering to themselves in empty rooms, tools had been spread out before several untouched repair jobs, and the car had been hosed but not soaped. By the time the phone finally rang, I damn near pulled it out of the wall.

"*What?*"

"Little antsy?" Sammie asked.

"What do you think? Hold it . . . We shouldn't be talking."

She laughed. "Man. You're a basket case. We won't be talking. I'll talk and you listen. Not that it matters. This is just an update anyhow. Fred Coffin's boys came down yesterday afternoon—Danny Freer and Bill Nathan. They haven't done much yet. Mostly poke through our notes and learn the cast of characters. They did talk to the owner—Alonzo. Remember Mickey Mitchell, a juvie shoplifter about ten years ago?"

I closed my eyes, trying to pull out that name. "No."

"He left town long since. Not a bad kid—a little screwed up. He stole a small item from Alonzo's shop back then. You ran the case, returned the item, had Mickey apologize, and got Alonzo to drop the charges. I was hoping that would mean something to you."

"I wish it did. I've done that kind of thing a lot. We all have."

She sounded disappointed. "Yeah. Well, anyhow, they were digging into it, for some reason. They're real tight-lipped. Not a fun-lovin' couple."

"I know Freer," I said distractedly. "He always seemed decent enough. How's the squad doing?"

"A little worse than before. Willy's p.o'd he's been dragged into it. Tyler's keeping it to himself, and Ron's looking like his dog was run over. The rest of them are walking on eggs. The chief's become a total pain in the butt—prickly as hell. Things've gotten real spit-and-polish around here. CYA's the standing order. Everybody's waiting for you to get a clean bill of health, but they can't understand the delay."

She'd delivered all this in hyperdrive, making it sound like some demented rap song. I didn't bother asking how she was holding up. "Any movement on the Boris case?" I asked instead.

There was a brief silence at the other end. "No. Not really," she finally said. "Kind of slipped off the front burner."

"Slip it back on," I told her. "You're in charge now. Is that a problem?"

"Hell, no. Might get our brains going again. How d'you want to work it?"

"Officially? Not at all—remember that. But if I were in your shoes, I'd be very curious about John Rarig. I was supposed to put his background under a microscope while you and Willy got to Marty Sopper through Marianne Baker. Maybe Ron can act for me—he's a natural. Tell him to get as many live accounts of Rarig's past as he can—not to trust the paper trail."

"I'll handle Marianne alone," she said, her enthusiasm plain. "I don't see Willy loosening her up one bit—too much like Sopper himself. He could work at it from the other end, though. Chat it up with Sopper's scuzzy friends. He'd be good with them."

"Fine," I encouraged her. "How 'bout the rest of your workload? If Tony's on the warpath, he's going to come checking. And you're one man short now."

"Don't remind me. I think we're all right for the moment. I heard several people in the Officers' Room writing the Boris thing off as a mob dumping, though. More talk like that, and Tony'll tell us to shut down the investigation."

I knew she was right. "Well, do what you can as fast as you can. It's the best we can hope for."

We hung up, she presumably feeling better, and I definitely deeper in the dumps. The more I stalked around the house, as if circling my problem in search of the slightest hope, the more convinced I became that my only salvation lay in keeping the Boris investigation alive. The fact that I had no say in that decision, however, made me feel like a drowning man within sight of a passing boat. It was a galling, belittling sensation, which threatened the calm I knew I had to maintain.

The phone rang again. This time it was Ted MacDonald, the news director of the town's radio station, WBRT. A lifelong resident, unlike Stanley Katz, and a far kinder man, Ted used an approach that was appropriately less self-serving than Katz's had been.

"Joe," he began, "I didn't want to crowd you when I first heard about this. How're you holding up?"

"In what context are you asking?"

He didn't take offense. "As a friend, off the record."

This was one of Ted's true talents and explained why he was the best reporter in town. He bided his time, made the effort to nurture his sources, and often waited until they came to him. He could only afford to do this, of course, because by now he had tabs on half the town's residents. Still, it was a pleasant contrast to the Katzes of the world and made me less inclined to hang up the phone on him.

"I'm waiting for the other shoe to drop," I said.

"Doesn't sound like Fred Coffin shares your sense of fair play. He's gone after you pretty hard in a press release we just got."

"Well, it's his investigation."

"Meaning there's something to find?" MacDonald sounded surprised.

"Meaning he'll come up with it if it's there or not. He's climbing the ladder, Ted. People like that see everything as an advantage. If he finds me dirty, then he's exposed a bad cop. He finds me clean, then he's a saint who shows no favorites. The man's in hog heaven."

"What are you doing about it?"

"Still off the record?"

"Yeah."

He'd never been known to break his word, but Richard Levay's caution came back to mind. "I'm waiting to see what the charges are."

Ted's silence spoke of his disappointment.

"It's not like I'm used to this role," I explained. "I've always talked to you and Stan from the other side of the fence. I'm sorry."

I hung up the phone, feeling even worse than before. There were no conversations left that weren't shadowed by the cloud hanging over me. Regardless of the topic, it seemed, the sticking point remained the same—was I lying or not?

And I hadn't even been formally charged yet.

Gail looked no better that night, coming home late as usual. This time, however, I noticed a skittishness that had been missing before. The sense of relief upon entering our home was absent. She didn't take off her shoes at the door, or use me as a sounding board for the day's frustrations. Instead of loitering in the kitchen where we spent much of our time together, she greeted me and continued upstairs, her coat still on, complaining of a headache and saying she was going to take a bath.

I left her on her own, listening from the darkened living room as she moved about upstairs. Later, after she'd been soaking for about ten minutes, I quietly went to join her, conscious of the house's somber quiet. She'd lit only one light in the bedroom, and when I opened the bathroom door to the misty sweetness of soapy hot water, I found only a candle lit.

"What?" she asked, a streak of pallor in the dark tub at the far end of the room.

"Just checking to see how you were."

"I want to be alone."

I closed the door and retreated to a rocking chair in the corner of the bedroom. I'd half expected the rejection—perhaps I'd even sought it out, to prove it was there, waiting to happen.

But with it, I felt an acute loneliness, which I now had to admit I'd also been anticipating. There comes a time in life, I'd discovered years ago, when emotional surprises all but peter out. It's not that they stop happening, but when they do, they carry the dull resonance of familiarity. Now that the wedge between me and my life had reached the two of us, I saw that its progress had been as swift, sure, and predictable as when the Titanic had borne down on that iceberg.

I sat in that chair, as I was sure Gail was lying in the tub, awaiting the inevitable.

She came out eventually, silent and brittle, wrapped in a robe she held gathered at the throat. I wasn't surprised when she slipped under the covers still encased in the robe.

"I take it today makes yesterday look good," I said.

"Yeah."

"You want to talk about it?"

"Not really."

She was staring at the twin peaks her feet made under the bedspread, her face tight and her brow furrowed. I said nothing more, but made no move to leave her in peace.

Finally, she yielded. "Remember what I said about wondering

when they'd fix the scaffold? Well, they have. Derby didn't just strip me of all the cases you might've been involved in. He's dumped me back into Juvenile, where I started. And I got the feeling that if any big cases come up there, someone else will handle those, too."

"Seems a little harsh," I commented.

Her face turned bitter. "He said it was for my own protection. The media and the public aren't allowed in family court, so I'll be able to keep functioning with only minimal distractions. What crap. The only thing he's protecting is his own butt. He figures if he can bury me from the start, he won't have to catch any more flak."

"What's there been so far?"

"The press has been leaning on him, questioning the integrity of the office. A couple of the low-rent lawyers around town went on record this morning about the same thing. You haven't even been arraigned yet, and I'm off to Siberia. I didn't think Derby would be such a politician."

I remained silent, thinking of her change of tone from twenty-four hours earlier. The pendulum would swing back into balance, as always, but that realization did little to lessen the sting of what I was hearing.

"You should've seen the new guy. Wolf? You haven't even met him. One week in juvie, and now he's handling some of my cases. Preppie bastard—couldn't keep the smirk off his face."

She pressed her hand against her cheek and closed her eyes. I could hear the stifled tears in her voice. "I know you're the victim here, Joe. I know all you've worked for is being threatened, and that I should be supportive and loving and all that shit. But to me, it's like it's all happening again—some big goddamn elephant coming out of the sky and landing on me like I was a bug, squashing you, me, everything we've got. It's just too close for comfort. Not enough time's gone by."

She turned to face me, and in the dim light I could see the wetness on her cheeks. "It's all coming back. The fears, the anger, the jitters. A photographer caught me in the street when I was leaving the courthouse this afternoon. I wasn't expecting it. He jumped out, holding that damn camera, and it all came back—that sense of not being in control, of being a victim."

She wiped away her tears, her eyes blazing. "It made me angry at you, Joe. Angry that you're a victim, angry that you've made me one again, angry that you somehow pulled me into this world of dopers and child abusers and careless, stupid people who kill because they don't have the brains to do otherwise. I used to sell houses to rich people, for God's sake. The hypocrite ex-hippie who kidded herself by joining all the right tree-hugger boards. It was working so well I could've faked it forever."

She pounded the bed several times with her fist, punctuating the next sentence one word at a time. "I'm tired of being raped."

She rolled over, turning her back to me. I sat motionless for a long time, sorting through what she'd said, pretending to be calm when all my insides were in turmoil. My trust in the pendulum had been reduced by the simple fact that, sooner or later, people ended up saying things they couldn't take back.

I knew what she was going through. The rape was fresh enough in both our memories. All her friends had been amazed at her ability to turn a catastrophe into a watershed, to use a trauma that destroyed many as a stimulus to return to law school, take the bar, and become a prosecutor. As friends, they'd taken comfort—even satisfaction—from her strength, using it for their own convenience to leave an unpleasant episode in their wakes. But I still shared her bed, and woke up to her nightmares, and lived in a house with as many locks and lights as a prison. I saw the subtle changes in how she walked down a street, how she stood in a crowded room, how she greeted previously unknown men with an inner wariness.

I knew the recovery for which she'd been justly applauded was still a fragile work in progress. What was destroying me now was that, while I'd been of help to her in the first event, I'd now become the cause of the worst setback I'd seen her suffer.

I stayed all night in the rocker, watching Gail toss and turn in fitful sleep, hoping against all odds that the few chips I had left in the game would turn our future around.

11

DANNY FREER AND BILL NATHAN CAME FOR ME THE NEXT DAY. With very short haircuts, broad shoulders, and stiff manners, they were models of the law enforcement stereotype— from the military-style mustache on Freer's upper lip to the superfluous sunglasses Nathan removed as I let them in.

"You two dig a hole deep enough to bury me yet?" I asked with a smile, extending my hand in greeting.

But gallows humor was obviously not on the agenda. Danny— older, more experienced, and visibly embarrassed— cleared his throat. "Joseph Gunther, you're under arrest for grand larceny and possession of stolen property. You're going to have to come with us." He began to recite the all-too-familiar Miranda warning.

I hesitated, watching his eyes, trying not to show the effect of his words. While I'd been braced for an encounter with these two, I'd always assumed I'd be dealt the same courtesies we usually offered our low-threat customers—either arranging a meeting at a lawyer's office, or simply issuing a citation to appear in court.

I was baffled and irritated by what I saw as theatrical nonsense.

Freer concluded by asking me if I undestood my rights. I ignored him. "Why all the razzle-dazzle, Dan? You don't have a warrant, do you?"

Nathan, his frustration boiling over into a young man's need for action, roughly spun me around. "Hands against the wall. Spread your feet."

Danny growled, "Cut it out, Bill."

A surge of noise outside made me look over my shoulder, out through the open door into the driveway. Climbing out of a series of cars and vans were reporters, cameramen, and technicians from several newspapers and radio and TV stations.

I dropped my hands from the wall, ignoring Nathan, and turned to face them both, all explanations suddenly clear. "Very impressive. Coffin's dog-and-pony show. No wonder you look like you want to be somewhere else. Where're we headed with this?"

"Woodstock," Danny said gruffly, looking at the growing crowd by the door.

Skipping the body search, Nathan grabbed one of my hands, slapped his cuffs on the wrist, and reached for the other. "You carrying?"

I indicated with my head. "Holster—right hip. That's it."

He finished with the handcuffs and then removed my pistol, slipping it into his jacket pocket. "Let's get the hell outta here."

I tried to catch Freer's eye. "Danny, you take me up there and call for bail, it's not going to stick. The judge knows me. You'll look like jerks."

Freer pursed his lips silently. Nathan, his face flushed, grabbed my elbow and pushed me toward the door. "Well, I don't know you from shit, and what I've been learning isn't too impressive, so why don't you just do the drill and shut up?"

I shook off his hand violently, hearing the first snap of a camera shutter from outside. Pure fury rose in my throat, choking my breathing. I stared at them both for a long couple of seconds, seriously considering making this a media event worthy of the name. The shame in Danny's eyes won me over, however, along with the absolute knowledge that all three of us right now had been reduced to simple puppets.

We walked the small gauntlet of bright lights, questions, and proffered microphones to the unmarked car they'd parked facing the street and then slowly drove away, swathed at last in cold silence.

They drove me straight to the state correctional facility in Woodstock, over an hour's drive north of Brattleboro. Normally, such a trip was only made after an arrest warrant had been served and a judge had dictated such conditions of release as would make a stay in jail unavoidable. In this situation, neither had occurred. As if dealing with some proven, stone-cold killer, Coffin had ordered Nathan and Freer to simply pick me up and deliver me for booking—an expeditious way of getting a menace off the streets. Except, as I'd told Danny, I was hardly that. Unless Coffin had something special up his sleeve, no judge in his right mind would jail me.

And from Freer's and Nathan's demeanor, I didn't think Coffin had any hidden aces. We were being made victims of a supercharged ego, inflated to the point of folly by ambition and publicity. It seemed both Gail and Kathy Bartlett had been accurate in their appraisals of the man.

The irony was—assuming I was right about how this trip turned out—Coffin had just allowed himself to become as manipulated as I had been.

Unfortunately, his fate would be short-term ridicule and his reaction long-term hell for me. It was therefore with no satisfaction that I sat in the backseat watching the countryside slip by.

With nothing tangible to either prove my innocence or explain Boris's death, I took advantage of the ride to ponder the few options I had left. Whoever was pulling the strings, for whatever end result, was counting on the legal system to be his dogged co-conspirator—the system I'd been brought up in, which was directing the other two men in this car, and which their boss was pushing to absurd extremes. Right now, all of us within it were being expected to serve the Rule of Law.

Except that I was beginning to consider the alternative.

If the puppeteer I was imagining truly existed, and was acting as I surmised, then the one thing he wouldn't know how to control would be a renegade puppet, acting on his own. Of course, that wasn't an insight I could act upon.

Yet.

Woodstock Correctional Facility had taken on the aura of a populist penal colony. Not only is it located on the main street entering what is possibly Vermont's most upscale village, thanks largely to some early Rockefeller largesse, but it butts right up to the sidewalk, around the corner from one gas station and opposite another, its unprotected front door within reach of any pedestrian. Turning Route 4's sharp corner onto Pleasant Street, motorists are given an open view right into the jail's exercise yard, predictably ringed by high fences and razor wire. It is a jarring sight, stimulating many a double take, and for me representing a typical example of the state's make-do pragmatism.

This, of course, was before I was supposed to be one of its guests. Now, as our car pulled into the unguarded parking lot next to the building—and despite my own hopes about the futility of this trip—I also remembered Woodstock's reputation for being cramped, over-crowded, and in need of repairs. Not that creature comforts were my primary concern. I was thinking of how someone of my profession might fare in such an environment, and a small knot of fear began forming in my stomach.

Freer and Nathan extracted me from the car and took turns securing their weapons in the trunk. Another of Woodstock's lesser-known sins is that it occasionally loses the keys to the officers' gun box, so the chastened have learned to trade being temporarily unarmed for being able to leave the place without delay after delivering their charges.

I was then led up the driveway, around the corner to the sidewalk, and up the few steps to the front door, my manacled wrists—as I felt it—like visual magnets to every passerby within sight. The odd absence of any press—given the publicity of our departure—didn't strike me until later. At the door, Nathan pushed an intercom button, announced our arrival to a disembodied voice, and swung the door back in response to an electric buzz.

We found ourselves in a gray cement-block cubicle, facing a second door, heavier, with a small armored window at head height. The ignored gun box hung on the wall next to us. To the round, pale face of the supervisor floating in the window, both my escorts opened their jackets to reveal empty holsters. The face nodded, there was a dull clank, and the steel door opened before us.

We stepped into another, slightly larger room, with a tiny cell in one corner, an equally small strip-search bathroom opposite, one scarred and battered metal desk supporting a computer, and a booking stand equipped for "mugs and prints." It was lit brightly enough to make us all squint upon entering. I saw, behind a curved bank of thick, tinted windows, the dim shape of the elevated control room operator, lording over a tilted panel of switches, intercoms, and TV monitors. Along one of the long walls, a second row of windows looked onto the prison cafeteria, where a few inmates could be seen listlessly wandering back and forth, barely glancing my way.

The heavy door slammed shut behind me, making me swallow hard, exposed in the harsh light.

Nathan handed the supervisor the booking affidavit, which he in turn carried over to the desk to be entered into the computer. Danny Freer turned to face me, his expression the only halfway sympathetic thing in the room.

He removed my handcuffs and indicated a metal straight-back chair. "Sit down, Joe. This'll take a few minutes."

He then picked up a clipboard and began asking me questions— age, height, weight, social security number, all the rest. As I responded to each, I saw through the corner of my eye the cafeteria windows slowly filling with gloating faces. Natural curiosity about incoming "fresh meat" had obviously been replaced by a widespread appetite for unprotected police officer. Word of my arrival had gotten out. Without comment, Danny moved to stand between me and the window, at which I heard a muffled outcry of protest. Someone began thumping on the thick glass.

"Okay," Freer said, his voice impassive. "Empty your pockets."

I did so slowly, allowing him to catalogue each item before he dropped it into a bag. Guards were now shouting at the inmates to back off from the window. My throat dry, fear overriding reason, I began to have doubts that Fred Coffin had stumbled in bringing me here—that maybe he was about to pull a rabbit out of his hat.

Danny, his routine finally finished, gave me a receipt and nodded to Bill Nathan, who picked up the phone on the desk and dialed the Windham District Court. I now cast a glance toward the windows and saw a crowd of men standing several feet away, their eyes upon me. Several of them grinned and made suggestive gestures.

Nathan lowered the phone and addressed his partner with disgust. "The clerk won't play. She's gone to find a judge."

We sat in silence for several minutes before Nathan began talking again, too quietly for me to hear. Finally, after the line had gone dead, he said, "Fuck you, too," and hung up with a bang.

He looked at Danny in disgust. "We gotta cut him loose—flash-cite him for arraignment on Monday. No bail, no conditions, no nothin.'"

Danny shrugged. "You surprised?"

He handed me the bag he was still holding so I could refill my pockets, and returned the clipboard to the supervisor. "Let's get out of here."

Nathan's face was closed down tight, his eyes narrow with anger. "I wanna mug and print him first, just for our records."

Freer shook his head. "In good time, Bill. Joe was right— Coffin fucked up. No point getting our shorts in a twist. Let's take him back."

Nathan's face colored. "He can hitch his way back."

Danny stared at him until his partner looked away, then he nodded good-bye to the supervisor and motioned toward the exit. We all three left without saying a word.

Gail met us in the driveway, hugging my neck as soon as I got out of the car, allowing Freer and Nathan to slip away without further embarrassment. Just as at the jail, there were no reporters.

"I heard it on the news," Gail said into my ear, still hanging on. "I can't believe he'd try something like that."

I rubbed her back, pleased beyond measure to have her in my arms. "Yeah—quite the sendoff. Everybody but the *New York Times*."

She pulled away far enough to look into my eyes. "How was it?"

"In retrospect, a slightly nervous drive in the countryside."

She scowled. "Coffin is such a prick. I'm glad Judge Harrowsmith handed him his lunch."

We began walking back toward the house. "Didn't put him on Nathan's good side, though," I said.

Gail stopped just shy of the door. "Joe. I want to apologize for last night."

I put my hand on her cheek. "Don't. There's no need. You are being victimized. You have a right to be pissed off."

"But not at you."

I laughed. "Maybe, but that's the way it works, isn't it?"

She shook her head in response, but I interrupted her before she could speak. "Gail, it's better to blow a cork at someone who loves you than at someone who wouldn't understand. God knows, I've run you over a few times."

The phone began ringing inside the house, so I jogged into the kitchen to answer it.

"I was hoping you'd be back by now," Sammie said. "That was some stunt. Doesn't give you much faith in the AG's office."

"Not that particular AG," I agreed. "On the other hand, since it didn't work, maybe he'll be a little more rational next time."

"Yeah." She didn't sound convinced. "Anyhow, I don't know that we'll be able to tie Marty Sopper to Boris's death, not if Boris was knocked off when we think he was. Willy's dug up a pretty good alibi for him—he was cheating on Marianne all that night with another woman."

"And it's solid?"

" 'Fraid so."

I thought about that for a moment. "Okay. What did Ron find out about Rarig?"

"That's looking more promising. He took your advice about working outside the paper trail, but he did it one better. He started calling people who knew Rarig as a kid—in Ames, Iowa, of all places. There'll be one hell of a phone bill next month, but I think it'll be worth it. From the few folks who remembered him, it doesn't sound like their Rarig's the same one we've got."

"A switch?" I asked.

"Could be. Hard to say exactly. Rarig's in his seventies, so anyone who knew him back then's pretty old, but their descriptions don't jibe with our guy. 'Course, to be fair, they also don't exactly jibe with each other, either. Still, I think we're barking up the right tree. Ron's still at it. He's hoping to find out why Rarig's never been back to Ames and never made contact with anyone there."

"He doesn't have any family? Maybe we could get some early pictures."

Sammie laughed. "That's why this is looking good. He was an orphan. There're some school pictures, and we'll be getting copies of those, but it sounds like real cloak-and-dagger stuff. Kind of cool."

I wasn't sure I would've phrased it quite that way. "Well, I'm glad it's going well. Did you get any feedback on the motorist from the other night?" I tried to temper my lingering anxiety by adding lightly, "The one I damn near shot?"

"Nope," she said without apparent concern. "Not a peep yet. We're still looking, though. By the way, I have an idea why Coffin tried his little throw-you-in-jail gimmick."

I shook my head at the phone, caught off guard by her sudden shift of gears. "Better stop there, Sam. You get on the stand, you'll have to own up to this."

"Not to worry," she answered, as she had before. "This is purely informational. I found out about that Mickey Mitchell deal—the shop-lifter you got Henri Alonzo to go light on. Alonzo told Coffin's two boys he felt you pressured him—says he was threatened by the uni-form—quote, unquote—and that in fact he wanted to prosecute. His theory now is that you had it in for him because he wanted to walk the straight and narrow, while you were just after brownie points with some snitch."

My mouth opened in surprise. "What? I never had Mitchell as a snitch. Before you reminded me, I didn't even remember who he was. And why the hell would I rip off Alonzo years later for a piece of bullshit like that?"

"Beats me," Sammie said. "But I think that's what Nathan and Freer were told to sell the judge from Woodstock. It does make you look pretty bad, you have to admit—especially with Coffin painting in the details."

I muttered something I barely heard myself and hung up, staring sightlessly out the window, my face flushed. Gail came in from the living room and cautiously stood beside me.

"Bad news?"

"It's not good." I checked my watch. "I'm going out for a while."

She looked at me, startled. "Where? You want me to come?"

"No. Thanks. And I better not tell you, either."

She followed me as I made for the door. "Joe, wait. If you're doing something connected to the case against you, you better think twice. Or at least fly it by Richard."

I waved my hand casually at her, crossing the driveway toward the garage. "Not to worry."

"Joe," she called out louder, an edge to her voice, "don't think you're a cop anymore. Coffin's just waiting for you to hand him something."

I faced her from the garage door. "I'm just going to clear something up. No big deal."

I got into the car and backed it into the open.

She walked up to my window, her face now tight with anger. "This is stupid and you know it. You're not in a position to clear anything up. That's not how it works. Let other people do their jobs, Joe. Don't mess it all up."

A sudden flash of rage ran through me. "How the hell can I make anything worse? I sit around on my ass, I'll not only get fired, I'll probably end up in jail. This whole goddamn thing's a frame, and it'll work because the system's making it work."

She slapped the side of the car door with her hand. "Yours isn't the only life on the line, you know," she shouted. "And you're not the only one feeling pushed around. You can't just disappear and play cop because you're pissed off."

I put the car into gear, feeling like I was about to explode. "We'll talk later. I gotta go."

We were both right, of course, which made matters worse, since for either one of us to back down, more than pride would be sacrificed. But in my self-righteous anger, I only saw that while we were both being victimized, I was the one with the most to lose, and the one best placed to do something about it—a male warrior instinct that belittled Gail's claim, made me feel subconsciously guilty and, predictably, twice as furious with Henri Alonzo.

The closer I got to Springfield, Vermont, where he lived, the more I resented his reckless intervention. An arrogant twerp at the best of times, he'd either gratuitously taken a poke at me when I was down and out, or he was up to something more sinister. Given the scope of everything that was swirling around me—a dead Russian, the CIA, an attempt on my life, and a steel-tight frame—it wasn't such a stretch to imagine Henri Alonzo as a willing pawn in somebody else's scheme.

My growing paranoia had become seductively rational, overriding all the warning signals that normally would have cleared my head. Gail might've been wrong about putting my trust in the system she'd so recently embraced. But I was dead wrong in taking my present impulsive course.

I'd totally overlooked the sequence of events that had stimulated me to make this drive—and the unseen hand that had carefully stacked them in place.

While Springfield has as distinct an identity as any other Vermont town, Alonzo's street seemed totally interchangeable with a dozen others I knew. Comfortably outfitted with trees, lawns, and sidewalks, the neighborhood was one of those post–World War Two enclaves, fated to travel the decades with no truly definable identity. Neither classic nor modern, bearing no particularly regional aspect, they all resemble the generic movie sets so common to films of the 1950s.

I parked opposite his house, the address of which I remembered from the night of the burglary, and crossed the fresh-cut grass to the front door.

He opened up as soon as my thumb left the doorbell.

"What do you want?" I couldn't decide if his tone echoed anger or fear.

I struggled in vain to stay neutral. "An explanation wouldn't hurt. Why did you come up with this cock-and-bull story about Mickey Mitchell? We both know it's total bullshit."

More slightly built than I, he almost cowered in the doorway. "I told them the truth."

"What truth? Mitchell was no snitch of mine. He was just a kid. We caught him red-handed, he swore on a stack of Bibles he wouldn't do it again, and you let him off the hook."

"I was pressured into that."

I felt like pinching his face in my hand, and totally lost control of my voice. "*Pressured?* You *fucking* little weasel. You told me you didn't want the publicity."

He stepped back nervously, and I thought for a moment he might slam the door. "I told you what you wanted to hear."

I paused, breathing deeply, feeling out of touch with my brain. "Henri," I tried again more calmly, "I don't understand why you're doing this. Did somebody pay you? Are you in a jam we could help you with?"

His eyes narrowed suspiciously. "What?"

My blood rose once more. "I'm giving you the benefit of the doubt. Maybe you can't help what you're doing. Does somebody have something on you?"

He straightened as if stung. "I'm a respectable man. I have nothing to hide. I have always followed the rules. You're a crook and now you've been caught. That's not my problem. Please get off my property."

I sized him up for a moment, considering that since I obviously had nothing left to lose, I might just pop him one for fun. But the adrenaline that had propelled me up here suddenly drained away, and I barely felt able to walk back to the car.

"I guess I had it wrong, then. You're just a nasty little bastard after all."

He didn't answer, choosing to look indignant instead.

I left him and drove back to Brattleboro on autopilot, my mind numb. At home I found a note from Gail, telling me she'd gone to spend the night with her friend Susan, that a little breathing room might do us both some good. She ended with "I love you," which I knew was supposed to be significant, but by then such sentiment had scant meaning for me. I was feeling as I had a lifetime ago—a teenage warrior in full retreat— empty, alone, beaten, and like the most disposable man on someone else's game board.

12

RICHARD LEVAY LOOKED AT ME CURIOUSLY, AS IF I WERE LOCATED at the business end of a microscope. "You realize what a jackass you've been?"

I chewed my éclair in silence. We were hunched across from one another in a window booth at the most fashionable coffee shop in town, a couple of blocks south of the courthouse where I was to be arraigned in half an hour. It was down the street from Dunkin' Donuts, whose more gluey concoctions I much preferred, but Richard had arranged the meeting and was far more discriminating than I. Also, I wasn't in the mood to argue about pastries.

"If arraignments didn't just happen to fall on Mondays in this county," he continued, "you *would* be cooling your heels in Woodstock right now. Coffin filed an obstruction of justice charge against you two seconds after he hung up on Henri Alonzo, and I seriously doubt the judge would've cut you slack twice in two days, not for something like that. In fact, I think the only reason Coffin didn't nail you just for publicity's sake, arraignment or no arraignment, is that he set the whole thing up from the start."

I gave him a blank look, realization only slowly dawning.

Richard shook his head. "You thought he was so full of himself he didn't know Harrowsmith wouldn't lock you up. He played you like a fiddle, Joe—got you to lower your guard, convincing you he was a jerk, and then he leaked that crap about Alonzo to Sammie so she could feed it to you and get you all fired up. Didn't you think it was a little weird the press was at your house when they busted you, but not at the jail or back home afterward? That's because he used them to turn your crank. He didn't tell them what jail you were headed to because he knew you'd be kicked loose. He was willing to look bad in the short run, but even his ego has its soft spots—he was only going to give them one photo-op."

He sat back in his chair. "You seen this morning's paper?"

"No."

"Well, it's a gift-wrapped present from you to Coffin—Katz's editorial is a sanctimonious warning to all us poor innocents to be wary of tin gods, meaning you and every other cop that's been held up for public admiration. If it ever comes time for Coffin to wax eloquent in front of a jury, he'll have more ammunition than he needs. If the public had any doubts about your guilt before, they're pretty much history by now."

I turned in my chair to face the window, sightlessly staring at the steady flow of pedestrians and traffic outside.

"I know I screwed up."

He took the time to tear off a piece from his croissant, dab it with some butter, and put it in his mouth. "Did you get anything out of him?" he asked.

"Alonzo? A lot of self-righteous indignation. Maybe Coffin did pull my chain, but I went up there 'cause I thought Alonzo might've been pressured somehow."

Richard gave me that familiar worried look. "Pressured how? He was robbed."

I was reluctant to feed his concerns. My theories were increasingly becoming mine alone, viewed by everyone else as paranoid ravings—not that waving guns at motorists and flying off the handle with Alonzo had helped my cause.

Wishing I hadn't brought up the subject, I explained: "In order for this whole thing to work, that brooch had to get into my pocket before the burglary. I don't mean slipped in there as I ducked under the tape—that would've been too risky. I mean earlier, like a day or more. I can't figure out the hows or whens of it, but when Alonzo brought up that crap about Mickey Mitchell, I started thinking he might know the who."

"But he didn't," Richard said.

"He held his ground."

Richard checked his watch and stood up, ignoring the rest of his croissant. "We better get going, and if I were you, I'd keep my fingers crossed that Coffin doesn't ask the judge to toss you in jail, *and* that the judge doesn't agree with him."

Arraignments in Windham County are scheduled for one o'clock, Monday afternoons, in the courthouse across the street from where the PD has its offices. They are democratic affairs, reminiscent of some soup kitchens I've visited. Twenty to thirty defendants mill around the second-floor hallway outside the clerk of court's offices, most of them without lawyers, waiting to be told what to do. They are a predictably scruffy lot, consisting of people one would expect to be lined up before a judge. Mostly men, a few of them try to spiff themselves up a bit, sometimes wearing other people's Sunday clothes. The rest don't bother, having been through the system often enough not to care any longer.

There is a tension in the air, although everyone's been told most arraignments are strictly routine—the standard price of admission to the legal maze. The building, with its many locked doors, armored glass, and watchful, armed court officers, instills an element of defeat in those being serviced, and the dehumanizing routineness with which they are dealt doesn't help.

Unless, of course, you're on the other side.

I remembered how I'd used the bureaucratic weight of the court to my own advantage in the past, implying that by some miraculous means, talking to me early on would somehow spare the person I was questioning from a slow strangulation by python-like red tape.

Now that I was on the threshold of the same journey myself, the memories of such behavior tasted bitter. Approaching the courthouse doors, and the cluster of journalists outside them, I realized for the first time that despite my best efforts—and even because of them—the fate being designed for me might in fact become reality.

This mood was not enhanced by hearing the first reporter say, "Here he comes," and being surrounded by a jostling herd of shouting, demanding people, some of them acquaintances, but whose friendship here mattered not at all. As we passed through the metal detectors, losing some of the crowd but picking up more on the other side, the torrent of questions fell on us like hail.

"Lieutenant Gunther, do you have any comments regarding the accusations made against you?"

"Are the charges true or false?"

"How do you feel about being here today?"

"Do you intend to plead guilty or not guilty?"

"Have you made any deals with the attorney general?"

"How do you feel about the way Fred Coffin's been talking about you to the press?"

"What about your confrontation with Henri Alonzo? He said you were pretty rough on him."

Richard had prepared me for this and had urged me to keep quiet. At the time, I wasn't sure how I'd fare, but it wasn't too difficult. Very quickly, the questions overlapped one another, blending into one long indecipherable babble. Richard pushed us through the throng, speaking for me, mostly with "No comments," slowly defusing the excitement our entrance had stimulated.

He led us straight to the privacy of one of the tiny conference rooms lining the second-floor hallway and left to find the court officer for the prosecution's "Information"—Vermont's version of a written indictment. He slipped back through the door a few moments later, accompanied by a small burst of noise from outside, and handed me the packet—the Information, the affidavit, and a calendar of relevant dates. My mood continued to deaden as I read through the charges and their possible sentences, feeling the full impact of the same judicial language I'd employed so often against others.

I finally put the packet down and stared out the window.

Richard hesitated before breaking the silence. "It shouldn't be too long. Forty-five minutes at most for any deals to be worked out by other defendants, and for the judge to review applications for public defender services. We'll be in the first group to be called, since you're represented by private counsel. After that, it shouldn't take more'n ten or fifteen minutes."

He tried to make it sound like an application for an auto loan, but I didn't have the heart to help him out. The silence swelled between us.

Finally, there was a knock on the door, a sheriff's deputy stuck his head in and said, "Five minutes, gentlemen," and we shuffled across the hall to the courtroom, rejoined by our phalanx of reporters.

There, the atmosphere was more controlled. All press except print reporters were restricted to the jury box, and all conversation—until the judge arrived—was kept to a dull murmur. Richard and I found seats in the gallery about halfway up.

Normally, the gallery was filled only with those waiting their turn, and maybe a few relatives or gawkers. Today, it was packed, including, it seemed, half the citizens of Brattleboro. Looking over my shoulder, I saw people standing shoulder-to-shoulder along the back wall, as if waiting for the start of a momentous event. Permeating the air was the almost constant snap and whir of cameras hard at work.

In prior times, high publicity cases like mine were given special treatment. They were processed through the back door at off hours and arraigned in something approaching privacy. Those days had vanished long since, for both appearance and efficiency, and I had been one to herald their passing. Now, I sat and watched case after case being rapidly dealt with—Judge Harrowsmith sitting high above like a hawk-nosed gargoyle. The inevitability of my turn coming up, coupled with the metronomic slowness of its arrival, made me feel increasingly stretched between numbness and anticipation.

When the moment arrived, it was thankfully undermined by the theatrical response of the press. Instead of feeling alone and exposed as I rose and walked past the bar to the defendant's table, I found everyone's attention was diverted by the sudden clatter of a dozen people in motion. The mechanical snap and whir of cameras rose up again like a swarm of locusts.

Harrowsmith frowned deeply as Richard, I, and Fred Coffin settled in.

This was the first close-up glimpse I'd had of Coffin, who was immaculately dressed, his hair stylishly long at the collar. He was tanned and good-looking and had an arrogant way of tilting his chin up slightly and looking at people from just off center, as if ready to dismiss them. He was also young, given his position and ambitions, and had the narrow face of a hungry man. I was in no position to be lacking in prejudice, but he gave me the creeps.

Judge Harrowsmith began our proceeding in the monotone of a seasoned professional, reciting my name and the charges against me, introducing both Richard and Coffin to the record, and asking the defense whether we'd received the Information and affidavit.

Richard stood, acknowledged receipt, went through his own automated routine of announcements and waivers, pleading not guilty on my behalf. He then asked the judge to release me on my own recognizance.

Harrowsmith addressed the prosecution, "Mr. Coffin, I'll now hear the State on conditions of release."

Turning slightly toward the cameras, the AG cleared his throat to better project his voice. "Your Honor, the affidavit before you is clear on the motivation and subsequent actions of this defendant. As the older, financially frustrated male companion of a wealthy woman—"

Richard was on his feet complaining, amid a small fluttering from the press. The judge, as sensitive as anyone to a photo-op, sat him down, with a warning to both parties.

Coffin resumed. "This man has obviously taken it upon himself to act utterly outside the law, not only daily conferring with fellow police officers, but also badgering and intimidating witnesses in the case pending against him."

Again, Richard protested, with similar results.

"The State is therefore requesting," Coffin continued, "the first three conditions, in addition to numbers five—reporting to the Vermont State Police barracks once daily—six—restricting Mr. Gunther to Windham County—fourteen—barring him from contact with any member of his department or anyone associated with this case—and seventeen—that in lieu of incarceration, he be issued an ankle monitor so he may be tracked at all times."

"Your Honor," Richard burst forth once more. "My client is one of the most highly regarded law enforcement officers in this entire state, with multiple commendations—worthy enough, in fact, to have recently been assigned as a temporary investigator to none other than the attorney general's office. The case against him is extremely circumstantial and, as we will clearly establish at trial, totally fabricated. This man," he said, pointing me out, yielding to a little grandstanding himself, "is totally innocent. The conditions put forth by the prosecution are so ludicrous I'm frankly surprised they didn't tack on a diet of black bread and water just to round things out."

The news hounds loved it, of course, but Harrowsmith squelched them by half rising out of his chair and glowering them into silence. He then announced his decision: I had to report to the state police once a day, not contact any colleagues, not leave the county, and sure as hell stay out of the case against me. Richard and I had 180 days to prepare for trial. The first three conditions Coffin had begun with were routine keep-your-nose-clean-and-show-up-for-court items and were not debated. The ankle bracelet wasn't mentioned again, either.

That should have been it, except the judge had one last bit to deliver to the cameras. "Mr. Gunther," he intoned, "whether guilty or not of the charges filed against you, you have recently demonstrated at least some pretty poor judgment. I do not argue your lawyer's high opinion of you. In fact, I will invoke it myself as being the precise reason you had better heed the conditions you've just been given. If I hear of you stepping out of line again, I will deal with it to the utmost of my authority."

With that, he sent us on our way—complete with noisy escort—having made me feel like the only mutt at a pedigree dog show. Given what Coffin had gained with his chicanery through the Woodstock trip and the leak to Sammie about Alonzo, I swore to never belittle his underhanded talents again.

I waited for Gail in the parking lot behind her office, sitting in my car, struggling to read a book, mostly trying not to think. She held long hours, pushed as much by her own drive as by the workload. I also knew her job to be a traditional haven from unhappiness. If she was feeling like I was, I might be waiting until midnight.

But it was only eight-thirty when I caught sight of her, which made me happy she wasn't overdoing it. I got out and showed myself under a nearby streetlight. I hadn't parked too near her car, allowing her to ignore me if she chose, and for the same reason I didn't call out. I knew she'd see me. She never ventured outside without carefully looking about—a caution I wished she hadn't learned so brutally.

To my relief, she didn't hesitate but immediately headed my way. I met her at midpoint and we embraced without a word, clinging to each other with exhausted desperation.

Finally, we separated long enough for me to take the briefcase she'd dropped and escort her to her car, parked as always under a bright light.

"How'd it go today?" she asked.

"You'll be reading all about it. They put a pretty tight leash on me."

"Which you'll be ignoring, no doubt."

I squeezed her shoulder. "No comment, much as I'd like to. Things settled down at the office?"

She tilted her head and smiled sadly. "I shouldn't complain. I've lost thirty percent of my caseload, and I sit undisturbed for hours on end. The whole place is as quiet as a library because everyone stops talking when I enter the room. Life's become very peaceful."

"I'm sorry, Gail."

She kissed my cheek. "It's not your fault. I forget that sometimes, but it's true."

"You doing okay at Susan's?"

She pursed her lips and silently unlocked her car door. "That a veiled invitation to come back?" she finally asked.

I hesitated before answering. In many ways, she knew me as well as I knew myself, which meant we both were aware of my options—and of how I might address them. "I wish it were," I said, "but given the restrictions on me, and Coffin's appetite, it might not be a good idea."

She relieved me of her briefcase and tossed it onto the passenger seat. "Joe, I know you can't say anything—I don't even want you to—but I also know you're going to have to do something about this, probably illegally. I told you earlier to let other people do their jobs to get you out of this. That was wrong, I guess, and pretty naive. Seems like that's a sure road to jail."

She was crying softly as she said this, and I wrapped her in my arms again, half wondering when I'd next get the chance.

She continued speaking into my shoulder. "I wish I could help you somehow."

"Just hang in there. This'll all sort itself out."

"I used to think that about a lot of things."

I stroked her hair. "You want to move back in anyhow? I could bunk with someone else. It would at least give you the comfort of being on home turf."

She shook her head. "I miss the company more than the surroundings. I don't want to live there alone, anyhow."

I pushed her away enough to look at her face. "Gail, we'll get through this. Even if I can't figure a way out and they throw the book at me, it won't mean jail time. That's just Coffin shooting his mouth off. Worst-case scenario, you'll end up living with a TV junkie or a supermarket security guard. Think of all the crap we've been through already."

She gave me a weak smile. "Yeah, I suppose."

We kissed and she slid in behind the wheel. I closed the door, and she rolled the window down. "Don't be a stranger, okay? Call me. I don't care how many times. You're going to need to hear a friendly voice."

"I will. I promise."

I watched her drive off into the gloom and stood there for several minutes, just listening to the town's steady vital signs. I hadn't the slightest idea when I'd be talking to her again. Whatever I did in the near future, it was almost a given it wouldn't suit Fred Coffin or Judge Harrowsmith. The way things stood, as Gail had admitted, the only road to freedom for me lay outside the system—a road I was either going to have to explore, or forever wonder why I hadn't.

13

THE PHONE RANG JUST BEFORE MIDNIGHT, AN UNGODLY HOUR IN a rural state. I was on the couch downstairs, half-comatose in front of the TV, surrounded by old newspapers, empty bags of junk food, a couple of dirty plates, and a bowl of melted ice cream. For the past three days, I'd been either checking in at the state police barracks, as required, or hunkering down here, eating poorly, not shaving, reading in the paper about everyone's outrage at rampant police corruption, and waiting.

I didn't mind the late-hour interruption.

"It's me," said Kunkle's voice. "Just listen."

I stayed quiet.

"Go for a walk up the street. Now." The phone went dead.

I hung up the receiver slowly. Something had come up in the Boris case, and Willy wanted to fill my ear with it, in direct conflict with a court-set condition—something I wasn't inclined to dismiss lightly.

I got up, went to the bathroom, and washed my face, watching myself in the mirror as I toweled off. The moment I'd been entertaining—purely as a notion—had finally arrived. Without the excuses of adrenaline or ignorance, on which I could have blamed my confrontation with Alonzo, I was willfully considering a violation of the rules I'd followed my whole life. The mildness of the affront made no difference. Brushing aside a court order was a big enough event that if the judge ever caught wind of it, he'd make sure I'd never forget.

I left the bathroom, put my shoes on in the living room, and, leaving the TV on and the house security system off, slipped out the back door. I cut through a small thicket of young trees on the edge of our property and emerged onto Orchard Street. From there, I headed uphill, away from the veiled glow of Western Avenue below.

It was a dark, clear night, and the stars overhead gave me more than enough light to see by, although I wouldn't have used a flashlight in any case. Taking Kunkle's cue, I was being unusually cautious. Coffin knew the burden of the restraints he'd put upon me—cooked up, no doubt, as much to force my hand as to keep me under wraps. In the 180 days we had until trial, nothing much was going to stimulate any headlines—unless I did something to change that.

Several times during my walk, I paused under a tree, enveloped in shadow, and waited. I saw a pet or two roaming its territory, a couple of 'possums and a family of raccoons. Once, a car drove by, forcing me into the bushes. But generally, I remained alone.

Willy hadn't specified where he'd contact me, and I hadn't expected him to. A Vietnam vet who'd specialized in long-range recons behind enemy lines, he was given to lurking in the night, finding, I expected, a form of inner peace that escaped him during the day. A friend of mine had once said there were two types of human beings—the simple complicated, and the complicated complicated. If ever there was a man who defined the latter, it was Willy Kunkle. In my experience, he was unique in regularly reliving his nightmares in order to quiet his own inner rage.

We met up near the crest of the road, where it borders one edge of Meetinghouse Hill Cemetery. I saw his shadow separate from one of the headstones to beckon me, and I climbed over the low stone wall to join him. In this vast, open spot, the stars gave a ghostly glimmer to all the marble and granite markers surrounding us like frozen gnomes.

"You check your tail?" he asked in a bare whisper.

"Several times."

He set off for the back of the cemetery, where the newer graves petered out at the edge of a field still popular with the local deer. I followed, my feet silent on the soft, immaculate grass. I found myself breathing shallowly, my mouth open, further adding to the absolute silence.

We finally stopped by a low bench inscribed with two names, located in a broad, flat area from which we could see anyone moving. The entire world seemed to end at a distant belt of trees, colored only in pewter gray.

"What've you got?" I asked in a low voice.

"First is what we don't got, which is Ron and J.P. Ron's out because that's the way Sam and I want it—he's got a young family, and he's too squeaky clean anyhow. He'd probably turn beet red before telling a lie, and then fuck it up anyhow. J.P.'s too much of a company man. He might be okay, but now's not the time to find out. And neither of 'em have military training, which the three of us do. I think that counts."

I didn't argue. The fact behind all this supposed calculation was that he and Sammie had decided to stick their necks out for me, for whatever reasons. I knew from experience I couldn't change their minds. The least I could do was to follow their ground rules.

"We got pretty good evidence Rarig's dirty," Willy went on. "Ron traced his career till he got into the Army and was shipped overseas. He was in on the D-day landings at Omaha Beach as a radioman and supposedly made it out alive, but that's where we think somebody pulled the switch. His whole unit was basically wiped out. They landed in the wrong place or something—I don't know—but they caught all hell and were written off."

Willy hunched over slightly on the bench, his body language expressing his pleasure. "But here's the good part: where the official Army unit history brags about him being a survivor, Ron dug up a hometown news article, written at the time, that has him listed as killed in action. There was a retraction a few days later, but we're thinking the paper got it right, and the feds had to scramble to cover it up. And I said, 'unit history,' right? That's because that's all there is on him. The Army lost his enlistment records—everything having to do with his identity. And remember Sammie telling you we were getting some high school yearbook photos faxed to us? Never happened. They called us back and said the books're missing for that year, not only from the

library, but from the principal's office as well. Before, the only complication was finding a way to have 'em copied."

"What about after D-day?" I asked.

Kunkle laughed softly. "All of a sudden, we have tons of records:
wounded in action, shipped back to DC and straight into a career at
the State Department. From that point on, we got rental information,
mortgages, country club memberships, driver's license, registration
forms—you name it. Like he was compensating for having no past
early on." He paused and then added, "He never married, by the way."

I played devil's advocate. "None of which tells us much. We thought
he was a spook almost from the start."

Willy was unfazed. "Yeah, well, the spook's in business again. We
been keeping a watch on his place, taking turns. This afternoon, he got
a visitor. Looked like a typical guest—old lady, white hair, bag of golf
clubs in the trunk—but her plates were from Maryland. I checked her
out, just for kicks. Name's Olivia Kidder, and her place of employment
is the CIA."

I raised my eyebrows in the darkness. This was either a curiously
coincidental time for old buddies to reunite, or a sign that something
was finally in motion.

"How'd you find out where she worked?" I asked a moment later.

"Routine check. I think most of their employees are out in the
open. I don't know what she does there, 'course. Hope to hell it isn't a
janitor or something. Anyway, the plan we cooked up was to hit 'em
tonight—see what they got to say. That's why I called."

"Sammie's still there?" I guessed.

"Yup. Kidder'll probably spend the night—long drive and all—but
we didn't want her to split tomorrow without having a crack at her. I
mean, what've we got to lose?"

I thought back to the conversation I'd had earlier with my reflection
in the mirror. "Nothing. Let's go."

Heading north in Willy's car, I began feeling increasingly at ease with
my decision. My chances of success were dim, but at a time when most
aspects of my life were in serious disarray, the simple act of riding

through the gloom was enough to make me believe in the possible again.

But not without misgivings. The sense of betrayal I'd felt on the night of the jewel theft, coupled with the maneuver Fred Coffin had pulled in court, was not to be eclipsed by some fresh air and a drive— especially when that drive could be taking me straight into more trouble.

I hadn't questioned the timing of Willy's visit to the Windham Hill Inn. If Olivia Kidder had indeed just arrived from DC after a long drive, it seemed unlikely she'd still be up. But he and Sammie had done their homework. As we crested the peak of the driveway and coasted into the parking lot with the engine turned off, I saw that while most of the inn's lights were extinguished, the same was not true of the room to the far right, a one-story wing that, through the window, looked like a piano-equipped library.

We'd barely eased out of the car and softly closed its doors before Sammie appeared out of the night like a breeze, her clothing dark, her eyes gleaming.

"They've been talking for hours, sitting about two inches apart like a couple of conspirators."

She gestured to us to follow and led the way under the stinking ginkgo tree to a large bush planted near the inn's far corner. From there, we had a clear view into the lighted room and could see John Rarig, as described, with a small, snow-capped, animated woman. From both their expressions, I could tell their topic was not a happy one.

Sammie pointed to a narrow set of stairs leading to a back porch. The door connecting it to the inn led directly into the library. "What do you say we invite ourselves in?"

I laid a hand on her forearm. "Hang on a sec. As soon as we go in there, we're opening ourselves to some serious problems. If these people choose to react like Alonzo did, Coffin'll land on us like God Himself. I'll end up in the slammer, and you two could be suspended."

"Fuck Coffin," Willy said without hesitation. "That bastard made me look like an idiot, saying you ripped off that brooch under my nose. He can drop dead, for all I care."

"I'm not worried, either," Sammie chimed in. "Besides, we got nothing to worry about." She pointed at the window. "They're up to something. They're not going to squawk."

Willy looked at me suspiciously. "You covering your butt all of a sudden?"

I smiled back at him. "Little late for that. But loyalty should have its limits. This is not a great career move for you guys."

His face soured predictably. "Loyalty? Spare me. You think you're doing me a favor, running interference so I don't get fired? I'm pissed off is all, and I'd love to shove something up Coffin's nose. I could care less about some stupid career."

I nodded. "Okay. Lead on."

We filed quietly up onto the porch. Sammie tried the doorknob, found it unlocked, and preceded us into the room.

Rarig and Kidder deserved credit. They didn't bat an eye—merely stopped speaking, sat back, and watched us line up before them.

Rarig smiled thinly, recognizing me. "Ah, Lieutenant. I thought you weren't supposed to be seen in such company."

"This is not an official visit," I answered, struck by his knowledge of my legal standing. I nodded to the woman by his side, hoping to throw them off balance. "Ms. Kidder. Nice to meet you."

Her face lit up with pleasure. "Very good. Trace my plates?" Her voice was clear and youthful, touched by a slightly ironic inflection. A successful veteran, I thought, of many a mental contest—and certainly no janitor.

"I did," Kunkle admitted. "And your place of employment."

Rarig addressed me again. "If not official, then what is this?"

I settled into an empty armchair. After a slight hesitation, my two companions did likewise.

"We thought it was time to clear things up a bit. Till now, we've been sticking to the legalities, like warrants and what-have-you. But as you implied, I'm working a little more independently at the moment, so I thought we might cut the crap and try being honest with each other."

Rarig raised his eyebrows. "I haven't been honest?"

Willy scowled at him. "Don't be cute."

Olivia Kidder was taking us in with the interested eye of a bird-watcher—silently waiting, I thought, for things to become more clearly defined.

"Your real name's not John Rarig," I said, gambling a bit to win her respect. "He probably died on the Normandy beaches in 'forty-four, or in a hospital back home as a result of his wounds. You weren't born in Ames, Iowa, and you haven't spent your whole career as a State Department paper pusher. You and Ms. Kidder came up together inside the CIA, which probably has a room full of identities like the real John Rarig's, just so guys like you can operate in daylight. You were a spook specializing in Soviet affairs, based in Austria, at least in the early years. What do you do for the Company, Ms. Kidder?"

She nodded slightly. "Please call me Olivia. I'm a glorified file clerk, really."

"Which is no doubt belittling both your talents and your position. Mr. Rarig, what was Sergei Antonov doing spying on you?"

He shrugged. "I don't know. Who is he?"

Willy muttered, "For Christ's sake," and Sammie shifted restlessly in her chair.

Rarig clarified his statement. "Lieutenant, if I was what you say I am, wouldn't you think me a little simpleminded to suddenly spill the beans just because you'd like me to? For all I know, your whole embarrassment with the attorney general is just a ploy to get me to trust you."

His patience exhausted, Willy launched himself from his chair and stood glaring down at John Rarig. With one lame arm dangling and his powerful right fist bunched up before him, he presented a conflicted image of impotence and fury—much more threatening than just an angry man. Rarig and Kidder watched him closely and, I noticed for the first time, with something approaching fear.

"You and Joe can play footsie all you want," Willy said in a low, tight voice, "but I'm not much of a bullshitter. You're dicking us around, maybe 'cause you whacked that Russian, or maybe 'cause you're a smoke screen for someone else. But our jobs are on the line, and I don't need some smartass fuck like you telling me fairy tales so you can pretend you're a virgin."

He leaned forward, placing that large, muscular hand on the arm of Rarig's chair, his face inches away from the older man's. "It wasn't all that tough digging up what we got on you, and it'll be easy to dig up more. The CIA are a bunch of fuckups. I saw it in 'Nam, and I'm seeing it now. So if you want to do this the hard way, that's fine with me. Sam and I are still legit, even if Joe's on thin ice, so we'll get the hell out of here, do our pissant paperwork, and come back to hang your balls from that vomit tree out there. Is that the way you wanna go?"

His speech was all the more impressive considering he'd just told me he didn't care about his job. And it obviously had an effect. Rarig sat blinking, pressed back against the cushion of his chair, even after Willy had straightened up.

Rarig glanced at Kidder, who nodded. He then smiled uneasily at Willy. Spook or not, he was in his mid-seventies—no longer capable of slugging it out, even with a one-armed man. But Willy could affect people that way in any case. It was the anger he carried within him—and the clearly feeble restraints containing it—that remained his most eloquent ally. And Rarig seemed to be a good listener.

"I wasn't saying we couldn't find some middle ground," he conceded uncomfortably. "But given the accusations you just made, I stand to lose quite a bit if I'm not careful. Isn't that reasonable?"

It was clear Willy would have been just as happy beating his brains out, but he looked over at me instead, sighed slightly, and sat back down.

I tried to keep the conversation moving our way. "It'd be reasonable if you made us some gesture of good faith. That's how middle ground is reached."

There was a long, thoughtful silence in the room.

"When you went down to Langley," Rarig finally asked me, "what were your impressions of Gil Snowden?"

I didn't ask how he knew about that, guessing Kidder had been his source. "That he knew more than he admitted, like you."

"Why?"

I rose to my feet and crossed to the door, putting my hand on the knob. "I guess Willy was right. We'll just have to do this the old-fashioned way."

Sammie and Willy were stopped halfway out of their chairs by Rarig quickly saying, "Snowden killed your Russian."

I stayed where I was, waiting for more. "My turn—why?"

"Because he thought Antonov was going to tell me something about Snowden."

"Was he?"

The older man shrugged. "We'll never know."

Irritated, I turned the handle. "Guess," I said.

Rarig hesitated and then gestured wearily to my chair. "Sit back down. It's a bit of a story."

We all three resumed our seats, which seemed to revive Rarig's self-confidence. "Would any of you like coffee, by the way? I should have asked earlier."

"Enough," Willy warned.

"Okay. I'm sorry," he said, steepling his fingers before his chin, his elbows propped on the arms of his chair. "Twenty-five years ago, when I was, as you guessed, working out of Vienna, we had a plan to make one of our defectors—let's call him Yuri—appear as if he wanted to return to the old country. He and his wife had been living in DC for years. He'd gotten a Ph.D. and had been working for our Army Intelligence, so the Soviets were definitely interested. We floated rumors he'd become unhappy with his new life, and that if the Russkies wanted him back, he'd have some nice stolen tidbits to help them let bygones be bygones. It was an attractive bait. He'd been working in areas sensitive enough that some of the Army Intel guys actually still did distrust him."

John Rarig shook his head at the memory. "He was a straight shooter, of course. I'd met him soon after his arrival, and he, his wife, and I became pretty close over the years. I was ordered to use that friendship to make this scheme look attractive to him."

"You didn't fight it?" Sammie asked, her own strong sense of loyalty stung.

Rarig pursed his lips. "I didn't know what was really going on."

Willy burst out laughing, to my irritation. "And you had your pension to think about. You guys are good. I thought I hung out with assholes."

In a touchingly protective gesture, Olivia Kidder reached out and squeezed Rarig's forearm. He smiled at her. "No. He's right. I'd been in the game since the war. Benefits were a real concern. I should've smelled a rat, but I was told the point of the plan was to use Yuri to lure a Soviet bigwig we were after out into the open where we could grab him. It meant the end of Yuri's work for the Army, but he'd had a good run, and he was well positioned for a cushy civilian job. But it was risky placing an old defector in a town like Vienna, so close to the Hungarian border, and I did put on blinders about that."

I looked at his downcast eyes as he spoke, and remembered his impotent yearning to return the inn to its utopian roots. In a job where the truth had been so routinely expendable, it had to have been tough not to make lying a natural reflex. His sudden openness, after such coyness moments earlier, made me very suspicious.

"Anyhow," Rarig resumed, "it all went bust. Yuri went to the meeting, somehow our grab team got lost, and Yuri was never seen again. We found out later the Soviet plan had been the exact reverse of ours. Something went wrong, though, and Yuri was killed. One source told me they overdid the chloroform. Not that we knew anything at the time."

Rarig, still looking at the rug, let out a small puff of air. "So, the Company brass came down like buzzards, trying to find out what had gone wrong. The problem was, there were several possible scenarios. One theory was that Yuri had in fact redefected, meaning everything we'd gotten from him over ten years was now suspect. Another was that some Russian mole within the Company had blown the whistle on our operation, thereby saving the Soviet target and getting rid of Yuri in one swoop. And then there was what turned out to be the truth, somewhere in the middle."

Sammie was looking understandably confused and fell back on her more conventional police training. "What happened to Yuri's backup?"

For the first time since he'd begun his tale, Rarig looked up at us, his face brighter. "Ah," he said, holding a finger in the air. "That, as they say, is the nub of it, or at least what they ended up focusing on at the end. Had Yuri been lost through carelessness? Had he shaken us off so he could make a clean run? I was inclined to look elsewhere, which is what brought me to focus on Gil Snowden. He was a Young Turk with a doting DDO, born into the right family tree, and with connections to burn. This had been his first overseas operation. I thought at the time he'd messed up somehow, but I could never prove it. His DDO threw a protective cloak over him and that was that. When the ax finally dropped, it fell on Yuri, predictably enough, whom they blamed for losing touch with his own team."

"What's a DDO?" Sammie asked.

"Deputy director of operations," Willy said sourly. "I met a couple of them in 'Nam. Assholes with rank."

Rarig smiled. "Crude but occasionally true. I wouldn't argue the point in this case."

There was a brief lull, after which I asked, not bothering to hide my incredulity, "That's it? Twenty-five years ago, you all get your pal Yuri killed, and that's why Boris or Antonov or whatever the hell his name is gets strangled on your front lawn? By a CIA boss, no less? You're going to have to do better than that."

Olivia raised her hand politely, like a student asking permission to speak. "Perhaps I can clear that up a bit. Have you ever heard of James Angleton?"

"Sure. He was your big counterespionage head for a long time."

She nodded. "That's right, for twenty years. He and John began at about the same time, as I did, for that matter. Hunting out moles became an obsession with him. He'd ruin a career on a rumor, or discredit a good defector on little more than a hunch."

"He took one of my defectors," Rarig added, "and locked him up for two solid years because he thought he was a double. He wasn't. And there wasn't one shred of evidence. Angleton was a sick man."

"In 1973," Kidder resumed, "just before the Vienna fiasco, William Colby was made director. One of the first things he did was to fire Angleton and dismantle his operation. He reduced counterintelligence from three hundred people to eighty, almost overnight."

She sat forward in her chair for emphasis. "The reason he did that was because counterintelligence zealotry was crippling the organization. Real or not, we'd become totally paranoid that everyone was reading everyone else's mail. So, after Angleton was retired—when Yuri came up missing—nobody wanted to return to the bad old days and go hunting for a mole. Nobody."

"Except me," Rarig said.

"But you had nothing on Snowden," I repeated.

Olivia Kidder explained more fully. "John found out through private sources that Snowden had been approached by the KGB immediately following Yuri's disappearance. No one knows what was discussed, and nothing ever surfaced to incriminate Snowden, but it was a damning piece of coincidence."

I finally saw where this had been heading. "And the KGB bigwig Yuri was being used to lure into the open was Sergei Antonov," I said.

"Better," Rarig corrected me. "It was his boss—my counterpart in the area—Major Georgi Padzhev. And it was Padzhev who supposedly contacted Snowden later."

I got up and walked to one of the windows facing the ginkgo tree, which was now shimmering like a ghost in the glow from the inn's lights. Rarig's and Kidder's appraisal of Gil Snowden matched my own gut reaction that he was connected to the attempt on my life in DC. To hear of an oddly similar scenario, in which someone actually had been killed, sent a chill down my spine. The more I hoped I'd found a dimly marked path toward vindication, the less I was questioning its highly dubious source—and the readiness with which it had been offered.

I turned to face them both, paying lip service to my doubts. "If Snowden's been so squeaky clean all these years, couldn't the meeting between him and Padzhev have been arranged so news of it could be leaked to you—just to make Snowden look bad?"

John Rarig laughed. "That's good, Lieutenant. That was a common ploy. The problem is only I got news of it, and since I was already known as pro-Yuri and anti-Snowden, I would've been a poor choice to discredit him."

"Gil Snowden was a small fish then," Kidder added. "Georgi Padzhev wouldn't have known or cared about him. Logically, a meeting between Snowden and Padzhev would have originated with Snowden, and handing Yuri to the Russians would've been the perfect way for Snowden to show good faith."

It was all so neat and tidy, and so conveniently unprovable. But paranoia's catching, and I was in need of answers. Still, I struggled.

"When I went down to DC," I said, "I was almost killed by a man with a knife the night before I was to meet Gil Snowden—a supposed mugger. But Snowden seemed to know all about it the next morning, which was unlikely unless he'd had prior knowledge. If you two are right about him, then why did he try to take me out? I'm a nobody, and everything I knew was shared by my department. Why such a high-risk move?"

"Because that was merely plan A," Rarig explained. "Since it failed, plan B's the mess you're in now."

"The CIA is framing Joe?" Sammie burst out.

"Snowden is," Kidder answered. "Whoever else might be involved is anyone's guess. That's why John and I are keeping such a low profile. Otherwise, we would have gone straight to the appropriate oversight committee and blown the whistle. As it is—and given what's happened to you—we're going to need more than a few hunches before we can show our heads and survive."

"The reason you've been targeted," Rarig said, "is because you have a reputation for doggedness. You don't give up. Snowden's a corporate animal. He knows that if you knock off an organization's primary mover—or better still, discredit him—everyone else will end up milling around in circles." He paused and then added, "Had any pressure lately to solve the 'Boris' case?"

"That's why we're here, wise guy," Willy said.

"But you're acting on your own, and at some risk to your jobs."

"He's right," I said. "Nobody's interested in Boris anymore. We're the only ones who think he's the key to all this."

Willy pointed at our hosts. "Then we better hitch our wagon to someone else, 'cause these two're getting ready to give you the screwing of a lifetime."

There was an uncomfortable pause while we all considered what he meant. He shook his head at our stupidity. "Jesus Christ. We been sitting here for God knows how long, listening to a bunch of teary-eyed war stories, totally missing the obvious. What've we got so far? That some CIA bureaucrat came flying out of Washington to whack a Russian on Rarig's front step so the beans wouldn't be spilled about some supposed conversation that took place a quarter century ago—a conversation which, of course, only Rarig ever heard about, and which never led to anything. Then, once the body's been discovered in a quarry Snowden couldn't have possibly known about, he shows his hand by inviting you down to DC, where he tries to get you killed one day, and then shows off that he knew all about it the next. And finally, just in case our taste for bullshit is still running strong, we're supposed to believe that, failing to kill you, he set up the world's fanciest frame on the assumption that without our fearless leader, the rest of us are going to act like chickens with our heads cut off." Willy stopped long enough to give us all an incredulous look. "Get real."

I cupped my cheek in my hand, staring at the opposite wall. My entire life was disintegrating before my eyes, and every time I tried to grab hold of it, the opportunity was pulled away. Willy had just done it again, throwing water on the hopefulness I'd been trying to ignite.

Stubbornness replacing reason, I argued the point. "Okay," I told him, "finish it up. If their story stinks, what replaces it?"

"Plain as the nose on your face," he said. "Rarig's brought in on the Yuri operation. He's supposedly Yuri's friend, the current Austrian field man, knows the lay of the land, the identities of his Soviet counterparts. He's perfect. But Rarig's getting long in the tooth, pissed off at the young bucks coming up like Snowden, and he sees a chance to make everything right. He'll sell Yuri to Padzhev for a tidy Swiss bank deposit, get out of the Company come retirement, and have a time bomb against Snowden—courtesy of Padzhev—in case he ever needs it. He farts around for a few years, dissipating any suspicions, and finally cashes in some of the loot, buys a Vermont inn, and becomes the country squire.

"Only things go wrong. Padzhev's old right-hand man shows up. He's Mafia now, driven by greed instead of the old red flag, and he threatens to squeal unless he's paid off. Rarig knocks him off, dumps him in the quarry, and sets up this whole frame against you to get both us and Snowden's people off his scent. He didn't count on that crummy tree, though, and on our tracing it back to him, so now he cooks up this cock-and-bull story because he knows if we swallow it, there's nothing we can do about it. We can't go charging into the CIA to bust one of their guys, and we ain't going to be able to persuade anyone else to do it for us."

It was, as I'd feared, as plausible as what Kidder and Rarig had told us; more so, in fact. The hopes I'd been stacking up against all logic—regardless of the consequences—collapsed.

As a cop, it was true that I'd become like a dog with a bone, making up in labor what I might have lacked in brains, depending on the evidence to light my way. Now I was at a loss. Nothing had clarity, and my growing inner turmoil was giving every hypothesis equal weight.

I rose to my feet one last time and walked to the door. "Willy's right," I said, feeling the pull of my own emotional exhaustion. "This is all just a bunch of stories. There's no reality to it anymore."

I opened the door and stepped out, seeing Sammie rise to join me, and hearing Willy exclaim paradoxically, "Jesus. You can't quit now."

Sammie caught up to me halfway across the lawn. "Joe, wait. What're you doing?"

I turned to face her. "I'm tired, Sam, and I've run out of ideas. I don't know what those two are up to—they're probably crazier than rats in a can—and I don't think they give a damn about us. Right now, I just want to go home. Maybe I'll come up with something in the morning."

"Willy was right about something else," she said as I turned away. "You can't quit."

I stopped again and placed my fingertip against my temple. "I know that up here," I admitted, "but right now I'm feeling like maybe there're some puzzles that just can't be worked out."

She looked into my eyes. "You gotta keep at it."

I didn't share her optimism, but at this point, their faith in me was quite possibly the only life raft I had left.

"All right," I finally said, fighting every instinct. "Get Willy out of there and we'll try hashing this out on the way back home."

14

WILLY, OF COURSE, DIDN'T SEE A RETREAT AS MAKING ANY SENSE at all. "You gotta be shittin' me," he snarled back in the car. "We just clobbered 'em in there. Right now, they're beating their brains out trying to keep alive. Jesus, if a bunch of dumb cops have 'em pegged, how far behind can the bad guys be?"

"What bad guys?" I asked, genuinely baffled that he'd left that conversation with anything that made sense. "Who do we choose from?"

He rubbed his forehead like a frustrated tutor. "Who cares? CIA, KGB, Russian Mafia—it doesn't matter. Those two old fossils're the lightning rod, and we just went from being part of the rod to being part of the lightning. The first shock was Boris. Whether Rarig iced him or not, his showing up was a sure sign to Rarig that his retirement days were over. Our hitting him tonight is the second shock. They have *got* to do something now. 'Cept if we cut 'em any slack, chances are they'll get away with it. We need to watch 'em like hawks."

"What'd you expect them to do?" Sammie asked.

"Move, for one thing. They're sitting ducks here."

"Hold it," I said. "What about your theory five minutes ago? Where Antonov was out to blackmail Rarig for a quarter-century-old indiscretion?"

Willy waved that away like a fly. "Bullshit smoke screen. I wanted them to think I was an idiot—think local, act local. You know, get their guard down. If what I said really happened, all Rarig would have to do is play dumb and keep his mouth shut. We don't have any proof. Why do you think they told us all that crap about Vienna if they didn't think their past was about to eat 'em up? They're sweatin' something out, and Antonov was just the tip of it. Rarig may not have killed him, but I do think he dumped him to buy some time."

He put the car into gear, swung it around, and drove out of the inn parking lot. "What we need to do is sit and wait—not keep flapping our gums."

He drove the quarter mile to where the driveway met the road, pulled over and killed the engine. "Right?"

Sammie was sitting in the backseat. Her voice was carefully neutral in the dark night air. "It does look like they're the only game we have."

I looked straight ahead, across the deserted road at the black wall of trees opposite. I found myself slowly emerging from the emotional air pocket that had almost swallowed me. The situation hadn't changed, but the company had. The two people we'd just left had learned to forecast the future using rumors, inference, and suspicion, while covering their own tracks sowing confusion and deceit. Theirs was a world of convenient realities, none necessarily based on the truth. Sammie and Willy, by contrast, inhabited a clear-sighted universe of cause and effect—they smelled a scent, and they followed it to the end.

Their simple lucidity was a welcome tonic.

"How've you two been working your surveillance so far?" I asked.

"Catch as catch can—no regular rotation," Sammie answered. "When one of us can carve out a few hours unnoticed, we spell the other guy. I think the chief knows we're up to something, by the way, but he's choosing to ignore us, so we've got a fair amount of slack."

"Okay," I said. "Let me help. I have to keep checking in with the state police, but I can reach my answering machine through my cell phone and pretend I'm still at home. And sure as hell I have more free time than either of you. Who wants to pull first shift?"

"I will," Willy said immediately. "Sammie was just on, and you're in no shape to do anything. Go home, get some sleep. I'll call you when I want out."

He drove us to where Sammie had stashed her car and left us there.

Five minutes down the road, she asked, "Feeling better?"

I laughed and rubbed my eyes. "Who'd have thought Willy Kunkle could ever pull you out of the dumps?"

Sammie drove into the Meetinghouse Hill Cemetery, where Kunkle had picked me up, and killed the engine. "This okay?" she asked.

I'd been so lost in thought, I'd barely noticed we'd stopped. I looked up and glanced around. "Sure," I said, but I didn't get out of the car.

She didn't press me, sitting quietly, waiting.

"Why do *you* think Antonov came to the inn?" I asked at last.

I saw her frown in the reflected moonlight. "I don't know," she said. "Maybe it was like Willy said—he wanted to put the squeeze on Rarig."

"All the way from Russia? Leaving behind the most lucrative black market in the world?"

"Then to kill him for some past grudge?"

"Okay. Why right now?"

Sammie remained silent.

"Try this on," I said. "When J.P. and I first visited the inn, Rarig played the genial host. At one point, he pulled out a recent *New York Times* piece featuring the place. It was very flattering—a big spread—but he kept it in a drawer out of sight. In the entranceway there are plaques from one gourmet magazine or another and the usual promotional material, so why not a blurb from one of the biggest publications in the country?"

"It say anything incriminating?"

"I didn't read it carefully, but I doubt it. He knew we were cops by then—local cops. Remember what Willy said? 'Think local, act local.' I think that's key. The one thing about that article is that the photographer caught Rarig only once, in a mirror, looking like he couldn't wait for them all to go away. You ever hear about the Windham Hill Inn before all this?"

"Sure—one of the fanciest around, along with the two in Newfane."

"Ever seen a picture of Rarig?"

She hesitated before staring at me. "No. You saying Antonov saw the picture in Russia, and that's why he came over?"

"The *New York Times* is known all over the world. Rarig's not his real name, and I bet it wasn't when he was operating overseas. After he pulled out of the business and came up here, as far as his old enemies are concerned, he fell off the end of the earth. And I'm not saying it was Antonov who saw the article. I think it was his boss."

"Georgi Padzhev."

"Right. I think Willy hit the nail on the head tonight without even realizing it. He thought Kidder and Rarig told us all about Vienna because it was on their minds. But they knew what they were doing—that's why they were so chatty. They were seeing how we'd react. Why, I don't know yet.

"I also think Willy's right about Rarig not killing Antonov but disposing of his body."

"Why one and not the other?"

"To buy time. Maybe to slip back into the shadows. Here's a guy who's spent his whole life with assumed names, foreign languages, probably even disguises, for all I know. He finds a body from the old days on his lawn. If he calls the cops, the press'll climb all over it, and we'll be digging into his past. Out of the question. So he dumps it—he knows where and when to go—and he washes his hands of it. 'Course, as Willy pointed out, he goofed. But it was a good plan."

"Just so he can go back to being an inn owner?" Sammie interrupted.

"People generally do things for a reason," I explained. "Burn buildings for the insurance, rob banks for the money. If killing Antonov and leaving his body was a message to Rarig, then hiding that body deprives the sender of any feedback—it forces whoever killed Antonov to do something more—something Rarig is hoping he'll see coming this time."

"Except we *did* find the body," Sammie pointed out.

"But nobody knows we linked it to Rarig, not officially."

Sammie slumped her head forward and placed both her palms against her face. Her voice was muffled by her fingers. "So what, Joe? What's it all mean?"

"What I *think* it means," I said tentatively, "is that Antonov was sent out to serve one purpose and ended up serving another. Padzhev saw Rarig's picture. Antonov flew over here to check him out. Somebody—maybe Snowden, maybe an old enemy of Rarig's, maybe even an enemy of Padzhev's—knocked him off and left his body as a calling card, which Rarig then tried to make disappear. Presumably, had he succeeded, Rarig was hoping things would end there—Padzhev might even think Antonov never got to Vermont. But the cat's out of the bag, so now we're all in for something more—what, I don't know. And I'm not sure Rarig does, either."

Sammie was staring out the window before her. "So, he actually doesn't know who killed Antonov, even though he fingered Snowden?"

"I think that's right."

"But Rarig remains a lightning rod of some kind, like Willy said, and for some specific reason."

"Right again."

"And Kidder's his inside contact."

"That's my bet."

"But if Snowden didn't kill Antonov, why did he try to kill you?"

I didn't answer at first. So many pieces of this puzzle were interconnected, seemingly on a three-dimensional frame, that I was finding it impossible to nail any one of them in place. "Maybe he didn't," I admitted.

She stared at me, her mouth half-open. "Then who, Joe? And who, if not Snowden, is framing you now?"

"I don't know, but I think it all hangs on Rarig."

As confusing, taxing, and seemingly futile as the night had been, I found for the first time in days that I could sleep soundly. A catharsis had been achieved, like the bursting of a dam, and it had released the almost paralytic pressure I'd been storing up for days. There were no obvious immediate solutions, of course. But where I'd seen only blank canyon walls before, now I was focusing on finding a way out.

My only regret, which clung to me like a dull and chronic pain, was that I couldn't share any of this with Gail.

* * *

Willy called the next morning. "Kidder flew the coop," he said. "Around eight."

"Back to Langley?"

"I think so. I tailed her for a while, but I didn't want to leave Rarig for too long."

"He stay put?"

"So far. Sammie's got him now. Something else, though—there's been a killing up in Middlebury. Another Russian."

I straightened, almost dropping the phone. "No shit."

"Yeah, Just came over the wire. A drive-by. Guy was a prof at the college. Supposedly an old-time dissident immigrant, dating back to the sixties. Got whacked in front of something called the Geonomics Center, on campus."

"No spook connections?"

"Not yet. No leads anywhere. Like I said, it's brand new. I'll dig into it, though, using the Boris case as camouflage. I got a friend in the department up there."

A beep echoed in my ear, indicating another call coming in. I hung up on Willy and answered.

"It's Sam," said the voice at the other end, sounding tense. "I got a bit of a situation here."

"What?"

There was a rustling sound, and another voice came on. "This is Rarig. We need to talk."

All semblance of last night's rambling host was gone. Rarig was clearly on edge. Something, I thought, was moving in the woods.

"I can't be there for several hours."

"You get here *now*."

"It'll mean missing my check-in at the barracks. They'll issue a warrant for my arrest."

"I can clear you of all that crap. I need you and your two friends, but it's got to be immediately."

"We going to Middlebury?"

It was a shot in the dark. I almost heard the thud as he fell.

"How the hell did you know that?"

"Who was the guy?"

"Nobody. They hit the wrong target. I need to save the real one. I can't reach him by phone, and anyway, I think they found him by tapping my line."

"Is that why they killed Antonov? To flush out the real quarry?"

"He read about Antonov in the papers. He got nervous and called me. Olivia came up to see what we could do. We thought we had a handle on it till this happened." His voice suddenly broke. "You're wasting time, Lieutenant. You coming or not?"

"Not yet, and you're not moving without backup, so don't bullshit me. What phone are you on right now?"

"Your partner's portable. I dug her out of her hiding spot. I can tell you people don't do this for a living."

"Don't be a smartass, John. You need us. Who's the guy we're supposed to be saving?"

"He's a defector. The one I mentioned last night that Angleton locked up for two years 'cause he thought he was a plant."

"Why not call in the cavalry?" I asked.

"It might be the cavalry that's hunting him." Rarig's exasperation was as clear as his voice was becoming loud.

"You're not going to give me your 'Snowden's-the-bad-guy' spiel again, are you? I'm a little less gullible today."

"God damn you, Gunther. I'm asking you to help me save a man's life. That's supposed to be what the police are for. I don't know who's trying to take him out, and I don't know why, but I've got to do what I can. I'll get you cleared of your legal problems—I've got the evidence you want—but I need you now."

"Give the phone back to Sammie and walk out of earshot."

I waited a few moments after Sam got back on. "He a safe distance away?" I asked.

"Yeah. Sorry for the screwup."

"I don't care about that. He's right. Snooping on people isn't our job. What do you think of all this?"

"That you leave the county? You'd be crazy. This creep's been lying to us since we met him."

"He sounds genuine now."

"He looks genuine, but it could all be cock-and-bull, and you'd pay the price big time."

"Willy called me about the shooting in Middlebury. That part's legit. How did it come down at your end?"

"I saw him through the window on the phone ten minutes ago. He was pacing back and forth, waving his arm. Then, all of a sudden, he flies out of the house, makes a beeline for me like I was standing in the middle of a road, and demands to talk to you on my phone. He is seriously worked up."

"This could be the break we're looking for, Sam."

I could almost feel her anxiety. "Jesus. It's all so tied up in knots, who's to tell? Willy says they use people like Kleenex. It's a hell of a risk."

"My other option looks like a dead certainty. Even if Richard gets me off, my career's toast."

She was utterly silent for a moment, before pointing out, "Rarig hasn't said what he wants yet."

"Put him back on, then."

A few moments later, Rarig demanded, "Are you in or not?"

"What's your plan?"

"My God. I hope to hell you're not on your department's SWAT team. All your hostages would die of old age."

"Sam and I are both on the team, and we're also alive to prove it. What's your plan?"

"I don't know yet," he conceded. "I need to get up there, find him, and get him to safe ground."

"You sure he's still in Middlebury?"

"He should be. When we moved him there, he and I picked out a priest hole he could use in an emergency."

"Is that where he called you from?"

"It doesn't have a phone. It has a signaling device he's supposed to trigger when he gets there, but he either didn't use it or he never arrived. That's why I want help."

"All right," I finally agreed. "I'll come, but alone. I won't jeopardize the other two."

He barely hesitated. "Fine, just get here."

15

I DIDN'T FLY OUT OF THE HOUSE AFTER RARIG'S CALL FOR HELP. IF anything, his impatience slowed me down, making me as careful as he seemed to have become impulsive. I packed a bag with every tactical necessity I could think of, including several weapons, and made sure the house was secure before I left. I longed to leave Gail a note and finally settled for a simple "I love you" on the icebox chalkboard, confident that sooner or later she'd see it.

The reason I knew she'd come by—maybe even move back in—was because I was also aware of how my departure would be received. For the violator of court-ordered condition of release to also be a cop compounds the sin exponentially. Any judge would feel the added insult—Harrowsmith more than most. None of which took into account the predictable howl from Fred Coffin's publicity machine.

Within a half hour of my no-show at the West Brattleboro barracks, a fugitive arrest warrant would be issued statewide, complete with description, photograph, and known contacts. One accidental sighting by a single cop anywhere in Vermont— and there were hundreds who knew me at a glance—would mean attention unlike any I'd ever received before. If Richard Levay thought he'd had a hard case before, he was about to start feeling like Clarence Darrow at the Scopes trial—assuming he didn't wash his hands of me altogether.

And yet I felt no real trepidation as I set out toward the Windham

Hill Inn. What I'd told Sammie had been the absolute truth. As I saw it, this was my only remaining option. It didn't matter if Rarig was lying about clearing my name. It didn't matter if we failed to locate his terrified defector. I wasn't entirely sure it mattered if nothing turned out as anyone was expecting. The point now was simply to create some random, spontaneous action—a move so utterly against my character that it would fall outside the boundaries imagined by whoever had set me up. As I saw it, I had to knock at least a single support beam to the ground and hope the whole structure followed suit.

These reflections so occupied my mind that when I reached the Windham Hill Inn and saw Rarig and Sammie waiting for me, it felt like I'd just hung up on them.

That impression was not shared by John Rarig. "You took long enough," he barked at me, pulling open my door.

I didn't bother responding. Grabbing a small canvas bag from the backseat, I asked, "Which one's your car?"

Sammie was watching me nervously. "You think this through?"

I gave her a half smile, following Rarig's pointed finger toward a dark green Ford Explorer. "The point is not to think—surprise the opposition into reacting."

She fell into step beside me. "You'll need backup."

"Maybe, but you won't be it. I don't need your busted career on my conscience—if it isn't too late already."

She jerked a thumb at Rarig, who was circling the car to get behind the wheel. "If he clears you, I'll be cleared, too."

I opened the back door and threw my bag inside. "Nice try, Sam. You already told me you thought he was full of shit."

She opened her mouth to say more, but I held up my hand. "Don't. Besides, I need you to stick your neck out in another way. If they find my car here, it won't take 'em long to start looking for Rarig."

"Right," she agreed, caught off guard.

"So ditch it somewhere and cross your fingers. Okay?"

The logic spoke for itself, but her voice was tinged with both sadness and longing. "Okay. Good luck."

I swung into the seat next to Rarig. "You, too. And promise me you and Willy will work together to cover your asses. I want you both employed when I get back."

I looked through the rear window as Rarig headed down the driveway. Sammie was standing in the parking lot, her hands by her sides, looking as vulnerable as a lost child in a bus station. I knew it was both momentary and misleading—that cool and decisive action would soon reassert itself—but in that brief moment, I was struck by the loyalty of the friendship between us and hoped to hell I hadn't burned her by proximity.

I waited until we'd gotten onto Route 30, heading north toward Middlebury, before I asked my still visibly tense driver, "Not that you'll tell me the truth, but who is it we're trying to save?"

He gave me a startled look. "You don't believe me? Then why are you here?"

"Personal reasons. Who is it?"

"His name's Lewis Corbin-Teich—at least that's what he goes by now. His old name's not important."

"Who made that one up? A committee?"

Rarig actually laughed. "No. He did. Like you said, personal reasons. He's a sentimental man. I just asked him to come up with something that couldn't be traced back to him or members of his family. That's what he chose."

"And he works at the college?" I was watching Rarig's hands on the wheel, the blanching of his knuckles. A field operative once, and obviously used to tension, he'd apparently lost the instinct over time. I hoped a little conversation would calm him down, for both our sakes.

"Yes. The language department. Russian's very big at Middlebury. There's a huge immigrant population there, a Russian/U.S. think tank, a refugee housing complex for Bosnians, lots of conferences and meetings throughout the year. That's why he fit in from the start."

"Weren't you worried someone would recognize him?"

"His own mother probably wouldn't. He wears a full beard, and he's had plastic surgery. He's just another guy with an accent now."

"You said Angleton locked him up and dismissed everything he had to offer. What happened after that?"

He paused to pass a slower driver on an inside curve, thankfully with no ill effects. "Two years later, other sources confirmed what he'd told us. Angleton never admitted being wrong, but he let him out—it was as close to an apology as you could get. Unfortunately, it also meant Lew was useless to us. I'm the one who came up with the teaching idea, set up the contacts, established the cover, and got him tucked away. The way we'd treated him was no different from what the Soviets did, but no one seemed to pick up on that. They were all hot to move on to the next item on the list."

He slid off the road slightly, spitting gravel up into the wheel wells. "Lew was so calm about the whole thing it almost made *me* suspicious. I would've hired a lawyer and sued their pants off, but he didn't care. Said he was just as happy he hadn't had to sell out his native land for his adopted one, and that the two years had given him lots of time to learn the language and love the region."

"He was locked up around here?" I asked, surprised.

"Yeah. In Vermont. We had a mountaintop radar installation back then—this was in the late fifties. It was very secluded, well guarded, manned by U.S. servicepeople. Perfect safe house for us. Lew was free to roam sometimes, always with a guard, and he got to know the woods and animals and seasons like a native, even though Angleton would push a button in Washington now and then and have him confined to solitary."

"Why?"

"No reason. Something would happen on the other side of the world—like maybe one of our agents would get caught and tortured— and revenge would be taken out on Lew."

It's been said that police officers—in a world where the most mundane traffic stop may lead to a gun battle—have to be slightly paranoid to survive. I wondered how much worse that must be for those inhabiting the smoke-and-mirrors world of intelligence gathering. It had to elevate paranoia to a whole new level and stamp those in its clutches with a permanent imprint.

I tried getting my thoughts back on course. "If Lew meant so little to you people, why kill him now?"

"I don't know. There was a connection between Padzhev, Antonov,

Lew Corbin-Teich, and me, but it's ancient history, and I can't see why it's resurfaced."

"Did Snowden play into it?"

"No. This was before his time." Rarig had come up onto another slower driver and was hanging back about two feet from his bumper. I could see the driver's silhouette as he repeatedly checked his rearview mirror.

"If we *are* entering a tactical situation," I said mildly, "you might want to start thinking about being alive when we get there."

He completely surprised me by suddenly applying the brakes and pulling over. "You're right. You drive."

Back on the road, I looked over at his profile as he stared out straight ahead. "You feeling all right?" I asked.

"Fine. I don't like to drive."

"I don't guess anyone else likes your doing it, either."

I didn't get a response, aside from a slight tightening of his jaw.

"It's been a long time, hasn't it?" I then said.

He didn't answer at first but turned away to look out the side window. We were on Route 100 by now, having abandoned 30 to cut up through Londonderry and Rutland to reach Middlebury more directly. I didn't press him, sensing my last words were still being digested.

Eventually, he said softly, "Yeah—long time."

"What's going on inside you, John?" I asked. "I'd kind of like to know before things get hot."

His eyes narrowed as he looked at me. "I'm not going to fall apart, if that's what you're worried about."

"Wouldn't you be, in my shoes?"

He gave me a rueful smile. "Okay. I thought I was free of this kind of thing, that's all. It's been a little strange—first Antonov, now Corbin-Teich. Whoever said you can't go home again was out of his mind."

"Lew must mean something special to you."

He went back to staring into some unseen middle distance. "A man comes to you one day, out of the blue, and volunteers to trade all he knows for asylum. He's up and coming in the KGB, protégé of an influential colonel. He's building connections, receiving favors, in line for a driver and a dacha and all the other capitalist treats the Communists pretend don't exist. His wife loves it, his kid's getting a good education, and yet he asks you to pull him out. Even in a noncynical world, you'd have to ask yourself, 'Why?' "

I ventured a wild guess. "The colonel was Padzhev?"

"Yeah. He and Antonov, like Batman and Robin, since Antonov was always the gofer. Lew was their latest project. But their enthusiasm had blinded them to his growing disenchantment. To them, it was a great game—Padzhev was a chess fanatic—but Lew kept looking beyond the job, to a corrupt society of unadmitted haves and have-nots, to the lie of equal opportunity and total employment. Not that our system was that much better. But as he saw it, we weren't hypocritical about it, and we were pretty much free to try to do something to change it.

"I didn't believe him at first. Angleton would've been proud. I thought for sure he was trying to pull a fast one on us. He gave us some information—to show good faith—and it checked out, but of course it would, so that didn't weigh much. But the more time I spent with him—the more I listened to him talk—the more I came to think he was the real McCoy. And with that I realized what he was proposing to give up."

Rarig shifted in his seat and stared at me intently. "Over that span of time, to me Lew Corbin-Teich turned from a prize catch into a hero of sorts. The irony was, of course, that I was totally alone there. My colleagues ended up thinking he was a born liar, and his countrymen labeled him a traitor and put a price on his head.

"But that was fine with him. He even asked me once, 'What did you expect?' Knowing everything that was going to happen to him, at least theoretically, he still went ahead. And the kicker is, he was right. After it was all over and I'd gotten him into Middlebury, it was like he'd arrived in Shangri-la. I used to kid him about campus politics—all those academics trying to nail each other's hide to the wall. He'd just laugh. It meant nothing to him."

"What about his family?" I asked.

"His wife didn't suffer much. She was a survivor and remarried well. His son was old enough when he left to take it in stride. He's in Russia still and apparently doing fine."

"Sounds like you became his family, in a way."

"Well, I guess there's always a bonding between defector and case officer. They even warn you about it. But when they treated him so badly and he bore them no grudge, something snapped inside me. Besides Olivia Kidder, I'd say Lew's the best friend I ever had."

I let a long reflective silence follow before rephrasing my original question, "So if it is Padzhev who's after him now, what's the motivation?"

"I said it *might* be Padzhev. And I don't know why. Padzhev took the defection hard. It was a personal failure, and it stopped his climb within the organization. I sometimes thought one aspect of the Yuri kidnapping was that since I'd been Yuri's case officer, snatching him would give me a black eye in return. In the long run, though, my career ended because I finally pulled the plug, not because of Georgi Padzhev."

"But it was connected, wasn't it?"

He frowned dismissively. "Vaguely. Things had been building to a head. The deal with Lew had left a bad taste, which didn't improve with time, but I wasn't as close with Yuri. His disappearance hurt mostly because of the stupidity leading up to and following it. It revealed how out of sync I'd become with the people I was working with. It took me years before I actually retired."

"Must've been weird finding Antonov under that tree—all those memories flooding back," I said, trying to take advantage of the conversation's confessional tone.

But he saw me coming. "I never said I found him."

His cautious reaction hit me with unexpected force. I slammed on the brakes, put the car into a skid, and pulled over to the edge of the road. "You're something else, you know that?" I yelled at him, feeling days of repressed anger finally exploding. "You go blabbing on about your walk-on-water buddy 'cause of his high moral tone, and then you cover your ass just like Snowden would. You're the one guy out of all of us who's risking nothing so far. My people have stuck their necks out on your say-so; I'm looking at jail time 'cause I decided to trust you; even Olivia, I bet, has put her job on the line for you. And you sit there playing hide-'n'-seek."

I grabbed the door and threw it open, almost losing it to a passing car, whose windy vortex blew around inside the passenger compartment. "Well, *fuck* you," I said, getting out and shouting back across the seat at him. "I've been dicked around by every bastard I've met so far, and I'm goddamned sick and tired of it. All that crap you fed us about turning the inn into a place for people to unload and to share. What a crock. You're as self-serving as all the jerks you've just been dumping on for the last half hour."

I slammed the door and walked to the back of the car, staring off at the distant hills, fighting to control my breathing. Never before had I lost it so completely—not even when Gail had been raped. I prided myself on keeping cool, keeping my emotional cards out of sight, maintaining a professional stance so that progress could take place, unimpeded by any histrionics from me.

And now I was standing by the side of the road, in the middle of nowhere, a warrant about to be issued for my arrest, having thrown the temper tantrum of a lifetime.

And I'd been worried about Rarig at the wheel.

He got out tentatively and took a couple of steps in my direction. "You okay?" he asked, his voice barely audible over the slight breeze.

I turned toward him, much calmer, actually feeling pretty good. "I'm in better shape than you are."

He nodded. "That's probably true. It was right, what you said."

"That you're a self-serving jerk?"

He looked slightly confused. "I guess. I meant about finding Antonov."

"And you're the one who dumped him in the quarry?"

He nodded. "I wanted to see what would happen—who might show himself next. I hadn't intended that the body be found. Just that someone might come looking. That's why I took such pains—wrapping him up in a tarp I later burned, ditching him in the boondocks. Lucky he was so small and light. I would've buried him if I'd had the time."

"So you put the finger on Snowden just to stir us up."

"No. He may've been Antonov's killer. I don't know why, but I don't know why not, either." He spread his hands to both sides. "I honestly can't tell you what's going on here, Lieutenant, but my friend is in danger. I've been out of things a long time. Alliances shift. I don't know who the players are anymore—who to trust. I'm sorry I upset you. I guess old habits are hard to break, especially when you're under pressure."

Mollified, knowing I really didn't have any choice but to follow the course I'd set, I returned to the car and got back behind the wheel. Rarig slid in beside me.

I didn't immediately start driving, however. I faced him instead and asked him point-blank, "You said you had the evidence to clear me. That was baloney, too, wasn't it?"

"I think the brooch was planted in your coat the night before the jewelry store window was broken—by a black bag crew who entered your home without your knowing it."

I just stared at him.

He stared at his hands. "But I don't know that for a fact, and I don't know who might've done it."

I let that sink in, grateful my motivation for being here hadn't hinged on that detail alone. Then I put the car into gear and pulled out. "Well," I finally said, "at least that's a start."

16

MIDDLEBURY IS AMONG THE MOST PICTURESQUE, ACTIVE, WELL-situated small towns in Vermont. Located halfway between Rutland and Burlington, on the state's western slope, it benefits from the twin charms of the rocky, tree-choked, looming Green Mountains on one side, and the gently rolling, fertile farmland of the Champlain Valley on the other.

With a quick glance at a map, one is hard put to even find Middlebury, dominated as it is by its urban neighbors, not to mention Montpelier beyond the peaks to the northeast. But closer scrutiny reveals something of its past importance. Not only does almost every longitudinal road converge for a moment in Middlebury, but the valley's sole railroad also cuts right through it. In odd contrast to today, Middlebury in 1820 was one of the largest towns in Vermont, a center of education, industry, transportation, and architecture.

It remains in many ways reminiscent of its heyday, filled with mansions, church steeples, and elegant greens. It also suffers for those same reasons. As a crossroads, it is pure bedlam, like an antique spring at the heart of a computer. Buses, trucks, trains, cars, recreational vehicles, and the thousands of people using them converge in a tangle of narrow, poorly designed, curvilinear roads contrary enough to drive a lab rat nuts. The irony is that around World War One, Joseph Battell, a major local benefactor, and the state's single largest landowner, declared the newfangled automobile such a menace that he tried to ban it from his road—the Middlebury Gap—which is now one of Vermont's chief tourist attractions during leaf-peeping season.

Today, as Rarig had earlier implied, the town owes its fame—and much of its commercial success—to the college named after it, created in 1800 as an alternative to the "ungodly" University of Vermont established by Ira Allen—brother of the often-drunk leader of the Green Mountain Boys.

Typical of most academic towns, however, this relationship is a distinct mixed blessing. The college is wealthy, tax-exempt, and archly proprietary. Owner of vast amounts of real estate, it pays little cash to the town while freely using its tax-fed infrastructure. Like a land-rich lord of yore, it sits atop a pristine hill, crowned with an assortment of architectural monuments—both stately and absurd—issuing statements either arrogant or beleaguered, and providing enough heated debate to keep the town in a perpetual lather.

None of this is evident to anyone passing through, of course, except perhaps the traffic problems. As Rarig and I entered the village's vehicular Gordian knot from the south, I was impressed as always by Middlebury's sheer sense of vigor. If internecine squabbling played a part in that, it was nevertheless a vital sign and, in this case, a healthy one.

I wended our way through the various curves opposite the stately Middlebury Inn, down into the crowded, bustling village proper, across the meandering Otter Creek, and up the opposite slope onto the broader, more open, carefully manicured campus. To the gritty, low-built, red brick of downtown, the college was a striking contrast, marked largely by broad swaths of color—green grass, broad, black avenues, and an imposing number of fortress-sized, light-gray stone buildings. If the traditional vision of academe was one of isolated hilltop serenity, this school fit the bill.

The image was enhanced, in addition, by there being very few people within sight.

I pulled up opposite one of the large buildings and looked around.

"What's wrong?" Rarig asked.

"This town just had a drive-by shooting, which means the local PD must be bristling right now. Why haven't we seen any sign of that, and why's the campus look so empty?"

"I don't know about the cops, but the administration probably issued an advisory to keep under cover. Lew says they've done that in the past when there's been some controversy. They tend to be a little hysterical sometimes."

"Can't say I blame 'em this time—people getting shot on the street. Where's the Geonomics Center?"

He pointed straight ahead. I noticed his hand was trembling slightly. "That's the Russian/U.S. think tank I told you about. It's a block or two down and to the left—Hillcrest Avenue. Why?"

"So we can avoid it. That's where most of the police'll be right now, collecting evidence. Where's that priest hole you told me about?"

"Seymour Street, near the railroad tracks. Turn around, go back across the river, take the first left and go up about a quarter mile."

I followed his directions, ending up in a distinctly poorer section of town, nevertheless lined by a row of tidy houses, however worn and in need of paint. Rarig guided me to the driveway of one of them, where we ended up facing an attached garage with an apartment perched on top of it.

He thrust his chin straight ahead. "Up there."

I glanced at the house beside us. "The owners know about it?"

"I'm the owners. I rent it out through a cover. They only know the apartment is used once in a blue moon by a guy who likes his privacy."

Rarig got out of the car, looked around nervously, and headed for the back of the garage. I followed him to where a narrow outside staircase led up to the second floor. The tension I'd noticed on the drive up was still fueling him like shoveled coal. I began to wonder about some of the ulterior reasons he might've had for wanting me along.

"It wouldn't matter anyway," he explained. "Even if someone did start nosing around. The stairs are wired to a silent alarm, and the door is armored. Lew would know somebody was coming. There's also an escape route, like a laundry chute, that he can use in an emergency.

It ends up in the basement of the house, near the bulkhead on the far side."

We reached the top, where Rarig extracted an exotic magnetic key from his pocket. He fitted it not into the keyhole mounted under the knob of the peeling wooden door, but into what looked like a knothole near the hinges. The door swung open the wrong way, and we stepped into a small antechamber equipped with a second door. Rarig closed the one to our backs. There was a loud mechanical click from in front of us. "Shutting the first frees up one of the locks of this one," Rarig told me. He pounded on the door with his fist. "Lew? It's John Rarig."

There was dead silence from the other side. Rarig's shoulders slumped. "I was afraid of this."

He fitted another, conventional key to the lock and led us into the apartment. I noticed as I passed the edge of the second door that it was equipped with some sort of electronic sensor.

The place was small, dark, tidy, and airless. It was also as empty and as still as a tomb. Rarig stood in its middle, his hands slack by his sides, looking around him like a homeowner whose house had just burned to the ground.

He shook his head. "God damn it," he said. "I knew he was in trouble."

I checked the rest of the place quickly, looking into the bathroom and glancing under the twin bed. It all looked as ready for occupancy as a fresh motel room, except for the fine layer of dust over everything.

"Show me where he lives," I told Rarig.

"That's the last place he'd be."

"It's all we got."

Reluctantly, he pulled himself away, closing both doors neatly, as if for future use.

I led the way back to the car, speaking over my shoulder. "He might be okay," I tried to sound upbeat. "He could've lost his keys and had to hole up somewhere else. Didn't you two have a plan for getting in touch in case something went wrong?"

Rarig glanced up from watching the ground before him. "He's supposed to leave a coded message on my phone ma—"

His voice trailed off. I followed his blank stare to the end of the driveway, where a car had just slowed to a stop. My whole body tensed, recognizing the universal blandness of an unmarked police vehicle.

The driver, surprisingly casual, swung out and approached us. He was wearing dark glasses, but I recognized him immediately as Jimmy Zarrillo, Middlebury's sole detective. As luck would have it, outside of the chief, Zarrillo was the only man in the entire department I knew.

"Hey, Jimmy," I spoke first, hoping against probability that this was purely a coincidence. "How're you doin'?"

Despite the smile my greeting evoked, his first words dispelled all hope. "From what I hear, better than you, Joe. What're you up to?"

He glanced at Rarig, now standing by the other side of the car, but switched to me as we shook hands.

It was all the time Rarig needed.

"Don't move."

His tone froze us both in place, still in mid-handshake. He was holding a semi-automatic on Jimmy, all nervousness gone.

Jimmy freed his fingers from mine, his eyes narrow with anger. "What the hell?"

"Put the gun down," I said sharply to Rarig, beginning to turn.

"Don't," he ordered. "Both of you—start walking toward the apartment."

"What the hell is this?" Jimmy half-whispered to me.

"Quiet," came from behind.

We disappeared behind the garage, out of sight of the road. I couldn't believe what had happened. Was Rarig in fact a Russian agent? Had he killed Lew Corbin-Teich for some reason I didn't know? Was he connected to the shooting of the professor outside the Geonomics Center? What little sense I'd thought I'd made of all this had become like water in my hand.

Once behind the garage, Rarig ordered us to put our palms against the wall and spread our legs. He then removed our guns, used our own handcuffs on our wrists, and took us upstairs to the apartment. There, he had us sit in separate chairs, to which he tied us with extension cords he salvaged from around the apartment.

"You two sit tight," he said. "I'll be right back."

Neither Jimmy nor I said a word.

After the door shut behind him, though, Jimmy asked nervously, "Talk to me, Joe. What's happening here?"

"I'm not sure," I answered. "Be quiet for a second."

We were both still. I couldn't hear anything. Not the sound of Rarig's footsteps going downstairs, not any traffic from the street. The apartment had all the acoustics of a bank vault.

"The place is soundproofed," I said.

Jimmy Zarrillo stared at me, half-angry, half-scared.

"His name's John Rarig. He's a retired CIA officer—at least I think he is. We're up here to try to save the guy who was supposed to have been shot this morning."

Jimmy looked incredulous. "What?"

"The guy who was killed was apparently the wrong target. They were looking for Lew Corbin-Teich. He's a teacher at the college and an old Soviet defector. Rarig was his case officer. But Rarig doesn't know who's behind the hit, and he thinks it might be CIA, so he couldn't go to his old buddies for help."

Jimmy was shaking his head. "Jesus, Joe. Do you know what all this sounds like? 'Supposed' this, 'we think' that, 'apparently' the other. It's like a goddamn fairy tale. Why'd he pull a gun on you, if you're working together?"

"Hold it," I cautioned.

Beneath us, we could feel a slight vibration.

"It's the garage door," I guessed. "He's hiding your car."

"He going to kill us?" Jimmy asked, his voice a note higher.

"I don't think so. Believe it or not, I think he's just trying to stabilize what you interrupted."

"*Me?*" Zarrillo burst out. "I just happened to see you. You know there's a warrant out for you."

"Yeah, I know. That's a total crock. Rarig thinks the same people who framed me are behind all this." I paused after saying those words, wondering if in fact Rarig had ever uttered them, or if I had just been allowed to fill in the blanks to keep me happy.

The door opened without warning and Rarig stepped back into

the room. This time, he sat down, extracting the gun again, but letting it hang loosely in his hand.

"Okay," he said, addressing us both. "I am sorry about this—call it universal damage control. I didn't want a long conversation out in the front yard. I take it Joe's filled you in?"

Jimmy glared at him contemptuously. "He gave me some bullshit about you being a CIA agent."

"Case officer," Rarig corrected. "Retired." A look of irritation crossed his face. "Look, you're in no danger. This apartment is a half-way house for an old friend of mine—"

"I told him," I said.

"You mention his name?"

"Sure I did. What do you think?"

He dismissed that. "Doesn't matter. All that'll change anyhow, assuming he's still alive." He addressed Jimmy again. "What I need is some time to save this man's life. You're just a victim of bad luck. Once Joe and I are done locating Lew—one way or the other—I'll tell your colleagues where you are and how to get you out, and that'll be that."

Jimmy looked around, made noticeably less anxious by Rarig's sincere tone of voice. "How long's that likely to be? I could starve to death in here."

"A day or two at most. I'm not saying it won't be uncomfortable, but I can't risk letting you go. And in case we're both killed, I'll make sure they have a way of finding out where you are. I'm sorry about the lack of food, but I didn't plan on this."

"Great," Jimmy muttered.

Rarig switched over to me and held up the handcuff key. "Can I let you go?"

"Not unless you want me to turn you in."

"I thought you'd say that. Nothing's changed, you know. We're still on the same mission."

"Sounds like Flash Gordon," I said, "which is what I should've realized from the start. I don't even know for sure you ever worked for the CIA."

His eyes widened. "*You* came up with it, and you hit the nail on the head, about the real Rarig being killed, and how the trail was erased. I didn't come knocking on your door."

I shook my head. "John—or whatever your name is—I let myself be conned this far because I was desperate to get out of my own mess. You told me you had the evidence to clear my name, and only after I was a wanted man did you admit it was bullshit. Now you've kidnapped a police officer and you're holding him against his will, and it's all on the strength of some spy story from the past that nobody can prove. I went with you this far—I admit that—but I can't go any further. I'm in too deep, I got nothing to gain, and I think it's time to face what I got to face."

Rarig rubbed his forehead with frustration. "Somebody tried to kill you, right?"

He didn't continue, so after a pause, I filled in the obvious. "Right."

"And somebody framed you for the jewelry theft."

"Okay."

"*Well, it wasn't me,*" he said, almost shouting, suddenly standing up and pacing the room. "I'm the sorry bastard who found a body on his front lawn. Don't you get it yet? We're both being jerked around. Somebody's after something, and we're just part of the plan. I was used to get the ball rolling, and you were framed to get you out of their hair."

He stopped in front of me and looked me straight in the eyes. "I could go home right now and let Lew be killed, if he hasn't been already. And you could turn yourself in and have your life as you know it come to an end—all because some sons of bitches figured things should turn out that way. Or you can fight back. Regain your life. Show them you're tougher than they think you are."

He brought his face closer. "These guys—CIA, KGB, Mafia, whatever they are—spend their entire careers manipulating people—the people they're against and the people who work for them. You and I are totally disposable. We mean nothing, and sometimes we're thrown away for no reason at all—to give someone a minute advantage, to make someone else feel a little better about himself, to allow some politician half a world away to say something without being a baldfaced liar."

He stepped back and looked at me sorrowfully. "You can let that happen if you want, but I'm goddamned if I will."

He turned back to Jimmy. "I am truly sorry you got mixed up in this, but that's the way things are, and if he wants to be your roommate for a couple of days, so be it. I'm not quitting."

The room's utter silence descended like a brick following his outburst. Jimmy looked at me and raised his eyebrows. "Why not go for it?"

"Are you kidding?" I asked him.

He shrugged. "I'm screwed either way. With you out there, I've got twice the chance of being found. I've known you for years. Him I just met. Do me the favor."

I sighed, tired of what seemed to have become an endless string of moral decisions, all stemming from a situation I didn't understand. I twisted around in my chair, offering my handcuffed wrists to Rarig. "All right. Let's get it done."

Rarig and I sat uneasily in the car, different allies than we'd been before, bound less by the lies and dubious perceptions that had guided us thus far, and more by an odd sense of survival. Wrapped in a moral white-out, I knew my only chance of staying alive now was to simply keep moving and hope I was headed in the right direction.

"You should've told me you had a gun," I said.

"It wouldn't have changed anything." This time, Rarig was behind the wheel, his earlier anxiety replaced by the tactical calm of a veteran. This was certainly more his type of battleground than mine. Still, as he backed the car out into the street, he showed a lack of self-assurance. "What do we do now?"

"Go to Corbin-Teich's apartment," I answered without thinking.

"He's not going to be there."

"It's where he left his life behind. There'll be traces of where he went."

Rarig looked at me strangely and began driving back toward campus, eventually entering a short, tree-shaded residential street. He pointed out an elaborate Victorian building with a fancy balcony clinging to the second floor.

"That's it," he said. "Upstairs."

"You got a key?"

Rarig patted his pocket and parked the car by the curb. We both got out, looking around cautiously.

"What happens when the locals find out their detective's missing?" he asked, casually walking toward the building's broad front steps.

"Given the way he approached us, I doubt he called it in," I answered. "Could be hours. 'Course, if he was due back at the station, they'll be looking for him soon—or if he's late for his next appointment."

Rarig looked surprised, hesitating on the top step. "I thought you were supposed to call in every time you left the vehicle."

"Patrol officers are. This was more of a thing between friends. The warrant on me isn't for anything violent, and my bet is there isn't a cop in the state who doesn't think Fred Coffin's full of crap. Jimmy just wanted to find out what was going on."

Rarig crossed the porch to a side entrance, pulling out his key ring. "Well, let's keep our fingers crossed."

He unlocked the door, which opened directly onto a staircase leading up, and proceeded ahead.

"He live here long?" I asked from behind.

"All the years he's been in Middlebury."

At the top, there was another door, unlocked, which let us into a large, pleasant, plant- and book-filled living room with broad windows, thick carpets, and comfortable furniture. It smelled faintly of pipe tobacco, old leather, and slightly dusty wool.

Rarig moved immediately to the phone and dialed a number. A moment later, he began speaking, his monotone making it clear he was addressing an answering machine. "This is John Rarig. If you hear this message and are looking for Middlebury police officer Jimmy Zarrillo, he is being confined at the address at the end of this message. It is an upstairs apartment, above a garage, fitted with a special security door, the keys for which have been left on a small ledge underneath the first step of the stairs outside. The magnetic key fits into a knothole near the top hinge, and the door pushes inward. The knob is a decoy." He then gave the address and hung up, looking over at me. "Satisfied?"

"If you weren't talking into a dead phone, sure."

He smiled, but without humor. "I called my private line at the inn. Before too long, I'll be reported missing and someone else'll connect the same dots we did. That message guarantees Zarrillo's survival and it buys us a little time." He then waved his arm at the apartment around us. "Okay—be my guest. He won't have left any tracks you wouldn't normally expect, though. Too many years living in the shadows—the trick to this business is to be who you seem to be."

"So no records of mortgages, phone bills, rental agreements, or anything connecting him to somewhere else?"

"Right." Rarig seemed almost pleased by this fact, as if—just temporarily—he was enjoying the pure tradecraft of it all.

But I wasn't put off. "Good—makes things easier."

He looked at me quizzically, but made no comment.

I began by making a general survey of the place, slowly walking through the kitchen, bedroom, bath, spare room, and office. I tried to pick up on the patterns of the man—what toothpaste he used, if he flossed or not, did his shampoo reflect a dandruff problem or not, did he like one- or two-ply. I counted mirrors, I looked at clothing, I noticed the degree of shine on his shoes, the type of literature he favored, the food and drink he liked, the artwork he found pleasing. I studied his choices in music and found several similar symphonies done by different orchestras and conductors. I discovered a love of plays—reading, attending, and directing them—from several signed production photos, a thick pile of annotated playbooks, and assorted memorabilia.

After almost two hours of this, Rarig finally showed his impatience. "Haven't found him yet? I saw you looking at the toilet paper."

"It's a character insight," I said. "I'll check yours out when we get back to the inn."

Rarig shifted his attention to the view outside the window. His earlier agitated gloominess had returned. "This is such a waste of time. He's probably dead by now anyhow."

"You two keep in touch over the years?"

"Pretty much. We had to be careful. Leave no traces."

"I bet he was good at that. Careful. Neat. A good planner."

Rarig glanced at me. "Yeah."

"A good actor, too," I added. "Conscious of how he projected himself. Always aware of how the audience was reacting."

Rarig allowed a half smile. "True."

"And for all that, a little insecure. Not only a man of habits, but fond of routine and happy to be placed in positions of imposed authority, where his title alone demanded automatic courtesy."

Rarig laughed softly. "Very good. A regular Sherlock Holmes."

"We'll see," I said with less confidence. "Is there a major theatrical building here?"

"The CFA, sure—the Center for Fine Arts. It's huge. They built it about four years ago."

"That's where I think we'll find him."

It was more than I meant to say—more definite—but I was reacting to Rarig's earlier cockiness. Like two men bobbing in the middle of an ocean, we were keeping alive not by treading water, but by competing on who'd be the last one to sink. It wasn't the kind of teamwork I was used to, but then not much at the moment was normal.

Predictably, Rarig dug in his heels. "Why?"

I crossed over to the door. "Because when you run, you run to familiar ground—someplace safe, close, and with any luck, dark. If I were a theater nut, I'd head for the theater. For Lew, I'm guessing it's a home away from home."

Without comment, Rarig followed me downstairs. We both instinctively paused at the bottom, peering out the door's glass panel at the street outside.

Everything seemed as calm as we'd left it.

We climbed off the porch, cut across the lawn, and quickly got into the Ford, irrationally appreciating its protection, even while surrounded by clear glass.

But our surprise, when it was sprung, came from closer by.

Willy Kunkle rose from lying behind the backseat, propped his elbow between us, and laughed when we both jumped. "Hi, guys. Miss me?"

17

"*JESUS CHRIST,*" RARIG SHOUTED.

Willy sat back, smiling like an idiot. "Saw it in a movie once. Couldn't resist it."

"What're you doing here?" I asked, already checking up and down the street.

"Don't worry," Willy said. "I'm not as dumb as you guys. Nobody knows I'm around." He pulled a portable radio from his inner pocket and keyed the mike. "You there, Sam?"

"10-4" came the familiar voice.

"They're baaaaack," Willy announced, laughing at the end.

He replaced the radio. "Except her, of course."

I pulled at my ear and sighed. "I should've expected this. You'll probably get fired—you know that."

Willy's eyes grew wide. "Ooh, that's a scary thought."

"You selfish bastard," I told him. "What about Sammie?"

He laughed again. "You know goddamn well she's why we're here. She thinks you set the friggin' sun, which you probably will before we're done. What's the plan, anyway?"

"I take it you found us 'cause of the car."

"Brilliant. Only took an hour or so. Small town. 'Course, there were two of us, and we knew to look around the college. I gotta say, though, for a guy with a price on his head, and the place crawling with law, you're not too discreet."

"How crawling *is* that, exactly?"

"The department here's got about ten or so. We spotted maybe three or four state cops as well. If you figure they divided the town up between 'em all, not counting the ones at the crime scene and a few to man headquarters, you get six or seven cruisers rollin' around. And I wouldn't doubt they got more coming."

"And you're sure nobody saw you?"

"Yup." He reached into his other pocket, pulled out a second radio, and dropped it on the front seat between us. "In case we get split up."

I picked up the radio and examined it. It was labeled "NewBrook Fire Department."

"What the hell?"

"I borrowed 'em," Willy admitted. "On my way through Newfane. I know the combination to their firehouse. They only carry a couple of miles, but I figured we might need a private frequency to talk on. We checked 'em out as soon as we got here—called around, pretending we were up shit creek. Nobody heard us as far as we could tell. So—you even *have* a plan? You been here long enough."

Rarig scowled at this rapid patter, but I was used to it. "As far as you're concerned, the plan is to go back home. We've got one long shot to check out, and then we'll probably be doing the same."

"Great. I like long shots."

I twisted around to face him fully. "Willy, I appreciate the gesture. I should've expected it. And if I really thought we had a chance of pulling this off, I'd even let you stick around. But things aren't going too well. We were discovered by one of Middlebury's finest and had to lock him up. You don't want to be a part of this anymore, and I don't want it on my conscience."

Willy was laughing again. "No shit. That's like kidnapping. And a cop, no less. Boy—you think you know a guy. No wonder you keep me around."

Now even I was getting irritated. "Willy, for Christ's sake. Fucking around is one thing—if you stick with us, you'll be an accessory. That's jail time."

Not bothering to argue, he opened the back door and got out. "We figured you'd say that." He pointed to the radio I was still holding in my hand. "You need any help, just turn it on. We'll hear ya. If nothing else, make sure it gets back to NewBrook. Don't want you busted for theft again. Bye."

He waved at us both and walked quickly down the street.

After a long, stunned silence, Rarig said, "I don't like that man."

"Yeah—well, he's an acquired taste. I wouldn't be without him, obviously whether I like it or not." I slipped Willy's radio into my pocket, turned off. "So where's the CFA?"

Rarig pursed his lips, and for a moment I thought the competitive edge between us was going to rear up into the open. The sudden appearance of two of my own troops, uncontrollable, unseen, and—to him—of unknown quality, obviously rubbed him wrong.

To head him off, I patted my pocket and said, "I'm not going to use it, whatever happens."

That gave him an out. "You may want to eat those words."

"Then so be it. I'm not going to turn my own professional suicide into mass murder."

He contemplated that for a moment and then pointed down the street. "Straight ahead across the intersection. Take a right when you hit South Main."

The CFA—Middlebury College's Center for Fine Arts—is one of three large structures lining the east side of South Main, just before it turns into Route 30 and heads off into the countryside. As a result of their location, they stand against miles of rolling fields, a lush green golf course, and have a spectacular view of the Green Mountains—all of which contrast violently with the buildings' bizarre architecture.

The southernmost two are athletic field houses, one looking like a soiled cluster of glued-together teepees, the other a Quonset hut with several Tootsie Rolls stuck to it. Both are connected by a tube-shaped umbilical cord.

Our destination was the newest of the three—as dissimilar from them as they are from each other, except in overall appeal. The Center for Fine Arts is a cob job of every building style known to Western civilization. In parts, its roof is flat, sloped, crenelated, and dormered, and apparently clad in everything from painted metal to slate. Similarly, its walls run from granite to brick to metal to peeling white clapboard, all butting together in cramped chaos. The front, with the most coherent appearance, is a shades-of-brown combination of frontier blockhouse, Norman castle, and federal office building, topped by a roof reminiscent of the sloped hull of the Confederate ironclad *Merrimac*, complete with gunports.

It is also cavernously huge, being built into the hillside, and at this time of year and day was largely dark and empty. When John Rarig and I stepped through one of the side entrances from the parking lot, I felt like a visitor who'd been shut in after closing time.

The art center's interior is its soaring redemption. As jumbled as the outside, here the architectural crisscross between new and old, granite and wood, seems playful, airy, amusing, and self-confident. From the building's middle space, an enormous stone wall thrusts up three floors to an elegant, fan-shaped wooden ceiling, lending to everything around it a paradoxical sense of lightness. Juxtaposed throughout this lofty, weighty, castle-like space are pits and balconies, masses of oddly placed and sized interior windows—some glassed in, some wide open—and an assortment of staircases, clinging to the walls as to a ship's side.

At present, it was all mysteriously dark, quiet, and foreboding.

That impression grew as we ventured from empty, overarching vestibule to silent, dim hallway to totally dark performance hall. There were several of the latter, some large, others built for either practice or black-box theater, but none containing the man we were after.

At each stop, depending on the lighting and the layout, we either looked around or Rarig shouted Lew's name into the void, identifying himself—only to hear his voice swallowed up by the gloom.

Finally, after an hour of this, frustrated by our lack of manpower and our ignorance of the floor plan, we were about to admit defeat. Rarig especially seemed to be running on ebbing resources. His mood, ever changing, had finally settled into a taciturn glumness, and mine was close behind. Failure here not only meant that Lew Corbin-Teich had spun away on his own, but it entailed my returning home empty-handed, to a reception probably rivaling the surrender of a child killer.

It was therefore with some relief that we finally got an answer to Rarig's last call.

We were standing in a doorway leading to the balcony section of what appeared to be—had there been any light—a very large stage area. Rarig's voice had just disappeared as usual, without echo or response, when after a pause we clearly heard the name *"John"* float by as if carried on a breeze.

Instinctively, we both stepped inside, shutting the door behind us, plunging us into a blackness so deep, I couldn't see my hands.

"Lew," Rarig asked, "is that you?"

"Whom do you have with you?" was the answer, coming from somewhere high and against the wall to our backs. It was a light, delicate voice, heavily accented, with the careful phrasing of someone who's learned the language too well.

"He's a friend. He figured out you might be here. Are you all right?"

"Yes, but I am not sure for how much longer. No doubt they are doing as you are, searching me out."

"That's why we're here," Rarig explained, as if coaxing a child. "To get you someplace safe."

"There may be no such place."

Rarig lost his patience. "Well, it sure as hell isn't here. Where are you, goddamn it?"

A soft chuckle. "That is John Rarig. Look to your left."

We did as instructed and saw a tiny, bright red dot hovering in the darkness. Following it, our shoulders rubbing the wall for reference, we groped forward, found a narrow set of steps, and climbed to the door of a small sound and light control booth wedged up against the theater's ceiling. The red light turned out to be from a pen-sized laser pointer, which our guide returned to his breast pocket as we joined him. A faint glow emanated from the equipment panel located at the base of a broad window overlooking a huge blank universe.

Lew Corbin-Teich was a soft outline of tousled hair and bushy beard, with an aquiline nose that came and went in the dim light as

' he turned his head. He greeted John Rarig with a bear hug and a kiss on each cheek, exchanging a few comments in Russian, which Rarig seemed to speak like a native.

Then Corbin-Teich turned to me and fumbled in the dark for my hand, which he shook energetically. "It is nice to meet you. I am Lewis Corbin-Teich."

"My pleasure," I said automatically. "Joe Gunther. Do you have any idea who's after you?"

His shadow shook its head, his voice sounding bewildered. "No. I was walking with Andrei to the Geonomics Center, where he had a meeting. I was merely keeping him company. He has been in low spirits since the passing of his wife. I heard an automobile approaching from behind us. I turned my head to look. I was nervous because I thought I had seen a man watching my house the night before. I saw the barrel of a gun in one of the windows and instinctively I fell to the ground. Andrei never saw a thing, and I never extended a hand to warn him. I was utterly silent throughout the attack. Speechless. Andrei died as if all life suddenly was pulled from him and only his clothes remained. He fell in a heap and never moved."

Corbin-Teich was weeping. Rarig placed one hand on his shoulder. "Lew, there was nothing you could do. He probably never felt a thing."

"Tell me about the man you saw watching your house," I asked.

Corbin-Teich's voice was strained. "It may have been nothing. I have been on edge ever since the death of Sergei Antonov. I no longer know."

I switched tacks. "Could your friend have been the target?"

"No, no. Andrei had no enemies. He was the gentlest of men."

"I heard he was a defector, too."

Corbin-Teich's rejection was absolute. "Ah, such nonsense. He was a poet. He left decades ago as a matter of conscience. No one missed him. No one cared, just as no one will care that he was shot down in cold blood."

Rarig administered more solace as I tried to keep Lew focused, although, truth be told, now that we'd found him, I had no idea what to do with him. Pure instinct was making me act like a cop.

"Did you get a look at the man who shot him?"

Corbin-Teich wiped his eyes with his sleeve. "I am sorry. Having all this return after so many years, it is a shock. I thought I had seen enough. I have become weak with old age. No, it is soft—that is what I have become. Forgive me. I understand what you are trying to do and I thank you. Yes—I did see the man, but I did not recognize him. His features were familiar. He was as they all were in the old days. But I did not know him personally."

"Why didn't you go to the other place?" Rarig asked.

"I tried. I ran after Andrei was shot, to the first phone I could find. I called you, and then I ran to go there. But I saw the automobile again, and I felt I could no longer stay in the open. I came here because I know it so well."

He stopped suddenly and looked from one of us to the other. "How did *you* find me?"

"That was Joe's doing."

"Lucky guess," I finished. "How long have you been here?"

"Hours. I have not paid attention."

"Rarig, you have any ideas what to do now?"

There was a pause before he answered. "No. I thought we'd just get out of town and go from there. Maybe hole up someplace for a while."

Great, I thought, but I didn't have anything better. I did, however, have one more question to ask. "Mr. Corbin-Teich—"

"Please call me Lew. It is a wonderful custom. I like it very much."

"Okay. You can call me Joe. I understand your friend had no enemies and you don't think he was the target, so don't misunderstand what I'm about to ask, but thinking back, do you remember the shooter ever taking aim at you, especially after he hit Andrei?"

There was a stunned silence. "You are thinking I was spared on purpose." It wasn't a question.

"I'm thinking it's possible."

"To lure *me* out?" Rarig asked. "I'm in the phone book, for Christ's sake."

I shook my head in the darkness, reviewing the conversation I'd had with Sammie the night we'd all met with Olivia Kidder and Rarig at the inn. "Not you—somebody else."

"It *is* possible," Corbin-Teich admitted, his voice harder now, its inflection suddenly reminding me that this man had once been a pro-tégé of Padzhev and a rising star within the KGB.

"The automobile," he continued, "had no reason to speed by. There was no other traffic, no other people on the street that I could see, and it was an automatic weapon, yet all the bullets struck Andrei."

"Who're you thinking of ?" Rarig asked me. "Padzhev? It still doesn't fit."

"No, not Padzhev. Someone else. Someone we haven't thought of yet. Someone who would benefit from getting things all stirred up. Killing Antonov on your front lawn, tapping your phone line to find Lew, staking out his apartment and then knocking off his friend in a fake drive-by. It all feels like somebody's trying to get something, or someone, to rise to the surface."

"Snowden must be behind it," Rarig said.

I shook my head. "If it's Snowden, then who's his target? Antonov's already dead, you and Lew could've been knocked off anytime. There's somebody missing in the equation."

"It is Georgi," Lew said softly.

"What is?" I pushed him.

"The target. It is Georgi Padzhev. Sergei Antonov would never do anything without Georgi's blessing, so we can assume Sergei was in this country under Georgi's orders."

"Probably because they saw your picture in that article about the inn," I added, excited that some of this might at last become untangled.

Rarig didn't answer, but I saw him run his hand through his hair as if considering the idea.

"Would Georgi Padzhev be after you?" I asked Lew.

"Not to kill me. We are old men now. The KGB is gone. All that is history. Georgi might want to talk, to reminisce, as old men do. I might like that, too. It is what John and I did, after all, for hours and hours. This image you have of the KGB, much of it is propaganda. Georgi Padzhev is no monster. He was a chess player, like John here, like many others. The pieces were human beings, it is true, and many died but not as Hollywood would have it. We didn't go around shooting people."

I didn't bother quibbling semantics. What did I really know, after all? "So Padzhev wants to reminisce. But he's old, he's now into the Mafia, and he has lots of enemies, which cuts down on his mobility. Antonov goes instead to check things out. But he's known as Georgi's henchman. Which means he's followed to Rarig's place, knocked off to lure out Padzhev, and Rarig's line is tapped for insurance. Is that what you're thinking?"

"Yes. That is possible. Sergei was not a henchman, as you say. He and Georgi were like brothers."

"So John told me," I said. "But John hiding the body confused things enough that Padzhev held back, unsure what was happening. In the meantime, we circulated Antonov's picture in the papers, which stimulated you to call John, which is how Padzhev's enemies located you. It's also why they probably framed me, to give themselves some breathing room. But they didn't kill you. They still needed bait to get Padzhev into the open, to show him that whoever killed Antonov was still in Vermont. Knowing Padzhev, might that work?"

"*I* think so," Rarig agreed. "Padzhev's a ruthless, ambitious man. One of the things Olivia told me last night was that he's fighting for his life right now, trying to hold off competitors. It's purely theoretical, but if he let Antonov's murder go unavenged, it could be used as a sign of weakness that would unite the opposition against him."

"I would agree with that," Corbin-Teich said. "The Georgi Padzhev I knew would never allow such a transgression. It was what made him so powerful in our organization."

"And why he went to such lengths to snatch Yuri," Rarig finished.

"So the people behind all this," I concluded, "are Padzhev's competitors from Russia, choosing the time and place for a showdown far from Padzhev's home base."

"It fits," Rarig said, "except for Snowden. Where's he belong?"

"You actually believe he killed Antonov?" I asked impatiently. "I thought that was just to get me all bent out of shape."

Rarig remained stubborn. "Then who tried to have you knocked off in Washington?"

My head was already hurting, and the thought of this extra complication pushed me away from the entire subject. "I don't give a damn anymore, at least not right now. Let's just get out of Middlebury so we can figure out what to do next."

"I would like that very much," Corbin-Teich said with obvious relief.

I took his elbow and guided him gently toward the door we'd entered. "Lead the way, then. The car's in the lower parking lot, away from the field houses."

We began traveling the quiet, darkened corridors and staircases like trespassers, pausing furtively to look around, keeping our voices low and our footsteps silent. In the dim light, I cast a glance at Lew Corbin-Teich, studying what I could see under what turned out to be masses of snow-white hair. The plastic surgery had obviously been of high quality, although not knowing the "before," I was hard pressed to judge the "after." Nevertheless, there was a stillness to his features, an absence of mobility that suggested a mask. Watching it, I couldn't help feeling his face embodied everything that had happened to me since discovering "Boris's" body. Nothing had turned out as it had at first appeared, and none of the subsequent explanations had been any more real than Corbin-Teich's remodeled appearance. Given what I'd been through these last few days, I couldn't help wondering how he'd survived half a lifetime of it.

Our silent progress stood us in good stead. Just shy of the building's entrance, we rounded a corner and saw two men in dark clothing loitering in the lobby, one of them with his eyes glued to the scenery beyond the plate-glass door.

We backtracked quickly but not before the other one saw us.

"*Stop*," he shouted, as Corbin-Teich grabbed my sleeve and pulled me back along the wall. Rarig was ahead of us, heading for a door to the left. I was about to follow when Lew yanked on me again. "No, this is better."

We slipped through a door on the right and vanished as into an absolute vacuum. From the comparative light of the hallway, we were now in total blackness.

Lew continued pulling at me, keeping me off balance. "This way. Follow me."

I sensed from how his voice vanished into thin air that we were in a huge room, probably another of the theaters, but this realization was of no use whatsoever as I stumbled down a sloping aisle, sightless and clumsy until falling down outright, brought low by a cluster of metal chairs that had been left in our path.

Corbin-Teich fell with me in a tangle, smacking my hand against one of the chair backs and sending the gun I'd just unholstered skittering across the carpeting.

Simultaneously, the door we'd used flew open, outlining our pursuer in silhouette, a pistol in his hand. Without thought, I reached for the front of Lew's jacket as he squirmed on top of me, yanked out the laser pointer he'd clipped there earlier, and pointed it at our pursuer. The tiny red dot stuck to his chest like an angry insect.

"*Freeze,*" I yelled, disentangling myself.

I saw the man's head duck down to look at the red dot, misinterpreting it, I hoped, for an infrared gun sight.

"That's right," I said. "Face down on the floor."

I saw him following my instructions as the door slowly swung to behind him. Before the light vanished, however, I was close enough for the laser alone to supply a poor substitute.

"Slide your gun over here."

He did as he was told. I picked it up, pocketed the pointer, put my knee into the small of his back and his gun to the nape of his neck, and frisked him for more weapons. I retrieved a dagger from a sheath strapped to his lower calf. I then dragged him over to the edge of the aisle, placed his hands between the legs of one of the bolted-down row seats, and snapped my handcuffs around his wrists.

I returned the pointer to Lew and asked him to search for my own gun.

"Where's your buddy?" I asked my captive, twisting one of his thumbs.

His voice was understandably tight. It, too, was heavily accented. "We help you."

"Right." I twisted a little harder, making him wince. "Answer the question."

He tried to wriggle away. "No English good."

"You Russian?"

"Yes, yes. Russian."

Lew Corbin-Teich was back, crouching by my side, my gun in his hand.

"Ask him who he is," I told him.

Corbin-Teich shot out a short, guttural question, which the other man answered with obvious relief.

"He says he works for Padzhev," Corbin-Teich explained. "That they were sent here to protect me from Edvard Kyrov."

"Who's he?"

Corbin-Teich rapidly asked a couple more questions and then translated. "He says Kyrov is an old rival of Padzhev. That he is a very bad man—a longtime criminal, even back to the old days."

The clear sound of a gunshot reverberated out in the hallway. I quickly moved to the door, opened it a crack, and squinted into the dim light. Rarig was standing over the body of the second man, having obviously doubled back from the door he'd used, to reemerge into the corridor behind his follower. It seemed clear he'd shot him in the back.

"Drag him in here," I told him.

He grabbed the man's feet and pulled him toward me. There was no blood on the carpeting.

After he'd passed by, I propped the door half-open so we could see what we were doing. "You just killed him, no questions asked?"

Rarig looked at me angrily. "I'm seventy-five years old, for Christ's sake. I'm not going to play around with some bastard like this. I just hit him in the back of the head. It was his gun that went off. Not mine."

I checked the body and found a pulse, slow but steady. There was no saying how bad an injury he'd suffered, though. Reluctantly, I undid half of the first man's handcuffs, and chained him to his buddy. "This one says they were sent by Padzhev to protect Lew—from someone named Edvard Kyrov. You ever hear of him?"

"Only by reputation. He's a crook—a black marketeer."

"He may be the one behind all this."

There was a noise from outside. We both scurried to the crack in the door and looked out as a young man wearing a small backpack trudged by, earphones perched on his head.

"I don't give a goddamn who anyone is right now, or says he is," Rarig whispered. "I just want to get the hell out of here."

In the light from the corridor, I could see his forehead shining with sweat. His job was done, or almost, and he'd spared no one, deserving or not, in achieving it—from possibly killing the man behind us, to using me from the start. His blatant self-service finally burned through the desperation that had been driving me, leaving me clear-eyed, furious, and decided on my course.

"Fine," I said, "but as soon as we get Lew to a safe place, I'm calling the cops. This thing is ending now. Is that clear?"

He nodded. "It's all I wanted from the start."

"You crap artist." I held out my hand. "Give me your gun."

His jaw tightened. "Not till we're out of here."

I exploded with rage. I took the dagger I still had in my hand and shoved its tip into Rarig's nostril, making his head snap back until it smacked against the wall. His eyes popped open with fright.

"Look," I said, my eyes five inches from his, "I'm sick of all this horseshit. Give me the fucking gun. Now."

There was no doubt he could have just shot me at close range, but my obvious disregard for any such logic persuaded him to merely push the gun into my hand.

I removed the knife. "Thank you. Now collect your friend and let's go."

Feeling his nose gingerly, he nodded toward the two men on the floor behind us. "What about them? What if they do belong to Pad-zhev?"

"I don't give a damn," I told him. "I've played this game long enough, and not a single person involved in it has turned out to be what they said they were." I walked over to Corbin-Teich. "Give me my gun."

He complied without comment. I noticed then that the unconscious man's arms were outstretched before him, his hands empty. My fury reignited, I swung back on Rarig, pushed him hard enough against the wall that the air flew out of his lungs, and went through his pockets as he doubled over in pain. I quickly found the Russian's pistol and added it to my collection.

"You asshole," I muttered to Rarig and spun him around to face the door, motioning to Corbin-Teich to join us.

"Simple plan," I explained to them, speaking softly. "We move quickly out to the parking lot, get in the car—me driving—and we leave town the fastest way possible, Route 30 heading south. Understood?"

Nobody made a sound. I pushed them out ahead of me, and the three of us marched down the hallway, turned the corner, and entered the welcoming daylight of the building's lobby. The sunshine, even fading as it was at the end of the day, made me feel for the first time that regardless of the consequences, I was regaining some measure of control. I knew it wouldn't make any difference overall. Fred Coffin and the court were still waiting to give me the run of a lifetime, and I still had no contrary evidence to stop them, but my temporary elation made all that immaterial.

18

W E WALKED IN LONG STRIDES TOWARD RARIG'S CAR, MY JACKET swinging heavily with its cargo of weapons, until Lew faltered and stopped, pointing up the curving drive that connected the parking lot to Route 30 above. "That is the same car. The man who shot Andrei."

Ruefully missing the two bodyguards we'd just left behind, I caught the small of his back with my hand and propelled him forward. "Keep going, Lew. One problem at a time."

But the car had me worried. It was poised motionless on the crest of the drive, as a lookout, which implied a number of things, all of them bad. Kyrov's men had probably followed Lew to the arts center—after flushing him outside the Geonomics building—and waited for Padzhev or his people to make an appearance. Now that we'd made a hash of that plan, things were likely to become a whole lot less subtle.

My newfound self-determination had lasted all of two minutes.

They waited until we'd climbed into Rarig's car, probably because they preferred us contained and possibly, I hoped, because they were slightly confused, Padzhev's men having mysteriously vanished from the equation. In any case, immediately after I started the engine, I saw a second vehicle slowly nosing down the road to our east, cutting off the only other exit from the parking lot.

"Look," Lew said from behind. Rarig and I both turned, expecting him to be pointing out the new car. Instead, he was staring at several men on foot, coming from around both ends of the building, a couple of whom had cell phones held to their ears.

I looked around, reading the terrain. It was mostly flat and open, lending itself to a cross-country run, but there were ponds and ditches and clusters of trees scattered about—and no doubt other obstacles lying just out of sight. Any errors now, I knew, might well prove the end of us.

I reached into my jacket and extracted Willy's radio. "Willy—you see what's happening here?"

His reply was immediate. "I see a black car at the top of the drive."

Sammie's voice followed. "And I've got a couple of guys walking along the front of the building toward your parking lot."

"I think we're in trouble here," I told them. "Better put out a May-day to the locals."

"Where do you want us?" Sammie said.

"I don't want you anywhere. I'm about to move—fast. I don't know where and I don't know how they'll react. Just stay out of the way and see what happens."

I was suspiciously surprised by her ready acceptance. "10-4."

I put the car into gear. "Fasten your seatbelts, gentlemen."

To confront either vehicle seemed counterproductive. The men on foot, however, were fairer game. I hit the accelerator and aimed straight for the two coming around the back of the arts center.

They were halfway across a broad pedestrian promenade spread out like an apron from the center's rear entrance, and, as I bore down on them, my intentions now clear, they stopped, pulled guns from under their jackets, and prepared to fire.

"Get down, get down," I shouted, veering back and forth to provide a poorer target. I didn't hear the gunshots over the roaring engine and the bone-jarring thuds as we jumped the curb, but a couple of crystalline holes suddenly appeared in the windshield like flattened bugs, and I felt a fine shower of glass sprinkle across my face. Through the web-like cracks, I saw both men jump out of the way at the last moment, their pistol muzzles still flashing. As we tore past, one of our side windows blew up with a crash, provoking a scream from Lew in the back.

"You okay?" Rarig shouted to him.

His voice was feeble over the wind now whistling through the various openings. "Yes, yes. I think so."

I heard Sammie's tinny voice, slightly muffled by my having returned the radio to my pocket. "Joe, top car's in motion, moving south on Route 30 to cut you off."

That was just one of my problems. Ahead, where I'd been hoping for a clean shot at the building's far end and the service road beyond it, I saw a low retaining wall barring my way, with only one narrow gap in it. I wrenched the wheel and headed in its direction.

Rarig yelled, "They're coming up behind us."

I glanced in the rearview mirror and saw that the second car had followed us onto the promenade and was moving to cut us off before we could reach the opening.

Rarig began pawing at my jacket. "Give me a gun."

Without looking, I swatted at him, hitting him on the side of the head. "Back off. You start shooting now, you'll probably kill one of us."

We reached the gap almost simultaneously, but my angle was better. The other car careened into my front left fender, pushing us up against the wall, but then it bounced away, thrown off course. I slammed on the brakes, hooked a right, and spun through the opening, heading for several playing fields and the golf course beyond. Out of the right corner of my eye, I saw the first car closing in from the southern service road with another vehicle in close pursuit. Sammie had yielded to instinct.

"How's the car we hit?" I asked.

"Still moving."

Ahead, the lay of the land again dictated my choices. To my front, all that open ground turned out to be hemmed in by trees, leaving only the right and left as possible escape routes.

"Go left," Rarig yelled, as if reading my mind. "Head for South Street."

That much was obvious. Speeding across the almost flat grassy surface, the second car was already closing in fast from the right. Sammie
seemed to realize our predicament. She peeled away like a sheepdog,
cut across behind me, and prepared to run interference between me
and the first car, which was rallying to shut me off on the left.

The terrain, as we all swerved away from the edge of the golf
course, began to roughen, making control that much more difficult.
I was now paralleling the edge of a wooded outcropping. To my rear,
I could see the second car closing in; to my left, Sammie and the first
car were jockeying for room, occasionally colliding as Sammie fought
to keep my narrow slot open. Ahead, since we'd now almost completed
a full loop, lay the lower access road off the art center parking lot, and
beyond it a grouping of houses, fences, and more trees. Whichever
route I chose, I realized, the end result was going to be a mess—possibly a terminal one.

Sammie was losing ground. All of us were leaping and skidding
badly by now, hitting small depressions in the ground, rocks, and
hillocks. My seatbelt was cutting into my lap every few seconds. But
Sammie's car was lighter than her opponent's, and I could see her
profile, tense and focused, as she struggled to maintain both position
and control.

It was becoming a simple matter of time—and Sam's suddenly
ran out.

The second car sideswiped her just as all three of us catapulted up
and over the access road, sending her into a pirouette and yanking her
from my sight as if she'd been attached to a cable that had suddenly
played out.

Keeping my eyes front, I shouted, "How is she? She okay?"

Rarig twisted around in his seat. "She's over on her side, but I think
she's all right. The spinning took most of the steam out of it."

He turned back and looked at me, speaking surprisingly calmly,
and added, "I think we're in trouble, though."

That, I already knew. With one car tailing me by only a few feet,
and the other one so close I could see the expressions of its occupants,
I saw my only hope was to negotiate a path through the houses ahead

and to the street beyond, losing both escorts along the way. I didn't hold out much hope of success.

"There's the cavalry," Rarig suddenly yelled, pointing to the right.

Through the side window, I could see the bright flickering of blue lights approaching from the south—out of town—presumably from backup units called in for mutual aid.

We'd run out of open ground. Our speed abruptly magnified by the proximity of trees, bushes, and outbuildings, we all three smashed through a fence, flew off some carefully landscaped terracing, skidded across the broad backyard of an enormous house, ricocheting off a shed and a swing set, and finally exploded onto the street between another house and its garage.

It was too much for the Ford. My steering wheel was wrenched from my hands as the car's front end plowed into the opposite curb, we spun around in a dizzying, weightless circle, surrounded by a medley of breaking metal and glass, and finally came to rest up against a tree, covered with icicle-like shards, enveloped in a sudden, deadening silence.

Not an absolute silence, however, since approaching at a fast rate was a screaming siren, bolstering what shred of hope I had left.

I should have known better.

Shaking my head to clear my vision, I saw men already clustering around our car, guns out, pulling open the doors, giving orders I couldn't understand. Beyond them, down the street, as I, too, was jerked clear by the scruff of my neck, I saw a state police cruiser come slithering to a stop, acrid smoke curling from under its shuddering tires.

The two officers inside never had a chance. Before their vehicle had even come to a complete stop, its surface began to implode under a torrent of bullets, its windshield becoming snowy white, its lights disintegrating and dying, its tires sagging onto the rims like horses shot in battle. In the deafening staccato of automatic gunfire, I reached for my own pistol, felt a shattering blow to the back of my head, and saw the Ford's seat come sailing toward me as my knees buckled.

Dazed and numb, my feet stumbling as if asleep, I was stripped of my weapons, hauled by my armpits to one of the pursuit cars, and thrown into the back next to Rarig and Lew. Without further fanfare, and with the south end of the street now blocked by the destroyed cruiser, both cars took off, tires screaming, toward the heart of the village.

South Street, broad and flat, is aimed at downtown like the straightest tine of a crooked, three-pronged fork, the other two extensions being Route 30 and College Street. Since Middlebury is like the hub of a wheel, however, with roads heading out of it to every cardinal point, logic dictated our doubling back on either one of those alternatives to avoid the village center.

But logic didn't entail Willy Kunkle. Screaming down Route 30, his blue dash-light flashing, Willy bore down on us like vengeance personified, forcing both our cars to swing right onto Main Street.

Swerving, cutting, driving up onto the sidewalk and scattering pedestrians, the three of us raced in a chaotic caravan, with Willy and our vehicle dueling like bumper cars. Through it all, the Russians were yelling at the top of their lungs and jumping in their seats like kids at a fair. Semiconscious, my hands still tingling and slow to move, I watched it all with a dreamy combination of clarity and distance, my brain shouting to do something—anything—but my body failing to act.

Across the Otter Creek bridge, where the town opens up beyond Merchants' Row to form an oddly shaped, tilted commons, Willy, like Sam before him, ran out of luck. Bouncing off one parked car, he hit another and was stopped dead in his tracks. Uphill, just shy of the inn, was the spaghetti-like intersection Rarig and I had entered earlier. Only this time, traveling in the wrong lane at terrifying speed, it seemed less a tangle of roads and more a lethal obstacle course. From every approach, there were cars, trucks, and RVs, all pressing in on us, their angry horn blasts floating on a growing distant chorus of emergency sirens.

We took the easiest way out, steeply up and to the left, free of downtown's clinging frenzy, onto the more open embrace of Route 7, heading north. From being surrounded by traffic and serried buildings, we were suddenly wedged between the forested slope of Chipman Hill to the right and the broad expanse of the Otter Creek valley to the left.

As soon as we'd broken loose, I felt my body press into the back cushion, the car's engine digging deeper as we abruptly picked up speed. Captive and without the slightest idea of what awaited me, I nevertheless shared the sense of relief expressed by the three cheering men in the front seat.

All of which ceased as we topped the rise just beyond town. Ahead of us, clearly visible in the fading daylight, sputtering red flares lined the sides of the road like the approach to an airfield. But instead of a landing path, they led directly to two parked cruisers, engine blocks facing us at a forty-five-degree angle. I instantly recognized a "deadly force" roadblock, set up to stop us at all costs. The cruisers would be empty, officers stationed at a safe distance to either side, weapons locked and loaded. In those scant few seconds, my eyes also found the standard "out"—a narrow avenue, crossed with tire-deflating spikes, that fleeing cars were visually encouraged to take to lessen the overall mayhem.

But my present company wasn't interested.

The front car almost leapt to the challenge, surging forward to push the two cruisers aside. It was a Hollywood moment—total testosterone fantasy—which our own driver was only too willing to follow, slamming on the accelerator.

The predictable results were more surreal than I would have imagined. Aside from the howling engine, there was total silence in the car, so what filled our windshield appeared as a silent movie. The lead vehicle, gunfire flickering from all windows, slammed into the cruisers, shoved them apart a few feet, and rose up on its rear wheels like a rocket taking off. Catapulting over the hoods of the police cars, deformed and blunted, it smashed down on the other side and skittered away, broken, twisted, and inert.

We burst through right behind in an eruption of sound. With metal tearing at metal, glass exploding like firecrackers, we, too, broke out onto the far side, slammed into the lead car, careened off it at an angle away from the hillside, and became airborne over the Otter Creek valley.

For an instant, the silence returned, to be split first by a single scream from the front seat, and then by a final convulsion of noise and destruction. We landed on our wheels, facing straight down the embankment, heading toward one hundred and fifty feet of near cliff— before we were stopped in our tracks by a single tree trunk. The door next to Rarig flew open, and like marbles in a chute the three of us were thrown farther downhill.

We had little time to assess whatever damage we'd incurred. Tangled in saplings and thick brush, hidden from the road above, we found ourselves dazed and cringing amid the random whine and thud of bullets flying just overhead, a result of the surviving Russians still shooting it out from the first car. Memories of war were so real in my brain, I thought myself back in battle.

I scurried over to where the other two were lying sprawled like sacks of coal, using any vegetation I could find as handholds against the steep slope.

"You okay? Lew—you okay?"

The old man passed his hand across his bloodied face. "I think so."

"John? We need to get out of here."

Rarig sat up, began to slide, and flipped over, grabbing some tufts of grass with both hands. He yelled out in pain.

"You all right?" I asked him.

"I hurt like hell."

A couple of bullets smacked into a young tree overhead.

"It'll get worse if we don't move."

"All right, all right."

I pointed toward the valley floor. "Straight down, as fast as you can. We'll stop when we reach better footing."

We did as I'd suggested, in a haphazard sliding tumble, seeing the college's distant lights across the valley, greeting the coming evening in blissful, Olympian serenity, perched on the far rise like a diorama of an era gone by. The contrast helped get me off autopilot. I looked for some landmark that might serve us once we reached bottom and found, poking above the trees, the pale shape of something that looked like a grain elevator, presumably lining the railroad tracks north of town.

A few minutes later, we reassembled amid acres of weed-choked gravel, the sound of distant gunfire almost stopped. I looked at my two companions in the coming twilight and asked them again how they were faring.

"I think I am not too bad," Lew answered, smiling happily at this near miracle. "A stiff neck, perhaps."

Rarig was less sanguine. He looked pale and winded, his eyes narrowed by pain. "I broke a rib or two. Hurts to breathe." He held his right arm across his chest, as if carrying an invisible baby.

I peeled the arm back and gently prodded the area beneath it. His sudden intake of breath guided me to a single spot just below his nipple.

"There's no deformity," I told him. "It's probably only a crack or a hairline fracture. Let me know if you feel like your lung's filling up, though."

"Swell," he muttered. "What now?"

"Keep your fingers crossed." I pulled Willy's beaten radio from my pocket, turned it on, hesitated a moment, and asked, "You guys out there?"

"Hey, there," was Willy's laconic reply.

Sammie was less laid-back. "Jesus. You made it? How are you? *Where* are you?"

"Within striking distance of the railroad tracks north of town, east of Otter Creek. I took a visual on what looks like a grain elevator. I think we'll head there." I glanced at Lew and then added, "Hang on a sec."

"Lew," I asked him, "what's the road closest to the tracks?"

"Exchange Street, but it connects to Route 7, so if you wish to not see all the commotion, perhaps another road might be preferable. A little farther west, there is a small covered bridge over Otter Creek, where Pulp Mill Road becomes Morgan Horse Farm Road. That is a far more discreet way of leaving town."

I paused before keying the mike again. Twenty minutes ago, I'd told Rarig our little clandestine operation had come to an end. That ambition hadn't changed, but I was acutely conscious of the mess we'd left behind. I was in no mood to deal with the Middlebury police, or anyone else who'd been shot at today.

I returned to the radio. "Are you both in the clear?"

"10-4."

"With a vehicle?"

"I got mine back on its wheels," Sammie said. "We're in it now, laying low."

"Good." I gave them Lew's directions and told them we'd meet them at the bridge in about half an hour—give or take.

It was slow going. Neither of my companions was in the prime of youth, and the longer we walked the more we all discovered just how pummeled we'd been. Rarig's rib kept forcing him to stop and gasp for air.

In over the time I'd allotted, therefore, and after carefully pausing at both the railroad tracks and Exchange Street, which proved surprisingly busy, we limped across the small, two-way covered bridge Lew had mentioned and emerged to see Willy and Sam sitting in Sam's dented car by the side of a small, grassy traffic circle, caught in the anemic halo of a nearby streetlamp. They were alone.

Feeling utter relief at last, not even curious why neither of them got out of the car to greet us, I escorted my two battered charges up to the back door and pulled it open.

A man with a gun was crouching in the rear seat. His accent made Lew's sound nonexistent. "Put up hands."

All three of us were too startled to follow orders. "What the hell?" I asked.

From behind me another voice, cultured and smooth, said, "Lieutenant Gunther, please do as he says. We don't have time to waste."

I turned around to face a tall, elegant man in a suit, flanked by two others, also carrying guns.

"Georgi," Lew whispered in astonishment, half to himself.

The tall man nodded as his companions quickly frisked us. "Dimitri. It's been a very long time."

Corbin-Teich stiffened slightly. "It is not my name now."

The other ignored him, addressing me with a slight bow. "I am Georgi Padzhev. You have no doubt heard of me."

"Yeah."

Padzhev raised his hand and signaled to someone in the darkness. An engine started up, a pair of headlights came on, and a large sedan rolled up behind Willy's car.

Padzhev gestured to the three of us. "I think it would be a little less crowded if you joined me in this."

I looked at him for a moment, studying his placid features. He, like Rarig and Corbin-Teich, appeared to be in his mid-seventies, but he carried himself like a man a good ten years younger.

"I take it we don't have a choice," I commented.

He moved to the other car and politely opened its rear door. "That is correct."

19

GEORGI PADZHEV SMILED AT ME. "JOSEPH GUNTHER—THAT I CAN recall without difficulty. Rarig and Corbin-Teich feel strange on the tongue. Dimitri, whatever possessed you to use Lew Corbin-Teich? It is so distinctly odd. I thought the idea was to come up with something out of the melting pot—something to help you disappear."

Lew didn't answer. Rarig glared at Padzhev and said, "Save it, Georgi. What're we doing here?"

But Padzhev apparently needed to dominate us a bit more, which, considering we were all tied to our chairs, seemed a little superfluous. "John Rarig I like. It is not so peculiar. It looked good in that *New York Times* article—very masculine. Much better than Philip Petty. I'm assuming that was fictitious, also?"

Rarig merely sighed, seeing the futility of a response.

We were in a motel room, somewhere between Shelburne and South Burlington—the three of us plus Sam and Willy—all with our hands and feet secured with coat hangers—crude, effective, and very uncomfortable. Padzhev was flanked by two silent men with guns. A couple more were outside. A television set, its volume muted, was tuned to a local news program. Images of Middlebury, pulsating with the red and blue lights of emergency vehicles, played over and over again.

We'd driven here in three cars, including Sam's, and had entered the room without formalities, indicating it had been rented beforehand. It was one of many cheap motels lining Route 7, which was interspersed with the shopping malls, car lots, and fast-food franchises that give the area its anonymous identity. In a state as small as Vermont, where newcomers—foreigners especially—tend to stick out, this spot was almost unique with its urban tendency to not notice or care. Padzhev had chosen well, at least for the short term.

He sat at the end of one of two beds, his elbows on his knees, his hands clasped before him, looking at us contemplatively. "What are you doing here? This is a good question. Do you have any idea of what has been going on?"

"Starting with Antonov?" I asked.

He shook his head slightly. "Antonov came over here because I wanted to speak with John Rarig—an old man's silly interest in the past, as it turned out. A folly. I meant the rest of it."

I wanted to draw him out—have *him* paint the picture for us. Rarig, his old cold warrior juices stirred, obviously thought otherwise.

"Edvard Kyrov took advantage of that folly to get you out from behind your defenses, knowing you wouldn't leave Antonov unavenged."

Padzhev nodded appreciatively. "Did you hide his body to protect me, John?"

Rarig's face hardened. "More to spare myself some grief."

I moved to defuse the tension slightly. "He was afraid Antonov had been dumped on his front lawn as some kind of warning, or a threat," I explained in a neutral voice.

Padzhev straightened, cupping his cheek in his palm. "There is a good deal of paranoia among people like us. It was an understandable reaction."

He rose and began pacing the floor. "Fortunately, it served both ends. Kyrov laid his plans carefully and well. Had it not been for your unintentional meddling," here he looked at Rarig, "I and my men would have been dead long ago, ambushed as we appeared at your inn to inquire about poor Antonov. Sad to say, that piece of good luck has not been enough. Certain elements have been conspiring simultaneously against me back in Russia, resulting in my having to confront them here, or not at all."

"You're talking about a showdown with Kyrov," Rarig challenged, his eyes bright.

Padzhev stopped pacing. "Yes. If I do not face him here, I will never survive the trip back, as you said, behind my defenses. That door has been shut tight."

I thought back to the countless conversations I'd had trying to root out this simple story—through all the complexities that had continuously blocked my way.

"So it was Kyrov who framed me?" I blurted. "To keep me out of the way and distract everyone from the Antonov case?" Despite the lies I'd been fed, I was still hoping I'd recognize the truth when I finally heard it.

Padzhev looked at me almost pitifully. "No. That was me. A couple of my men bypassed your home's security system, placed the gem in your pocket, staged the burglary, and let your colleagues leap to conclusions, helped, I must admit, by a small donation to Henri Alonzo's bank account, in exchange for some theatrical raving. I needed breathing room as much as Kyrov."

He suddenly looked amused. "Although you almost upset the applecart, pulling out your gun in the middle of the street and waving it around. You scared poor Nicolai half to death."

I stared at him in disbelief.

He studied my expression for a moment, and then asked, "Why did you do that, incidentally? He was only tailing you. It seemed like such an overreaction."

I closed my eyes—no wonder he'd vanished without a trace. "What about the attempt on my life in Washington?" I asked.

Now he was the one looking confused. "What attempt? That would not have served me in any way."

"Nicolai didn't try to kill me there?"

"No. He's never been to Washington. He was tailing you home so he could plant the brooch later."

"Snowden arranged the hit on you," Rarig stated flatly.

But Padzhev gave him a quizzical look. "There's a name from the past. Why would he?"

"Stop it," I shouted in frustration, sensing the same fruitless cycle starting over again. "What're you going to do with us? Why're we being held?"

Padzhev sat back down. "Yes, well, that is pertinent enough. I need your help."

For the first time, Willy stirred. He laughed sharply and said, "Right—that's pretty fucking likely."

Georgi Padzhev smiled again. "It might be. Lieutenant Gunther, I gather you have a particular friend named Gail. Isn't that correct?"

"You son of a bitch," I said softly.

"Perhaps," he only partially agreed. "But I need to be extremely practical at the moment. As you might imagine, I have much to lose right now, so I'm inclined to be quite ruthless. Your friend Gail hasn't a hope of living unless you lend me a hand. That goes for all of you."

"I don't think so," Willy said. "She may be his big squeeze. She means squat to me."

Padzhev didn't even look at him. "Quite. So, Lieutenant, do we proceed?"

"Doing what?" I asked. "I'm not in a position to help anyone do anything."

"There you are mistaken. You have access to information, to manpower, to equipment. You also have a knowledge of the local terrain and its occupants. For outsiders like myself and my companions, those are significant assets. And it is my belief that so long as I control Ms. Zigman, you and your colleagues—regardless of any belligerent outbursts—will be of assistance."

Sammie finally broke her long silence. "How do we know you have her?"

Padzhev nodded to one of his men, who stepped out of the room, leaving the door barely ajar. Moments later, the man I'd pulled my gun on in traffic stepped inside. In the bright light, the similarity between him and my supposed Washington mugger was vague at best. But I no longer cared. Next to him was Gail, her hands tied behind her back, her mouth covered with tape. They filled the doorway long enough for us to recognize her, and then they vanished. Only the memory of her eyes boring into mine remained.

The effect of this on me at first was too big to handle. Seeing Gail trussed up, her eyes filled with desperate appeal, I knew her panicky memories, like mine, were filled with images of past violence and impotence. It went beyond anger, frustration, or shock. Combined with the psychological beating I'd already taken, it felt like a confirmation of doom.

But only for a moment.

During the next few minutes, like the survivor of a presumed lethal fall, I began feeling the initial, choking upsurge of fear draining out of me, to be replaced by a numb single-mindedness. The legal and moral complexities that had once all but stopped me cold faded next to my need to help Gail. With one move, Georgi Padzhev had suddenly simplified my life. It occurred to me, in one of those odd asides one often makes amid crisis, that he must have been quite good at his job.

"What would you like me to do?" I asked him, surprised at the steadiness of my voice.

He smiled at his success. "I need more than just you, Lieutenant." He eyed Sammie and Willy behind me.

Sammie didn't hesitate. "I'm in," she said, sounding stronger than I knew she felt.

"You can go fuck yourself," was Willy's response.

Padzhev's pleasure merely increased. "Excellent. I will share with you a little of my predicament, so you can see for yourselves what I need."

He resumed his restless pacing. "I am, as they say, a stranger in a strange land—land that Edvard Kyrov chose well before my arrival. I am hoping that advantage has also made him overconfident."

He paused to look at me directly. "He has been whittling away at my forces from the moment I arrived, and I think he may be about to launch a final assault, which he will no doubt do as soon as he learns of my precise whereabouts. What I hope to do is to use that momentum to his disadvantage—to select a site, attract him into it, and eliminate him using means he won't suspect I have."

"And which you're hoping we'll supply," I suggested.

He bowed in appreciation. "Exactly. What I'm looking for is the type of device your police forces use to track your opponents, along with the expertise to operate it."

Willy burst out laughing. "A bug? You want us to bug the guys who're after you? You been watching too many movies."

"Actually," I quickly added, and I hoped diplomatically, "what you're referring to is usually only available to larger departments. We've never had anything like that."

Padzhev gave us a long appraising look, obviously reassessing our usefulness.

I tried to buy us a little time. "What did you have in mind, anyway? How were you thinking of planting them on Kyrov's people?"

He frowned and waved his hand idly. "Oh, we have a fairly good idea where a couple of them are, from time to time. Our numbers aren't great enough to turn that to any tactical advantage, but if we could get close enough to attach such a device to even one of their vehicles, then we might use it to find the others until, eventually, they all could be either tagged or eliminated."

He was rubbing his chin with one of his knuckles, lost in his own thoughts. The unlikeliness of his scheme suggested the limitation of his options—a point belied by his calm manner—and it occurred to me that if, in fact, we did turn out to be useless to him, our lives were basically forfeit. He was struggling to stay alive—not to win some abstract advantage over his enemy— which, as ironies had it, meant it was up to us to supply him with hope.

Luckily, Sammie did just that. "I have an idea," she said, the nervousness in her voice showing she'd reached the same conclusion I had.

Padzhev looked up at her. "Yes?"

"There is a way to track people using satellites. It's called the Global Positioning System, or GPS—"

Padzhev scowled. "We are fully aware of what it is, Miss. It is not my interest to know where *I* am on a map. I wish to know where *they* are."

"I know, I know," Sammie protested. "Let me finish. It's not hard to turn that around—to plant a GPS transmitter on someone, and then receive that signal off a satellite to find out where he is. Biologists do it to track migration patterns."

Padzhev's expression cleared. "The collars they put on animals. Of course. And you have access to that equipment?"

Again, Willy laughed, but Sammie protested loudly. "Yes, we do. It's not connected to our department, but I know where to get it."

I hadn't the slightest idea what she was talking about. She had recently been involved in helping the Brattleboro selectmen establish new "no-fire zones" within the town borders, to limit the possibility of firearms accidents in and out of hunting season, but that had involved mapmaking, not GPS.

"How do you plan to do this?" Padzhev asked her.

She shook her head. "I tell you, you won't need us anymore."

His eyes narrowed. "I told you I needed your expertise as well."

"And I don't trust you farther than I could spit."

He pursed his lips. When he spoke again, the tension in him was easier to see. "I don't have time to negotiate. If you wish to die right now, fine. If you wish to live a little longer, then go get what you need. It is your choice to believe me or not, but I will tell you that if I make it out of your country alive, you will be set free. What I'm asking you to do will be in the best interests of all of us. Edvard Kyrov and his people will not be so inclined. It is your choice."

"I want the Lieutenant with me," Sammie said.

Padzhev didn't hesitate. "Fine, but I keep all the others, and I give you an escort." He leaned forward and cocked his head toward the TV set. "And keep this in mind: there are no guarantees. Kyrov is no longer the only person looking for us. Everything depends on your speediness. The more time you take, the more imperiled we all become, and I will not hesitate to eliminate your friends if I feel either Kyrov or the police are too close."

I saw Sammie's jaw harden as she stared back at him. "We're wasting time."

We drove back to Brattleboro in one of Padzhev's cars, with Sammie and me in front and one of the Russian gunmen in the back. He didn't say a word the entire trip, but neither of us assumed he couldn't speak English. Not that we cared anyway. Our course had been chosen for us.

Which naturally made me think of how other people were faring.

"Does anyone in the department know you went up to Middlebury?" I asked.

I watched her in the dim glow of the dashboard. It wasn't quite dawn, and we'd all been through the wringer. She was strained with fatigue and tension, and I wondered how much longer she could function on nerves alone.

"Ron was supposed to be faking things for us," she said. "He refused not to play some part, and we thought we'd be back before he got into trouble. Considering the shootout, though, I think we can kiss that idea good-bye. Plus, not only did Willy abandon his vehicle when he smacked that other car's rear end, but he identified himself when he called for backup. The chief may've been playing silent partner to our little escapade, but he's going to have a tough time covering for this one."

"I am sorry," I murmured.

Sammie's voice took on a false heartiness. "Nothing to apologize for. You've been shafted from the start. As far as I'm concerned, I'm still doing my job."

"That might not hold up in court."

"Yeah, well . . ." She turned toward me suddenly. "You're going to have to keep a low profile when we hit town. Coffin made sure your picture's plastered all over the place, like a regular Jesse James."

"What's the plan, by the way?" I asked. "Or does present company make that a bad question?"

For the first time in too long, she smiled broadly. "Hell, no. In fact, the more the merrier." She looked up into the rearview mirror and said loudly, "Hey, Vladimir. You speak English? 'Cause you better be a part of this if you want your boss's plan to work."

The man's response was slow and heavily accented. "My name is Anatoly."

"Good. Pay attention. We're going to hit up an outfit called Cartographic Technologies for what we need. They're civilians—high-tech mapmakers. Came in on the wave of the computer revolution. They use mapping to piggyback other data— demographics, vegetation distribution, political affiliations, watersheds, even 911 addresses. They work in the same building we do, upstairs, and they got computers and printers and fancy Internet connections up the wazoo. What

I'm thinking is, we approach them like this whole thing is a superse-cret, high-security undercover job—that all this publicity about Joe has been a smoke screen to get the drop on some bad guys. We can make 'em Russian and pretend you're an adviser from the feds. You understand?"

Anatoly merely nodded.

"What makes you think they'll have what we need?" I asked.

"They were the ones who documented the no-fire zones. We got friendly, since I like all that gadgetry, and they showed me a lot of the other stuff they do. That's when I saw one of those transmitters."

I was doubtful, but I kept it to myself. Whether she believed in her own plan or not, Sammie had bought us time, and right now that was good enough. If Padzhev was heading for the kind of fight he described, anything was possible, including our being able to get Gail and the others out of harm's way.

It was still dark when we reached Brattleboro, and drizzling slightly—that predawn hour when, from my days as a young patrol-man, I'd always envisioned the buildings and empty avenues as parts of an abandoned, life-size train set—an image enhanced by the traffic lights endlessly, quietly blinking, cautioning no one—blurry washes of red or yellow flashing dully on the scarred shiny surface of the streets.

Sammie headed toward Grove Street—and the entrance to the Municipal Building's parking lot—but passed it by, pulling onto Wil-liston just beyond—a rarely traveled, narrow, one-way street, which, after she'd killed our lights, turned as black as any urban back alley.

We moved silently on foot across the front of the intervening State Office Building to the edge of our parking lot, pausing in the gloom of the bordering trees to watch for any activity. Given the police depart-ment's location on the ground floor, it seemed to me an enormous risk to use the rear entrance, even assuming the usual skeleton crew was hunkered down over coffee or filling out reports.

But that wasn't Sammie's intention. She led us not to the rear but to the side of the building and a broad metal fire escape leading up to a locked steel door on the second floor. There she paused, extracted a set of keys from her pocket, fitted one to the lock, and let us in.

She smiled at me as she quietly pulled the door to, explaining the unauthorized key. "Thought it might come in handy someday."

The second floor was dimly lighted and as still as a tomb. The three of us walked halfway down its length before ducking into a dead-end alcove, stoppered by a glass-paned door marked "Cartographic Technologies."

Sammie tried the knob, found it locked, and dug a wallet out of her back pocket. From it, she extracted a thin piece of rigid steel wire with a hook on the end. I wondered if she and Willy weren't spending too much time together.

Instead of picking the lock, however—a movie stunt I'd never seen work in real life—she slipped the wire between the door and the jamb, searching for the lock's button release mounted along the edge. There was a distinct snap; Sammie straightened, turned the knob, and ushered us across the threshold. Anatoly remained silent throughout, but I caught him giving Sammie an admiring glance.

We entered a single, large, high-ceilinged room, ghostly pale from the streetlights below filtering through a long wall of tall windows. The room's center was occupied by a large table, strewn with dimly perceived papers, and all around the periphery, squatting like toadstools on every available flat surface, was a tight row of softly contoured, mismatched computers, monitors, printers, scanners, fax machines, and other things I couldn't identify, all dark and silent except for a scattering of green and amber operational pilot lights that took us in like the eyes of patient beasts. There was a quiet, steady hum in the room and the faint odor of warm plastic.

"Now what?" I asked, still looking around.

"We wait till they show up," Sammie answered. "There's an old vault in the far corner there—they use it for storage—but it'd be a good place to stash ourselves, just in case someone else walks in."

We carefully followed the direction she'd indicated, found the room-sized vault, and borrowed three office chairs to make ourselves comfortable, surrounded by piles of boxed documents and rank upon rank of rolled-up maps.

* * *

Three hours later, only Anatoly was left sitting in a chair. Sam and I had made beds of the boxes and were fast asleep when our silent companion shook us awake, his finger to his lips. We could hear outside the vault, now tainted with the pallor of early morning light, people entering the outer room, laughing, talking, and moving things around.

Sammie sat up, rubbed her eyes, and moved her tongue around the inside of her mouth. "Christ," she whispered. "Wish I could brush my teeth."

Yawning, she stood up, stretched, and added, "Let me go in first. Might cut down on the heart attacks."

With her departure, Anatoly exhibited the first signs of nervousness I'd witnessed so far. He sidled up to the doorway, his face tense and his right hand under the flap of his jacket, resting, I was sure, on the butt of a gun.

After a small outburst of surprised chatter and a few laughs, Sammie stuck her head back into sight and invited us out.

Standing in the middle of the room were two very tall, slim women, both with bright red hair and freckles. I'd seen them before in the corridor—God knows they were hard to miss—but never realized they worked here.

Sammie made the introductions: "This is Abby and Judy Coven— the sister act of Cartographic Technologies. My boss, Joe Gunther, and our colleague Anatoly, who's playing a little coy with his real identity."

Abby, the one with the most hair—a flaming bush that almost engulfed her head—raised her eyebrows. "Ooh, that sounds interesting."

Judy, a little shorter, and with straight hair in a pageboy, looked at me and added, "Especially in the company of the most wanted man in Windham County." Her expression was considerably less appreciative than her sister's.

Sammie scratched her cheek. "Yeah, well, that's what we'd like to talk to you about. You expecting anybody this early? Any meetings or anything?"

Judy shook her head. "No, why?"

Sammie walked over to the front door, which was shielded from view by a freestanding room panel. "I was wondering if it would be all right to lock the door, just while we're talking."

Judy didn't answer, but Abby was obviously intrigued. "Sure. We have a clean slate till eleven."

We heard the lock snap shut, and Sammie reappeared, wearing her most affable smile. "Why don't we all sit down?"

We ended up in a circle, parked on a variety of desk chairs, including the three we rescued from the vault. The arrangement reminded me of a therapy session.

Sammie cleared her throat. "The reason for all the cloak-and-dagger is that we're working undercover—probably the biggest case any of us has ever been on. That's why all the cock-and-bull about Joe. We had to make it look like he was on the run."

"You did a pretty convincing job," Judy said flatly.

"That was the point. If we hadn't, he couldn't've gotten in tight with the gang we're after."

Judy, like me, seemed to be trying to recall which television show this came from. "I hadn't heard about any gangs," she said.

"You wouldn't have," I spoke up. "We're not talking about street thugs wearing colors. This is bigger, and more dangerous." I jerked a thumb at Anatoly. "I don't want to go into too many details, but since we're asking for a favor, it's the Russian Mafia. Anatoly brought it to our attention. Vermont isn't great pickings for them, but it is a perfect place to lie low. And that's something we want to stop."

Judy still looked totally unconvinced. Her sister was smiling ear-to-ear. "This is great. What do you want from us?"

Sammie leaned forward in her chair. "Remember that GPS thing you showed me a while back—the satellite transmitter? We were hoping to use a few of those to track this gang's cars."

Judy surprised me by bursting out laughing. "This must be legit. Only the Brattleboro cops would think of bugging a car with a caribou collar. How in God's name were you going to attach the thing? Wrap it around the bumper?"

Sammie was taken aback, but I took hope from Judy's first show of interest. "Couldn't we hide it in the trunk, or somehow attach it underneath?"

"You could, but it wouldn't work. Those transmitters are line-of-sight devices. Their antennas have to be visible to the satellite for their signal to be picked up. They'd only work if you glued them to the roof." She paused and added, "Which might actually work if they're driving eighteen-wheelers, or some other tall truck."

There was a disappointed silence in the room until I asked, "You said, 'those' transmitters. Did that imply there're others?"

Abby smiled broadly, and before her sister could stop her, she blurted out, "Sure there are. We've got eight of them right here—"

Judy held up her hand. "Hold it. Hold it. How do we know what's going on here? We can't just give you a bunch of stuff and wave you out the door. Abby's talking about cutting-edge equipment—the hardware equivalent of Beta copies—samples. Companies lend them to us so we can work out the kinks. If they get into the wrong hands, we're in serious trouble."

"By 'wrong hands,' you mean competitors, right?" I asked. "That wouldn't be a problem here. These are crooks, not patent thieves."

"And," Sammie added, "we'll draw up a document right here and now, assuming total liability."

I resisted knocking her on the head for that one, nodding in agreement instead.

Abby got to her feet. "Come on, Judy. Lighten up. You know darn well we're expected to beat the shit out of those units—and lose 'em, too, if it comes to that. That's why we got 'em in the first place, *and* we signed a waiver."

She crossed the room to one of the cabinets, unlocked the top drawer, and returned with a plastic box. She opened it, extracted what looked like three small wafers, and laid one in each of our hands. "Latest technology. Designed to track birds in flight."

I cradled it in my palm, barely feeling its weight. "This talks to a satellite?"

Abby looked pleased at my incredulity. "Yup. And—what's better—it's more powerful than the collar we showed Sammie. I can't say we've ever put it in a car trunk, but the makers say it should work. We've only had 'em for a week or so."

I held it up to the light and examined it more closely. I then fixed Judy Coven eye-to-eye. "They would be perfect."

Judy bit her upper lip thoughtfully. "Abby's right," she finally admitted. "We're not at risk as much as I said. I would like that document, though, in case things do go sour. Companies like ours are plowed under all the time by one lawsuit or another, and I don't feel like joining them, especially over some deal you won't tell us anything about."

Sammie rolled her chair over to one of the desks and grabbed a sheet of paper. "Done."

I turned the wafer over to Abby Coven. "How do they work, exactly?"

She dropped it back into the plastic box. "The tradeoff is the power supply. The larger units can emit pretty much a continuous signal, so the satellite can track it around the clock. Depending on the size and configuration of the battery, the unit will work from a few days to several months. These little guys can't do that. They talk to the satellite periodically. The less they talk, the more the power source lasts. We heard they've used units kind of like these on monarch butterflies. 'Course, those emitted only once every few days, so they'd last for weeks. In any case, the rate of frequency can be programmed in."

"And how are they picked up by you?"

This time, it was Judy who rolled her chair across the floor, stopping before one of the computers, which she switched on. "The technology is called GIS, for Geographical Information System. Just as an example, here's a grid of downtown Brattleboro." She tapped on the keyboard a few times, and brought up a colorful, slightly fuzzy version of a topo map, with the elevations marked in earth-colored hues, complete with a shadowing effect that made the screen look three-dimensional. I instantly recognized the confluence of the West and Connecticut Rivers, with the looming mass of Mount Wantastiquet hovering on the New Hampshire border.

"What we receive from the sending unit—via the satellite—," Judy continued, "are the coordinates for latitude and longitude. Those are logged into the computer and appear on the screen as a single white blinking dot."

A dot like what she'd just described magically presented itself. "I'm cheating here," she said. "The units aren't activated, so I just entered in some data. The fastest those wafers can work is once every ten minutes, so every ten minutes you'd get a new dot on the screen, assuming the unit was moved."

"How long will the battery last at that rate?" I asked.

Judy looked up at me. "I don't remember. We haven't really fooled with these much."

"A week," said Abby from behind us. "That long enough?"

It wasn't a question that bore much thought. "Should be," I said.

I tapped the screen with my fingernail. "You can call up all of Vermont, just like you did Brattleboro?"

"Yup."

I pointed to several small boxes containing numbers. "These are the coordinates?"

Judy hesitated. "That's where they'd show up. This is fake, though—I mean, I wrote them in. Real data looks different. It fluctuates a lot. The Department of Defense corrupts all satellite-linked GPS readings somewhat—some kind of paranoid antimissile hangover from the Cold War. They call it 'selective availability.' Part of the program here corrects for that, though, so it's nothing much to worry about."

Anatoly spoke for the first time, slowly and carefully. "This is legal, outside the military?"

I laughed, thinking of how improbable that would seem to a life-long resident of the old Soviet Union. "Yeah—pretty neat, huh?"

I turned back to both Coven sisters, suddenly concerned, and pointed at the oversize computer. "The problem is, though, that all this only works if you've got one of those and know how to work it. Isn't that right?"

Judy's hands fell from the keyboard and she looked at the screen in a new light. "Yes. I'm afraid so."

"Where're you going to be operating from?" Abby asked.

Sammie and I glanced at each other and then at Anatoly, who gave a barely perceptible shrug. "We don't know yet. It might be dangerous, though. You couldn't be there, if that's what you were thinking."

Abby smiled. "I like a good time, but I'm not *that* interested. Maybe we could manage it all from here and send you the results."

That piqued Sammie's interest. "How?"

"Simplest way would be over the Net—as e-mail. It would be slow, but unless you have the right equipment and a trained operator, I don't see how else it would work. This way, all you'd need was a laptop with a modem and access to a phone line."

"And you two at the other end," I added. "I don't know how that part would work. If things got hairy, you could be spending a lot of time in that chair."

The Covens exchanged looks.

Anatoly pulled at my sleeve and whispered, "This is not good."

I got up and walked with him to another part of the room, keeping my voice low. "Maybe not, but it's all we got. You can stay here with them, babysit us, or tell your boss you canceled the whole idea on your own."

He didn't answer, his choice already clear.

"Could be good publicity," Sammie was coaxing the two sisters.

I was amazed at her callousness. In point of fact, these women could also end up with their reputations and business ruined. But I added, almost instantaneously, "And maybe some compensation. I know better than to speak for the chief on financial matters, but we've found money before for emergencies like this."

After a telling silence, Judy finally nodded. "Okay, what the hell. I'm assuming you don't have a laptop?"

We all shook our heads.

"We'll set you up with everything, then. Just make sure a full inventory is added to that document you drew up."

Sammie laughed at the pure absurdity of the suggestion. "You got it."

20

GEORGI PADZHEV OPENED THE DOOR OF THE MOTEL ROOM HIM-self, his eagerness transparent. "Did you get what we need?"

Sammie, entering behind me, hefted the canvas bag she had looped over her shoulder.

Rarig and Corbin-Teich were sitting at a table in the corner, their hands free. Willy, I noticed with no surprise, had only graduated from coat hangers to his own handcuffs, his muscular right wrist still attached to his chair.

"Where's Gail?" I asked.

Padzhev gave me a distracted look, reaching for Sammie's bag. "She's fine."

I stepped in front of him and slapped his arms down. Anatoly immediately grabbed me from behind and shoved a gun in my ear. I kept looking at Padzhev. "Where is she?"

The muscles in his face quivered briefly as he fought for self-control. He then muttered something fast and harsh to Anatoly, who steered me outside, down the walkway, and into the abutting room. Gail was sitting up on one of the beds, no longer bound or gagged, but looking like hell. A guard was lounging in a seat by the window.

Anatoly said, "You have two minutes," and shoved me toward the bed, taking up a station by the door.

I sat next to her and took one of her hands in mine. "How're you holding up?"

She smiled wanly. "If I knew you'd be this much trouble when we met, I don't think I would've made the effort."

That cut deeper than she'd intended. I looked at the floor, thinking how right she was.

She touched my cheek. "Joke, kiddo—I wouldn't change a thing."

"I wouldn't blame you if you did. I wish the hell I could."

"What's going on, anyway?"

"It's boiling down to an old-fashioned shoot-out between two rival Russian gangs. I'm just hoping we all get out of it alive."

"Who's 'we'?"

"You, me, Willy, and Sam, plus some guy from Middlebury and John Rarig. They might have more hostages than they got soldiers by now."

She watched my face for a long moment, and then asked, "It's pretty bad, isn't it?"

"It could be. I've been told so many lies by now I'm the last one to know what's what. But I think the top guy here—Georgi Padzhev—is fighting to stay alive, pure and simple. He's far from his base, cut off and outnumbered, and so desperate for help he's got us working for him."

Her face registered surprise. "How?"

"He's holding you over my head. Sammie and I just got him a fancy bugging system he's hoping will tell him when the opposition's too close. I don't know what the hell good it'll do."

Anatoly pushed himself away from the doorframe and tapped his wristwatch.

I kissed Gail and stood up. "I love you. I'll do what I can."

She nodded and smiled encouragingly. "I know."

Back in the first room, Padzhev had spread his new toys on one of the beds. Rarig and Corbin-Teich were standing at its foot, looking like two spectators at a game of solitaire.

"This is quite excellent, Lieutenant," he said as I entered.

"Sammie fill you in?"

"Yes, she did. I hope we can rely on your two operatives in Brattleboro."

"You can send somebody down there to shoot one of them as insurance, if you want."

He looked away from the computer and the small pile of wafer-thin transmitters and fixed me with a stare. "I will if you think it necessary, just as I will shoot your girlfriend in the head if you step out of line."

I stared back, feeling my face flush. It was time for me to do everything possible to avoid such confrontations—to be amenable, affable, and helpful. To fade into the woodwork until I saw an opportunity to act.

"I appreciate that," I finally said and jutted my chin toward the electronic pile on the bed. "How do you plan to use this stuff?"

His study of me lasted a few seconds longer, before he stepped away and resumed his nervous pacing. "From what I understand, the best advantage it gives us is if we occupy a stationary position."

"That's true," Sammie agreed. "If we were getting the information in real time, it might not be, but since it's going to be e-mailed to us, that'll slow everything down. Our staying put means that much less data to be crunched down and forwarded."

Padzhev paused by the bed and picked up one of the transmitters again, turning it over in his hand. "So we are the fort and they are the attacking army—a fort before which they will abandon their vehicles and render all this utterly useless." He tossed it back, barely hiding his disgust.

"That was plan A," I suggested, "when we thought we were dealing with much clunkier transmitters. What we need is to find a way to plant the bugs on the people, not their cars."

He gave me a sour look. "If we could do that, Lieutenant, we could also kill them, which happens to be the whole point of this exercise."

"We have to figure out a way they'll pick up the bugs themselves," Sammie said, stimulated, I thought, by Padzhev's worsening mood, which was beginning to concern me, too. "Like the Trojan horse."

He lifted his face, intrigued. I felt we'd become courtiers to his fickle king, finding any way possible to prop up his spirits—and extend our own lives.

"How?" he asked, reasonably enough. "What would they want of ours?"

"Weapons," I answered.

There was dead silence in the room. "The one thing you both have in common, as you pointed out," I continued, "is you want to kill each other. If you leave behind a cache of arms—like they'd been abandoned in a panic—they'll probably be picked up and distributed."

He frowned. "And used against us."

"A few extra aren't going to make much difference. We only have eight bugs. We could plant them in eight gun butts."

"Screw up the sights," Rarig suggested.

Padzhev shook his head. "They would check for something like that. The Lieutenant is quite right—they must be of obvious value."

He buried his hands in his pockets and leaned back against the bathroom door, taking us in like a challenging teacher. "So now we are in need of a fort with walls a mile thick—someplace we can control, where we know the terrain, and into which our opponents will have to penetrate on foot, allowing us to intercept them by eavesdropping on their positions."

"Someplace high and lonely?" Corbin-Teich asked softly.

Rarig looked at him meaningfully. It struck me then that Corbin-Teich had been almost mute since being bundled in here with the rest of us, overwhelmed and perhaps quite frightened by all the fireworks. Or so I'd thought.

Padzhev watched him carefully. "You know of such a place?"

"With only one narrow road, eight miles long," Lew admitted, sounding like he was reaching far back in time.

Rarig seemed to have made the same decision I had, about buying time with cooperation. "You have a map?" he asked. "I know where he's talking about."

Padzhev didn't move, but one of his men immediately produced a road map of the state, spreading it open at the foot of the bed. Rarig leaned over it, slowly extending his finger and tapping it in the middle of Vermont's so-called Northeast Kingdom, a remote, sparsely populated, harsh, and beautiful area, famous for its desolate, forested land and the independence of its inhabitants.

"There's a mountaintop here that might suit your needs," he said. "It worked for us forty years ago."

I suddenly remembered what he'd told me earlier of how and why
Lew had come to know Vermont. "That the old radar site you were
talking about? Where he was held under wraps for two years?"
Lew smiled wistfully. "It was well known for good hunting."
The irony of that was lost on no one.

Rarig's mountain was as empty and unmolested as he and Corbin-
Teich had foretold, but their description had missed the hostile vast-
ness of the place. As we drove in a caravan up miles of narrow, broken,
blacktopped road, the edges of which disappeared into the bordering
vegetation like liquid, I began feeling we'd left one world for another.
Vermont is famous for its trees and mountains, but mostly as a backdrop to a rural domesticity that has stamped the state for well over a
hundred years.

The reality of Rarig's radar mountain was something else entirely.

The Kingdom, of course, has always been a separate entity from
that other, bucolic image. Poorer, colder, and less inhabited than the
rest of Vermont, it remains the most stalwart reminder of the Ice Age's
grinding havoc. Where sections just slightly south and west of it reflect
the ease of long summers, gentle springs, and recreational winters,
the Kingdom stays aloof. Hard, harsh, and stark, it is the symbol of
what has given New Englanders their tough reputation. This mountain
reflected all of that, and more.

The entrance to its single access road had been subtlety itself—a
winding country lane, dotted with the occasional modest home,
gradually becoming narrower, darker, and less friendly. By the time
we'd reached the first of two unlocked steel gates, it was clear we were
no longer among the inhabitants of this region. Where once military
trucks had rumbled freely back and forth, trees now crowded the
ragged edge of a scarred pavement barely wide enough for a single car.
Overhead, blocking the light, branches reached out for one another
like slow-moving dancers.

Had the road been dirt, as they are all over the state, the contrast
would have been less jarring—we'd have been using yet another temporary man-made incursion into the wilderness, prone to washouts,

overgrowth, and winter's annual ravages. But this was a government-built road, still in remarkably good shape, lying on the ground like some vestige of a vanished civilization. I thought of Mayan ruins, ghost towns, and abandoned factory buildings—images of hopes lost, people displaced, ambitions thwarted—and the dread that had been rising in me since leaving the motel in South Burlington suddenly overflowed.

Padzhev had chosen to make that motel room the means to deliver the eight doctored weapons, faking a scene of hasty retreat. He hadn't told us how he'd tipped Kyrov to our whereabouts, but the urgency with which we'd left had injected a mood of genuine desperation in everyone. Padzhev, it was clear, was gambling everything on this tactic, and as we drove farther up the mountain, leaving a familiar world behind, it occurred to everyone, I think, that our chances of returning alive were very slim.

Rarig had told us this mountain was one of the tallest in the Kingdom, and the higher we drove the more easily I believed him. Not only did occasional gaps in the trees reveal views stretching for dozens of miles, but the vegetation began to reflect an exposure to unremitting harshness. Like hundreds of other sites strung out along the nation's eastern coast like baubles on a necklace, this radar installation had been chosen for the breadth of sky available to it—sky that also carried snow and wind and rain from miles away, sometimes at terrible velocity. The more we climbed the more the trees, the bushes, and even the boulders took on a hunkered-down appearance, like the shoulders of miners kept too long in the pit.

The temperature, too, spoke of altitude and exposure, and I slowly realized a threat none of us had considered during our beleaguered calculations. It was nearing the start of fall, when the weather could turn capricious, and nowhere else in the state was that more likely than right here—exposed on a mountain in Vermont's bleakest environment.

Unless we were lucky, and the elements held off, none of us had enough warm clothing to survive what was dished out so commonly in these hills. And through the open window of the car, the tang of brittle cold air told of a coming menace.

* * *

Apart from where we'd dropped off two sentries on the way in, our first stop came about eight miles up. The road suddenly widened, the trees pulled back, and we found ourselves on a broad shelf of land—flat, overgrown, and appointed with a broad, tidy scattering of bruised and discolored Quonset huts, their rigid uniformity at odds with the raging growth crowding around them—weeds, bushes, and stunted trees had overtaken once-mowed yards and trimmed walkways, making the whole look like a long-abandoned playground.

Rarig and Corbin-Teich stood by the cars, the latter transfixed by the metamorphosis of a place he'd once known as a small but bustling military base.

I walked over to them. "Big change?"

Corbin-Teich seemed in shock. "This was the United States to me. Men in green and khaki. Everything 'shipshape.' It was I who mowed many of the lawns here, just so I could do something."

"How many people lived here?" I asked, impressed at the number of buildings.

Rarig shrugged. "Two hundred, maybe, give or take fifty. I don't know. It was a small village, really—housing, mess, dispensary, mail room, all the rest." He jerked his thumb toward the cloud-shrouded peak above us. "The installation is another two miles up. After satellites replaced radar stations in the sixties, they sold the whole thing to a couple who tried turning it into a toy factory. They could've done it, too, except that the woodchucks drove 'em off the mountain—gangs on skimobiles, shooting guns, terrorizing them. In the wintertime, the snowdrifts get so deep, the huts turn into huge moguls, irresistible to the half-wit, twenty-something crowd. The locals figured since it was once government-owned, it now belonged to them. After the couple retreated back into the valley, the place was stripped clean, and what the punks couldn't steal, they destroyed." He shook his head. "Take a look around, assuming Prince Igor'll let you—you won't believe what people are capable of doing."

I wondered at his tour-guide tone of voice, but Rarig had progressed from the nervous excitement I'd seen grip him on our trip to

Middlebury. Now he seemed fatalistically resigned, as if his present situation was merely a logical, if delayed, extension of all that had gone before.

Padzhev overheard that last remark and approached us from a small conference he was having with the eight or so men he had left. "The prince has no objection. In fact, we need to find that telephone line you mentioned in the car, to see if it is connected."

"Should be," Rarig said. "The wardens still use it sometimes. We'll have to tap in down here, though, 'cause the only actual phone outlet is on top of the mountain, where the radar towers are."

"You seem to know a lot about it," I commented.

He smiled slightly. "Old man, old memories. I've come up here a couple of times since those days. This is one of the few old stomping grounds still available to me."

"You did not tell me," Corbin-Teich said.

"No. I figured your memories of the place were a little different from mine."

Padzhev gave instructions to his men, most of whom fanned out, and then turned to us, gesturing like a nanny urging her brood to run and play. "Go, go. We don't have much time to establish our defenses. Once Kyrov finds the map we left behind and convinces himself it isn't a trap, he'll be rapping on our door without much delay."

I glanced toward the car holding Gail and the still-handcuffed Willy Kunkle. A guard stood beside it with his arms crossed.

Padzhev shook his head. "No, Lieutenant. You may have some tender moment later on—perhaps. Right now, I need you out there." He pointed toward the overgrown compound.

With some imagination, I could still see what Lew had called home so long ago. I'd spent enough time on bases in the fifties to recognize the traces, as of dinosaurs in ancient soil. The huts were arranged like neatly placed railroad cars, among a grid of now patchy asphalt. Everything, although strictly utilitarian, had been built to last and had even endured the ravages Rarig had mentioned.

Not that considerable effort hadn't been made to destroy it. Every building I entered had been mauled by the passage of violence, frustration, and pain. Room after room was gutted—holes punched in the Sheetrock, heating ducts torn from the ceilings, floors pried up. The wiring was gone, the windows broken, the doors smashed, the tile bathrooms ritualistically reduced to rubble with sledges. Graffiti was everywhere, most of it vile and raging, lashing out at a world too far away to hear— or care.

And yet it all stood, often reduced to curved metal walls and foundation only—as seemingly indomitable a monument to human engineering as any Roman ruin. I could walk its shattered byways as tourists do in Pompeii, and as easily picture the place in its heyday, all the way down to the bustling communal dining room.

Anatoly found me standing in the middle of a particularly ravaged building, its insulation streaming from the rounded ceiling like stalactites. "You come," he ordered.

I followed him outside and across the compound to a small, nondescript building not far from the access road. Several of our group were standing around the gaping door. Beyond them, sitting in the gloom, was Sammie, the laptop balanced on her knees.

Anatoly gave an order and the group parted to let me pass. Padzhev was beside Sammie, looking unhappy.

"I'm not a phone technician," she was saying. "I'd feel a whole lot more comfortable if we just kept looking till we found a terminal point."

Padzhev addressed me as I entered. "This is a singularly inopportune time to start dragging our heels."

"Or to cut corners that could screw everything up," I answered. I turned to Sam. "He want you to splice into a line?"

"Yeah. It's stupid. Getting all this junk and running the risk of hooking it up wrong. Christ knows how many wires there are."

Rarig spoke up from outside. "You find the line?"

Sammie answered. "Yeah, but it's more like a cable. And there's no connection that'll fit the computer."

Rarig shoved his way inside, laughing. "No kidding. All this was state-of-the-art at the time—jam-packed with stuff. I can pretty much guarantee a connection at the top, though—that's where the few people who use this place call out from. Push comes to shove, and you still want to fight 'em off down here, you can direct things from above using a radio."

Padzhev scowled angrily and for the first time showed his mounting impatience. "God damn it. I want to see where those bastards are, not hear about it thirdhand." He shouted something in Russian and then said, "Get out. We'll go up."

We went in one car—Sammie, Padzhev, Rarig, and myself with one man driving. The others had been given orders to dig in, set up crossfire zones, and otherwise prepare for an onslaught. Nothing had changed in our status since we'd arrived here—the sentries below had reported nothing, and none of us had been given cause for alarm—but the tension was rising nevertheless, as it might have upon the approach of a hurricane on a sunny day.

The trip to the top was distinctly different from what we'd already seen. The road remained the same, but the bordering vegetation, from a hodgepodge of trees, brush, and meadow, now became a uniform stand of stunted, thick evergreens, giving the narrow road the appearance of a carefully groomed path in a tightly knit English garden maze. In contrast to the wild abandon of the compound's woodsy jungle, this looked almost lovingly maintained.

But it also had an ominous undertone, for the higher we climbed—turning corner after corner, always wondering what lay ahead—the more the clouds enveloping the peak began to press down upon us, decapitating the already low treetops and making us feel we were crawling between two unmovable forces, destined to be snuffed out entirely.

And there was no relief from this menace at the top, for as the trees finally pulled away, as if dragged down by the mist, there loomed out of the pale void three gigantic, towering, steel-clad structures—vaguely defined, unfamiliar in form or function, and utterly, threateningly immense.

"My God," murmured Padzhev, his eyes riveted outside the streaming windshield.

Instinctively, the driver stopped the car.

Only Rarig was smiling. "Impressive, huh? Those are the radar towers—five of 'em. Tallest one's sixty-five feet. The radar dome designed for that one would've made it look like a kitchen stool, but the whole site was decommissioned before they got it in place." He pointed to a sturdy shack ahead and to the right. "That's the telephone hut over there."

Our driver pulled over and we emerged into a freezing, wet, windblown environment that cut through our clothes and coated our faces with moisture. The air was a uniform gray, visibility extending to no more than one hundred and fifty feet.

Sammie looked around, her computer case held to her chest. "This is creepy—like a black-and-white sci-fi movie."

Ahead of us, as if in response, a metallic moaning was followed by a loud thump as a wide door swung open on a long, low-slung building across the road from the towers.

Rarig's only comment was "Old computer building, where the scope dopes number-crunched the radar data." He pointed to the shack's front door. "Someone's going to have to blast that lock off."

Padzhev nodded to the driver, who extracted a gun from under his coat, pointed it at the lock, and pulled the trigger as we all instinctively shied away. Absorbed by the mist, the shot sounded like a damp firecracker.

Padzhev pulled the door open and gestured Sammie through.

The interior was simplicity itself—four battered walls, one tiny barred window, and a shelf with a single phone line curled up on it like a garter snake, all covered with dust. Padzhev looked around, obviously baffled.

Rarig interpreted his expression. "With everyone leaving, and vandals tearing the place apart, this is all the powers-that-be want to waste money on. Even then, they have to replace the lock every once in a while. The wardens bring their own phones when they come."

Sammie put the computer on the shelf and clipped the phone line into its back.

"Guess we better let Olivia know where we are," I said casually.

Sammie's sole reaction was a minute hitch in her movements as she continued setting things up.

"Who's Olivia?" Padzhev asked.

"One of the two women at the other end of this deal," I explained, grateful Anatoly hadn't been chosen to join us. I glanced out the open door. "I doubt the computer's going to like all that humidity."

Padzhev growled at the driver, who stepped outside, closing the door behind him. One down, I thought.

Sammie looked around her. "Wish I had a chair. I can't type on this shelf."

Padzhev got the hint. "I'll go find something."

As soon as he left, Sammie turned to me. "Olivia Kidder?"

I kept my voice low. "What options have we got? This god-damn scheme of his isn't going to work. Sooner or later, Kyrov'll get the upper hand and eat us for lunch. We need help."

We heard voices outside the door as Padzhev shouted something to the other man.

"Set everything up, and if you get a few seconds to yourself, send an SOS to Judy to be forwarded to Kidder."

"Snowden'll probably intercept it," Sammie warned.

"Then e-mail Tony Brandt and make sure he gets briefed by Kidder. Somebody's going to have to tell the cavalry who's who up here."

The door crashed open, making us both jump, and Padzhev and the driver hauled a huge, dented steel box into the room. "Will this work?" he asked, panting.

Sammie perched herself on it, placing the computer on her lap. "Great. Thanks."

A nervous twenty minutes later, she looked up from the keyboard. "Got it."

Padzhev sat next to her and peered at the glowing screen. Floating in its middle, like an island on a black sea, was a multihued, three-dimensional slice of map, with a mountaintop at its center. "That's us?" he asked.

"Yup." She touched the screen with her fingertip. "We're right here, and that thin black line squiggling down there is the road. The Quonset village's here."

Padzhev stared at it as though it were a crystal ball, which we were all hoping it was. "No sign of anyone else?"

"Not yet. The two women at the other end are going to keep watching till they see a change. Then we'll get an update—assuming the Trojan horse worked. If it didn't," she added grimly, "then I guess the next thing we'll hear is a knock on the door."

21

WE WERE BACK IN THE VILLAGE IN ONE OF THE LESS DESTROYED huts, most of us bundled into piles around the floor, trying as best we could to keep warm and catch some sleep. Outside, in the darkness, Padzhev and his men had rigged a few booby traps around a marginally defensive layout, which I knew in my gut would finally prove futile. Sammie was stuck on the mountaintop, staring at her unmoving screen and no doubt feeling like a Popsicle by now.

I looped my arm around Gail's shoulders and she snuggled up closer, as much for the body heat as for the company.

"Joe?" she whispered.

Padzhev had finally left us alone together only a few minutes ago, and given the mood of our last conversation back in Brattleboro, we'd been taking our time getting reintroduced, letting body language do most of the work.

"Yeah?"

"What's going to happen?"

I gave her shoulder a squeeze, murmuring into her ear. "Nothing good. When all hell breaks loose, I'll do what I can to get us out of here, but it may be too late. I am sorry."

"You were hardly in control of things," she protested.

"I went to Middlebury."

"Versus what? Sitting around home waiting for the inevitable?"

I had nothing to say to that. What had seemed at the time like an act of independence was now looking more like the fate of a lemming. It wasn't something I could argue.

She sighed. "Well, I don't want to be here, but I'm glad we ended up in the same place at the same time. When you left— when you went underground—just after our fight, I couldn't believe how much it hurt. I hated what had been done to us. I didn't know if we'd ever see each other again, or how it would be if we did."

I laughed softly. "And now here we are—some romantic evening."

She kissed my cheek. "I'll take what I can."

But I'd felt her lips trembling.

I sensed it first, before I heard a sound, like the smell of a storm before the first drop of rain. I was already peering through the gloom at the hut's front door when a shadow darkened its threshold. I quickly shook Gail awake as Padzhev began issuing orders in Russian.

"Layer up—as many clothes as you can beg, borrow, or steal. We're headin' up the mountain."

I left her scrambling among the odds and ends we'd salvaged from the motel room, the car trunks, and each other and stumbled across the debris-strewn floor to where Padzhev was directing his men.

"My people and I are going up the road."

He looked at me irritably, interrupted in midsentence. "What? Why?"

"Sammie must've given the alert. We going to get weapons?"

He let out a sharp laugh. "That's not very likely."

"Then get us the hell out from under your feet."

One of his men asked a question. Padzhev's face contorted with pure rage for an instant, and I thought he might lash out. But he clamped it back down and pointed at the door instead. "One car for all of you, and one of my men goes along, with orders to kill anyone who steps out of line. Leave."

I pointed to Kunkle, who'd spent the whole night with his one arm cuffed high above him to one of the only solid pieces of plumbing still attached to the wall. "Him, too. Give me a key."

Padzhev swore in Russian, said something to the man next to him, and left us. The man silently handed me a handcuff key and went after his boss.

I jogged over to where Willy was sitting with his back against the wall. As I freed his hand, pale and cold to the touch, he snarled, "Fucking Russkies. If I didn't like 'em before, I hate 'em now."

He snatched his hand away as soon as I let go of it and buried it under his left armpit, briefly closing his eyes. "Jesus Fucking Christ."

I hooked his elbow and dragged him to his feet. "This is about to turn into a battlefield. We're heading for high ground. You got anything more to wear? It's going to be even colder up there."

He looked around, unsteady on his feet, and pointed to a ratty blanket. I threw it over his shoulders and steered him to where Gail had gathered Rarig and Corbin-Teich near the door. Our bodyguard, presumably a non–English speaker, watched us warily and gestured that we should head for the cars.

Outside, the first trickle of dawn's light had dampened the sky with a wash just pale enough to make the horizon stand out. Overriding that faint, mountain-etched line, however, was a low ceiling of clouds, far more bruised than what had enveloped the radar site the day before. We cut across to the cars, working our way through the tall weeds and underlying trash. Around us, Russian voices rang out in short bursts, and men could be seen running from one position to another as Padzhev fine-tuned his defense. At no point had we been given any idea of the numbers rallied against us, and at no point had I been led to believe it was anything less than twice our own forces.

We were bundled into a vehicle and driven up the now-familiar tree-encroached lane to the mountaintop. Halfway there, the mists of yesterday returned, wetter this time and worsened by a strong steady wind we hadn't felt in the village.

When we emerged from the car ten minutes later, however, the contrast was more fully revealed. The temperature, already unseasonably cold, had dropped another fifteen to twenty degrees, pushed there by gusts that forced us to avert our faces just to catch a breath. The few extra layers of clothing we'd scavenged were about as effective as tissue paper.

Bent over, our arms linked, Gail and I half-ran to the telephone shed. A guard Padzhev had left with Sammie met us at the door, weapon drawn, looking nervous. He held up his hand to stop us, but we brushed him aside and stepped into the shack. He didn't follow. Summoned by his colleague, he left to help escort the others into the nearest radar tower.

Sammie, encased in so many layers she looked like a ragtag, bloated snowman, was still sitting on her metal box, the computer on her lap. From what I could see of her face, she looked utterly exhausted.

I pulled the door closed behind us, cutting off the blast, if not the sounds of its buffeting as it hammered on the thin wooden walls.

"You okay?" I asked her.

Her voice was muffled by whatever it was she'd pulled across her mouth. "Yeah. Hey, Gail."

"Hey, yourself. You look like your clothes are the only things holding you up," Gail answered.

I could tell by the corners of Sam's eyes that she'd smiled. "Probably right. Take a look."

She swiveled the computer around so we could both see the screen. The familiar map face was there, but now it was covered with a spray of eight small white dots. They were most concentrated about halfway up the slope.

"Where is that?" I asked.

"The village's front door . . . Hang on. Another one's coming."

In response to a small beep from the machine, she hit a few keys, wiped out the picture we'd been looking at, and summoned its successor. It appeared in sections, stack by stack, slowly, with deliberate care. The end result showed the dots spread out, closer by.

"Inside?"

She glanced up at me. "Yup."

The radio yelped next to her, making both Gail and me jump— Padzhev shouting for an update. Sammie keyed the mike and calmly described the picture before her.

Several minutes later, the computer beeped again, starting the process all over again.

"Has this been worth it?" I asked, feeling distinctly odd about the true meaning of what we were watching.

"I know it doesn't look like it, but I think so. I saw 'em coming early on. I could tell Padzhev how to move his troops around. It'd be better if we knew that each dot stood for every bad guy, instead of a sampling, but it's better than nothing."

As soon as the picture became clear, she called Padzhev on her own and told him what had changed. "Plus," she then added, putting the radio back down, "it may have helped us. Remember that scrambling thing the Department of Defense does to GPS readings that Judy told us about? The selective availability? Last night, I got an e-mail from Abby Coven: She said she noticed the flickering in the numbers had quit all of a sudden—that her computer didn't need to correct them anymore. So she got on the Internet to ask around and found the selective availability on eight of the twenty-four satellites up there had been turned off—the eight servicing this part of the world."

I had told Gail of our subterfuge earlier. "Do you think it's Olivia Kidder?" she now asked.

The door burst open violently, helped by the wind, and the man I'd brushed aside stood before us, gun still in hand. "You come," he shouted.

I heard the computer beep yet again as we were hauled outside. "Hang in there, Sam. I'll be back," I shouted over my shoulder, unsure she'd been able to hear the second half of the sentence.

The guard, frustrated, angry, and obviously scared, pushed us toward the tallest tower. Clad in rusty, corrugated steel sheets, it stood hulking like some symbol of Armageddon, thrusting out of the earth like an enormous square column, its top swallowed whole by the gray, swirling mists. I wouldn't have been surprised upon entering it to find it extended both into the ground and straight up for thousands of feet.

Reality, of course, told otherwise. We were half-thrown into a dark, cold, thunderously noisy steel cube, the exact dimensions of the tower's footprint. The floor was concrete, the ceiling and twenty-foot-high walls metal. There was an enormous elevator shaft to one side, next to a steel-grid stairwell, and the biggest, most robust piece of scaffolding I'd ever seen running from the floor through the ceiling—presumably to support the huge radar dome Rarig said had never been put in place. Otherwise, the whole room looked like an abandoned warehouse building, utterly lacking the exterior's air of malevolence.

Rarig, Corbin-Teich, and Willy Kunkle were grouped together near the entrance to the stairwell, apparently waiting for us.

"How're things with Sam?" Willy asked.

"She's fine, but it's heating up in the village," I answered, just as my escort slammed me in the back with his hand.

"You *quiet*," he shouted.

"Up yours, asshole," Willy answered.

The other guard pulled Rarig by the sleeve and gestured up the stairs. "Go."

Rarig led the file, followed by Corbin-Teich, the guard, me, Gail, Willy, and the man who'd shouted at us.

The stairwell was totally encased—a square, metal, windowless silo—and the stairs themselves, made of welded, open gridding, stretched up out of sight into the pitch black void, switchback-on-switchback, lending an additional sense of fantasy to our climb.

Whether stimulated by this, his own natural restlessness, or some private grand plan, Willy, just shy of where visibility yielded to total blindness, suddenly announced, "Hey, boss. You sick of this shit yet?"

I caught his meaning instantly—a now-or-never chance to turn the tables, which, given our other options, sounded good to me. After the man behind Willy let loose with his expected *"Quiet,"* I yelled, *"Yeah,"* grabbed the right wrist of the Russian above me, swung him around, and slugged him in the gut. Out of the corner of my eye, I saw Willy spin on his heel, catch his man full in the face with his elbow, and send him tumbling down the stairs, his gun clattering against metal.

Willy had swung from the high ground, and his man had all but fallen into thin air. My position had been just the reverse. Even doubled over by my blow, my opponent landed up against the wall and then used it to brace himself. With my hand on his wrist, still held overhead, I found myself vulnerable to a good left hook to the ribs. The air rushed out of my lungs and my eyes filled with sparkling light.

Instinctively, I hit him close enough to the groin to make him pull back, and then Gail took over.

Standing below us, she grabbed his coat collar and hauled on it with all her strength, jamming her leg against the wall in the process. He staggered forward, caught his shin on her leg, and hurtled down the stairs. As he passed Willy Kunkle, Willy gave him one sharp, clean blow to the larynx. There was an odd sound from his throat, and he fell like a bag of rocks on top of his struggling companion.

All three of us were on them in an instant. Willy grabbed the gun from the dying man's hand and held it to the other's head, as Gail and I pinned him in place.

"*Don't move,*" Willy shouted.

The hapless Russian froze.

"Let me shoot the bastard."

I took a deep breath to clear my head. "Relax. It's over."

I frisked our victim, locating another pistol and a pair of handcuffs. I pulled them out, laced them through the railing, and snapped them around his wrists. "I think this'll be enough. Check the other guy."

The guttural noises had stopped coming from him. Willy groped for his pulse, said, "He's dead," and went through his pockets.

Gail had eased off the survivor and was sitting on one of the steps, her back against the cold, rattling wall. I leaned over and took her hand in mine. "Glad you were there. You did great."

She gave me a weak smile. "Compared to what?"

"We'll be finding out soon enough." I turned to Willy. "What'd you get?"

He held up two guns. "Plus extra magazines and another set of cuffs."

I stood and looked up at Rarig and Corbin-Teich, who'd been watching us in stunned silence. "You two keep climbing. John, you know what's up top?"

"Two more levels like the ground floor, then the roof. It's flat with a railing around it."

"Okay—top floor and wait. And take this." I handed him one of the guns. "Just make sure you know who it is before you shoot."

They began climbing into the total darkness above. I looked at Gail closely. "Your choice. Stick with us, or go with them."

She pointed at me.

Willy had peeled off the dead man's coat and jacket and now handed the former to Gail, donning the latter himself. She accepted it without comment. Her silence didn't trouble me too much, since I recognized the set of her face—she was in her version of combat mode, which I knew would stand her in good stead, at least for the moment.

I undid the other Russian's cuffs and ordered him to give up his coat. He did so without protest.

"You all set?" I asked Willy.

"You bet," he said, smiling broadly.

"Then let's see if we can find that other gun and go round up Sammie."

Outside, daylight was getting stronger—a dark pewter now—but the wind and the cold were as intense as before. We ran doubled-over to the nearby shack and piled inside like late arrivals to a departing elevator.

Sammie stared up at us in bewilderment. "What's happened?"

"The rats have grabbed the ship," Willy said. "What d'ya got there?"

She showed us the screen. "Padzhev just announced they're pulling back. He's got about three men left. They should be here any minute."

"Will the Covens know if you disconnect?" I asked.

Sammie's mouth half opened. She'd spent so much time here, bent over her screen, that it had probably become like a lifeline to her. "Yeah," she said tentatively.

I reached over and unclipped the phone cord from the back of the computer. "Then they're officially off the hook, and so are you. Let's go."

I helped her to her feet, dumped the computer on the shelf, and headed back over to the tower.

"Now what?" Willy asked, as we slammed the door against the wind.

I looked back at the access road through a crack in the door.

"We bolster our manpower. Get the guy we left on the stairwell down here."

Sam and Willy left together. Gail sidled up next to me and shared my observation point. "It's so weird, knowing what's happening, but not hearing anything—not a single gunshot."

"I think that's just about to change," I said, half to myself.

Looming out of the swirling gray with startling speed, a car came skidding to a sudden stop near the telephone shed.

"Step on it, guys," I yelled over my shoulder.

The three of them appeared, Willy and Sam dragging the wide-eyed Russian between them.

I grabbed him by his collar. "You wave your friends over here when I tell you, but no words. Understand?"

He shook his head. "No. I will not."

I looked back outside. Padzhev, holding his arm against his side with his other hand, staggered out of the car, followed by three others, Anatoly among them.

"Persuade him, Willy," I ordered.

Willy laughed in the Russian's face, pulled out his gun, and ground it into the other man's groin. Almost nose-to-nose, he said, "Wave, shithead."

Across the way, Anatoly had opened the shed door and was shouting something at Padzhev.

"Now," I said.

I pulled back the door and Willy thrust his captive's upper half into the opening, where he began waving like a maniac.

Still looking through the crack, I saw Padzhev catch sight of us. "Okay. Enough. Close the door."

Padzhev had turned away to summon the others, not noticing Kunkle yanking our decoy out of view like a rag doll.

"They bit," I announced. "Cuff him again, then let's give 'em a proper greeting."

Willy returned the Russian to the stairs, where Sammie attached him to the nearest railing, warning him, "One sound and you're dead."

We then all drew our guns, Gail standing behind me, and moved just out of the doorway's immediate line of sight.

Moments later, their caution dulled as much by their desperation as by our ruse, Padzhev and his three followers banged through the door, one of them even falling as he entered.

Sammie, Willy, and I grabbed our three and threw them to the ground, our knees in their backs and our weapons thrust in their ears. Gail stamped her heel onto the outstretched right hand of the man who'd tripped and kicked the gun he dropped across the floor.

I had Padzhev under me, writhing in pain. "*Nobody move*," I shouted at the top of my lungs.

With the instinct of cornered animals, all four of them became utterly still.

I addressed the back of Padzhev's head. "You know better than I do that we got about thirty seconds to do this. We're armed, you're armed, and Kyrov's hot on your heels. He'd just as soon see all of us dead. One choice: you want to join forces?"

"Yes," he said, and followed it with an order in Russian.

I stood up, patted Gail on the back, and returned to my viewing spot. The shadow of a man—more ghost than substance—slipped out of the woods and hid behind Padzhev's abandoned car.

"Okay, boys and girls," I said, "time to go up top."

I helped Padzhev to his feet and steered him toward the stairs.

"Where are we going?" he asked.

"We don't have too many options," I explained. "This is a rein-forced steel building, with one way up. If we can control that, we ought to be able to last for a few days at least."

From the sound of his voice, I guessed Padzhev to be near the end of his rope. "To what end, Lieutenant?" He stopped in mid-climb and turned to me. "It is I Kyrov wants. Why not satisfy his need?"

I pushed him along. "Because sacrificing you will get us nothing. He doesn't want witnesses. And I want you for my own anyhow—you're going to clear my name."

Padzhev laughed tiredly and shook his head. "Such an optimist."

I didn't bother telling him what my hopes were based on. Until I saw otherwise, the SOS I'd had Sammie send via computer rated right up there with putting a note in a bottle.

We continued climbing until we couldn't see into the darkness. "*Rarig*," I shouted. "We're coming up—with Padzhev and company."

I then muttered to Padzhev, "Tell your people to holster their weapons, in case Rarig thinks you're trying to pull a fast one."

Rarig's disembodied voice confirmed my suspicions. "I better like what I see, Georgi, or people are going to start dying."

Padzhev gave the order to his men. Slowly, the darkness paled to a light gray, and through the latticework of switchbacks above us, we could just make out the entrance to the second floor. I moved to the front of our line, crossing the threshold first. I paused there, my hands by my sides. "Rarig?"

"Where's Padzhev?" he said from behind one of the huge scaffolding pillars, a continuation of those below.

"Right behind me." I gestured for Rarig's old nemesis to appear.

Padzhev wearily stepped into the half-light, still holding his wounded arm. "Philip—John—it is all but over. No more games."

God only knew that in the duplicitous world these two called their own, there was always more room for games. Maybe for once Rarig heard something he could finally believe, or maybe, like Padzhev, he'd run out of gas at last. In any case, he stepped out into the open, the gun in his hand pointing somewhere at the floor between us.

"What happened?" he asked.

Padzhev gave a half-shrug. "We are on the same side, after all these years."

"Kyrov's just outside," I explained. "What's the layout up here?"

Rarig pointed behind us. "I think we should go up one more flight. The light's better on the stairs, so we can see who's coming, and there's an interior ladder to the roof as a last resort."

"Done," I said, and stepped aside to let him lead the way.

Corbin-Teich met us on the third-floor landing, looking glad for the company, even if it did include his old boss. "I have been looking outside," he said nervously. "There are men all around. At least ten of them."

"That's about what we counted," Padzhev confirmed. He stepped onto the floor and looked around. This third level, like its predecessors, was stripped clean except for a few small piles of trash. The radar scaffolding dominated its center, and the elevator, frozen in place, stood with its doors open, blocking the otherwise open shaft beneath it. Across from us was an open door leading to a tiny exterior platform, and in a small room to our right, a ladder led to a square hatch above— the escape route Rarig had mentioned. Enough light poured through these two openings to make a view of the staircase pretty clear.

After looking around, I returned to the others. "Okay, everybody— weapons check. Who's got what, and how much ammo do we have?"

Our inventory consisted of twelve handguns for the eleven of us, pretty evenly divided between ten millimeters and .40 caliber. Ammunition came to about two magazines per weapon. Only Lew looked a little uncomfortable, handling something he probably hadn't touched in forty years. Given his increasingly removed, almost dreamy state of mind, however, I didn't think it was going to matter much.

The plan, such as it was, was simplicity itself—we would guard the stairwell, shooting at anyone who came within sight.

To give us a slight advantage, we gathered together a pile of metal rubbish, including a loose bulkhead we found cast aside on the roof, and used it to barricade the threshold. Then, as an afterthought, we also threw enough odds and ends down the short stretch of stairs facing us to prohibit anyone from making an unimpeded run.

After that, it was sit and wait. Which took all of five minutes.

Willy had just stepped out onto the landing, to benefit from the stairwell's acoustics, when he leaned back inside and announced, "Company."

We helped him back over, took up positions, and started listening to the crash and rumble of the wind on the building, trying to discern any stray movement in its midst.

We found it with the single sharp clang of something hard hitting metal, like the toe of a shoe against one of the steps. Moments later, the vague shape of a head moved against the dark background of the landing beneath us.

Instinctively, I opened my mouth to shout the standard police warning not to move, when Anatoly's muzzle flash exploded right next to me. In that split second of lightning clarity, I saw the man below spin like a top and vanish from sight. He never knew what hit him.

Willy looked disgusted. "So much for waiting till we see the whites of their eyes."

But my own disgust ran deeper, and Gail picked up on it instantly, placing her hand gently against my back. "They are here to kill us."

I glanced across at Padzhev's pinched features. His arm was obviously causing him growing discomfort. "They're here to kill *those* bastards," I barely whispered.

But she was right. I was no longer a cop—I hadn't been for a long time now. Worse, I was now operating out of desperation. Niceties like verbal warnings and taking prisoners were as appropriate here as in a feeding frenzy.

But I still couldn't come to terms with shooting a man in cold blood.

There were more sounds from below, furtive, tentative, unaccompanied by anything visible. Sammie jogged over to the door leading to the small exterior platform to see what was going on outside the building. All she got for her pains were two shots which ricocheted inside the large room like lethal marbles in a tin can.

"Nice, Sam," Willy said to her. "Maybe you can call in some artillery next."

She gave him a baleful stare and came back, saying nothing.

A voice speaking Russian echoed loudly up the stairwell. Padzhev and his men listened quietly, and then Padzhev responded with an abrupt one-liner.

Willy smiled grimly, seemingly in his element. "What d'ya bet that meant, 'Fuck you'?"

"You should know," Sammie muttered.

There was a sudden blast of gunfire from below and a stuttering of blinding flashes. Bullets came screaming through the gridwork before us, bouncing off the walls and ceiling, careening among the obstacles we'd laid out, like crazed hummingbirds hungry for blood.

We hit the floor and covered our heads, feeling the thud of spent missiles falling around us. In the background, we could hear the dull thunder of footsteps pounding up the stairs.

Willy, his cheek bleeding, cradled his one good arm on the barricade, oblivious to the fusillade. "Come on, come on, come on," he kept shouting, and then began to fire. The rest of us joined him a moment later, and in the bursts of acrid light, we saw two men fall, entangled in our barrier, and three more behind them turn tail.

The silence that followed emphasized the ringing in our ears.

I motioned to my cheek and asked Willy, "You okay?"

He touched the wound gingerly. "Yeah. Didn't even go through."

"Went through this guy," Rarig said, his voice trembling with adrenaline.

We looked at one of Padzhev's men, seemingly resting with his back against the barricade. His shirtfront was stained bright red. Without hesitation, Gail scrambled over on her hands and knees and checked his pulse. She shook her head at me. Two of the other Russians dragged him to one side and distributed his gun and ammunition among them.

I glanced at Lew Corbin-Teich, who was sitting around the corner from the door, his back to the wall, his eyes sightlessly on the opposite wall. His gun was resting on the floor between his legs.

I scuttled over to him and put my hand on his shoulder. "Lew?"

I wasn't sure what to expect—from nothing to a frightened scream. Instead, he turned his head and looked at me calmly. "I am fine, thank you." He then handed me the gun. "I do not believe I will be using this, however. I might have been of service in a situation like this very long ago. But I realize now, despite even this, that I am not who I once was."

I took the gun and returned to the others, doubting he was alone in his sentiments.

There was a longer wait before the next assault, and when it arrived, the reasons for the pause became instantly clear. Another barrage from the stairwell's nether depths was accompanied by a second, long-distance offensive from outside, with a shower of automatic gunfire through the exterior door Sammie had peered from earlier.

Now, instead of bullets bouncing in front and over us, they came from behind as well, commingling in a hail that sent us scrambling uselessly for cover. The very steel walls we'd depended upon for protection became the allies of our attackers, redirecting their shots in patterns we couldn't anticipate.

As before, Willy stood his ground, this time with Sammie and two of the Russians beside him, but they were paying the price, flinching and falling under the deafening onslaught.

And then Rarig yelled, "*Grenade.*"

Rolling across the floor toward us was the cylindrical missile from a grenade launcher. Anatoly was in midsprint almost as soon as Rarig let out his warning. He fielded the grenade like a ballplayer, tossed it underhand back toward the door, and dove to his right for protection.

The explosion occurred just outside the building, riddling its corrugated wall, and turning it into a ragged, daylit doily, each hole of which threw a shaft of light across the bitter, smoke-filled air. Anatoly lay still where he'd landed, caught by a piece of shrapnel.

I staggered to my feet, my head thrumming from the effects of the blast, and gestured to the ladder leading up to the roof hatch. "Get out, get out. Willy. Sam. Get the hell out."

I grabbed Gail by the arm and thrust her toward the small room with the ladder, hauling Corbin-Teich to his feet to follow her. Little by little, the others fell into line, some barely able to walk—Padzhev supported by a bleeding Corbin-Teich—until only Sam, Willy, and one of the Russians were left at the barricade.

Sam crouched long enough to slam another magazine into her gun and shouted to me, "Get them out. We'll be right there."

I did as she said, pushing, prodding, yelling at the others to hurry, until at last only Padzhev was left on the ladder, struggling up with one hand and being pulled along by the scruff of his neck. Mercifully, inside the small room, we were shielded from most of the lethal ricocheting.

I wedged myself alongside the room's small doorway and called out to the three of them, "Now. Go. I'll cover you."

Only Sam and Willy made it. The Russian turned to follow and caught a slug to the side of his head, falling to the floor as if dropped from thirty feet.

The other two ran by me, Willy first, because of his arm, then Sammie, who positioned herself across from me as Willy began to climb. He was almost to the top when the first head appeared around the corner of the stairwell door. I fired at it and ordered Sammie to go.

She hesitated and then obviously realized now was not the time. Halfway up the ladder, however, she stopped, hooked one arm around a rung, drew a bead through our door to the one at the barricade, and said, "Okay, your turn."

I retreated as she fired several shots to cover me, until my head was even with the backs of her legs.

"Go," I shouted, and we both scrambled as fast as we could, up and through the roof hatch above. There, Willy was lying on his stomach, waiting for anyone to come into view.

The contrast between the roof and the room below was an assault on the senses. Instead of being catapulted from chaos to calm, we found ourselves surrounded by the equivalent of a minor hurricane. Freezing wind tore at our clothing, cut off our breath, and worked in pulsating gusts to drive us off the roof's flat surface. Bleeding and dazed, most of us either staggered to retain our footing, or simply gave up and fell to the cold steel plating.

Leaving Sammie with Willy at the hatch to watch our backs, I crawled around to check on the others. Padzhev, his head cradled in Corbin-Teich's lap, looked almost beyond help, his eyes glazed and his face expressionless. Rarig, holding a stomach wound, lay on his side, turned so he could catch his breath in the gale. Gail was sitting cross-legged, her back to the wind, several guns in her lap, trying to force her numb fingers to redistribute our remaining bullets among a small cluster of magazines. She was grim but determined, looking up as I appeared and saying, "Jesus Christ, Joe. Is this what it's like?"

I wasn't sure I understood and then realized I'd heard only some part of a raging internal monologue. But the light in her eyes spoke well of her spirit, so I gave her a kiss and left her alone.

Back at the hatch, Sam and Willy were deep in conference.

"What's going on?" I asked, stretching out beside them.

"Nothing," Willy answered.

"I think they pulled back," Sammie said.

Willy opened his mouth, but Sam caught his arm to quiet him. "Listen." She got to her knees to hear better. "Listen. It's gunfire."

"What the hell?" Willy dragged himself to the edge of the roof, where the wind smashed off the side of the tower and came up at him like a solid wave. "There're people down there," he shouted back. "People in tactical vests. *Good* guys." Barely keeping to his knees, he began waving his arm and yelling to those below, oblivious to the fact that we could barely hear him just ten feet away.

Minutes later, a megaphoned voice floated out of the open hatch as from some subterranean deity. "You on the roof. This is the FBI. Put down your weapons and come down the ladder unarmed."

Sammie looked at me, smiling from an exhausted face. "I'll never dump on e-mail again."

22

TONY BRANDT AND I SAT IN A SMALL CONFERENCE ROOM DOWN the hall from Jack Derby's office. It was two weeks after the FBI, accompanied by Gil Snowden and members of the Vermont State Police, had plucked us from the center of Edvard Kyrov's vengeful crew.

There had been a flurry of bureaucratic activity since then, during which we survivors had been questioned, debriefed, and discussed behind closed doors like problematic visitors from a distant planet. Gail alone had been cleared almost immediately—a right, she'd asserted later with a laugh, awarded to all deputy state's attorneys who'd been kidnapped on the job.

Rarig, Padzhev, and, as it turned out, Anatoly had been taken to the hospital in various states of disrepair, where they were all recovering. Lew Corbin-Teich, after a long talk with Snowden, returned to Middlebury and teaching, having decided his blown cover mattered little in a post-Soviet world. Snowden had also had a chat with Rarig, although less, I thought, to debrief him, and more to rub in the fact that it was he who'd joined forces with Tony to save us after hearing of Sammie's SOS. I didn't doubt this would have little effect on Rarig's paranoia, confident that he'd come up with some wild theory to explain it.

I, on the other hand, was perfectly happy to accept things at face value again, including the fact that the mugging in Washington had in fact been just that. Snowden showed me DC police documentation revealing that my attacker had been caught trying to stick another tourist in the ribs a week after I'd left town, and had been ruled insane by the court. More nut than predator, he hadn't been after money but thought he was ordained to rid the city of trespassers—which explained why he'd been lurking around a war memorial instead of some back alley.

That conversation had taken place at our house, over coffee, and I'd taken the opportunity to ask Snowden some additional questions, like why I'd been invited down to see him in the first place.

"I had to find out what was going on," he'd told me. "We'd seen the articles about Antonov's death and had Philpot confirm his identity at the ME's office in Burlington. I knew how tight Antonov was with Padzhev, and that Padzhev was involved in a major power struggle back home, with international implications. But I was also in a bind. I couldn't ask the FBI to run the case, since no federal crime had been committed, and we're not allowed to operate on U.S. soil. So, I figured if I asked you to Washington, your suspicions might push you to dig deeper than you might otherwise. The mugging was a happy coincidence, falling right into my lap—I used it to spur you on. I actually didn't even know about it till you told me. And I did my best later to keep you interested—I told the RCMP, for example, about Antonov being a point man for the Mafia and asked them to leak it to you."

"Then why did you run interference for Rarig?" I'd asked. "Pulling his high school pictures just before they were mailed to us?"

He'd shaken his head at the memory. "With Olivia Kidder suddenly involved, it was getting out of hand. I wanted to slow things down a little." He'd paused then and added, "I'm sorry you got so messed up in the process. If I'd known Padzhev was going to plant that brooch on you, I never would've used you as a bird dog in the first place. Things got away from me."

His commiseration had sounded nice, but I hadn't kidded myself. I knew damn well that if he'd had to do it over again, he wouldn't have changed his tactics much. It wasn't in the nature of either the man or the organization he worked for to treat people like me as anything more than pawns.

Perhaps responding to this, I'd needled him a bit. "Rarig said you're a crooked, ambitious, well-connected backstabber—and implied Padzhev's had you in his pocket since the mid-seventies."

Snowden had only laughed, denying none of it. "Yeah, I know. That's why I love how this turned out. It's driving him nuts seeing me look good."

Of the Russians I was told little. The feds had gathered them up, the dead and the living, to be taken to parts unknown, but I did find out Kyrov himself had slipped through the net. I'd worried that their taking possession of Padzhev might end any chances I had of clearing my name, but Padzhev had come clean, and Snowden made sure the Vermont Attorney General's Office knew how and by whom the brooch had been planted in my jacket pocket.

Other legal details had been addressed: Rarig's disposal of Antonov's body, Willy and Sam's unorthodox view of their job descriptions, and, of course, the little matter of my violating those court-issued conditions.

All but the last were being handled with "extenuating circumstances" kept firmly in mind, although Tony had been sorely tempted to rid himself of an utterly unrepentant Willy Kunkle, something Sammie had headed off by saying that if he went, she did, too. Not that I'd believed Tony in the first place—he'd ended up barely slapping their wrists.

I was beyond such special treatment, of course. My problems went outside the department. They even exceeded Judge Harrowsmith's reach, had he been inclined to help. By ignoring almost every condition levied upon me, I had guaranteed my own dismissal from the police force and unwittingly awarded Fred Coffin at least a consolation prize.

Which was why Tony and I were now sitting in Derby's conference room. All I could rally in my defense was a lifetime in law enforcement, a good performance record, and the hope that Vermont's small cadre of decision makers might see their way clear to making an exception in my case. But those were slim chances. I had thumbed my nose at the court, regardless of circumstances. Even if they didn't hit me with time, fine, or probation, I'd still be saddled with the commission of a crime. And thereby lose my career.

There'd been but one strategy left, and to his credit, Jack Derby had thought of it. Since there seemed to be no way to duck this particular legal bullet, Derby had called on the one man in the state with the power to make it simply disappear.

The door opened and Derby stepped in, accompanied by Gail. "Thought you'd like to see a friendly face," he said, as they both sat down.

I watched them cautiously. "Do I need one?"

Derby laughed, removing any doubts. "Just so you can celebrate. The governor'll be granting you a pardon later this week. Your record's clean."

I'd been preparing myself for a likely disappointment, knowing pardons were all but unheard of, especially from a tough-on-crime governor like our current one. Now I didn't know what to say.

Derby removed the need, his own obvious glee needing further outlet. "Better still," he added, "it also means Fred Coffin's been handed his lunch by the same man he was ass-kissing for a judgeship. I love it when irony works in your favor. Apparently the governor's a big fan of yours—and not so big on ambitious nitpickers."

"Coffin's been fired?" I asked, stunned by such a reversal of fortune.

"Oh, no, although he'll probably wish he had been. He's still at the AG's, and unless he quits, nobody'll let him forget how this turned out. Given his track record, payback'll be terrible."

He paused, brought up short by having flown his colors so openly. When he spoke again, it was in a much more muted tone. "Well," he inaudibly slapped the tabletop and rose to his feet, "I'll leave you to it. Congratulations, Joe. I couldn't be happier for you."

He leaned forward, shook my hand, and was gone.

Tony got up also, smiling to himself. "I didn't realize Fred had pushed his buttons quite so hard. Interesting working in a state this small."

He paused at the door, looking back at me. "See you tomorrow morning?"

I smiled and nodded. "Thanks, Tony. I appreciate it."

He shrugged. "I blame it all on Kunkle. He's a bad influence on you."

I sat still, staring at the polished tabletop after he'd left, lost in thought. Gail reached out and squeezed my hand. "How're you doin'?"

I leaned forward and kissed her knuckles. "Let's get out of here."

Jack Derby's office was on the second floor of a bank building located downtown on Main Street. When we stepped out onto the sidewalk, the evening rush hour was clogging the road. Brattleboro wasn't designed for heavy traffic and had never figured out how to deal with it. I looked up and down the block, thinking of all I'd seen happen in this town, feeling a great sense of relief to be back on familiar ground.

"You didn't answer," Gail said, her hand in mine.

That I hadn't, although less from willfulness than from simple inability. Inside, I was still as cut up and bloody as I'd felt sitting in court, listening to Coffin describe me as the frustrated, impotent, older boyfriend of a rich, indulgent woman. Self-serving name-calling by an arrogant politician, perhaps, but with elements of painful truth. Combined with everything else that had been hitting me at the time, such debasement had seemed in context. But I hadn't been a total victim through all this. Few people truly are. Ahead of me was the task of sorting through the extent and nature of my own culpability—alone and with care. And that included scrutinizing Coffin's portrayal of my relationship with Gail.

I gently squeezed her fingers, and led her toward the crosswalk. "I'm okay. But I'll feel better after you treat me to a Dunkin' Donut."

Gail came along without comment, but I felt her eyes on me as we waited for the light to turn green.